The Alphabet of Heart's Desire

The Alphabet of Heart's Desire

by

Brian Keaney

www.hhousebooks.com

Paperback ISBN: 978-1-910688-37-3
Kindle: 978-1-910688-38-0

Cover design by Bustles Lloyd
Typeset by Polgarus Studio

Published in the USA and UK

Holland House Books
Holland House
47 Greenham Road
Newbury, Berkshire RG14 7HY
United Kingdom

www.hhousebooks.com

For Rosie

The room is an appalling mess. The entire floor seems to be covered with books. They lie half open, or piled precariously one on top of the other. At a desk by the window, heaped with yet more volumes, he is frantically searching for something, wild eyed and dishevelled, pulling papers out of drawers, throwing them recklessly behind him and cursing loudly. Then suddenly, with a cry of triumph, he holds up to the light a small brown phial, carefully, fearfully scrutinising it in order to check that it is not empty.

Satisfied that its contents will suffice for his immediate purposes, he crosses to the other side of the room, somehow finding a path through the piles of books to where a small table stands against the wall. On the table is a decanter half filled with wine and a solitary wine glass. He puts down the phial and pours a glass of wine. Then, picking up the phial again, he takes out the stopper and, with trembling hand, adds a few drops of its precious contents to the wine glass. He hesitates for a moment, then quickly pours in the rest. He sits down on a chair beside the table and drinks the wine at one draught, as if it were ale and he a workman on a hot day. When the glass is empty he smiles, leans back in the chair, and closes his eyes. After a little while the muscles of his face begin to slacken, the glass slips from his hand, falls to the floor, and shatters.

For a long time he remains motionless until suddenly there is a knock upon the door and his eyelids flutter open. Uncertain of his surroundings, he stares sleepily about him. The knock comes again, the bedroom door opens, and the maid peers uncertainly into the room. She glances first at the broken glass on the floor and then at her master.

'What the devil do you want?'

'Please sir,' she begins, 'begging your pardon for disturbing you an' all, but there's a visitor downstairs.'

'A visitor?'

'Yes sir.'

'Well, who is it?'

The maid shrugs. 'I don't rightly know, sir. He's a foreigner of some kind.'

'A foreigner? Whatever do you mean?'

'I think you'd best come and see for yourself, sir.'

There is a long silence 'Very well, I'll be down in a moment.'

The maid withdraws but he remains sitting at the table for some considerable time before at last he can summon the energy to stand up, cross the room, weaving through the towers, and make his way downstairs. He has no idea who might be visiting him at this hour and he cannot imagine what is wrong with the maid that she could not elicit the fellow's name and business. She seemed positively off-hand, shrugging her shoulders like that. He ought to talk to her about her attitude but it is not the sort of thing he finds easy. Besides, he is so inestimably weary.

What he encounters in the kitchen, however, banishes all such thoughts from his mind: standing beside the maid, his mahogany complexion in stark contrast to her pasty cheeks, is a man of about his own age dressed in loose-fitting white robes. Upon his head he wears a soft white hat, not unlike a Chinaman's.

What such a man can be doing in the middle of the Lake District, far from any port, is quite beyond Thomas's comprehension. Yet there is something distinctly familiar about him – those dark eyes glistening, the grave, almost noble, almost judging countenance. Thomas feels sure he has seen this fellow somewhere before but he cannot for the life of him think how or where that might be.

The stranger bows elaborately. 'Mr Thomas De Quincey, I believe?'

He nods. 'And who might you be?'

'I am nobody of consequence,' the stranger replies. 'I am only here to give you this.' He holds out his hand and in his open palm there nestles a small silver locket upon a chain. 'She asked me to return it to you, at the very end.'

PART ONE

The Basis Of Taxation

Anne

Fathers, step-fathers and uncles. They're the commonest culprits – speaking from everything I've heard, and from what I've seen myself. Except in the case of servants, when it's generally masters or young masters that's responsible.

A girl is brought up to do as the man of the house tells her and that's what she does. Often enough she's so young when it happens she don't understand what's going on. Take me, for instance. I was twelve years of age – I looked older, I know, but I was just twelve. A child.

I'm not trying to make out I was innocent. You don't grow up innocent in Limehouse. But I was ignorant. I saw things but I didn't always know what they meant. And I wanted to believe there was good in the world, and that the good would win out over the evil in the end, and that all would be as God intended. That's what they tell you when you're a babe, ain't it? And until you stop believing that you ain't grown up.

My mother only took up with Harold Lampton because she couldn't see her way clear after my father was swallowed up by the Thames. He was coming home late one moonless night with his best friend, who was known as Hawking Sam Hartley, or just Hawk, and not on account of him going around with a leather gauntlet and a trained bird, I should say, nor even because he had a curved nose like a bird, but simply because he was always hawking and spitting, whatever company he was in. Great gobs of green filth. The inside of that man's lungs must have been a terrible sight.

Anyway, the pair of them was more than a little the worse for drink, when my father stumbles over the corpse of a dead dog, gives a cry of surprise and a curse, and tumbles head first into the water.

Hawk waited for a long time to see if my father was going to climb back out again and no doubt he coughed up a great deal of green oysters while he was doing so. But my father did not reappear. So round Hawk comes to see us with a sheepish expression and the news that my mother is fresh made a widow.

My mother and I wept and wailed, as you might imagine, and when the news got round our neighbours dropped by, some to offer sympathy, and other in the hope that there might be a drink, or a bite to eat, or even a pipe of tobacco going, which there weren't. And that was that. From then on we had to shift for ourselves.

In Limehouse, like anywhere else, things can very quickly turn to the bad if you ain't got no support of any kind to cling to. So we looked to Hawk. He clearly felt a bit of guilt about what had happened and to begin with he came round to see us a lot and helped out with a bit of food now and then, and even managed to get us some work making baskets – but there weren't a lot of money in it and never enough work, neither.

Then one day he didn't come when we expected him. We was waiting on the canes to make more baskets but there was no sign of him. So off I went to the ale house that he was known to frequent to ask if anyone knew what had become of him. Of course everyone there knew Hawk and right away they told me he'd been named by a magistrate as being part of a gang of bit-fakers passing what they call *counterfeit* coins and as a consequence there was a warrant out for his arrest. Most of them was of the opinion that he'd gone on board a ship and weren't likely to be seen in these parts again. I kept asking questions but they just sniffed and shrugged and went back to their drinking. They'd told me what they knew and there weren't nothing further to be added. So that was the end of Hawk as far as we was concerned and the end of the baskets as well.

My mother was very cast down. I suppose that while Hawk was around she still felt in touch with my father in some fashion but now he was gone as well she felt my father's death the stronger. I tried to rouse her but all the spirit was gone out of her, like a dog that someone had poisoned, and she wouldn't be jollied. So I decided I'd best take matters into my own hands.

Some of the women in our lane used to sew hammocks for sailors. I asked around and they told me where to find the man in charge of the trade. His name was Mr Hazel and he had a chandler's shop at the back of St Mary's church. I persuaded my mother this would be the way out of our predicament and though she showed little enough enthusiasm, she came with me to see him.

Mr Hazel was a short, wizened little man with a face like an apple in February, and the look of a man who'd tasted something nasty and couldn't forget it. When we entered the shop he was writing in his ledger and he raised his eyes from his reckonings, looking us up and down like he was estimating our value. After a moment he made a tutting sound with his lips, as if to show he was disappointed with what he'd seen and his eyes glassed over. Trying not to let this daunt me, I told him we was respectable women that had fallen on hard times and we understood he might be able to offer us work sewing hammocks.

'Very neat and tidy is sailors,' Mr Hazel said when I'd said my piece. 'Neatest people in the world, you'll find. So it's no good offering them anything badly-made, no good at all, because they won't buy it. Won't even look at it.'

I told him we was very neat workers.

He looked doubtful.

'Show us your hands.'

We spread out our hands on the counter, palms facing upwards.

Mr Hazel shook his head. 'They don't look like the hands of hammock makers,' he said.

'We haven't had a lot of experience making hammocks, right enough,' I told him. 'But you won't find more willing workers anywhere in Limehouse.'

'Willing is neither here nor there,' he said. 'A dog might be willing. But I ain't going to pay him to sew hammocks.'

'Just give us a try.'

Mr Hazel sighed like the world was out to do him an injury but he showed us into the back room and provided us with needles and canvas. Then for the next half hour we plied those needles as best we could while he sat out front and went on scratching away in his ledger as if he had all the deeds in the history of the world to record.

Now the truth is that we weren't neither of us great with a needle, and canvas ain't easy to work with, neither. What you really need is a palm thimble, which, of course, we didn't have, otherwise you're forever stabbing yourself in the hand. So after a while I went out to the front of the shop and asked Mr Hazel if he could supply one. He looked as though he couldn't believe his ears.

'Leather don't drop from the sky,' he informed me. Then back he went to his pen and ink.

I felt like telling him that I knew as well as he did where leather came from. Didn't we live down the road from a tannery and didn't we know all about the stink when the wind was in the wrong direction? But I held my tongue and went back to work. Try as I might, without the palm thimble I was continually getting blood on the canvas.

After an hour Mr Hazel came into the room and examined our work, holding it out in front of him like a pair of soiled breeches.

'Waste of good canvas,' was all he said.

I practically went down on my knees and begged him to give us another chance, promising we'd get ever so much better with practice, but he would not be moved and we walked out of there no better off than before, and me with me palm all stabbed and sore.

So when the landlord came round for his rent at the end of that week we had nothing to give him. Mr Gillespie was a tall, thin man with a face that long, a horse would have been proud of it. He was always dressed in a black topcoat and battered hat. His tenants used to call him The Undertaker and it had always been my father's joke that he was in mourning for the loss of his purse. When my mother informed him of our circumstances I was quite certain we'd be out on the street that very night but to my surprise, and to my mother's also, Mr Gillespie had a speech prepared. No doubt he knew all about my father's death already. People round there had little enough to do but gossip.

Mr Gillespie cleared his throat and then began. Bill Chambers was a decent man, he said, and he had always thought of him as a friend rather than a tenant, which surprised me greatly because I'd never seen Mr Gillespie display any obvious signs of friendship towards my father, nor anyone else for that matter. His only friend was the rent, as far as I could tell. But I held my peace and listened. He would not see us homeless, Mr Gillespie continued, not on any account. He would do the right thing by us.

My mother was greatly cheered by these words but of course it soon turned out that his speech was a deal finer than the actions that came after it, as is very often the case with the promises of those who have more money than the rest of us.

Our building was not the only property he managed, Mr Gillespie informed us.

Well, naturally, my mother said, Mr Gillespie being a *personage of considerable resources.*

Where she got this last phrase from I can't imagine since my mother was not an educated woman by any stretch of the imagination. Mr Gillespie may have had a similar thought because he looked quite startled but then he nodded gravely as if it was only right and proper.

'I have another room I would be prepared to offer you at a much lower rent,' he said, 'and I shall conduct you there myself.'

He announced this as though we would be travelling in a coach and four but as it turned out it was just a short walk around the corner.

Before we could go any further, however, there was something that had to be made clear. My mother was deeply and profoundly grateful, she assured him, with a little bob, and she knew that her poor dead husband would be looking down on Mr Gillespie from heaven at this moment and blessing him for his generosity.

Mr Gillespie nodded again as if he entirely shared her conviction.

'The only trouble being, Mr Gillespie, as how we don't have no money at all,' she went on. 'Not so much as a farthing.'

Mr Gillespie looked entirely unperturbed. 'That's the whole beauty of the arrangement,' he told her.

My mother gave him a sideways look. 'What arrangement is this?' she asked. Her voice had turned sharp and prickly.

'Nothing untoward, my dear Mrs Chambers,' he continued. 'Nothing in the least untoward. You may be assured that everything will be above board and entirely shipshape because that is the way I do business. But if it would please you to follow me, all shall be made clear.'

Mr Gillespie had long legs and my mother and I had only short ones so we was obliged to scuttle along the road to keep pace with him. As he walked, he hummed tunelessly to himself and I was sorely tempted to ask him what he was humming only I thought he might take offence.

The room we'd been living in until then was nothing to speak of. The walls was mouldy but there was a proper window with glass in it, a table and three chairs and two good mattresses. The building was a bit broken down and there was always rats running up and down the stairs and of course the smell from the tannery when the wind came from the east was frightful – but the wind wasn't always from that direction and the other tenants was a decent lot on the whole. Obviously, there was a few bad apples, like you get everywhere. Down in the basement there was a collection of thieves that would have taken the steam off your piss and sold it back to you as a cure for scurvy. But we never had nothing worth stealing and, anyway, most people knew my father and they either liked him too well to do us any harm, or they took one look at his fists and thought better of whatever mischief they'd been planning.

This place that Mr Gillespie was taking us to was a very different matter indeed. Very different. The entire population seemed to be sitting about on low walls or standing at street corners chewing on clay pipes and staring in front of them like they was half asleep or sick. You never seen more miserable-looking people in your entire life.

Mr Gillespie took no more notice of them than they did of him. He turned down a lane that was so narrow we had to go in single file, then under an archway and into a filthy looking courtyard where a dog with a stick tied to its tail was running round in circles barking and a gang of half-naked children was throwing stones at it. They stopped when they saw us and disappeared into various dark doorways, though I knew very well they was watching us still from the shadows.

There was a smell from a cesspit somewhere very close at hand and it was that strong you could have cut it with a knife and spread lard on it. I looked at my mother to see how she was taking all this but she didn't look back. She had made her face as empty as the people we'd seen on the way in here.

Mr Gillespie led the way across the courtyard, being careful not to step in any of the puddles, which was probably wise because it hadn't been raining, and turned into one of the buildings in the far corner. He opened a door and showed us an empty room. It was smaller, damper and dirtier than the place we'd just left. The floor was spread with rotten straw, there was a window in one wall patched with a bit of rag and not a stick of furniture to be seen.

He must have read my thoughts because straight away he said, 'I can let you have a table and a couple of chairs,' as if he was making an offer of *considerable generosity.*

My mother nodded her head, encouragingly. 'Very nice, Mr Gillespie,' she said, hoping he might come up with some more suggestions.

'Now I'll show you the other room,' he said.

My mother and me looked at each other in astonishment. Whatever did he mean? He couldn't possibly be offering us two rooms. It didn't make no sense.

We hurried after him as he led the way back into the hall and stopped before a door beneath the stairs. He took a key out of his pocket and I wondered at this for it was not normal where we lived to provide a lock on an apartment. A bolt on the inside if you was lucky and that was it. When he opened the door I saw that the room, if it could really be called a room since it was scarcely bigger than a cupboard, was almost entirely taken up with a great copper pan that sat on top of a brick hearth. Beside it there was a couple of buckets and some wooden beaters.

'What's this?' my mother asked.

'This, my dear Mrs Chambers, is the arrangement I mentioned earlier.'

It seemed that Mr Gillespie had decided that my mother and I was going to become washerwomen and this was how we would pay our rent. A boy called Perk would bring the dirty linen in a basket every other morning and collect the clean garments. Perk would also bring us fuel for the fire, which fuel we were at all times to keep locked in this room. Mr Gillespie was most particular on this point. On no account was we to contemplate selling fuel to any other person or persons, no matter how strongly they should seek to persuade us. If we did, Mr Gillespie would hear about it for he had his 'sources of information'. He looked very stern when he said this. Of course we agreed. What choice did we have?

Perk, whose full name, he later boasted, was Anthony James Perkins, arrived the very next morning pushing a cart laden with a table and two chairs, an immense wicker basket filled with dirty laundry, a bundle of kindling, some logs and a bar of lye soap. He looked about eleven years old and puny with it. I thought it a marvel he could even push the cart across the yard but I soon discovered that there was no job Perk was not prepared to tackle. He had a very high opinion of his own abilities and regarded himself as an authority on any subject you could name.

We was not the first to be installed as Mr Gillespie's washerwomen, Perk informed us almost as soon as he arrived. 'Won't be the last neither, I shouldn't wonder,' he added with a grin. 'No-one lasts very long at this lark.'

Before us, according to Perk, there was a one-eyed Irish woman called Maggie O'Sullivan who'd died of consumption within eighteen months and before her a woman called Mrs Taylor. No one knew her first name and she hardly spoke to a soul. Six months she lasted. Then she fell on the ice in the courtyard and broke her hip.

'After that she just give up,' Perk told me. 'I come round one morning, puts me head in the room and she's lying on the straw, the colour of marble.'

'When have you ever seen marble?' I asked. I was annoyed because he seemed to be taking so much pleasure in other people's misfortunes.

'I get around,' Perk said. 'I see all sorts of sights and, what's more, I intend to make something of myself. I shan't be Mr Gillespie's laundry boy forever.'

'Oh, and what shall you be?'

'A man of business.' This last he said with an air of the most *supreme* confidence.

The clothes that Perk brought us was very soiled indeed and our first attempt to clean them was nothing like good enough in his opinion.

'I ain't taking them away,' he said. 'Mr Gillespie will just send them back again. You ain't soaked them, have you?'

'Course we did,' I told him. 'Soaked them overnight in cold water, boiled them all morning in the copper.'

'Cold water!' Perk says scornfully. 'My word you're green, ain't you?'

I took a swipe at him with a wet shirt but he ducked out of the way.

'You have to soak them in piss,' he declared.

'In piss?' I said. 'Don't be daft!'

But my mother only nodded her head and sighed, 'I should have thought of that myself,' she said.

So from then on we saved our own piss for soaking the clothes in and I spent most mornings up to my elbows in it. I expect I went around smelling of it, though it made little enough difference for the cesspit that was perfuming the air when we first arrived turned out to be in the basement directly below our room so we was never free from the stink of it.

That was our life in Burley Court, an endless round of drudgery with barely enough money for bread after Mr Gillespie had deducted the rent from our wages. Nonetheless, we could survive. Our condition was low enough, there was no getting away from it, but it was not so low that my mother needed to go taking up with Harold Lampton. Yet that was what she did. And that, rather than my father's death, is the root and source of all the difficulties that have pursued me ever since that time. Even so much as glancing at Harold Lampton was a mistake she should never have made. I knew that as soon as I set eyes on him. And so would you if you saw him. Imagine a face that wanted more than anything to tear your throat out. That was Harold Lampton.

It was a Sunday when she brought him back for the first time. She'd met him in St Mary's graveyard of all places. She used to go there every so often to visit the grave where her parents and all my brothers and sisters was buried. When I was younger I used to go with her but there weren't that much there for me. I'd never met her parents and there weren't even a proper headstone to record their names and dates, just a hump in the ground and a small worm-eaten wooden cross sitting crooked on top of it. As for my brothers and sisters, well, frankly, I didn't like to think of them lying there in the cold earth. It gave me a funny feeling, like I had no right to be standing above them, or walking around in the weather with all the freedom of a living, breathing soul.

What exactly Harold Lampton was doing in the churchyard that morning I wouldn't like to say. Of course he told my mother he was visiting his parents' grave just like her but I don't believe that for one minute. Harold Lampton weren't the kind to go visiting people's graves, not unless he'd put them in the ground himself and he wanted to look down on them and laugh. If I was to hazard a guess I'd say he was there that Sunday looking for a victim and when he saw my mother his eyes must have lit up.

He was a tall thin man with thick dark hair and dark eyes. He'd once earned money as a prize-fighter at travelling fairs, or so he told everyone, and he was fond of stretching out his arms on either side of him to show his reach. Lightning Lampton was the name he had gone by. His professional name, he liked to say, stretching out the word *professional* like he stretched out his arms.

He looked at people from under a pair of heavy black eyebrows and there was something about that look that was... well, like a storm coming. People stepped to one side to avoid him on the street. And they was right to do so because he was full of a cold, hard anger that seemed to come from some place deep inside him and was always trying to find its way to the surface.

He didn't show that side of himself to my mother to begin with, of course. He went out of his way to be charming but I could see right through him because charm was something that didn't come naturally to him. It was obvious to anyone who wasn't determined to believe otherwise that he was putting it on.

For the first few weeks after he moved in he behaved himself. He'd go off in the morning saying he was going to the docks looking for work, and maybe he did work, though if he did, I doubt it was honest. Leastways, he'd come back with money in his pocket. But then he started spending more and more time in the ale house and he very soon began to show his true colours.

My father had been inclined towards the drink, I won't deny that, and like any man he could lose his temper when he'd had too much. But it was like a passing cloud with him. He raged against the world, and anybody that had the misfortune to be standing in his way at that particular moment was liable to feel the back of his hand. But it all blew over soon enough. The next morning he'd go round looking red-eyed and feeling sorry for himself for an hour or two but pretty soon he was back to his usual good-humoured self.

Harold Lampton was a different kind of man altogether. He carried his anger around with him everywhere he went, nursing it like it was his baby, and feeding it with little tidbits of grievance, and he was provoked as easily as a wounded animal. A real turk he was, and if any man crossed him he would reach for a weapon in the blink of an eye. Anything that could cut, or tear, or bludgeon another man's body.

We was both very soon frightened of him. My mother did everything she could to keep him happy but that only annoyed him even more. He would imitate her voice back to her: 'Oh yes, Harold, of course Harold, certainly Harold,' he'd say mockingly. Then he'd reach out one of his long arms and take hold of her face with his thumb on one side of her jaw and his fingers on the other and he'd squeeze her until she yelled. Then all of a sudden he'd give her a shove so that she'd fall over backwards and he'd stand there, looking down on her and taking a rich pleasure in her terror.

At first he regarded me as nothing more than a nuisance. *Your darling daughter*, that was what he called me. 'What's your darling daughter doing here?' he'd say when he'd come back from one of his drinking sessions. I knew that was my cue to get out of the house as quickly as I could so that he could get at my mother.

I was just a child, like I say, but I knew what men and women did together. We only had the one room and when my dad was alive I used to lie there at night a few feet away from them and pretend to be asleep while he climbed on top of my mother and took his way. But at least he had the decency to wait until it was dark.

Harold Lampton didn't care what time of day it was. Once my mother sent me out in the middle of the afternoon for a couple of meat pies and when I came back he was taking her up against the wall. I stood there, frozen for a moment. Then he looked round and saw me staring at him with his breeches down around his ankles and his hairy arse on display and he gave an evil grin.

'Look Marjorie,' he said, 'Your darling daughter's here.' Then he took my mother by the hair and twisted her head round so she could see me.

I'll never forget the look on her face. Helpless, that's what she was. Like an animal being led to the slaughter. I put the meat pies inside the door, turned round and run away.

All of that I could have lived with, bad and all as it was.

But then he got tired of my mother and started on me. I hadn't even had me monthlies. He bided his time, waiting for an occasion when he could be certain that my mother would be out for a good long while. Then poor old Mrs Dawson who lived in the room above us gave him his chance. She was dying from a lump on her chest that was eating her insides out. So my mother went and sat with her for several nights to keep her company before she went off into the darkness on her own. That was Harold's opportunity.

On the second night he came back from the public house earlier than I expected with a funny look on his face. All smiles he was. I knew straight away that was a bad sign. He didn't know how to smile properly. It didn't come naturally to him. All he could manage was a kind of sly look, like a fox's grin.

He sauntered over to the table, all the time keeping his eye on me. I understood that I ought to get out of the room without further delay but he held me with his eyes and I just couldn't do it.

Then he sat down at the table and folded his arms. 'You and me don't much like each other, do we?' he said.

I didn't know what to say.

'You're in the way, that's why,' he said. 'Understand me?'

I nodded.

'So I'm going to give you a chance to earn your keep. Then maybe we'll get along a little better. Would you like that?'

I nodded again. I had no idea what he was talking about.

'Come over here,' he said.

I glanced towards the door but it seemed to be miles away.

'I said, come over here.' His sly look had disappeared now. Instead, he flashed me a look of such *viciousness* from underneath those dark eyebrows that I could hardly stay on my feet for fear. I walked shakily across the room and stood in front of him.

'Kneel down,' he said.

'What?' I looked at him in confusion. The only time you knelt down was to say your prayers but I was pretty sure that Harold Lampton didn't want me to pray for his soul.

'You heard me.'

I got down on my knees

He took hold of my hair in his left hand and held it fast. I saw now that he held a knife in his other hand. He must have been holding it out of sight the whole time. He'd planned the whole thing all right.

'If you don't do exactly as I tell you I'm going to cut your face open,' he told me. 'Understand?'

'I couldn't even speak but he didn't wait for an answer. 'Undo my breeches,' he told me.

I undid his breeches. His thick, ugly cock reared up at me. There was a smell off it like old cheese.

'Put it in your mouth,' he ordered.

I looked at him in astonishment. I'd never heard of anything like this.

He brought the point of the knife up to my neck so that it was right against my skin. 'Do it!'

I bent my head over his lap and took his cock in my mouth. He gave a moan of pleasure and I hoped that would be all he wanted. But of course that was just the start. The hand that gripped my hair forced me down until my throat was full of him. Panic took hold of me and I started to retch but that didn't concern him in the least. He pulled my head back and then pushed it down again, up and down, working it faster and faster and all the while I thought that I would choke on him. Then all of a sudden he gave another great moan and he shot his bitter seed into me.

Afterwards, when he had taken his cock out and done up his breeches he looked at me, still kneeling there too frightened to get to my feet. 'Enjoy the taste of it?' he asked.

I said nothing.

'You'll get used to it.'

Tuah

Let me say from the very first that Mr De Quincey was unworthy of her. He was addicted to opium and, like all addicts, he could not be relied upon. But perhaps you think I am unfair? You think I have my own axe to grind? That is a wonderful expression, is it not? It was a Scotsman who first taught it to me. Captain McKerras. A clever man with crooked teeth and a piece of his left ear missing. A man who liked to drink rum and sit in his cabin laughing at his own thoughts while the running of the ship was left entirely in the hands of Bosun Mortimer.

Be careful of Mortimer, the captain told me once, when he was in his cups. That man has his own axe to grind. I looked at him in confusion and he took great delight in explaining the meaning of this saying.

'I am wasted on the ocean, Abdul,' he said afterwards. (Abdul was what they all called me.) 'I could have been a natural philosopher. I could have been a statesman.'

This was something that he often said and whenever he did so, he would reach up with his hand and touch his mutilated ear like a mother reaching out tenderly to stroke her infant child.

It was Captain McKerras who taught me English. Both

everyday words, as he called them, and the Lord's Own Words from his Bible. Very difficult to understand I found the Lord's Own Words yet I took a kind of solace in the sound of them and they seem always to be with me. *This is my comfort in my affliction: for thy word hath quickened me.* That was the captain's favourite line and in time it became mine also. For there is indeed a comfort to be found in language, even though it is not my own, and in the end it is the only comfort left to me.

As you might imagine, I do not often move in polite society but at times, by some chance or other, my path will cross the paths of ladies and gentlemen who, upon hearing me quote the Bible are so greatly taken aback that they cannot decide whether they ought to be pleased at this display of piety from a savage or offended at the sound of scripture on the tongue of an infidel. They are quite dumbfounded at the monstrosity I present. I am an insult to their understanding. Some, of course, ask me to perform some more.

I only faintly remember my uncle, who was a great Bomoh, which you would call a witch doctor, that is if you were to call him anything at all which I very much doubt since you would be most likely to regard him as entirely beneath your consideration. Regrettably, his face has quite passed from my recollection now, along with so much else, but I do recall him telling me this: wherever you go boy, whatever people you find yourself amongst, and no matter how harshly they behave towards you, always treat their gods with great respect and in time they may come to look favourably upon you. He meant the gods, of course, not the people. People do not change so easily.

In time. What a dreadful phrase that is! A locked door behind which lies a world of suffering.

My uncle could see things that were yet to come. Not clearly. He told me once that it was like looking at the clouds, that the pictures in his mind shifted and changed and the more closely he tried to look at them, the further away they seemed to get. Nonetheless, he foresaw the destruction of our village and his own most violent death. And he understood that there was no avoiding it.

My childhood, which I came to regard with an aching fondness, was nonetheless a far from easy one. My father was drowned before I was born when his fishing boat was caught in a storm, and my mother died giving birth to me. This much I was informed of by my uncle upon whom fell the burden of my care. He had neither wife nor children of his own who might have softened his hard edges and as a consequence he had little patience with me. For my stupidity he would beat me regularly but he also taught me much that would serve me well in the great trial that was to come. Especially, he showed me how a man can withdraw into himself so deeply that anything can be endured, however terrible.

Nowadays, when in my mind I hear my uncle speak, it is more often than not in English that he warns me to respect the local gods and in English that he tells me of the pictures in his mind that come and go like clouds. My own language has deserted me. I am a savage with no words of his own except those that I have borrowed from Captain McKerras's and his Lord. *My soul melteth for heaviness: strengthen thou me according unto thy word.*

I was nine years of age when I was first taken from my village. The men who took me were Dutch traders, though of course I did not know that then. I had never seen white men before. I did not know that there were many different kinds of white men, that they spoke many languages, each of which they believed was their Lord's language, and fought amongst themselves – that they travelled the seas looking for other people to fight with. I had never seen a vessel larger than a fishing boat, and no one used boats for anything but fishing.

I was sitting outside my uncle's hut drawing pictures in the dirt with a stick when Lotong came running towards me. Behind him were almost all the other men of the village. They were carrying their spears and I knew immediately that something was wrong. Lotong was a man upon whom the gods looked favourably, until that day at least. He was tall, brave and proud and the other men looked up to him as to a leader but that day there was confusion written on his face and also fear. I had never seen Lotong look afraid and my heart seemed to stop beating as I watched him running towards our hut. I think I sensed even then that my childhood had come to an end.

My uncle must have seen the men coming too for he stepped out of the hut and asked what had happened. They all looked at Lotong and he announced that a great sailing boat had come to the island, far bigger than anything anyone had ever seen before, and that Layhoe and Boenga had been walking on the shore and had seen it arrive.

My uncle nodded and looked about for Layhoe and Boenga. There was no sign of Layhoe but Boenga stepped forward and described again the great ship that had appeared near the island, and how a smaller boat had descended from it and how, when it had drawn near the shore, he had seen that the men inside it were as white as ghosts. He had been afraid but he had not run. He and Layhoe had stood their ground and waited to see what would happen next.

'And what did happen next?' my uncle asked.

'The white men got out of the boat and stood there watching us. After a moment Layhoe told me to stay where

I was while he walked forward to meet them. But one of them was carrying a large knife and as Layhoe reached him, without any warning he thrust the knife into Layhoe's belly. Layhoe cried out and fell to the ground, his blood running out onto the sand, and I turned and ran back to the village the quickest way I could.'

My uncle nodded. He did not look angry or fearful or even surprised at this news, only tired. 'It has come at last,' he said.

'What has come?' they asked, gazing at him in wonder.

'The end of our peace,' he told them.

'But what must we do?' Lotong demanded.

'It makes no difference what we do,' my uncle replied. 'They will kill us all.'

Then everyone became angry and began talking and shouting at the same time, calling my uncle an old fool and a coward and all manner of other names. Finally Lotong raised his spear and they all fell silent. 'We will attack them before they attack us,' he said. 'Either we will take vengeance for Layhoe and drive them away or we will die with honour.' The others all agreed this was the best thing to do. My uncle only stared into the distance as if he had lost all interest in the discussion.

By now most of the women and children of the village had heard the news and were gathered around, their faces full of terror. Lotong told them to flee into the forest. Then he set off with the other men following.

I looked at my uncle but he said nothing. I wanted to go with the men but when I followed them for a few paces they pushed me away and told me to run and hide. So I went back and tried to persuade my uncle to come into the forest with me but he only shook his head. In the end I ran into the forest by myself and looked for somewhere to hide. I could not see the women or the other children. I was so frightened that I could not decide whether to climb a tree or to hide among the bushes. First one idea seemed better, then the other. I was still trying to make up my mind when I heard the first shot.

I did not know what it was for I had never seen or heard a pistol before but I immediately understood, though I do not know how, that it meant killing. Death was in the very sound of it. So I thrust myself into the middle of a thorn bush, not even noticing how my skin was torn, and I waited. I heard more shots and cries and I thought of what my uncle had said, that they would kill us all.

I spent all day hiding in the thorn bush. I did not dare come out even to drink, though I was desperate with thirst. In the middle of the afternoon I heard the sound of men coming through the forest and then I saw them. I could not study them well from where I lay but I could see enough to know that everything about them was strange – their clothes, their hair and of course, their pale skin. I counted six of them. They passed by without noticing me and I lay there hardly daring to breathe. A little later I heard them returning and I could see that this time they were dragging one of our girls with them. It was Tarjong who had been my friend and with whom I had often played in front of my uncle's hut. Her hands were tied and they led her like an animal. I wanted to weep at the sight of her but I was too frightened to allow the tears to come.

Only when it grew dark did I creep out from my hiding place. First I looked for some water to slake my thirst. Then I decided to see if I could find somebody to tell me what I should do. As soon as I drew near the edge of the forest I could see the glow of a fire near the shore and I knew that was where the white men must be. I went very carefully, creeping first towards our village; but there was no one there except my uncle. He lay on the ground outside his hut and in the moonlight I saw that his throat had been cut. I sat down beside his body and now I *did* weep, but silently.

After some time I got to my feet again and began to search for a weapon of some sort but there was nothing in the village I could use, not even a stick. Either the men had taken all their spears and knives or the white men had stolen them. So I picked up a large stone, thinking I might smash one of the white men's skulls with it, and crept down towards the beach.

They had made a great fire and they were sitting around it, drinking. Tarjong was lying stretched out on the ground, her arms and legs tied to four stakes, and one of them was on top of her. She was sobbing while he grunted like a pig and the other white men shouted encouragement. The sound of their language was strange and ugly. Two of the men from my village were sitting on the ground nearby, their hands tied behind their backs, their heads bowed in shame. I wondered what had happened to the rest. Were they all dead, like my uncle? Or were they still hidden?

I tried to decide what it would be best to do but it was hard to think with the sound of Tarjong sobbing in my ears. Perhaps if I waited until they were all asleep I could untie her, and the other two. I was thinking about what I might use to cut their ropes when there was a shout close behind me and an arm came round my throat. I struggled furiously but it was hopeless. A white man lifted me from the ground and carried me into the circle. Then he pinned me to the ground, and his companions tied me up and placed me alongside the two men from my village. There I remained for the rest of the night while the white men continued to drink and to sing and to take it in turns to lie on top of Tarjong. By the time the last man had satisfied himself she was no longer sobbing. From that day until we were all sold and separated, I never heard her utter another word.

Thomas

Today, in the school room, after they had finished their arithmetic and were sitting on the Turkish carpet with its intricate design of orange and blue flowers that Thomas never grew tired of trying to unravel, Flossy announced that she was going to read to them from a new book she had been sent by her brother James in London. Thomas considered Flossy to be the prettiest lady in the whole world, as well as the kindest, and he tried to imagine what her brother in London might be like. Not unlike her, he decided. Perhaps very tall, certainly very handsome, and always smiling.

Flossie's creamy skin and blond hair reminded Thomas of one of his sisters' dolls. He secretly envied his sisters those dolls, and if the truth were known he would dearly have liked to have played with one, to have taught it lessons, to have put it to bed, to have confided his secrets to it, as he had seen his sisters do. He sometimes imagined a game in which he addressed a doll of his own called Flossy and told it stories. The doll would sit up nicely to listen and it would be ever so well behaved. There would be no naughtiness with Flossy.

But he knew his mother would have thought such a game very wrong for he was not a baby any longer and, what was more, he was a boy and would one day have to make his way in the world like his father. He would join the Company and seek his fortune in some distant land across the seas where the scent of spices blew upon the wind. All his education was no more than a preparation for that day. It was what his mother expected of him and Thomas must not disappoint her. He feared his mother's displeasure above everything else for it tore away his excuses like a pitiless wind tears the leaves from the trees and left him without words to defend himself. So he put all thoughts of dolls out of his head and settled down to listen to Flossy's story.

The story, Flossy told them, was from a land on the other side of the world called Arabia where there were vast deserts of yellow sand and where golden palaces glittered under a burning sun.

Thomas's interest was immediately engaged. The other side of the world where fortunes could be made by any man who had the courage to reach out and take them! That was where Thomas himself was one day bound to go, and already he could see the shining towers and fierce light, and he himself riding through it like a prince.

The people who lived in this country wore long white robes, like Jesus, Flossy told them, but they were not good like him. Indeed, the rulers of this land were dreadfully cruel and treated their people as though they were slaves.

'But why do the people put up with such treatment?' Thomas asked.

Elizabeth, who was nine, already knew the answer to this question. 'They have no choice, Thomas,' she informed him. 'Anyone who does not obey them is instantly killed.' She looked at Flossy for confirmation and after a moment Flossy nodded gravely.

Not for the first time Thomas wondered how Elizabeth knew so much, and about so many different things. Like him, this was the first time she had heard the story and yet she instinctively understood the ways of its characters. She was three years older than him, of course, but even so. Sometimes it seemed to Thomas that Elizabeth knew more than the grown-ups. He would never be as clever as her, no matter how hard he tried. For Elizabeth just knew things without even having to learn them even though her world, just like his, was bounded by the borders of Greenhay.

'I would run away,' Mary declared. She was seven. Despite this, Thomas was disdainful of her opinions. Mary believed she was pretty and this thought had quite turned her head. She did not try to think about anything properly and behaved so foolishly that Thomas was quite ashamed of her. For example, she screamed when she saw an earwig and when Thomas carefully picked it up and watched as it frantically waved its pincers about, she insisted that touching it would poison him.

'They cannot run away,' Flossy told Mary. 'There is nowhere else for them to go.'

'What about the desert?' Thomas asked.

'No-one can live in the desert,' Flossy informed him. 'It is too hot and there is no water. Now, I want you all to listen carefully for this is a story quite unlike any you have heard before.'

As Flossy began to read it soon became clear that this was indeed a story like none that Thomas had ever heard before. It was a story in which he could lose himself entirely, a pleasure he had never enjoyed so fully until that day.

The hero was a boy called Aladdin, a poor boy, but a cheerful one, who lived with his mother in Baghdad, a great city that was as full of its busy inhabitants as a nest of ants. Thomas could picture the streets in which Aladdin played cheek-by-jowl with beggars, pick-pockets, water-carriers, fruit-sellers, letter-writers, match-makers, fire-eaters, errand-boys and gangs of ragged children who lived in the midst of all this bustle like fish in water. Thomas decided he would live in just such a city when he was older.

One day, Flossy continued, Aladdin was playing a game of chase with his fellows in the street when a stranger approached him and asked whether he was the son of Mustapha the tailor

'I am, sir,' Aladdin replied, 'but my father died a long while ago.'

'This is a most fortunate meeting, Aladdin,' the stranger exclaimed, 'for I am your uncle and I have been searching for you for some time. I was told you might be found playing in these streets and the moment I set eyes upon you I knew you from your likeness to my brother.' He asked where Aladdin lived and then instructed him to tell his mother that he would be visiting them shortly.

When Aladdin ran home with the news his mother was greatly surprised. 'I knew your father had a brother,' she said 'but I have never met him and I always believed that he died many years ago.'

Nonetheless, she set about preparing the best meal she could from the little store of food that they possessed, and when the house was filled with delicious smells of cooking the stranger arrived, laden with gifts for them both. There was food and wine and rolls of cloth finer than Aladdin's mother had ever possessed. After they had thanked him profusely for his presents, they all sat down to eat and he began to tell them about himself. He was a merchant by trade, he explained, and he had been out of the country for many years.

Thomas nodded eagerly at this description for it was exactly like his father: a merchant who has been out of the country for many years; a man of power, wealth and mystery; a man who could travel the world at will.

During his absence, the visitor went on, he had amassed a great deal of wealth. Now that he had returned to his native land, he was determined to improve the lives of his closest family.

'I don't believe him,' Elizabeth announced as Flossy paused for a moment in her reading. 'It's a trick.'

Thomas looked at her in shock. He had been delighted with the stranger's benevolence, sharing Aladdin's excitement without question. Yet all the time Elizabeth had been listening and weighing the stranger's words, and now she had reached her decision, which she pronounced with that certainty so typical of her: The stranger was not to be trusted. And Elizabeth was always right. Indeed, now that she had spoken, he could quite clearly see that the stranger's story was a pack of lies. All the same… He looked anxiously at Flossy for confirmation but she merely smiled and carried on reading.

The following day the visitor returned with a fine suit of clothes for Aladdin. He wanted to show his nephew the parts of the city the boy had never seen before. They would visit the street where the sultan had his palace and where all the wealthy nobles lived. Therefore, Aladdin must dress accordingly. The boy was thrilled and, feeling like a lord, put on the fine clothes, which fitted him perfectly. Then he and the stranger set off.

It was not long, however, before Aladdin realised that instead of going towards the heart of the city, they were travelling in the opposite direction, towards the desert lands that lay beyond the walls.

Here Thomas glanced across at Elizabeth in acknowledgement of the accuracy of her prediction and in return she gave him a knowing smile.

When Aladdin asked where they were going the man who had claimed to be his uncle took from his bag a piece of cake. The boy was hungry for they had been walking for some time, so he took the cake eagerly. Then the man began telling him a story so full of marvels it made Aladdin forget all about the sultan's palace. Only when they had left the city behind and come to a narrow valley between two mountains did the story cease and Aladdin come to his senses.

He looked around in amazement and realised that while he had been listening to the story he had been under some kind of spell. Upon understanding this, he felt very frightened and would have run away immediately but the false uncle said, 'If you will but stay a moment I will show you something even more remarkable than that story.'

The false uncle gathered sticks and built a fire. When it was burning brightly he threw a powder upon it and muttered some magic words. Immediately the earth opened up in front of them, disclosing a square flat stone with a brass ring in the middle.

'Beneath this stone,' he declared, 'there lies a great treasure that no one else may touch except you, Aladdin, and if you will do exactly as I tell you it can be yours.'

Aladdin was still very much afraid but the thought of that treasure made him bolder and indeed Thomas immediately felt bolder too. So Aladdin grasped the ring and pulled. The stone came away much more easily than he had expected and there beneath was a great dark hole and a set of steep stone steps leading downwards.

'At the foot of those steps you will find an open door leading into three large chambers,' said the man. 'Go through these chambers without touching anything at all or you will die instantly. The chambers lead into a garden of fine trees, heavy with fruit. Walk on till you come to a niche in a terrace where you will see a lighted lamp. Pour out the oil that it contains and bring that lamp to me.'

Thomas could see that dark hole in the ground with the most complete clarity. And he could see, also, the terrible dilemma that Aladdin faced. The man who had claimed to be his uncle was obviously a magician of great power and cunning. He had lied already about the visit to the sultan's palace. There was no guarantee that he was not lying now. But the thought that in the darkness lay a treasure on which only he could lay his hand would surely torment him for the rest of his life if he refused to descend the stone steps and seek it out. Poverty or riches, that was the choice. Safety or cowardice. A boy should be ashamed to be a coward. Everyone knew that. Aladdin, it seemed, was of a similar mind for though he hesitated for some time, he agreed at last to do as the magician suggested. Then the magician took a ring from his finger and gave it to him.

'If you find yourself in danger, rub this ring and help will come,' he promised.

To Thomas's dismay that was as much as Flossy would read for one day. Now it was time to practise their handwriting, she announced, leaving Aladdin considering his quest as he took the ring.

'Oh please, Flossy!' Thomas said, 'just a little more.'

But Flossy was adamant. She stood up, crossed over to the blackboard and wrote:

The Magician placed his ear to the ground and listened.

Thomas stared at the blackboard in surprise. The sentences they copied for writing practice were generally a great deal less interesting than this, even his favourites like,

Of all the fine birds that fly in the air,
None with the Peacock, for beauty compare.

'Why did he put his ear to the ground?' Thomas asked after a moment.

Flossy gave him a patient smile. 'Story time is over now, Thomas,' she said. 'We are practising our handwriting. No person who cannot write a fine clear hand, can call himself educated, now can he?'

Thomas shook his head.

'Very well then.'

After the lesson, when they were allowed out into the garden, Thomas sat on the grass beneath his favourite tree, a great horse chestnut, and discussed the story with his sisters, for his mind was so full of the wonders of the Eastern lands and Aladdin's adventure that he could think of nothing else. Mary, who was busy making a daisy chain, did not have a great deal to say about it. She liked the story but she thought Aladdin would have to be very foolish indeed to go down into the hole. She would not do so whatever the magician promised her.

Elizabeth was a great deal more interested in the magician than in Aladdin. 'How do you think he knew that only Aladdin could touch the lamp?' she asked.

'By magic, of course,' Thomas replied. This seemed such a simple question that he was surprised to see Elizabeth frown as she considered it.

'Yes, but what kind of magic?'

Thomas was not entirely sure what Elizabeth was driving at. Finally he said, 'He probably just made a spell and then he knew. After all, if you can do magic, you can do anything.'

Elizabeth shook her head. 'The magician couldn't touch the lamp himself, could he? That was why he needed Aladdin in the first place. So you can't do anything, even with magic.'

'If I were a magician,' said Mary, suddenly tearing her daisy chain apart, and throwing it away, 'I would make it so that you could eat whenever you like, not just at meal times.'

The other two ignored this interruption. 'You know that

sentence Flossy made us copy out?' Elizabeth continued.

Thomas considered it. 'The Magician placed his ear to the ground and listened,' he said. 'What about it?'

'I think that was how he did it. He put his ear to the ground and listened.'

'Listened to what?'

'To all the footsteps in the world and somehow out of all of them he recognised Aladdin's and knew that he was the only one who could bring him the lamp.'

'But how did he know?' Thomas asked.

'Because the footsteps were a kind of language.'

Thomas gazed wide-eyed at his sister and could not speak.

Anne

I *considered* murdering Harold Lampton while he was asleep. All it would have taken was a big enough stone to smash his head. Or I could have just cut his throat with his own knife. There'd have been a proper kind of justice about that. But I knew I'd never have the nerve to go through with it. He'd only have woken and seen me standing there with murder in me heart and God knows what he would have done then.

Besides, I had no wish to be hanged. When my father was alive he used to take me with him to Tyburn whenever anyone notorious was executed. There'd be a great crowd of people, talking and laughing and feeding their faces with pie, and fellows going round singing ballads about the prisoner on his way from the salt box. My father would lift me up onto his shoulders so I could get a better view and I always did my best to act like I was enjoying myself for his sake. When the executioner led the cart away and the poor prisoner was left dangling there, jerking about in *agony*, I cheered heartily along with the rest, fierce enough to lose me voice, especially when the poor cove kept going long past his time. But the truth was, it sickened me. Killing ain't the sort of thing I take pleasure in.

There weren't no point telling my mother what Harold

had done. Even if she'd believed me, she was as much under his thumb as I was. I couldn't just run away, neither, because there weren't nowhere for me to go. It was the middle of November, the streets was cold and getting colder with each passing day. In the mornings the ground was white with frost and it looked like we was in for a repeat of the previous winter – that had been terrible harsh, especially for the bushed and seedy, on the streets and in the park.

One morning in January on the way to buy some bread I'd passed a ragged looking boy sitting on a doorstep all hunched up against the cold. He looked about six or seven. When I was making my way back home again he was still there, in exactly the same position. I told myself I ought to take care in case he tried to rush me and filch the loaf. That's a common enough game among the kids.

I put the bread in my coat and made my face as fierce as I could to show I weren't no push over. But, as I got closer, it seemed to me that he didn't look right at all. Much too still to be natural. So I stepped up closer, to get a good look, all the time keeping very *cautious*, and suddenly I saw he'd croaked.

A week later a bundle of rags outside St Mary's Church turned out to be an old woman in the same condition. After that it was commonplace. All through January and February I saw corpses left on the street for days on end. That weren't how I planned to end my days.

I asked myself what my father would have done if he'd been facing a problem like this – he always considered himself a bit of a philosopher. London, he used to say, may look like a collection of buildings to you, but it ain't. It's a collection of ladders. Everywhere you look, you can see them. Up they go into the bright blue sky above us and down into the darkness below. And there's always someone standing on the next rung. So what you've got to do – and here he'd wag his finger in the face of anyone willing to listen to him – is find the man on the rung above you and make him your friend. That way you'll always keep in work.

As it happens my father didn't always keep in work, and there was long periods when the man on the rung above seemed to be looking the other way. But all the same, he was in work more often than he was out and not just on account of his broad shoulders neither but because he was well-liked by people and whenever labour was being hired his face would stand out from the crowd.

So I looked around for the person on the next rung of the ladder and I realised it was Perk. Now that weren't an admission I was particularly happy to make. But Perk it was, whether I liked it or not. So one morning when he'd delivered our latest basket of dirty linen and was taking away the clean clothes I followed him out to the cart.

'Can you keep a secret, Perk?' I asked.

His eyes lit up. He loved to feel important. 'Course I can,' he said, putting the basket of clean clothes into the cart. 'Everyone tells me their confidences.' He tapped the side of his head with his finger. 'There's more secrets in here than there is shit up a horse's backside.'

He thought he was sharp as a razor.

'So come on then! What's the news? Don't tell me you're in the family way?'

I tried to fetch him a slap across the side of his face but he ducked out of the way too quick and grinned back at me. 'You'll have to be a lot faster than that to catch me a wallop,' he said. 'All right then, you ain't knapped. So what is it?'

I looked back towards our door but my mother was inside, most likely sorting through the clothes to find the ones with the worst stains. I looked around the courtyard. There was a group of old women standing about in one corner, huddled in their filthy old shawls, like a lot of old crows. They was craning their necks in our direction and I knew they'd have dearly liked me to give them something to gossip about but they was too far off to hear what I had to say. All the same, I kept my voice low.

'I'm running away from home.'

'Is that all?' he said scornful. 'I thought you was going to tell me something worth hearing.' He stooped down to pick up the handles of his cart.

'Wait a minute!' I said. 'I need your help.'

'Oh, help, is it?' Now he looked interested. 'Well, that's a *saleable commodity*.'

'I ain't got no money.'

'Then what you wasting my time for?' The look of interest disappeared and he set off with the cart once more.

'You wouldn't know the answer to my question, anyway,' I said, turning away. I knew he had too high an opinion of himself to let that go.

Sure enough he stopped in his tracks. 'All right then, Miss High and Mighty, what's your question?'

'If you was me, and you needed to run away but you didn't have no-one you could go to – no friends, no family, nothing – what would you do?'

He thought about it for a moment. Then he said, 'I'd go to Mrs Dempsey on Spencer Street.'

'Where's Spencer Street?'

'Off the Mile End Road.'

'And who's this Mrs Dempsey?'

'She's a woman that takes in girls what are willing to work.'

Now this was a surprise. I'd never heard of a woman like that before. 'Would she take me in?'

Perk shrugged. 'Only one way to find out.'

Just then my mother put her head out of our door and asked whether I was going to stand there chattering all day long or come in and do some work. So I couldn't ask no more questions. Perk went off with his cart, whistling to himself, and I went back to the smell of sweat and piss.

But all morning I thought about Mrs Dempsey, trying to imagine the kind of woman she might be. I fixed on a plump, motherly sort of creature with rosy cheeks and a kindly smile. As to the kind of work she might have to offer, I hadn't an inkling.

In the middle of the day my mother sent me out to get us something to eat. and I decided to take my chance there and then since every hour I waited was an hour that Harold Lampton might turn up.

It was bitter weather with a gritty kind of sleet in the air. All the same, the streets was crowded with every manner of person, respectable or otherwise. Boys selling boot laces and girls selling combs, old men selling walking sticks and old women selling oysters. There was a crowd around a chestnut seller, half of them just there for the warmth. Gentlemen and ladies was harder to find for this weren't a *prosperous* area by any means. But there was a few clerks with their wigs on crooked and their hands stained with ink, frowning to themselves as they hurried along, counting other people's money in their heads, no doubt. Every so often a gang of jack tars would come thrusting down the road with their chests sticking out, and there was plenty of out-of-work labourers lounging about on street corners with their hands in their pockets and their hats pulled down low. But I had no time for any of them. I was intent on putting as much distance between me and Harold Lampton as I could manage.

Spencer Street turned out to be much further up the Mile

End Road than I'd imagined but I found it in the end. There was a second-hand clothes shop at one corner and I stepped inside to see if anyone could direct me to Mrs Dempsey's.

A man was sitting behind the counter, reading a book. When the shop bell rang and he got to his feet I saw that he had a twisted back.

He looked me up and down, his eyes taking in my *measurements* and without even wishing me good day, he said, 'I can't say I've much in your size, my dear, but I daresay a girl who had some skill with a needle could soon rectify that.' He had such a strong Scots accent I had difficulty making out what he was saying at first.

'I don't want to buy nothing, sir,' I told him, 'I was only wondering if you could tell me where I could find Mrs Dempsey.'

He frowned and gave a kind of half-smile, like I was a box someone had given him and he couldn't work out how to open it. 'And what would you be wanting with Mrs Dempsey, may I ask?'

'I have some business with her,' I said, trying to sound as *confident* as I could.

'Business, is it?' he repeated and I could tell there was mocking in his voice but I pretended not to notice. 'Well, I'm not the kind of man to stand in the way of business. You'll find Mrs Dempsey on the other side of the street. Count ten doors and knock on the eleventh and tell her Hunch-Backed Archie says good morning when you see her.' He sat down again and picked up his book but I could feel his eyes boring into my back as I went back out into the street.

Mrs Dempsey's house did not present a very *encouraging* face to the world. It was three storeys high and large enough to have been grand at one time. In better days someone had introduced the walls to a coat of whitewash but whatever attraction these two had once possessed had long since vanished. The windows was all either boarded up or blinded with curtains the colour of dirt and the whole building had a sickly look, as if it might collapse and die at any moment. I knew in my heart I was making a mistake but I'd come too far to back out of it now.

I stepped up to the front door and brought down the knocker sharp. I was trying to make myself feel *confident* but I was beginning to suspect Perk might be a good deal less knowledgeable than he made out. The door was opened almost immediately and a man-servant appeared at the door. At least, I assumed he was a man-servant for he was dressed in knee-breeches and a frock coat. But he was a bully fellow who carried himself with a swagger.

'What do you want?' he demanded

'I want to see Mrs Dempsey.'

He grinned, showing a set of teeth that belonged on a horse. 'Run along, little girl. This ain't no place for you'

He started to shut the door but I put my hand out and stopped him. 'I want to see Mrs Dempsey,' I repeated.

A woman's voice called out, 'Who's there, Jeremiah?'

Jeremiah turned his head. 'A girl asking to see you, Mrs Dempsey.'

A moment later Mrs Dempsey herself appeared in the passage and Jeremiah stood aside. She was about as far from my dream of a kind-hearted, motherly creature as you could have got. Tall and thin, her skin was stretched over her bones, like someone that had been dead and gone to Peg Tantrums for a week. She had long dark hair and the coldest pair of green eyes I'd ever struck. It was hard to tell how old she was. She looked older than my mother but there was no end of powder and paint on her face and she was wearing a sack-dress of blue silk that might have graced a fine young lady.

'What do you want?' she demanded and her voice was like flint.

All my courage was draining away into my boots but I somehow found enough to say, 'I was told you took in girls that was prepared to work hard, ma'am.'

Her expression changed and her cold green eyes seemed to glitter. 'You' heard correctly,' she said. 'I do.'

'I was wondering if you might have a vacancy for me.'

She nodded her head slowly and the faintest of smiles crept over her face. 'Do you know, I think I might,' she said.

Tuah

The Dutch men who had captured me were not regular slavers. In this I was perhaps fortunate, if you can call it good fortune to be taken from one's home, chained in the hold of a ship and half-starved, before being sold in the market to the highest bidder. They were men whose trading had not gone well and who had decided to make up for their losses by a little dealing in human flesh. Thus there were no more than a couple of dozen of us imprisoned in the hold.

All the same when I was first led like Jonah down into the belly of the Dutch men's vessel I was overwhelmed by my misfortune. In the darkness below deck the air was filled with the smell of shit and fear. Now that everyone I knew had been killed it felt to me as though I was to be buried alive in a wooden grave. The crew did not care to dally amongst us. They manacled our hands and feet and left us with just three buckets for more than twenty men and women before disappearing up the ladder into the light of day and shutting the door behind them.

Years later when the Reverend Hewitt of St Mary's Church in Stepney told me of the ten plagues of Egypt, it seemed to me that the ninth, the plague of darkness, was the worst of all for the very thought of it recalled me to those first hours of my captivity. *And the Lord said unto Moses, Stretch out thine hand toward the heaven, that there may be darkness over the land of Egypt, even darkness which may be felt.*

That was how it seemed to me, as though the darkness in which we dwelled was something more than just a lack of light. It was something that I could plainly feel lying heavily upon us all, a thick layer of shame that was the very manifestation of our slavery.

We did not speak much to each other. The misery of our condition had taken such a hold upon us that we could scarcely summon up the will for conversation but in time I learned enough to know that we had all suffered the same fate. The others, mostly men, but a few women, were from another island. They too had seen the ship approach, watched as the white men drew steadily nearer, and then been taken by surprise at the suddenness of the attack. They too had fled into the forest but the white men had pursued them and dragged them back to the ship. Now, they had no idea what the future might hold for them, nor did they greatly care. Their spirits were entirely broken. We might have asked with Job, *and where is now my hope? As for my hope, who shall see it?*

The crew did not waste much time upon our welfare. Three of us were given the job of emptying the buckets. I was one. The other two were a young man called Baschoot who told us he was eighteen years of age, and an older man called Appol who said little but who reminded me of my uncle, something about his eyes, I think, some glitter of ancient wisdom. He looked as though he still retained some sense of who he was, whereas all the others seemed entirely lost. It was Appol who explained to me what the Dutch man intended when he pointed first at the bucket and then at me, and as we walked together up the ladder carrying our pails of shit he whispered to me to have courage for I was not dead yet. But it did not seem to me that there was much to distinguish my existence from death.

On the third day of my captivity four of the crew came down into the hold in the middle of the morning, as was their custom and ritual, to supervise the emptying of the buckets. One held a torch, two more held pistols and the fourth carried a bunch of keys. As they descended into the hold their faces contorted like demons in disgust. They made their way over to each of the three of us in turn. By now I knew what to expect, so once I had been unlocked, I picked up the bucket, trying to spill as little of its contents as I could – for it was full to the brim as always and I was not yet accustomed to the motion of the ship.

We went before our captors, up the steps and onto the deck. Here I stood for a moment, blinking as my eyes grew accustomed to the light of day, and in that instant Baschoot acted. He hurled the contents of his bucket over the Dutch men who cried out in dismay at being showered with shit and piss. Then he made a run for the side of the ship, intending to throw himself overboard. Since there was no sign of land it was clear that he had chosen death before slavery. But that was not a choice the Dutch men would allow him. At least not on those terms.

Before he could clamber over the bulwark two of them laid hands upon him and, though he struggled, he was easily overpowered; for the days spent in darkness with little food had left him weak, as it had all of us. While these two held him firmly down, a third tied his hands behind his back. By now, many more of the crew had come running and they were all talking noisily to each other.

Then a hush fell upon them as the captain strode up. He had not been among the men who had landed on our island but I had seen him when they first brought me to the ship. A tall, thin man, his pale blue eyes seemed to give off a cold power, or so I fancied. He took his time, looking hard at each man who stood on the deck, including me. Unable to meet that awful gaze I hung my head, terrified that he would think I was partly to blame for what had happened. The crew looked almost as worried and they were entirely silent as if each man feared for his life. As I think upon it now, it seems to me that perhaps they did.

At last he spoke. I did not understand his words then but I could see that some crew members started, clearly surprised at the terrible sermon that he preached. When he was finished they all drew either pistols or swords and set about carrying out his orders. A great many of them went down into the hold and I assumed they meant to massacre us all.

I trembled as I waited for the killing to begin, for despite everything that had befallen me, I did not want to die. But to my surprise, the prisoners were all brought up onto the deck where they stood looking frightened and bewildered while the crew remained very grim, their weapons at the ready.

Then the captain gave an order and a man stepped up with a pot of something black and sticky. From it came a stink that I had been smelling ever since my arrival on the ship, without truly being aware of it, as though it were the very spirit of the vessel. He knelt beside Baschoot who still lay on the deck, looking about with wide, frightened eyes, and he began to paint the black substance on Baschoot's face. It was tar, of course, as I later learnt.

It must have been hot because Baschoot cried out in pain and tried to pull his head away but another man bent down, seized his hair and held him still until his whole face was covered. Nobody spoke, neither crew nor slave as Baschoot whimpered like a beaten dog.

At last the man with the brush stood up and stepped back out of the way and the man who held Baschoot's hair released it. I was wondering how difficult it would be for Baschoot to wash the thick black substance from this face and whether he would be badly blistered when the captain gave a further order and one of the crew stepped forwards with a lighted torch in his hand, bent down and set Baschoot's face alight.

I was so shocked I could not keep myself from crying out but my cry was nothing to the screams that came from Baschoot as he thrashed about on the deck in agony and the smell of burning flesh mingled with the smell of burning tar. I do not know how long the whole thing lasted. Perhaps it was only a few minutes but it seemed to me that it would never end. I could not bear to watch and yet I dared not look away for fear I might attract the attention of the captain and meet the same fate as poor Baschoot.

That day I learned a great and terrible truth, that it matters not how bad things seem to be, there is always worse that can befall a man.

After some time, Baschoot's screaming ceased and he lay still. The flames died down and it was possible to see the ruin of his face. Then the captain spoke again and two of the crew members picked up Baschoot by the arms and legs and threw him overboard into the ocean, where he sank slowly beneath the waves. Immediately a group of sea-birds began circling overhead and I hoped he would not rise again and let them eat the burnt meat off his face.

I remember noticing that one of the Dutch men was still stained about his shirt with the shit that Baschoot had thrown at him and I thought to myself that he would always wear that shit upon his body however long he lived and he would always smell of it; it would be his mark, and he would forever be *a fugitive and a vagabond.* It made no sense, I knew it even then, but there was some tiny scrap of comfort in the thought.

After Baschoot's punishment we were all locked in the hold for the rest of that day and the night that followed with neither food nor water.

Following that incident, no-one else tried to escape his fate. How many more days passed before we came in sight of land I do not remember but they were many. I do recall that for three days in a row our ration of food was increased. Then, on the fourth day the motion of the ship ceased and we were brought up on deck to find the ship anchored and tied up in a great port. Our clothes were taken from us and we were made to stand still as buckets of cold water were thrown over us and we were washed with rags and then rubbed with oil by grumbling crew members. I had thought myself beyond debasement now yet there was in this treatment something that humiliated me still further.

Then we were led off the ship in three groups, each man or woman tied at the neck with a noose and joined to the others like animals. The dockside was crowded with men, some rolling barrels back and forth, others carrying chests or sacks, others wheeling barrows laden with boxes and others still standing around in groups talking loudly. They paid us little heed but I looked around me in amazement at so much activity. Here for the first time I saw men whose faces were as far blacker than mine as my face was blacker than those of the Dutch men. I saw, too, that it was these black men who did the work while the white men stood about, talking and issuing orders.

I saw too that some of these white men had the most extraordinary hair which lay in rolls upon their heads. Later, of course, I understood these to be wigs but at the time this seemed but one more bewildering aspect of the world into which I had been snatched.

We were made to climb on board a horse-drawn cart and were taken from the dock, down a long straight road with what then seemed to me to be great tall buildings on either side. There were many people coming and going along this road and here, for the first time also, I saw women dressed in bright clothes, strolling in ones and twos and calling out to the sailors who laughed in reply.

From time to time a passerby might glance in the direction of myself and my fellow captives but in a moment his glance had sought out some other diversion and we were quite forgotten. Slavery, it was clear, was nothing out of the ordinary here. *For we are strangers before thee, and sojourners, as were all our fathers: our days on the earth are as a shadow, and there is none abiding.*

For a long time after I was first captured I did not understand why the Dutch men had taken us. I even believed at first that they might be intending to eat us. It was Appol who explained that they would sell us when they reached the next port. Even then I did not completely understand, for his way of speaking was not exactly the same as in our village, but more particularly because I had no understanding of what it truly meant to sell another human being. I was but a child even though I was tall and strong for my age, and I had passed my infancy, moreover, on a small, untroubled island.

After seeing how the Dutch men had treated Baschoot, I was certain that there was no wickedness to which they would not stoop. So when at last we came to a market place where a great crowd of people were assembled and the cart drew to a halt beside a raised wooden platform I was by no means certain that they did not mean to kill us there and then to entertain the crowd, whatever Appol might have said. But the Dutch man who had been leading the cart stood up on the platform and began calling out in a loud voice and many of the populace gathered round to look at us. Most of them were white but there were darker faces among them, too. I searched them all for any signs of pity but saw nothing only idle curiosity on most and an air of concentration on some, such as you might see on a man who is considering how he might manage some task which he has set himself. These were the ones who had come to do business, not merely for entertainment.

Suddenly there was a disturbance in the crowd as a great fat white man pushed his way to the front. There was some laughter at the sight of him for he cut a most remarkable figure. Most of the other men were simply dressed in black coats and black or brown leggings but this fellow wore an elaborately-embroidered scarlet topcoat, a mustard waistcoat and white knee breeches. On his head was perched a heavily powdered wig and in his hand he carried an ebony cane topped with silver. Of course, I knew nothing of fashion at this time. Yet even I could see how much he stood out from among the other white men and not just on account of his great belly. He was a man who had chosen to make a spectacle of himself in defiance of his fellows.

He pointed to me and asked the Dutch man something. The Dutch man grinned, climbed off the podium and onto the cart where he took hold of me and turned me round so that I faced away from the crowd. Then he put his hand upon the back of my neck and pressed down hard until I was bent over double. I could hear the crowd hooting with laughter behind me but I could not understood what was happening or why I was being made to stick out my arse in this way. Then I remembered a story I had heard once from another boy about two of the men who lived in our village and my heart sank.

When I was allowed to turn around once more, the fat man seemed to be arguing with the Dutch man. I suspected they could not agree upon a price and I tried to judge how the argument was proceeding from the tone of their voices and the expressions on their faces. I prayed to my uncle and to all the spirits of my village and of this place too, though I did not even know its name, that the fat man would not be prepared to pay the price the Dutch man wanted.

Suddenly another voice interrupted and a small, determined looking man pushed his way to the front of the crowd. I noticed that half of one of his ears was missing. He said something to the fat man who answered him curtly and waved his hand dismissively but the small man only smiled back at him, an odd smile. Half his mouth curled upwards but the other half stayed where it was. It made him look as though he mocked the fat man. Perhaps he did, for the fat man looked indignant and shouted something at the little man, who shouted back at him. Now the fat man's face clouded over with anger and he strode over towards the little man, his belly sticking out before him and his cane raised in the air. I thought he would knock the little man down and that would be an end to the episode.

But in an instant the little man had drawn a long knife. At this the crowd drew back and the little man pointed the knife at the fat man's belly. The expression on his face was still one of amusement but there was a glint in his eye that made it clear that this was not a game he played – he was quite prepared to spill the fat man's guts upon the ground should it prove necessary.

The fat man looked at the knife and muttered in disgust before turning on his heel and striding away, much to the amusement of the crowd, many of whom called out what were obviously insults. Then the little man put his knife away and took out his purse. After that, it was not very long before I climbed down from the cart and was led away back to the dock from where I was taken on board the little man's ship, the Laurel Bower.

Take therefore no thought for the morrow: for the morrow shall take thought for the things of itself. Sufficient unto the day is the evil thereof.

Thomas

Flossy's features were solemn, as were the faces of the four children ranged before her. At the far end of the room were the toys with which they were accustomed to play, but these were not in use today: the dolls' house was closed, the lead soldiers were all packed away in their boxes and the rocking horse was still. This was not a time for laughter and play.

As Flossy began to read, Thomas recalled how only weeks before in this very same room she had read them the story of Aladdin. Then the world had seemed to be opening up before him, a treasure chest of possibilities, of adventures and of great deeds. Now all those possibilities had withered away and the world was cold and empty, and their hearts were filled with pain.

'After the disciples had gone back to their homes, Mary Magdalene stayed behind at the entrance to the sepulchre, weeping.'

Flossy was almost weeping herself. Her voice cracked with emotion and threatened more than once to break down entirely, but she pulled herself together with an effort and continued.

'Then she stooped down and peered into the tomb and there she saw two angels robed in white, who said to her, "Woman, why do you weep?" Mary Magdalene replied,

"Because they have taken away my Lord and I know not where they have laid him." No sooner had she said these words than she turned and saw Jesus himself standing beside her, though at first she did not recognize him. Jesus said to her, "Whom do you seek?" And, supposing him to be the gardener, she replied, "Sir if thou hast borne him away, tell me where thou hast laid him and I will take him away." Then Jesus called her by name saying, "Mary," and immediately she recognised him and said, "Master."'

The tears were running freely down Flossy's cheeks as she closed the book, unable to read any further. Thomas's eyes remained fixed on her, as did those of his brother and sisters, and the room was entirely silent except for the loud ticking of the clock which now suddenly began to strike the hour, making Flossy jump. She put the book down on the table in front of her, produced a handkerchief and blew her nose in a most unladylike way.

A question was troubling Thomas. He knew this was not the time to ask it, and his mother was always telling him how irritating it was to ask questions at the wrong time. He knew he was a nuisance. He knew that he was a disappointment to his mother. He had understood that for as long as he had understood anything at all. But he had to know the answer to his question because it was important to understand things and this was something that did not make sense. Flossy had chosen this passage to read to them because it was connected to Elizabeth in some way, so he had to try to understand it properly, particularly as Elizabeth was not here to explain it to him. He would ask Flossy. She would not cut him down like his mother might. She would make everything clear.

He waited until she had put away her handkerchief. Then he said, 'Why didn't Mary Magdalene recognise Jesus at once?'

Flossy considered the question for some time. It was obvious that she found it difficult to answer. Finally she said, 'Because he was transfigured.'

'What does transfigured mean?'

Now Flossy sighed deeply and Thomas dearly wished that he was cleverer and did not have to trouble her so. 'It means that he was shining and beautiful,' she informed him. 'Now come along all of you, it is time to go downstairs.' With that she stood up and the children dutifully followed her out of the door, leaving the school room exactly as they had found it that morning, apart from the big book of bible stories lying flat upon the table where Flossy had set it down.

Their mother was already seated at the dining table when they arrived. She scarcely looked up as Flossy brought them into the room, curtsied and took her leave. Then, without a word the children took their places at the table and waited while Susan, the maid, brought in the dishes of cold sliced ham and limp vegetables. This was not one of the cook's most impressive offerings but the entire household had been upset by what had happened the night before and nothing was quite as it should be. The children bowed their heads while their mother said grace; then they all began to eat.

Mrs De Quincey put her food into her mouth quite mechanically, apparently unaware of what she was eating. Thomas watched her for a while, then considered the ham on his plate. The pinky-grey colour and spongy texture made him feel sick. He set down his knife and fork. He had meant to do it quietly but the extra care that he devoted to the action somehow only succeeded in making him more clumsy and his cutlery clattered on his plate. His mother looked up and regarded him sternly. The icy wind of her anger began blowing across the table towards him.

'You must eat, Thomas,' she announced.

'I'm not hungry.'

She frowned. 'It makes no difference whether you are hungry or not. If you do not eat you will be unwell. Do you think that would help our situation?'

'No, mother.'

'Then eat.'

Thomas put a piece of ham into his mouth but it was like eating wet, salty cloth and he set down his knife and fork again in despair. His eyes were beginning to fill with tears.

His mother regarded him coldly. 'If you will not eat Thomas, then you had better leave the table immediately. You may wait in the school room until the meal is over.'

The other children watched in silence as, head bowed and eyes downcast, Thomas left the room.

Once outside in the hallway he shuddered with the effort of restraining a sob, wishing desperately that he had more control of himself. Then he stood still, listening. The house was quite silent, except for the ticking of the hall clock. The servants were all in their own quarters, eating their meal. A thought came to him that was both terrifying and yet completely irresistible.

Perhaps Elizabeth might be transfigured.

He made his way towards the back of the house, slowly and timidly at first, then more quickly until he reached the rear staircase, which he ascended on tiptoe. He was very aware that he was being deliberately disobedient. There could be no excuse and no proper explanation. He was defying his mother's explicit prohibition. People were coming to prepare Elizabeth for her last journey and no-one was to see her until they had done their work. That was what she had told them. Thomas had thought this sort of preparation was the doctor's job but his mother had shaken her head. 'The doctor's job is to cure, Thomas, and where it is not possible to cure, then at least to understand.'

Thomas was confused. He had always relied upon Elizabeth to interpret what his mother told them. But Elizabeth was gone. On his own, he was doomed to infuriate his mother over and over again with his endless questions and his obstinate behaviour. There was nothing he could do about it because he was simply not clever enough to know what else he ought to do. He never would be clever enough. And yet he was possessed by an overwhelming, dizzying desire to understand the causes of things.

The door to Elizabeth's room was locked but the key had not been taken away. It waited invitingly in the lock and Thomas accepted the invitation, taking it between his finger and thumb, turning it easily, then pushing open the door and stepping inside.

The room was not at all as he had expected. The bed which was normally against the far wall had been moved into the middle, its headboard towards him so that he could not immediately see his sister. Beyond the bed, the window had been thrown open and the midday sun blazed out of a deep blue sky, like Aladdin's sun. Despite the open window the room seemed hot and there was a smell which he could not identify but which pricked at his nostrils.

Carefully, he closed the door behind him, making as little noise as possible. Then he walked slowly forward. But as soon as he could see the bed properly he stopped and, despite himself, gave a cry of horror. Nothing in his life, no country scene nor any story told by Flossy had prepared him for this.

There was blood all over the sheets and the top of Elizabeth's head was a hideous bloody wound. It was as though someone had taken an axe to her skull. The sight made him grow dizzy with horror. He knew he ought to turn and run, for now that he had cried out in the silent house it was only a matter of time before his mother arrived and discovered him. But he could not move, it was as though some spell had been cast upon him. He had entirely lost control of his body and his legs were rooted to the floor.

Outside, the wind got up and the curtains billowed furiously into the room but Thomas did not see them; his gaze was fixed on his sister's body and the terrible mess that had been made of her head. He suddenly understood that her hair had been shaved away and the top of her skull had been deliberately cut open, that someone had tried to stitch it together again with black thread but that they had made a poor job of it. This was why his mother had not wanted him to see Elizabeth's body. She knew exactly what had happened because she had allowed it to take place. Perhaps she had even ordered it… But why?

He had no idea how much time had elapsed when the door he had so carefully closed was thrown open and his mother appeared in the doorway, her eyes blazing with anger.

'Well, Thomas,' she said, her voice as cold and hard as the voice of death itself. 'Now do you see what comes of disobedience?'

Anne

I know what you're thinking. Why did I cross Mrs Dempsey's threshold? And why did I stay? I must have known what kind of a house it was. I must have seen I'd be no better off there than at home. So I must have wanted that kind of life for myself, else I wouldn't have stopped there five minutes. I'd have been out of that door like the hounds of hell was after me.

Well it weren't that simple. Because nothing is ever that simple, leastways not for people like me. That's one of the things I've learned in life, though I'm the first to admit I ain't learned much. Not that learning *necessarily* solves anything, anyway. Thomas was full to the brim with learning, like a rain barrel in November, but it didn't make his life one bit easier.

Of course I quickly understood what kind of house it was – I weren't that much of a baby. I knew what men paid women for, I just didn't know when I knocked on that door that there was houses like Mrs Dempsey's where they went to do it out of the weather. Until then I'd only seen women like that *plying their trade* in the street. I'd watched them ducking down alley-ways, standing up against walls and trying their best to keep out of the light. So I thought all doxies was street-walkers. It never occurred to me that a group of them might live together in a house, with doors and beds and proper china cups, and everything nicely taken care of so that the wind didn't get where it shouldn't.

But like I say, I soon worked it out. When Mrs Dempsey introduced me to the girls on that first morning and I saw how they was all young and healthy but they lay in bed half the morning without so much as an anxious look and then when the evening came they painted their faces and put on fine dresses, it was obvious to anyone what was going on. The gentlemen came to the house in ones and twos looking jolly and talking in loud voices. Mrs Dempsey poured them brandy, and they drank her very good health. Then they went upstairs with one or other of the girls and there was all kinds of giggling and moaning coming from the rooms for a little while. Afterwards, the gentlemen left, some looking very pleased with themselves, others looking shame-faced. Well, obviously I'd have been dim-witted not to work out what game they was playing. And I weren't dim-witted. So, why did I stay?

Because Mrs Dempsey was clever, that's why. She never did anything in a hurry. She was a thinker and a planner and a schemer and a woman that could outwit her own shadow if she needed to. So when I turned up at her door like that, it didn't take her very long to see what I was worth. She drew me into her net with all kinds of treats and favours like you might go about taming a wild cat

The very first thing she did was give me the best feed I'd had in years – maybe in my whole life. She sent out Cecille, who was the only one of the girls up and about at that time and told her, 'Be sure to bring back something that will put some strength into this girl's limbs.'

Cecille was tall and pretty with big blue eyes and very dark hair hanging down her back like silk and she tutted and fussed about the *condition* I was in. 'But don't you worry, queen,' she said, 'we look after our friends at Mrs Dempsey's.'

There was lots more talk like this but I forget it now. All I remember was that I'd never felt so happy in my life. They liked me. Mrs Dempsey liked me. Cecille liked me. They wanted me there. They was going to look after me. I was out of the storm, safe and secure. The wolf had gone past without so much as catching the scent of me.

Cecille came back shortly after with an eel pie big enough to feed a *regiment* of soldiers. The smell of it was so good that when she put it on the table I swear I burst into tears. And there was some kind of drink to go with it, something in a green glass bottle that I never learned the name of. Mrs Dempsey poured it into a china cup and told me to sip it slowly. It was very sweet, and on that morning I fancied it had the flavour of cherries. Certainly, it was like nothing I'd ever drunk before, and it warmed me all the way through. I sat there, melting into the chair, like the snow thawing out on the first morning of spring.

By the time I'd finished that pie, the other girls was up and about and I was introduced to them one by one. There was Charlotte, or Charlie as she called herself. She was sweet, full of smiles and plump with apple dumplings that would have looked perfect on the prow of a ship. Her blonde hair and blue eyes put me in mind of a china doll – not that I'd ever had a doll to call my own but I'd seen them in shop windows and coveted them often enough.

Then there was Suzette, a real long-meg who could make her face look terrible stern like you was in no end of trouble before suddenly throwing back her head and laughing. Suzette spoke much less common than the other girls. A proper lady, she was, or so I thought at the time. What's more, she was *musically talented*, as I learned later that day.

Mrs Dempsey had a brand new piano in her drawing room and Suzette sat down and played the most *beautiful* music I had ever heard. And she could read and write into the bargain which was a great mystery to me in those days. Whenever Mrs Dempsey wanted anything done in that line of work, she'd give the job to Suzette who could read off the words on a letter or set them down smartly on a sheet of paper without so much as a frown on her face.

Finally there was Muriel and Estelle. They was twins. Both was small, or petite, as they called themselves, and dark with flashing eyes. On that first morning I fancied they had something of the gypsy about them, though later on I learned that their mother was a seamstress from Cheapside and their father a costermonger who lived behind St Paul's before he got the flux and died.

When I had eaten so much that my belly ached and all the girls had introduced themselves, Mrs Dempsey announced that it was time I had a wash.

'A wash?' I said. This was unexpected.

'Well, I don't like to mention it, my dear,' she said, speaking to me in a more *confidential* tone than my own mother had ever used, 'but the smell off of you would melt the candles in a cathedral, and that's the God's honest truth.'

I was *mortified*. Not that I even knew the word at that time. That was something Suzette taught me very much later, along with a great many other words, for she seemed to carry no end of them around in her head. But *mortified* I surely was, to be told that I stank, in front of all those lovely young women who seemed to me to be the very height of beauty and *refinemen*t. You can see I didn't know much about either of those two things but that was how I was when I walked into Mrs Dempsey's house. Green as grass and smelling like a cess-pit.

Mrs Dempsey herself disappeared during the washing as if she was too *delicate* to witness such a thing, though in truth there was nothing at all delicate about her. Mrs Dempsey would do whatever was needful for her own survival. But she had her position to preserve. She was above the ordinary run of the house. Mrs Dempsey *issued instructions.* She didn't bother herself with carrying them out. That was for other people.

It was Suzette who took control, as she always did in Mrs Dempsey's absence. She told me to take off me clothes and though I was shamed to do so in front of such *dazzling specimens*, I did as I was told and they all made light of it, laughing and joking like we was playing a great game, so that after a while I didn't feel too bad. Then Charlie brought in a pail of water and a sponge and she washed me all over. And I do mean all over. Not just my face and hands. But places that had never known such attention in my few short years. I bit my lip and *surrendered to the sponge*. There was no other choice for me.

Then Mrs Dempsey came back with a linen shift and a pale blue linen dress both of which was finer than anything I'd ever worn before. I never saw my own clothes again. Perhaps they was sold – more than likely they was burnt.

I suppose, if I thought about it at all, I told myself there would be other jobs for me to do at Mrs Dempsey's, washing and cleaning and the like. A house like that would need to be looked after, that only stood to reason, and I was a girl who weren't afraid of hard work. Deep down I must have known this didn't add up – but deep down is where we bury people when they die and we don't expect to find they've dug their way out again the next morning and are sitting down to breakfast.

I weren't an only child. My mother had six chits before

me, every one of them buried in the graveyard along with her parents – I was the only one what survived. 'You was determined to stay alive,' she told me once when I asked about my brothers and sisters. We was in the graveyard together at the time, standing in front of the grave with our heads bowed. 'Death came a calling for you many times but you always sent him packing,' she went on.

And that was how I thought of myself. A survivor. No matter how hard trouble came looking for me, it couldn't drag me down because it was my instinct to stay alive. So maybe that's another reason I didn't walk out of Mrs Dempsey's, make my way back home, and deliver myself up to the *tender mercies* of Harold Lampton. I made a reckoning, without even realising it, that whatever awaited me in Mrs Dempsey's I could deal with it better than I could deal with Harold Lampton. If I went home again, he would surely be the death of me.

Harold weren't the sort of man to take my disappearance lightly. I'd slipped out of his clutches and I knew he couldn't abide that. Even though he'd said I was a nuisance, even though he'd made it plain I was in the way, that didn't mean he was content for me to just walk out of the house and not come back. As far as he was concerned it was up to him to decide whether I came or went. He was in charge and he made the decisions. I was just something to be disposed of, like goods in a warehouse.

So it weren't no great surprise when he turned up at Mrs Dempsey's in the middle of the afternoon two days later looking for me. Those two days had been the most pleasant of my life, it was like I'd been floating around in a dream. To my surprise Mrs Dempsey hadn't given me any work to do. None at all. I'd done me best to help out with keeping the place clean and tidy but no one had seemed bothered whether I lent a hand or not. I didn't know what to do with myself, to tell you the truth. I mostly just followed after the girls listening to their chatter. At night I slept on a rug in a corner of the sitting room under a pile of shawls and an old cloak of Charlie's. And I'd have been perfectly happy to carry on like that but I knew in my bones it couldn't last and I was right.

Harold Lampton was blind drunk when he appeared at the front door. I could tell as much from his voice even though I was only listening from the first floor landing, being too much of a coward to even peer round the bannister to catch a glimpse of him. It was Jeremiah who answered the pounding on the door, naturally, and Jeremiah that described what happened to me afterwards

'He was standing on the doorstep, swaying from side to side like a man on board a ship,' he told me, 'the two eyes of him burning like lanterns on a foggy night.' For a man whose principal occupation was knocking other people down, Jeremiah had quite a way with words.

'I've come for the girl,' Harold said and he spat on the ground when he said it and ground his own spit into the dust.

'I don't know what you're talking about but you've no business here,' Jeremiah told him. 'Now be off with you.'

'I told you, I've come for the girl,' Harold roared. 'And I ain't leaving without her.'

'What girl would you be talking about?' Jeremiah asked, patient and polite as a draper with a lady.

'You know perfectly well who I mean. Her name's Anne and she's a little vixen that needs to be taught some manners.'

'There's no-one of that name here,' Jeremiah said and he started to close the door but Harold put his foot inside. Big feet Harold had and he wore great strong boots as hard as iron. So the door stayed open. Then he drew out a knife and showed it to Jeremiah. 'I'll find her for myself, then,' he said. 'Now stand aside unless you want me to spill your guts all over your hallway.'

So Jeremiah stood aside without another word and Harold walked straight past him. But he got no more than three paces down the hallway before Jeremiah hit him over the head with a cosh that he always kept handy inside his coat. Jeremiah knew all about hitting people over the head so Harold Lampton went down like a sack of coal and he didn't get up again. After that everybody made their way down into the hall to see what had happened.

Tuah

Captain McKerras had not gone to the market in search of a slave. He had merely been drawn by the crowd gathered around our cart and was then filled with loathing at the sight of the fat Dutchman dressed in brightly coloured clothes who was examining my arse with such thoroughness.

The captain had a great dislike of Dutchmen. 'Everywhere I sail, I find a bloody Dutchman sitting on his backside in the port, counting his silver,' he would often complain.

When the captain had taken a drink or two, and before he became so thoroughly drunk that his head slumped upon his chest and he fell to snoring, he would often set forth his views upon the nations whose ships contested the waves. 'The Portuguese believe they discovered the world,' he would say. 'The Spanish believe they mapped it. The Dutchman believes he has bought the world and the Frenchman believes he can steal it. But they are all entirely deluded for the rightful owner of the world is the Englishman and the Scotsman is his man of business.'

Of all these nations, however, it was the Dutch who most aroused his ire. 'I would not give a Dutchman's fart,' he would say about something that particularly irritated him, and when the food was bad he would hand it back to the ship's cook with a grimace and tell him to go serve it to a pig, or if he could not find a pig then no doubt a Dutchman would be glad of it.

He was, I came to see, a lonely man who considered himself set apart from his crew both by his status and by his wits, of which he had a very high opinion. He had not found his rightful place in the world he had left behind and he had gone to sea in the hope that there at least his talents might be recognised. But the wooden world was no different from the one upon which he had turned his back. The men obeyed him but they did not love him. Nor did they rightly understand him, despite being closeted up alongside him for so long.

It is my belief that the captain bought me, at least in part, as a way of occupying his time and using his mind, as a diversion from his loneliness. There is much to do at sea, of course, but there are also many empty hours when the wind is constant, the sails are set, the course is fixed and there is nothing but sea and sky to contemplate. At any rate he took the burden of my education upon himself, setting aside an hour of each morning, except Sunday, for the task of teaching me English. To begin with his method was very simple. He would point at objects, tell me their names and I would repeat them. This might take place in his cabin but more often we walked together about the ship.

Whenever we encountered Bosun Mortimer during these perambulations, the man would give us a dark look and spit over the side of the ship. The Bosun had not been happy about my coming on board. I would bring bad luck, he had warned, but his protests had been waved aside by the captain.

Bosun Mortimer was a huge man with a great black beard like a spade, and a face that looked as though it had been made of clay and then trodden upon by a drunken crowd. Though surrounded by water, he did not believe in washing and at all times he gave off a stink like rotten meat. 'I don't like the world and the world don't like me,' he used to say. And it was true. No one liked him. The crew suffered him as they suffered weevils in the biscuits and rats in the hold.

Relations between the captain and the bosun were always somewhat strained. The bosun made no secret of the fact that he regarded the captain as a fool and the captain readily returned the compliment. My arrival on board served to aggravate the situation even further.

One day, when the captain was sleeping off one of his drinking bouts in his cabin, I had been ordered to clean the decks by the bosun and I made the mistake of leaving a broom outstretched upon the deck. When he came back later to check up on my work he stumbled over the broom and hit his head upon the mast with such a thump that those nearby turned at the sound. When he had recovered his wits, he was so infuriated that he shook with rage and I knew immediately I would be beaten.

He had me tied to a stanchion and he whipped me himself. I do not know how many times for I passed out before the end. *Wherefore doth a living man complain, a man for the punishment of his sins?*

Afterwards, when I was cut free and lay slumped upon the deck, coming back into a confused consciousness of the terrible pain in my back that was all torn and bloody from the knots in the whip, he stood and pissed upon me, laughing as he did so. From that day onwards, if I was slow to carry out any task he would ask me if I wanted him to piss upon my back again. It was a joke he never tired of repeating.

The captain was extremely angry when he learned how I had been flogged. Mr Gilbert, the ship's doctor, told me this as he removed the dressings from my back a week later. Apparently, Captain McKerras had woken from his drunken slumber and called for me. When he was informed that I was receiving treatment from the ship's doctor he had demanded to know what had occasioned it.

'Someone must have told him about the bosun pissing on your back,' said Mr Gilbert, 'and that sent him into a rage. The captain don't hold with abusing the men, says he leaves that sort of thing to the Dutch. Anyway, he marches straight up to Bosun Mortimer with a pistol in his hand, cocked and loaded. He puts the pistol to the bosun's head and asks him to name one good reason why he shouldn't blow his brains out then and there. You know what the bosun told him?"

I did not understand everything that Mr Gilbert said for my English was but poorly developed at this time but I understood this was a question that I could not possibly answer so I shook my head.

'*You need me to run this ship* – that's what he said and he didn't so much as turn a hair at the sight of the pistol, neither. I reckon if Death himself came looking for Mortimer with his scythe in his hand, the man would stand up straight and defy him. So anyhow, there they were, the two of them, face to face, with the whole crew looking on and not a man among them daring to breathe. Of course it were the captain what gave way in the end, as the bosun knew he'd have to. For one thing, it don't matter what a man does, you can't go blowing his brains out just because you're feeling put out, specially not just because a nigger's been flogged. And for another, the bosun was quite right. He's the man who keeps the ship afloat and all of us making headway along the great blue highway. All right, the captain sets the course and takes the helm when he has a fancy to, but that's about it.'

I had been quite unaware of this postscript to my flogging for immediately I was cut loose, two of the crew had carried me to Mr Gilbert's cabin where he at once gave me a dose of laudanum before commencing to bind up my wounds. It was my first experience of the drug and I suspect that Mr Gilbert administered far too strong a dose, for I was in a confused state for the rest of that day and the following one. Moreover, I was filled with such an enormous weariness that I could hardly raise myself from the floor in order to eat. Despite this, the drug did not entirely take away the pain of my back. Instead, it filled my head with thoughts which seemed so luminous and of such powerful import that the pain of my back became almost an irrelevance.

Chiefly, my thoughts were of my uncle. Over and over again I came upon him lying on the ground outside his hut with his throat cut open and his blood spilled upon the dry earth. But though he was dead it seemed as if he spoke to me somehow, whispering to me to get it quickly and bring it to him, though what 'it' might be, I could not make out. I searched his hut, trying to find something that might satisfy him but everything that he owned lay in pieces on the floor. I picked up a few shards of broken pottery and tried without success to fit them back together again, all the while weeping at the thought of how much I was disappointing him.

The next day but one I was back at work, my chief task, in those early days, being the swabbing of the decks. A layer of salt and grime was forever being formed upon those planks, and the crewmen assured me that it would rot and warp the wood if it were not washed away. In addition, the filth that sea birds seemed to delight in depositing had to be removed. Then, finally the boards must be rubbed smooth with a sandstone so that no splinters might form. The moment I was finished one deck it was time to start again on another. Within a few days of being taken on board the Laurel Bower I had come to know those decks as intimately as a lover knows the body of his beloved.

My mind was still greatly befogged that morning and it seemed to me as I gazed closely upon the deck, that there were pictures within the grain of the wood, faces that leered and mocked me or gazed upon me with a tender sadness as if they knew some awful truth about me that I myself could not comprehend. I became convinced, moreover, that those faces had not just then appeared but that that they had been always there, locked within the wood, like spirits or like some other order of being entirely. Only now that my eyes had been opened through suffering, was I able to see them. But soon enough the faces faded and I was left with nothing but the salt-encrusted planks and the burning pain of my back.

When it was clear after some weeks of swabbing decks, that I was beginning to understand what was said to me, it was decided that the time had come for me to climb the rigging. For my training in this I was given over into the hands of a young seaman known to all as Nimble Peterkin, a slim, fresh-faced fellow with a great deal of curly red hair, a beard that seemed to grow only in patches, and a ready smile that was at its widest when he climbed the rigging – which he did with so much grace it was like a kind of dance.

As I prepared to go aloft for the first time I was watched by all the crew to see how I would acquit myself. Bosun Mortimer in particular stood planted at the foremast with a hungry look upon his face. I knew that he was hoping to see me overcome by fear, or better still to see me climb to a great height then lose my footing and topple down upon the deck, my body smashed and broken. *Be sober, be vigilant; because your adversary the devil, as a roaring lion, walketh about, seeking whom he may devour.*

Indeed, Mr Thomas, the quartermaster, a small neat man with bright blue eyes who delighted in gossip and whose nickname was Jolly James, had warned me that morning to be extra careful on the ropes. 'For that same cotton shirt and breeches that you now wear formerly belonged to a boy called Adam who grew too free and easy up there and lost his footing. Broke his neck when he hit the deck.'

Jolly James had come out from his cubby-hole along with all the others to see me climb. I do not know whether his tale of Adam's fall was a true one or merely some invention of his own to add to my unease but I determined not to give him, or any of them, the satisfaction of seeing me quail. I took the rope firmly in my hand and I began to climb.

As it turned out, I found no difficulty whatsoever in mounting the rigging. The higher I climbed, the more exhilarated I began to feel. It seemed to me that in this aerial kingdom I had found a greater freedom than existed anywhere else on board and as I learned more about the business of managing the ropes and canvas I took real pleasure in the thought that by the simple action of furling or unfurling of the sails, I could influence the whole course and destiny of the Laurel Bower and its company. *But they that wait upon the Lord shall renew their strength; they shall mount up with wings as eagles.*

It was Nimble Peterkin who informed me of the ship's business, which I had not thought to enquire about until that time for there was so much else to learn. It had not occurred to me that the ship might have some greater purpose other than simply to sail the waves like some great restless beast.

'Opium,' he told me as we stood side by side nearly two hundred feet above the deck on the topgallant yard with the roar of the wind filling our ears and the seagulls riding the currents of the air down below us. 'We pick it up in India and bring it to the Chinese you see, on account of them having such a great appetite for it. Their government don't particularly like us supplying them, mind, but the captain knows a deal more tricks than a Chinaman. So he talks to them nicely, or he bribes them, and if that don't work then we makes our way secret-wise like an eel slipping through a fisherman's grasp.'

'But what is this opium?' I asked.

Peterkin frowned at me. 'You know very well what it is.'

'How could I?'

'On account of Mr Gilbert giving you a dose of it only two weeks back to stop you thinking about them stripes upon your back.'

'The medicine?'

'Aye, it is a right handy medicine when it's properly managed. But that's not why them Chinamen desire it. For a start they don't drink it in wine, they smokes it. And they does so because they likes it. No other reason. The more they gets of it, the more they wants it. I've seen 'em in the smoking houses, scores of them, and not just in China neither. Back home and all. Englishmen, Chinamen, any other kind of men you might care to mention, lying one next t'other on the floor like the wounded and the dying, and all of them wanting just one thing – more.'

'You think it is a bad thing, then?'

'No thinking about it, Abdul. It's got to be a bad thing. Ain't no way it can be anything else. What makes you want more, makes you weak. That's why the Chinese government don't want us bringing it in.'

'Then why are you…?' I struggled for the words.

'Why am I a party to it?'

I nodded.

'A man has to live. Simple as that.'

After that, he would say no more.

Thomas

He heard the clock in the front parlour of Greenhay striking nine o'clock and a small sigh escaped his lips, though he was careful to make sure that no one else heard it. Almost the entire household had been gathered together on the lawn since six and the air was beginning to turn chilly, though it was mid-summer and still pleasant enough out of doors, if such an occasion could ever be called pleasant. They were awaiting the return of the carriage that would contain Mr De Quincey, a man whom Thomas had scarcely seen more than a handful of times in his entire life; indeed, Thomas was not at all sure that he would recognise his father were he to meet him in the street; except, of course, that he would not meet him in the street for Mr De Quincey would not be out and about, taking a pleasant stroll in village, town, city or the English countryside: Mr De Quincey was dying, and had returned to England for the express purpose of ending his time on Earth in a respectable location and surrounded by a respectable household.

The servants all knew this. They understood, moreover, that each and every one of them was a part of that respectable household and, since Mrs De Quincey had instructed them to line up and wait outside the house, then line up and wait outside the house they must, howsoever long it might take for the carriage to appear. Mrs De Quincey had gone to meet her husband at Bristol and their return together had been expected for the last three hours.

Thomas risked a glance in the direction of William. His older brother was sitting on the low wall between the lawn and the flower beds, whittling a stick with a pocket-knife. He happened to look up at that very moment and Thomas quickly turned away, but he was too late to avoid a scornful look.

William's arrival at Greenhay the previous evening was an event to which Thomas had been eagerly looking forward, despite the sombre occasion that had necessitated his brother's return. The older boy was as much a stranger to the household as Mr De Quincey, having lived for a time with his father in Lisbon and then having been sent to a boarding-school in Lincolnshire where he had remained until a few days ago, not even returning in the school holidays. Thomas had even less recollection of William than of his father; indeed, he had spent a great deal of time during the last fortnight trying to imagine what his brother might look like.

He had waited impatiently all day for the arrival of his brother's coach and when it had finally appeared at the end of the drive he had run out to meet it. A sturdy looking boy in a stiff collar, black coat and striped trousers had descended and regarded him with obvious distaste.

'Don't tell me you're Thomas,' he had said.

Thomas was crestfallen. 'Yes, I am,' he admitted.

'God! What an awful little runt you are.' William turned to the footman, who was struggling to take down a trunk from the roof of the carriage. 'I say! Careful with that box. The catch isn't very reliable.' Then he marched off towards the house, leaving Thomas to follow miserably after him.

It had already been decided that William would share Thomas's room and so immediately after dinner, William went upstairs and began a detailed examination of the bedroom's contents while Thomas stood warily in the doorway, watching. It did not take William long to come across Thomas's stone sitting in pride of place on the mantelpiece. Thomas had discovered it a few months earlier in the garden: it was uniformly grey, the grey, Thomas liked to imagine, of an elephant's hide, very smooth and almost triangular in shape. Thomas had liked the feel of it in his hand when he first picked it up and after he had taken it into the house and washed it, he liked to press it against his cheek and imagine the long, dark tunnel of history through which it had travelled to arrive at this moment of cherishing.

'What on earth is this?' William demanded.

'It's my stone,' Thomas told him.

William gave him a pitying look. 'Your stone!'

Thomas bowed his head, unable to meet his brother's gaze.

With a sudden burst of energy, William crossed the room, opened the window and flung the stone outside. 'Stones belong in the garden,' he said, 'not in the bedroom.' He closed the window. 'What else have you been hoarding away up here?'

Thomas shook his head. 'Nothing.'

William's eye fell upon the leather bound notebook that lay face down upon the bookshelf. Thomas immediately darted across the room in an attempt to reach it but he was too late. William had already picked it up and opened it.

'A true account of the people and history of Gombroon,' he read. 'Gombroon? Where on earth is that?'

'It is a country I have invented,' Thomas said.

William's eyes widened. 'A country you have invented?'

'Yes.'

William considered this for some time. Finally he said, 'Tell me, what is the principal industry of this imaginary country of yours?'

'The principal industry?'

'Surely that is not too difficult a question! From what do its inhabitants derive their wealth?'

'I hadn't thought.'

'You hadn't thought! What a pitiful condition the economy of this country must be in. Look here, who is the ruler of these Gombroonians, if that is what you call them?'

'I suppose I am.'

'You, the ruler? I don't believe you are fit to rule a line on a piece of paper. Very well then, perhaps you can tell me this: on what basis are your subjects taxed?'

Thomas shook his head. 'I don't know.'

William replaced the book on the shelf. 'You are the most complete disappointment that could possibly be imagined,' he said.

Not another word had been exchanged between them since that conversation. Now they stood on the lawn along with Thomas's remaining older sister, Mary, and Richard who, at six years old, was judged old enough to take part in the arrival party, unlike Jane and Henry who were allowed to remain untroubled in the nursery. Behind them stood the servants, arranged in order of precedence. All of them had been that way for hours.

Sunset came and went but none of them left their stations. William whittled his stick to nothing and put away his pocket-knife. The clock in the drawing room struck nine and Richard was sent to bed. The clock struck ten and the servants muttered among themselves but not one of them was prepared to be absent when Mrs De Quincey and her husband arrived.

It was nearly midnight when a collective decision was reached that they should move in one body out of the grounds, on the chance of encountering the travelling party on the road, though spirits were low and few among them still expected their master to arrive at so late an hour.

Thomas, more asleep than awake, trailed along towards the rear of the procession, clutching the hand of Milly the parlour maid. Behind him, Mary's hand was held firmly by the cook, Mrs Danforth. William declined to hold the hand of anyone and sauntered along with his hands in his pockets, looking as if nothing about this whole business could possibly concern him in the least.

To everyone's surprise, they came upon the party bearing Mr De Quincey within five minutes of setting out. The carriage was coming at so slow a pace that the fall of the horses' feet was not audible as anything more than a gentle rumble until the servants were almost face to face with their master and mistress. The first clear notice of the approach was the sudden emergence of the horses' heads from the deep gloom of the shady lane. A gasp of surprise came from the servants, and an answering whinny from the horses at this unexpected meeting.

What struck Thomas as the carriage came into full view was the mass of white pillows against which his father was reclining. This and the hearse-like pace of the procession recalled vividly to his mind the memory of his sister's funeral and he felt himself almost buckle at the knees, overcome with sudden sadness.

The servants now began to return towards the house in advance of the carriage. Thomas, who had been towards the rear of the party but was now at its front, was still so deep in recollections of Elizabeth's funeral that he did not notice his brother William sidle up beside him until William was bending towards him and practically breathing into his ear.

'Do you remember the other Jane?' William asked.

Thomas had been so firmly convinced that William had resolved not to speak to him ever again that he was quite at a loss for words.

'The one who died,' William added bluntly.

Of course Thomas knew who William meant. The other Jane was the sister who had died before Elizabeth. Thomas had been no more than five years old at the time and the details were very vague in his mind. He had some idea that she had been treated harshly by someone, a servant perhaps, but it was something that was never spoken about.

William shook his head. 'You know nothing, do you?'

'That's not true!' Thomas objected. 'I know about Elizabeth.'

Instinctively, both boys glanced around in case Thomas's words had been overheard, but no one was paying them the slightest attention.

"Do you know why I was sent away?'

'To go to school, of course.' Even as Thomas spoke the words he was conscious of their inadequacy. If that was the beginning and end of the matter William would surely not have asked the question.

'I was sent away because I was difficult to manage,' William hissed.

Thomas did not find this information in the least surprising, though it did somehow chill him, as though his brother were some malevolent spirit come to plague him, and the two boys continued to walk in silence for some time. Then William inclined towards Thomas once more. 'Have you ever wondered about the chief industry of Greenhay?' he whispered.

Thomas looked at him blankly

'I see that you have not,' William continued. 'It has never occurred to you to ask such a question. What about the basis upon which its citizens are taxed? You have not considered that either, I suppose.'

Thomas shook his head. He could make no sense of his brother's questions.

'Then I shall enlighten you, little brother.'

Thomas's gaze had been fixed on the ground in front of him, for he was so exhausted by his ordeal that it would have been the easiest thing in the world for him to stumble and pitch headlong onto the stones of the road. But there was something about the tone of William's voice that made him glance up. Even in the darkness of the lane it was clear to him that William's face wore a most peculiar expression, as if he were filled with a very great anger but at the same time as if he found that anger oddly amusing.

'The basis of taxation in Greenhay is obedience,' William told him, 'and the chief industry of our little kingdom is death.'

With these words, he moved away from Thomas and his face changed back to its customary expression of barely concealed disdain.

Anne

No doubt Mrs Dempsey had been expecting Harold to show his face from the moment I entered her house, for she always *calculated* things in advance, and now that he'd been dealt with, she lost no time proceeding with the next stage of her plan. She was a great one for plans.

I'd hidden in Charlie's room. Now that the fuss was all over she was standing in front of the mirror brushing her hair and I was peering out of the window watching Jeremiah making his way along the alley that ran behind the house. He had Harold Lampton thrown over his shoulder like a sack of coal. I was just about to ask Charlie what she supposed he'd do with Harold for I still weren't convinced I was rid of him entirely, when the door opened and Mrs Dempsey entered.

'Come with me, child,' was all she said.

At these words my heart stopped beating and my legs turned to water. I was quite certain she intended to throw me out on the street then and there. I'd proved too much trouble and she would wash out the household without delay, like a doctor doing a purge. Of course the truth was that I was the most *valuable commodity* in her house just then but like a fool I didn't understand what I was worth.

To my relief, instead of showing me the front door she led the way upstairs to the very top of the house where Muriel and Estelle shared a room. At the end of their corridor was a door I hadn't yet opened though I'd explored most of the house since my arrival. It suddenly came to me that she was going to shut me in this room as a punishment for drawing Harold Lampton upon them and my relief was immediately replaced with dismay. I decided my best course of action was to throw myself at Mrs Dempsey's feet and plead for mercy. But by the time I'd come to this decision she'd already opened the door

The room was small and almost entirely taken up with a wooden bed and mattress. Mrs Dempsey sat down on the bed and waved her hand for me to do the same.

'Now then, Anne,' she said when we was sitting side by side, 'I am going to show you something that I was obliged to learn for myself when I was your age and I am doing this because I believe it may be of considerable assistance to you in the years that are to come.'

'Yes, Mrs Dempsey,' I said though I hadn't the first idea what she was talking about.

'Tell me,' she continued, 'have you ever seen a map of England, or indeed a map of any other country?'

This was unexpected but I nodded my head all the same. My father had come back from the docks one day and rolled up in the sleeve of his coat was a map that he'd bought from another labourer who'd taken it from a ship. My father was very pleased indeed with his purchase, telling my mother and me that he'd paid a favourable price because the fellow who sold it to him didn't understand its true value. 'He weren't no more than a mutton head,' my father repeated several times, chuckling heartily to himself.

He unrolled the map with great care and spread it upon

the floor of our room, weighting down each of the corners with his own shoes, his knife, and a stone bottle that had once held strong drink but had long since stood empty.

He explained to us that the shape on the paper was a picture of the coastline and all the countryside of England, Scotland, Wales and Ireland, and the dots and letters stood for the towns. I thought it a beautiful thing and shared my father's delight. But while my mother admired the colours and the lively pictures of the winds and of sea serpents that decorated the edges, she quickly grew tired of the map itself. She was of the opinion that my father would do well to sell it as quickly as ever he could lest that pack of thieves that infested our basement should get wind of it. 'For if there's anything of value to be found within a mile of here, those villains will sniff it out before the world is a day older and lay their pox-ridden hands upon it.'

My father accepted the truth of her opinion and the map was sold the following day, though not for quite as much money he'd hoped. All the same, the sight of it spread out upon our floorboards had made me fully aware of what I'd only half understood until that time, that this great country of ours ain't no more than a lump of rock floating in a great expanse of sea. I understood also, that there was plenty other such lumps of rock both near and far and that the chief business of the world was to ferry goods from one of these lumps to another.

I didn't say a word of this to Mrs Dempsey of course for I assumed she would not be interested either in my father's pride or in my own clumsy understanding of the *mercantile world*. But in this last assumption I was wrong for it was of trade and shipping that she now began to talk.

'Look up at the ceiling,' she told me. 'Do you see that stain in the far corner? Does it not seem to you that it resembles the outline of a country such as you might come across depicted on some map?'

'Well, yes, I suppose it does.'

'I want you to imagine a ship, sailing round the coastline of that country, stopping at ports to take on board supplies and trade with the natives. Can you do that?'

'I think so.' It seemed a very strange thing to ask, that I pretend the mark left on the wall by some ancient flood was a kingdom I could sail around. It weren't at all the sort of pastime I would have expected a woman like Mrs Dempsey to engage in. I turned and looked at her curiously but her eyes was fixed firmly on the stain so I regarded it again and tried to believe in this game of make belief since she seemed to consider it so very important.

'Very well then, Anne. Now I want you to concentrate as hard as ever you can upon that picture of a ship sailing into port. You have seen plenty of ships in the docks, I am sure?'

'Yes, Mrs Dempsey.'

'Then imagine it is your own ship. Consider how the sails snap in the wind and how the sailors spring to their tasks, keeping the course that their captain has planned.'

'But I don't think the sailors would be very happy to find a girl on board their ship, Mrs Dempsey.'

'It is not their ship, Anne. It is yours and they are all your sailors. They will be happy or sad as you desire them to be. Likewise, the natives they encounter in this strange county will be savage or gentle, and the inns wherein the sailors board will be full of pleasure or misfortune, as you alone decide. Do you understand me?'

'Yes, Mrs Dempsey,' I assured her, though in truth I was understanding less and less as the conversation went on. The words she spoke made perfect sense but why she had brought me to this room and shared this *vision* was quite beyond me.

Mrs Dempsey got up from the bed. 'Then I have done my best for you,' she announced. 'Now this evening you must begin to work for me and I hope you will do your very best to give satisfaction.'

'Oh yes, Mrs Dempsey.'

'Good. Then I will send Suzette up to talk to you presently.'

She left me sitting on the bed, terrified to hear my work would now begin in earnest. All the stories I'd told myself about cleaning the house or running errands crumbled away to dust. What a fool I'd been! Anyone could see this house was like a great windmill and its sails turned solely for the purpose of a man's *secret pleasure*. Now the time had come for me to put my shoulder to the mill wheel. For this, I had run away from home.

As I sat there, *contemplating my ruin*, Suzette entered the room, carrying a small blue glass bottle in her hand and smiling sympathetically. She sat down on the bed beside me.

'I have come to explain the rules of the house,' she told me.

I nodded. I'd always imagined there must be rules though so far I hadn't been able to work out what they might be, other than that Mrs Dempsey was in charge and Suzette was her lieutenant.

'Every man who is invited to enter this house does so as a guest of Mrs Dempsey,' she continued. 'A guest. Do you understand what that means?'

'Course I do.'

'No man is ever to be made to feel unwelcome and no man is ever to be mocked or belittled. A man's dignity is a very delicate thing. Even though he might be as strong as Samson, his dignity will be no stronger than a bird's egg. Do you follow me, Anne?'

'I think so...'

'The worst thing you can do to a man is laugh at him and

the gravest insult of all is to laugh at what he carries between his legs. If there should ever be cause to talk about it, and there are men who will wish to hear such talk, then you should always tell him that his cock and balls are the finest you have ever seen. Oh, and lastly, it may be that from time to time a man loses his courage and cannot do the deed for which he came here. Then you must thank him for his kindness, as if he were only considering your feelings, and assure him that there will always be another occasion. Do you understand all this?'

'I'm not sure.'

'The man is always in the right. That is the principal thing to remember. Unless, of course, he should seek to do you real violence. God forbid that should happen, but if it ever should, you must scream at the top of your lungs and Jeremiah will be through that door and upon him like a dog after a rat.'

I must have looked *utterly terrified* at this for she put her arm around my shoulders. 'Do not distress yourself, Anne,' she said gently. 'I have never known such a thing to happen in Mrs Dempsey's. Most of the men who visit us are no more than babies without their breeches. In any case they get a good look at Jeremiah when they step through the front door and that's enough to keep them in their place. As for Mr Bayliss, whom you will be entertaining this evening, he could no more do you violence than he could take off his own boots.' She said this last with a smile and I wondered what she might mean by it. Who was this Mr Bayliss and why could he not take off his own boots? Now she held up the blue glass bottle. 'I have something else to give you besides advice,' she declared.

'What is it?'

'Oil.'

I looked at her in *complete bewilderment.*

'You must rub it between your legs.'

I took the bottle from her and pulled out the cork. The smell was strange and sweet.

'It will make things a great deal easier for you, I promise.'

That evening, there I was sitting in the parlour along with the others, listening to Suzette playing the piano when Jeremiah announced Mr Bayliss.

The first thing I thought when I clapped eyes on him was that what Suzette had said about him being *incapable of violence* was entirely false. He would surely crush my body beneath his without even realising it for he was a great fat, red-faced gundiguts with lips as thick as rope and eyes like a pig. My second thought was the desperate hope that before any such thing could happen he might drop down dead on the staircase since he could barely get his breath from walking the length of Mrs Dempsey's hallway.

Mrs Dempsey made a great fuss of him, as if he was one of her oldest and most valued friends. She remarked on how very well he was looking and she told Charlie to pour him out a glass of brandy without delay.

Mr Bayliss accepted both the compliment and the brandy as though they was no more than his due and his great thick lips twisted into a smile but from the moment he entered the room I was the subject of his real interest. His eyes was fixed on me like a couple of magpies feasting on a dead dog and I felt myself tremble and shake under that *terrible scrutiny.*

'Anne is the newest member of our household,' Mrs Dempsey informed him. 'She has only just recently joined us.' She said this, as though conveying a piece of news but I was in little doubt that Mr Bayliss knew all about me already and that I was the very reason he had entered under our roof.

He sipped his brandy and his gaze travelled up and down my body. 'A very great asset she will prove I am sure,' he replied. And then to me, 'Are you a willing girl, Anne?'

Everyone in the room but Suzette whose eyes was fixed upon the piano turned their heads to look at me.

'Yes sir,' I muttered.

'That is what we like to see, Mrs Dempsey,' Mr Bayliss said. 'The bloom of youth and a willing disposition. What more can anyone ask for?'

When my father was alive there was a lane not far from where we lived called Petty Drake and in that lane a man called Three Fingered Harry used to keep a stall selling live eels that he brought fresh to the market every day in a tin bath. He had a wooden block and he would hack those eels to pieces for the customers. I'm told it was on that very same block he accidentally chopped off his two missing fingers. But it was the eels that concerned me when I was a little girl far more than Harry's missing fingers. The chopped up bits of them used to squirm about and wriggle long after they'd been severed from each other. Three Fingered Harry had just the one tooth in the middle of his mouth, so long and brown you could have used it for a clothes peg. Mostly he was silent but at odd times, he would grin down at the bits of eel and remark, 'They don't know they're dead'. That single phrase was his only bit of conversation but, like his tooth, he got good value from it.

When Mr Bayliss finished his brandy and declined a second glass saying that he believed he would ask Miss Anne to entertain him further, I felt like one of them eels, bloody and squirming and convinced I still lived when really I was well and truly dead.

Up the stairs I went with him behind me, panting like a *terrible ogre* from a nightmare. Several times he had to stop to catch his breath but it was still too soon when I opened the door of the little room at the top of the house and he followed me inside.

He sat down on the edge of the bed with a great sigh and it seemed to me the whole room shook from the weight of him. Then he stayed very still for a long time, staring at me with a strange kind of look on his face so that I wondered was he in pain. I wanted him to speak, I wanted to know what he was thinking about, I wanted to shout at him to get on with it or go back downstairs and leave me alone – but I couldn't say a word. I felt like I'd never even learned to talk. So instead, I just stood with my back to the door, looking back at him and waiting.

'Take your dress off,' he said, at last.

I took off my dress, fumbling with the laces like a child. My fingers seemed swollen to the size of sausages. All the time I was aware of him watching me like a cat watches a bird it plans to make a meal of.

'And your shift.'

I pulled it over my head. Then I was standing there completely naked while he continued to look me up and down, judging me, matching me up against some idea of a girl that he carried around in his head, the girl Mrs Dempsey had sold him, no doubt. Finally, he seemed satisfied. 'Help me off with these breeches,' he ordered.

I did as I was bid, though it weren't no easy matter, the cloth being so plastered to his body with sweat that it felt more like skinning an animal than pulling off his clothes.

To my surprise when the breeches was at last peeled away, there weren't no obvious sign of his cock and for a moment I wondered did he have one at all. But he guided my hand to where it was, buried deep in the great sack of his belly. I very nearly asked him how he knew where to find it but I recalled Suzette's advice about a *gentleman's dignity* and passed no remark.

What I could find to take hold of was small enough compared to Harold Lampton's great monster but it seemed to give him every bit as much pleasure for he moaned out loud when I touched it. 'You're a good girl, Anne,' he told me.

I wanted to reply that I was anything but a good girl but I held my peace as well as his cock.

What followed was a tricky business. I soon learned that the fear I would be crushed was quite unfounded. Mr Bayliss did not propose to climb on top of me at all and in truth I think the great sack of his belly would have made such a thing impossible. Instead he bade me sit upon his lap with my legs astride and instead of him mounting me I must mount him.

I had only the vaguest of notions what I was about and all the time I kept losing track of his small cock in the vast mountain of his belly but eventually I succeeded. Then he took hold of my sides and forced me down upon him which was very painful even with the oil that Suzette had given me. I cried out with the pain of it and his eyes lit up, as if this was what he had longed for most of all. He held my body clamped within his great fat hands, and grunting with the effort he moved me up and down upon his cock like a man trying on a pair of gloves, until his eyes rolled in his head and he whimpered and whined like a dying animal. The only mercy was that the whole thing was over much more quickly than I had expected.

Afterwards, there was some blood which he wiped from his cock with a cloth that lay upon the bed. I didn't remember seeing that cloth there earlier and it occurred to be that Mrs Dempsey must have placed it there for this very purpose. Then he lay back down upon the bed, shut his eyes and very quickly began to snore.

Tuah

In telling this tale I am conscious I have made it seem as though I learned English without any great effort. The truth, of course, was very different. For many months I was like a simpleton, nodding where I should have shaken my head, grinning hopefully where I should have looked downcast. The replies I made were stumbling and often nonsensical. But slowly I began to understand the life of the ship and learn the words I needed to hold my place within it. *The heart of the prudent getteth knowledge; and the ear of the wise seeketh knowledge.*

Peterkin had explained to me that opium was The Laurel Bower's business, the reason every man had come on board and the means by which they meant to make their fortunes. Now I began to see how that business was conducted as the ship left the open sea and slowly navigated its way down the steaming waters of the Hooghly River, stopping every few days to allow Captain McKerras to go ashore. Afterwards the opium was brought on board in cedar wood chests where it was treated by the men with the greatest reverence. *If therefore ye have not been faithful in the unrighteous mammon, who will commit to your trust the true riches?* Then it was stowed carefully in the hold under the watchful eye of Mr Priestley, the First Mate.

I have not spoken much of Mr Priestley hitherto, perhaps because there was not much to say of him. I do not mean that he was an individual of no significance, for on the contrary, it was well-known among the crew that his uncle was one of the most powerful men in the Company. But he was a man whose purposes were obscure, a man who kept the closest possible guard upon his words and deeds. Indeed, his very thoughts seemed to be imprisoned behind his dark, brooding eyes.

He was the tallest man on board, so tall that he was forever stooping to avoid hitting his head upon doorways, but as thin as a shadow and the only man who shaved his beard every day. It was rumoured that he wrote at great length in a ledger each evening and it was widely believed that this record was kept solely for the Company's benefit – and that this was the real reason for his presence on board. Every man was careful what he said in Mr Priestley's hearing, including Bosun Mortimer. Even Captain McKerras himself was always a great deal more guarded in his manner towards Mr Priestley than towards any other man, and this was true even when the captain was in his cups.

Because of the opposition of the Chinese to our trade, the Laurel Bower never once set down on the mainland of that country. Instead, we dropped anchor off the coast of Lintin Island in the mouth of the Pearl River where a great many other ships were also to be found riding at anchor. Some of these were respectable merchantmen, carrying cargoes of wool and cotton, but many more, like the Laurel Bower, were laden with opium packed in wooden chests. In addition, amongst these seaworthy vessels there were a number of abandoned hulks that had been left to rot by their owners and were now used as floating warehouses by the smugglers. In their little boats, some of which were very roughly made indeed, these enterprising individuals threaded their way in and out of the larger ships like mosquitoes in search of blood. They generally came on board the Laurel Bower by night, talking in low voices with the captain and Mr Priestley in the captain's cabin, before emerging once more to carry off our cargo and dispose of it by ways and means known only to themselves.

To be moored off the coast of Lintin Island for any length of time was not a situation the crew much cared for. The air was foul and the anchorage perilous, the sight of so many broken masts and black rotting hulls cast a profound gloom over us all, and if our arrival chanced to coincide with the monsoon season, as it did on one occasion, the ship was lashed all day and all night by rain so fierce and incessant that no man dared go above deck. Captain McKerras would sit in his cabin reading his bible for hour after hour. Certain passages he would make me repeat after him until I learned them by heart. One of his favourites was from the Psalms: *They that go down to the sea in ships, that do business in great waters, these see the works of the Lord and his wonders in the deep. For he commandeth and raiseth the stormy wind, which lifteth up the waves thereof. They mount up to the heaven, they go down again to the depths; their soul is melted because of trouble.*

The first time he made me repeat this I asked him what the word 'soul' might mean but although he spoke at great length upon the subject I could make no sense of his answer. But lately, as old age creeps over me, I often think of that psalm, for my soul was indeed melted when I was taken on board the Laurel Bower and forever after it was a strange, misshapen thing. Elsewhere in the Psalms I have read: I*t was good for me to be afflicted so that I might learn your decrees* and perhaps that is true.

It was during a spell of particularly bad weather that Captain McKerras became sick. His illness began with a dry cough that seemed a small enough matter but very quickly progressed to a terrible deep hacking, the force of which bent him double. In no time at all he was shivering and too weak to leave his bed. From that day onward Mr Priestley assumed command; he did so without any fuss, but it was as if he had been waiting for this moment, and it was immediately obvious that he understood all the business of captaining a ship so the crew accepted their new master without question and seemed to settle to their work with less complaint than when the captain was in charge. Indeed under Mr Priestley's command the Laurel Bower even seemed to sail more smoothly upon the water.

The care of Captain McKerras became my job. I brought him his meals and did my best to keep him clean. Mr Gilbert came to see him each day, often to draw blood from the captain's arm, a practice which he assured me was absolutely necessary to rid him of the poison but which only seemed to me to make the captain weaker.

'What he really needs,' Mr Gilbert declared repeatedly, 'is Fever Tree Bark.' But it seemed that the ship did not possess any of this precious commodity. The Dutch controlled the supply and were not prepared to share it with anyone. Instead, therefore, Mr Gilbert had recourse to laudanum. 'It is the next best thing,' he assured me as he perched like a crow on a stool beside the captain's bed while I sat cross-legged in a corner of the room.

In Mr Gilbert's opinion the captain's infection was the consequence of a deliberate act of policy on the part of the Chinese. 'They know how poisonous their cursed island is. That is the reason they force us to tie up there for weeks on end. They hope to kill us all without so much as firing a shot or wielding a blade.'

'You think the captain will die then?' The thought of life on board without the protection of the captain dismayed me greatly for even though he was gravely ill, I knew that the others would be reluctant to lay hands upon me in case he should recover and learn of it. But were he dead I would be entirely at their mercy.

Mr Gilbert clasped his hands together and put his head to one side, frowning as if this were a very difficult calculation. 'I have seen many a man recover from just such a fever and take no lasting harm,' he said, 'but I have seen many more who were utterly undone by it. Captain McKerras is a stubborn man. He will not easily surrender his grip upon life and we must take heart from that.'

Despite Mr Gilbert's optimism, the captain diminished daily, growing old before my eyes as the fever burned away steadily inside him. He scarcely ate a morsel other than a few spoonfuls of hardtack biscuits mashed up in water to make a kind of gruel. Very soon the bones of his face stood out beneath the thin fabric of his skin so that his eyes seemed too big for his head.

At the height of his illness the captain began a strange whispering as if he were unburdening himself of some great store of secrets he had hoarded up throughout his life. So much had happened to me since the arrival of the Dutch ship off the coast of my island that you might have thought I would be quite unmoved by this and yet it unnerved me greatly for the captain stared at me so intently, and with so much anguish, as if he suffered under the burden of a terrible secret that he needed to convey to me and it put me in mind of the dream I had endured after my lashing in which my uncle had repeatedly whispered to me even though his throat was cut.

I tried as hard as I could to understand what the captain

was saying, leaning over him and putting my ear right by his mouth, and at last his words became clear to me. Over and over again he repeated, 'I love you, Abdul.'

You might think this would have pleased me but it only made me feel extremely uncomfortable. I knew well how the rest of the crew would mock and jeer if they heard him and I prayed that he would stop. 'It is merely the froth of his mind, brought to the surface by his sickness,' I told myself. 'It will subside in time.' And in time it did subside, though the silence that replaced it was just as worrying in its way.

The day that the muttering ceased I learned from Mr Gilbert that Mr Priestley had decided to return to England. The doctor came to tell the captain this news in person but the captain only stared glassily back at him. It was a decision that was popular with the men, Mr Gilbert assured me, for they had been away from their home country for more than three years now and some of them had left behind wives and children.

'All but Mr Priestley and the bosun are going round with hearty smiles upon their faces,' he continued.

'But I thought it was Mr Priestley's own decision,' I said.

Mr Gilbert nodded. 'Aye, but we was due to make one more journey between Kalkut and Lintin, see, and Mr Priestley hates to throw away the profit for the sake of the captain's health. It's not the kind of thing the Company takes a great shine to. When they authorise a ship to trade on their behalf, they do not like to see the schedule changed.'

'The captain did not fall sick on purpose.'

'That's not the way the Company will see it,' Mr Gilbert replied. 'A man who makes an undertaking should be as good as his word. That's the long and the short of it as far as they're concerned. Besides, Mr Priestley believes the captain will not last much longer so the sacrifice will be in vain.'

'Then why has he decided to return?'

'Mr Priestley is a cautious man. He knows the captain has his own connections. He won't risk upsetting them.

Although he gave no sign of understanding Mr Priestley's news, from the day that the decision to return to England was taken Captain McKerras began to recover. At first it was barely discernible. He looked a little less like a dying man, though still you would not have given very good odds on him ever getting up from his bed and resuming his former life. But day by day he became more alert and took more nourishment. Finally, one morning when I entered the cabin with his bowl of gruel, he frowned at me and struggled to raise himself on his elbows.

'Gently now, captain,' I told him, as though I were trying to manage a wild animal that had just appeared in the cabin. 'Take it easy, sir.' I squatted down beside the bed and showed him the bowl of gruel. 'I've brought you something to eat.'

'Abdul?' His voice was as weak as an infant's and so hoarse as to be unrecognisable.

'Yes, captain.'

'What has happened?'

'You have been very ill, sir.'

'Who is in charge of the ship?'

'Mr Priestley.'

He groaned and sank down on the bed once more. I tried to persuade him to take some gruel but he only shook his head and pushed it away.

But each day after that, he grew a little stronger. Within a fortnight he was out of bed and sitting in a chair, reading his bible. A week later he ventured out of his cabin for the first time and by the time we were in sight of England he was able to walk about unaided. Yet though the men all addressed him as captain, he made no attempt to resume command, only looking about with a kind of weary bewilderment as if he could not understand how he had ever involved himself in the business of sea-going.

PART TWO

The Painted Screen

Thomas

The estate of Laxton was situated in the heart of Northamptonshire, not far from Corby. The house, which stood in some ninety acres of parkland, was an imposing, block-like building with two substantial wings and a scattering of outbuildings trailing at its skirts like chickens following a mother hen. It had been constructed at the end of the previous century from a creamy yellow local stone that, Lord Carberry had informed Thomas not long after his arrival, was to be found nowhere else in the country and was very much sought after these days for buildings of the grandest sort. Lord Carberry made this declaration with a considerable degree of satisfaction, as if the quality of the stone and its universal desirability – indeed, its very existence – was something for which he had been personally responsible.

Thomas had not expected to find himself spending the summer amid such grand surroundings and even after a week with the Carberrys he was still adjusting to the change in fortune. The invitation had come about because his mother, feeling her son's presence during the long vacation to be somewhat too much for her increasingly brittle nerves, had decided it would be a good thing for him to find some task that would relieve her of the burden of regarding his dissatisfied countenance at every meal time.

Lady Carberry, though at least ten years younger than his mother, was an established friend of the family and she had always held a favourable opinion of Thomas's intellect. When, in correspondence, Thomas's mother had expressed the opinion that her son was in need of occupation, Lady Carberry had recollected the disorder into which her books and manuscripts had been descending over a period of some years and proposed a solution that had proved amenable to all parties: Thomas would organize her library.

Of all his mother's friends, Thomas considered Lady Carberry by far the most intelligent. He enjoyed her company greatly and believed that she brought out the best in him. In Lady Carberry's presence, he became somehow cleverer, more confident, more truly himself. It was as if he were breathing a different and more rarified air, an air that was both healthier and also subtly intoxicating. Although by no means an acknowledged beauty Lady Carberry possessed a potent attractiveness nonetheless – that thick, lustrous brown hair cascading down her back, those very intense blue eyes which regarded the world with such graveness but were capable, also, of an ironic amusement, and that long, slightly masculine face with its characteristically determined expression. Moreover, she seemed to possess the gift of moving easily between the generations so that in his mother's company she appeared older and altogether more conventional, while in conversation with seventeen-year-old Thomas, she seemed almost like an older sister. At times when she was listening to him speak on some complicated intellectual subject, there was the faintest hint of a raised eyebrow that seemed to convey such a wealth of unspoken understanding, Thomas found himself dizzy with anticipation.

Lord Carberry was a great many years older than his wife. Thomas did not know how many years exactly but he strongly suspected that the noble lord would not see fifty again. He was stout, with little patches of broken veins upon his cheeks and possessed a irritating habit of repeating, 'Very good, very good,' at regular intervals whenever he was being told any piece of news, whatever its import. Indeed, Thomas suspected that Lord Carberry would greet the news of his own funeral with the same, cheerfully meaningless phrase.

His lordship seemed to have no interests of any kind other than admiring his house, riding to hounds, drinking port and sleeping throughout the afternoon so that Thomas pitied Lady Carberry, yoked to such a limited individual. However, despite his faults, Lord Carberry was by no means ill-humoured and he seemed quite content to allow his wife to have her own way in almost everything. Thomas could only suppose that this provided her with some measure of compensation for the apparent tedium of their life together.

The only other guests at Laxton were a Mrs Schreiber, a mutual friend of Lady Carberry and Thomas's mother, and her daughter, Margaret. Mrs Schreiber was about the same age as his mother, Thomas believed, for she had told him when they were first introduced that they had been friends as girls. However, to Thomas's eye she looked a good deal older, being altogether shrunken in frame, the flesh of her face seeming entirely hollowed out, as if she had once been a more substantial woman. This air of being no more than a remnant of her former self, combined with the rather ancient-looking wig that perched uneasily upon her head, gave her the appearance of having been preserved and stuffed for posterity. The only thing about her that seemed to be truly alive were her eyes which were as small and dark as currants. Much of the time she sat in a corner of the drawing room, those dark eyes flitting restlessly about and an expression of settled anxiety upon her face, as though she lived in the expectation of the gravest news.

Margaret Schreiber was perhaps eight or ten years older than Thomas and as plump as a Christmas goose. She regarded him at all times with an air of severe disapproval and treated his efforts to make conversation with the utmost suspicion, only volunteering information about herself or her opinions with reluctance. He learned from an announcement made by Lady Carberry at dinner shortly after he arrived that she was engaged to be married to a Mr Edward Dunwoody who had an estate some sixty miles from Laxton. 'A sound fellow,' Lord Carberry declared, looking up from his meat at the mention of Miss Schreiber's fiancé. 'Knows a thing or two about horseflesh. Recognises a good fetlock when he sees it, what?' He looked very pleased with this last comment, grinning around the table until Lady Carberry gave him her sternest frown, whereupon he returned, somewhat chastened, to the clearing of his impressively laden plate.

Edward Dunwoody himself joined them for luncheon the following day. In his mid-forties, he seemed impossibly tall and thin. His red hair was receding at the front and his thin lips were arranged in a perpetual sneer. He contented himself with frowning and nodding in Thomas's direction when Lady Carberry introduced them, as if Thomas were not entirely visible to him, and spent almost the entirety of his visit complaining angrily about the state of the county's roads which he said were nothing short of a disgrace and an insult to the good people of Northamptonshire. Three times on his journey to Laxton he had been obliged to dismount and lead his horses through low-lying land that had become flooded for the lack of proper drainage – three times, no less! It was a matter on which he was considering litigation, for a valuable animal might easily be injured in such conditions.

Lord Carberry agreed that this was indeed a serious matter. A man depended upon his horses.

Exactly so, Dunwoody continued. He had spoken to the Lord Lieutenant about it last year on the occasion of the ball at Bellingford House but the man had only laughed uproariously as if he thought it all a great joke.

'Eglinton's not a bad chap,' Lord Carberry ventured.

'But he lacks seriousness,' Dunwoody continued, determined not to be mollified. 'The condition of the roads is not a matter for jest.'

There was a great deal more of the same before Dunwoody departed later that afternoon. The only good thing about his visit, as far as Thomas could see, was that he put Margaret in a much better mood, so much so indeed that she volunteered to play the fortepiano and sing for them that evening. Unfortunately she turned out to have almost no ear for music, playing the instrument without any kind of feeling whatsoever, rushing through passages that should have been played slowly and fumbling those that required dexterity. Her voice was tolerable in the lower register but set Thomas' teeth on edge when she reached for higher notes. By the end of the evening he was thoroughly glad to retire.

The following morning Lord Carberry left the house early to see a man about a chestnut mare he was thinking of buying. After luncheon Mrs Schreiber and Margaret set off for Northampton to visit an eminent physician whom Mr Dunwoody had recommended – Mrs Schreiber's health, Thomas was unsurprised to hear, was a matter of some concern. They had at first been reluctant to make such a difficult visit (especially given the condition of the roads) but Lady Carberry had insisted they take her best carriage and dispatched two of her ablest footmen along with them.

Thomas and Lady Carberry were left in sole possession

of the house and for some time they sat together in the morning room reading companionably in a pair of armchairs. Then Lady Carberry set down her book and Thomas did likewise, waiting for the announcement that he knew was to come.

'As you know, Thomas,' she began, 'For some years now I have been deeply interested in religion.'

Thomas was well aware of her ladyship's interest since it was the basis of her friendship with his mother.

Recently, Lady Carberry continued, she had begun a systematic study of theology, but there were many points with which she had been experiencing difficulty. As she made this confession she gave a small sigh and added, 'Oh Thomas, you cannot imagine how much I envy you.'

Thomas regarded her with astonishment. 'But why ever should you envy me, Lady Carberry?'

'Because you are a young man, Thomas, and you have received a young man's education. You are familiar with the languages of the ancient world, which is such an inestimable advantage, whereas I have been taught no more than was judged appropriate for a lady to know, in other words scarcely anything at all.'

Thomas was so greatly flattered to hear Lady Carberry speak to him in this confidential manner that he found it difficult to concentrate as she leaned forwards in her chair to explain the particular conundrum that was perplexing her at this moment.

'I have repeatedly read the statement that Our Lord began his mission upon earth by preaching the need for repentance,' she declared.

Thomas nodded. The need for repentance, of course. But even as he forced himself to focus on her words he was noticing the scent that surrounded her and that somehow summoned up in his mind images of woodland flowers, dappled glades and animals untroubled by human presence.

'The difficulty I find,' she was saying, 'is that nowhere in the Bible can I discover any reasonable grounds for this assertion. Indeed I am beginning to wonder, if it is not too presumptuous a supposition on my part, whether there might possibly be some error in the translation of the Bible into English.'

She gazed at him expectantly and Thomas realised that she was hoping for some sort of guidance from him. He ransacked his mind for something intelligent to say in response. Surely, such a fine Greek scholar as he was, he could be of some assistance. Had not one of his school masters had expressed the opinion that 'this boy could harangue an Athenian mob better than you or I could address an English one', and so... But this was not the sort of question he was used to pondering. What was the Greek word for repentance? Of course! The confidence Thomas always felt when pronouncing on matters of scholarship came flooding back.

'Perhaps it is a question of translation,' Lady Carberry,' he suggested. 'The word metanoia that appears in scripture is invariably construed as repentance, but whenever a word is translated there is always a process of adjustment to make it fit an existing concept in the second language.'

'I'm not sure I follow,' Lady Carberry said.

In my judgement,' Thomas continued, 'metanoia could more accurately be translated as spiritual transformation.'

Lady Carberry's eyebrow lifted perceptibly. 'And what is it that we are to transform?'

'Why, our intellects of course. A new spiritual revelation has been established and we must transform our mental faculties in order to apprehend it.'

Lady Carberry considered this. Then she nodded and

closed her book smartly. 'I have made up my mind to learn Greek,' she declared. 'And you must be my tutor, Thomas. If you will agree, of course.'

Thomas caught his breath at the prospect. 'Certainly Lady Carberry. I would be most honoured.'

'I must warn you, it will not be easy,' Lady Carberry said, an almost skittish look coming into her eye. 'You and I will be forced to spend long hours in the library together and I am afraid you will find me a very poor scholar.'

'I cannot believe that, Lady Carberry.'

'Oh but it is true. I shall need you to be a very stern school master indeed.'

Anne

After Mr Bayliss's visit, the little room at the top of the house became mine and I spent long hours there entertaining gentlemen, or just lying on the bed, alone. Mr Bayliss himself came back to see me two or three times a week to begin with but after that first time he never asked me to sit astride him again. What he wanted instead was just as difficult in its own way and like nothing I've ever been asked to do since.

First of all, to my surprise, he taught me to sing *London Bridge Is Falling Down*. I knew it well enough already, like every child does, so it weren't difficult for me to learn but his version was different to mine. The words was fancier, and he was *most particular* about those words. If I got them wrong he got cross and then I had to tell him I was sorry and promise to try harder. Then we'd start again and carry on until I got it right.

Of course, the singing weren't the only thing he wanted. I didn't get away with it that easy. While I was singing I also had to use my hands on his cock to 'bring him to a froth', as he put it, and I had to learn the way he wanted it done, very gently at first, then firmer and faster, but not too fast and not too firm neither, else he yelped like a dog that's got itself under a horse's feet.

I asked Charlie if this sort of thing was normal, for I only had my father and Harold Lampton to judge by and I'd never heard my mother singing to either of them. Charlie had come up to my room with some bread and a basket of whelks – they was all very good to me in those first days, especially Charlie, who was like an older sister. When I asked her about the singing she laughed out loud but she said there weren't no telling what a man might want. A fellow came to see her regular for a year and all he ever wanted was for her to piss on him. I thought she was having me on when she said this and I told her I wasn't as green as I looked but she shook her head and swore blind it was as true as she was standing there. That was what he wanted and that was what she did.

'You're telling me he paid for you to piss on him?'

'Course he paid. Mrs Dempsey wouldn't let him out of the house if he didn't pay.'

'What if you couldn't, though? What if you didn't need to go?'

'He always came at the same time and on the same day. So I used to drink a glass or two of ale beforehand just to be on the safe side.'

I gave her a hard look because I still weren't sure she was telling the truth.

'You think that's peculiar,' she went on. 'There's a gentleman comes to see Suzette once a month that likes being beaten.'

Now I stared at her with my mouth wide open.

'You'll hear it when he's here. Everyone in the house can hear it.'

'She beats him?'

'First he does the deed, then she tells him what a bad boy he's been and she wallops him on the backside with a leather strap she keeps hanging on the back of the door for that very purpose. Ask her, if you don't believe me.'

I didn't ask her, because after hearing that I was a little bit scared of Suzette but I did see the strap on the back of the door when I went into her room a couple of days later. So I knew then that it must be true.

Apart from Mr Bayliss, none of the men Mrs Dempsey found for me wanted anything out of the ordinary. Certainly no one asked me to beat them or piss upon them. Truth is, my age was enough. I was still a child, and still looked like a child and that was all they was paying for – to stick their cocks into a little girl, that was the great attraction. They all seemed to think they was very fine fellows for doing so and they obviously expected me to agree, which of course I did, that being part of the bargain.

As far as I was concerned they was all a bunch of maggots and the only difference between them was the length of time they took. Some of them had hardly started before the whole thing was over. Those were the best ones because they was gone the soonest. Others seemed to take forever, grunting and panting like their lives depended on it. The very worst was the ones what called me names and cursed, like they hated me, even while they was shoving themselves into me. Full of a dark anger against the world, they was, and me never certain they wouldn't do me some terrible mischief. I only ever breathed easily when they was out of the room.

I finally came to understand what Mrs Dempsey had been showing me when we'd sat on the bed and had our little talk about the damp spot on the wall. I discovered the value of her gift too, though at the time it had seemed to me like she was wandering in the head. Looking at that damp patch and weaving stories around it took my mind off what was happening to me. A man older and a good deal uglier than my father might be rooting away between my legs like a pig in a trough but all the time I was imagining myself sailing around those foreign countries with their forests full of unknown creatures, brightly-coloured birds and dark-skinned natives peering at me from among the trees.

Despite my fear of Suzette and the strap hanging on the back of her door, it was her what told me the truth about Harold Lampton. She asked me to come with her to Hunch-Backed Archie's one afternoon. It was from Archie's shop that all our dresses, shoes and stockings came, for Mrs Dempsey had a *reputation to uphold* and she liked her girls well turned out. Archie bought clothes cheap from people of quality who'd died before their time, or so Charlie told me, for Archie would never tell you straight out how he came by anything. If you asked him, he would only tap the side of his nose with his finger, which was as good a way as any of saying mind your own business.

Archie was the first man I ever knew that was interested in books. He weren't just interested in them, neither. He placed more store by books than he did by anything else. On those occasions, when I called into the shop with one or other of the girls he'd be in the middle of reading and he'd keep us waiting for a great length of time before he closed the book with a sigh as if it pained him to loosen his grip on the words and turn his attention to everyday things.

But that was all in the future. This particular afternoon was the first time I'd been outside the door of Mrs Dempsey's house since my arrival. I'd been terrified that the minute I set foot on the pavement Harold Lampton would reappear and pounce on me.

When Jeremiah had walked off down the alley that day with Harold slung over his shoulder like a roll of carpet, I hadn't felt relieved. Far from it. I knew what Harold

Lampton was like and I didn't believe I'd seen the last of him. As soon as Jeremiah came back that morning I'd run down the stairs to ask him what he'd done with Harold.

Jeremiah grinned. 'I set him down on a bench somewhere,' he told me.

'But what about when he wakes up and comes looking for you?'

'I'll worry about that when it happens.'

It seemed to me that he'd be *well advised* to take the matter more seriously and I tried to tell him so. He might be walking down the street one day and suddenly find himself with a knife stuck between his ribs. For that matter so might I. But Jeremiah wouldn't listen. He just insisted that he could look after himself well enough.

I decided to confess my fears to Mrs Dempsey. She was sitting in a little drawing room at the back of the house where she spent a great deal of her time. It was gloomy in there with the curtains half closed and just one candle sputtering in its holder. There was a big old clock in one corner with the hands stopped at ten to six and a stuffed bird in a glass case up on a shelf. On the table in front of her a set of fortune telling cards was spread out. She had a great fondness for consulting those cards, though she seldom told anyone what she saw. I stood in the doorway until she looked up and beckoned me in.

'Mrs Dempsey,' I said, going to stand in front of her and trying to make myself bolder than I really felt, 'I need to talk to you.'

'Then talk.' She turned over a card and looked at it sternly, as if it had no right whatsoever to be sitting there upon her table.

'It's about Harold Lampton. How can we be sure he won't come to the house again?'

She looked up from the card and frowned, as though she didn't rightly understand what I meant. Then she said, 'I expect Jeremiah gave him a good talking to when he came round.'

'I'm not sure Harold Lampton's the kind of man to listen to a good talking to.'

'Perhaps not.' She turned over another card and nodded as if it told her no more than she already knew. Then she put down the cards altogether and looked at me for some time with her head on one side, like I was a piece of furniture and she was trying to decide where to put me in the room. Finally she said, 'Perhaps you'd better not go out of doors for a few weeks, Anne. Stay inside like a good girl and I'll consult the cards. When it's safe to venture out I'll let you know.'

Then she went back to her fortune telling and I went back upstairs to my room but I weren't reassured. I thought both her and Jeremiah was *gravely underestimating* Harold Lampton. No doubt he'd bide his time but he wouldn't forget what had happened.

It was nearly a month after my talk with Mrs Dempsey that Suzette suggested I go with her to Hunch-Backed Archie's. I was surprised because although it weren't exactly disobeying Mrs Dempsey, it was going against her advice and generally speaking what Mrs Dempsey said was law. But she weren't around that afternoon. Where she was I had no idea because Mrs Dempsey didn't tell anyone her business, she'd simply announce that she would be out on a particular morning or afternoon, and Suzette would be left in control.

So when Suzette asked me to go with her to collect a dress that Archie had altered for her, I hesitated.

'The air will do you good, Anne,' she told me. 'You're starting to look like something that's been growing in the dark.'

So I went along with her, but I wondered all the same why she needed me at all since she was only going to pick up a dress and carry it back to the house.

The outside world was a shock at first – the cries of people, the ringing of bells, the neighing of horses, the clatter of carts, the smell of smoke and dung and baking, the feel of the breeze against my face and the great traffic of common folk, passing up and down the street, some in a tearing hurry to go about their business, other dawdling and staring about them like visitors at a fair ground. It fairly knocked me off my feet and I stood outside Mrs Dempsey's door, swaying like a leaf on a tree until Suzette took me by the arm and marched me across the road like a child that has barely learned to walk.

We stepped inside Archie's shop and as we waited for him to look up from his book I remembered how boldly I had told him I had business with Mrs Dempsey only a few weeks before and the look he'd given me in return, half mocking, half pitying.

Archie placed a ribbon in his book to mark his place and shut it carefully. 'Good afternoon, Suzette,' he said, 'and good afternoon, young lady. We have met, of course, but we haven't been introduced.' He spoke as though we was all standing together in some nob's drawing room.

'This is Anne,' Suzette told him. 'Keep her in mind if you come across something nice, something that would go well with those lovely blue eyes of hers.'

I found myself blushing. No one had ever mentioned the colour of my eyes before.

'I will certainly do that,' Archie said. 'Perhaps you will allow me to take a few measurements, Miss Anne?'

I looked at him in surprise. Then I nodded. A moment later he had lifted up a flap in the counter and was standing beside me with a measuring tape in his hand. He measured my waist, the length of my skirt, my sleeves and finally my bosom, which would have shocked me greatly once but which now seemed a very small liberty indeed. Then he returned to his place behind the counter and wrote the measurements down in a notebook.

'Thank you for your patience, ladies,' he said, looking up. 'I will go and fetch the gown now.'

While he was gone, I had a quick nose round the shop. There weren't very much to look at. In the window stood a dressmaker's form with a dusty looking ivory gown hanging on it. Beside it, an even dustier gentleman's cocked hat and a pair of cracked leather gloves. A gentleman's top coat was pinned up against a wooden frame and a pair of yellow breeches below it. In the far corner of the window was a collection of wigs on wooden stands. Behind the counter stood a row of sacks stuffed with clothes waiting to be sorted and through the doorway into which Archie had vanished I saw many more such sacks.

After a few minutes Archie came back with Suzette's gown and handed it over. It was lavender-coloured silk, trimmed with lace.

'A most elegant piece of work,' he observed.

Suzette nodded, reaching out greedily to take it from him.

'A very fashionable lady once wore this gown,' Archie continued, holding it just out of her reach.

'No doubt she did,' Suzette agreed.

'You'll tell Mrs Dempsey that, won't you?'

'Tell her what?'

'That a very fashionable lady wore this gown.'

'I'll tell her.'

'Not everyone could lay their hands on such an item,' Archie continued.

'I don't suppose they could. You're a very special man, Archie.' Suzette raised an eyebrow as she said this and she reached out her hand once more for the gown.

It seemed to me that for the briefest of moments a flash of anger showed in Archie's eyes. Then it was gone and he handed over the dress.

We bade him good day and left the shop, the doorbell clanging behind us. There weren't no exchange of money. That would be dealt with by Mrs Dempsey. She fed us and clothed us and put a roof over our heads but all the money we earned with our bodies was hers to give and take as she pleased.

As we was making our way back to the shop, Suzette said, 'I asked you to come with me, Anne, because I don't like to see a girl made a fool of.'

'What do you mean?'

'That fellow who came to the door looking for you.'

'Harold Lampton, you mean?'

'I don't know what his name was. The one Jeremiah hit over the head.'

'What about him?'

'He's dead, you know?'

'What?' I stood in the middle of the road so that she had to pull me out of the way of a cart horse.

'Jeremiah doesn't leave a job half done,' Suzette went on. 'It's not his way.'

'Are you sure?'

'Course I'm sure. I haven't been working at Mrs Dempsey's all these years without learning how she does business. She employs Jeremiah to keep things tidy. So if someone has to be disposed of, Jeremiah disposes of him good and proper. He doesn't come back again to make trouble for us all.'

'What did he do with the body, then?' I still couldn't believe that Harold Lampton was no more.

'I don't know. Probably dumped him in the river. He's not going to tell me, is he? He's not going to tell anyone. But Jeremiah has his ways and means, you can be sure of that, and nobody causes him trouble twice.'

We was outside Mrs Dempsey's by now and Suzette put her hand on the door handle but I stopped her. 'So why has Mrs Dempsey let me believe he's still alive?' I asked.

Suzette sighed and looked at me like I had no more sense than the stuffed bird in Mrs Dempsey's parlour. 'Why do you think, Anne?'

'I don't know.'

'So you wouldn't go back, of course. Now, don't let on to a soul that I told you, all right?'

As we went back inside I realized that she was right to look at me in disbelief. Mrs Dempsey had led me around on a piece of string and I had let her do it. Not only that, but I had thanked her for the privilege.

Tuah

I was entirely unprepared for London. Despite the excitement that went through the crew, passing from man to man like a fever as we drew closer to port, I had no real idea what to expect. For years I had scarcely placed my foot upon dry land, and suddenly I found myself set down in the midst of the greatest city in the world, a place with a heartbeat that reverberated on the other side of the ocean. Yet I was without any proper understanding of what a city really was. I had no idea how it functioned, nor what it meant to chart a daily course through its narrow lanes, its treacherous alleys and its great broad highways. All of that I would have to learn.

The first thing that struck me when we came into port was the noise. Even while I was still on deck, the hubbub of the city reached me, like the sound of bees at work in a gigantic hive. A great welter of human voices and animal cries all mixed up with the trundling of cart wheels, the grinding of stone, the hammering of metal, the banging of timber and the mighty creaking and groaning of all those buildings as the restless population swarmed back and forth in their constant frenzy of activity.

All the arrangements for the captain's disembarkation

had been made by Mr Priestley. He had dispatched messengers with letters while Captain McKerras sat silently in his cabin, seeming entirely unconcerned with his own disposition. His sickness had left its shadow upon him and he was not the man who had appeared at the slave auction three years earlier to rescue me from the fat man in the scarlet topcoat. He would not now have been prepared to involve himself in another man's quarrel. He preferred to watch the world go about its business without the slightest indication that he wished to participate.

For days I had wanted to ask him what would become of me when we reached our destination but I had not dared, at first for fear of what his reply might be and later because I suspected that he did not know the answer himself. Nor did I possess the courage to seek out Mr Priestley and put my enquiries to him. Instead, I merely waited and I told myself that there was no point in worrying since I had no power to change anything. Yet though I repeated this advice to myself over and over again, I still could not help dwelling on the possibility that I might be taken to auction once more, or, worse still, left in the hands of Bosun Mortimer who would delight in doing me harm.

When I learned from Mr Gilbert that Mr Priestley had heard from the captain's brother and that he was imminently expected on board, my anxiety reached its peak. Would the captain's brother accept responsibility for me as well, or would I be left behind like unclaimed baggage? I began creating a picture in my mind of what this brother might be like. An individual of considerable power and influence, I imagined him to be, tall and elegant, with the captain's quickness of mind but possessed of all the gravity that the captain lacked. So convinced was I by this portrait that I assumed the sharp-eyed hunchback who limped on board and knocked on the door of the captain's cabin that first afternoon in dock must be a servant sent to convey his master's intentions. The idea that he might be the captain's brother never even entered my head, despite the looks and nudges that I saw the crew give each other. But it was not long before the door opened once more and the hunchback stood in the doorway holding a wooden box I had often seen in the captain's cabin and that I knew well contained his personal papers. Then the truth became clear to me and I saw that there was a resemblance between the two men, slight but unmistakable. I saw, too, that the hunchback was considering me with some interest.

'Is this the boy?' he asked in a voice that immediately reminded me of the captain's.

I had been squatting with my back against the wall of the cabin but now I got to my feet and tried to look respectful, sensing that my fate was about to be decided.

Captain McKerras appeared behind his brother. 'That's him,' he agreed.

'You will come with us,' the hunchback said. Then he and the captain walked off the ship, with me trailing in their wake, almost overwhelmed with relief and yet still anxious beyond measure.

If the din of London had seemed great on board, once we were on dry land it was almost overwhelming. Dock workers were busy loading and unloading cargoes, men staggered like ants under the weight of enormous bundles, or pushed carts piled high with sacks of grain while others argued fiercely, spitting on their hands and striking bargains, shouting with laughter, or roaring with anger. Reunited family members eyed each other warily, friends threw their arms round one another, sailors exchanged hopeful banter with hard-faced women or stood pissing against walls and cursing their own aim. Everywhere, too, there were animals.

Dogs barked, cocks crowed, horses and cattle and pigs dropped their dung wherever they stood and ragged children darted back and forth to collect it in pails. Through all of this I threaded my way after Captain McKerras and his hunchback brother, terrified that I might lose sight of them and be swallowed up in an instant.

At last we stopped where a driver stood waiting patiently with a horse and carriage. The hunchback spoke to the driver, then he and the captain got inside and sat facing the front. I crouched on the floor at their feet. Then the driver got up in his seat and took hold of the reins.

'You have not asked me about the shop,' the hunchback said once we were in motion.

The captain shrugged. 'How fares the shop?' he asked, sounding as though nothing in the world could be of less interest to him.

'Fortunately for you it fares well,' his brother replied, 'otherwise you would have nowhere to fall back upon.'

Captain McKerras raised one eyebrow. 'I am not yet altogether undone,' he said.

'But the Company are not best pleased, or so I hear. Nor do I think that fellow Priestley will be quick to take your part.'

'I am finished with the Company,' Captain McKerras said curtly. 'And with Priestley too, damn him.'

'No doubt. But are they finished with you?'

The captain leaned out of the cab and spat upon the street. Then he sat back once more, his eyes half closed. 'You have not changed a whit, Archie,' he said. 'You still insist on looking at the world through the wrong end of a spyglass.'

'Why should I change? The rich continue to die before their time and I continue to live beyond mine. That is a kind of equilibrium that I have no wish to disturb.'

This was how they spoke to one another – in riddles. And much of it, of course, above my head.

No more was said after that until the carriage drew up in front of a row of tall houses. I quickly scrambled out so that the two men could get down. Then Archie paid the driver while the captain and I waited in silence. When the carriage had driven away, Archie produced a set of keys and led us through the back door of one of the houses into a room that was almost entirely filled with clothes. They lay everywhere in great heaps, or stuffed tightly into hessian sacks. We passed swiftly through this room into a hallway where more clothes stood about, then upstairs to a second floor where I glimpsed yet more bundles of clothes and up once more to the top of the house where, instead of clothes, there were books everywhere, books in crates, books in boxes, books arranged on shelves and books lying scattered upon the floor. New books, old books, great thick leather-bound books and tattered books that were scarcely more than bundles of yellowing paper.

The captain picked up some volumes that were heaped upon an armchair, handed them to his brother and sat down heavily in their place. 'I am unspeakably tired,' he announced.

Archie put the books down on top of some others. Then he stood in the middle of the room for some time regarding me with a frown before turning back to his brother.

'What is the boy's name?' he demanded.

'Abdul.'

'Can he sew?'

'Of course he cannot sew.'

'Can he reckon money?'

'No.'

'Can he read?'

'No.'

'Then what in God's name can he do?'

He is very good upon the rigging.'

'Unfortunately, we have little need of rigging here.'

Archie McKerras turned back to me. 'We will have to find a use for you,' he said. 'You cannot remain idle.'

'Yes, sir.'

'Is there any whisky?' the captain demanded.

'Of course there is whisky.'

'Then leave the boy alone and fetch the bottle.'

Archie disappeared briefly and came back with a bottle of whisky and a couple of glasses which he filled. He handed one to the captain and sat down opposite him.

The captain sipped his whisky and licked his lips. 'Are the whores still keeping you busy?' he asked.

'Whores are always in need of finery.'

'And that is all that you provide them with, I trust.'

Archie McKerras gave his brother a long, hard look.

'It was a joke, Archie.'

A scowl crossed Archie's face and it struck me, watching the two men, that they seemed to have resumed some old disagreement begun long before the captain went to sea and too well-rehearsed to need openly articulating. Preoccupied with settling into their positions of mutual irritation they had almost forgotten my presence.

'I read the most extraordinary poem last week,' Archie said after a while. 'It was about a sailor whose life was ruined by a single error of judgement.'

The captain swirled whisky around in his mouth and swallowed. 'I can assure you that my life is not ruined,' he said.

'I was not talking about you,' Archie said. 'I was talking about a poem.'

'I am not sure I believe you.'

'Believe what you like. You are not the centre of creation, Donald.'

'I make no claim to be.'

'It is one among a collection of poems that has been causing something of a stir of late. Lyrical Ballads, they are called. Coleridge, that is the fellow's name.'

'Never heard of him.'

'But you will, Robert. You will.'

The captain turned to me then and for the first time in several days he addressed me directly. 'Rags and poetry, Abdul,' he said. 'This is what I have returned to.'

Thomas

Thomas and Lady Carberry worked together in the library for a couple of hours each afternoon. Thomas would set some exercises and when Lady Carberry had completed them, they would read over them together. She was far from being a poor scholar as she had claimed, and he was seldom obliged to correct her, but on those occasions when he did so, their proximity, as he leaned across her to point out some error in her translation, produced within him a sensation of heat, of excitement, of sweetness that, he told himself, could only be the satisfaction that came from communicating knowledge.

Mrs Schreiber remained in the drawing room while Thomas and Lady Carberry pursued their studies but Margaret took to walking around the terraces just outside the library and from time to time, when he looked up from his work, Thomas was sure he saw her staring in through the window, though she always looked away again immediately.

The Schreibers' visit was of shorter duration than Thomas's, and the day before they left Margaret approached Thomas when he was walking by himself in the grounds. He saw her coming towards him as he sauntered amid a stand of beech trees that Lord Carberry was fond of telling anyone who would listen, had been planted nearly a hundred years earlier by his great grandfather after he had won a great deal of money betting on the outcome of a horse race.

Thomas stood and awaited her, since it was evident that she had come here expressly to seek him out. He presumed that she intended to bid him farewell, though he was surprised at this for hitherto she had not shown any great inclination towards civility.

'Good morning, Margaret,' he said.

'Good morning, Thomas.'

'I am sorry that you will be leaving Laxton tomorrow.'

'You surprise me. Will you not be overjoyed to have Lady Carberry all to yourself?' You and she are thick as thieves, are you not?'

She said this with such obvious malice that Thomas was taken aback. 'I confess, I do not understand you,' he replied.

Margaret raised one eyebrow and lifted her chin so that she might look down on him further than she did already; for although she was of little more than average height, yet she was still inches above Thomas.

'I hope that Lady Carberry and I are friends,' Thomas continued.

'Let us hope so indeed. Shall we walk?'

They set off along the path that led between the trees.

'You are a very clever young man, Thomas.'

'It is kind of you to say so.'

'And yet you are the most complete fool as well.'

Thomas stopped. This was too much! 'Did you seek me out this morning with the express intention of insulting me?' he demanded. He felt his face going red and he struggled to control his speech.

'I sought you out to offer you a piece of advice.'

'Oh really? And what might that be?'

'There are two sides to Lady Carberry.'

'May I remind you that we are both guests in Lady Carberry's house. She has placed her entire household at our disposal.'

'Her generosity is not at issue,'

'Then what is, pray?'

Margaret gave a little shake of her head, as if dismissing the question. Then she began to walk again and, after a moment's hesitation, Thomas joined her. 'Men are so very weak,' she told him.

'I dare say you find them so.'

'It is not I who seek out their weaknesses. Tell me, Thomas, you do not think very highly of Mr Dunwoody, do you?'

Once again, Thomas was taken aback, this time at the abrupt change in topic.

'He seems a very...worthy man.'

She gave him a withering smile. 'Edward has been a good friend to Lord Carberry for many years.'

'I do not doubt it.'

'He said it has been like watching a bee drowning in honey.'

'I will hear no more of this!' Thomas turned and marched off in the direction of the house.

'Take care, Thomas!' she called after him.

One afternoon, towards the end of his stay, while Thomas was in the middle of explaining to her ladyship why the imperative was used for the Lord's Prayer in Mathew while in Mark the same word was rendered as an imperfective, Lord Carberry entered. He stood just inside the door, looking a little uncomfortable, as if, perhaps, he was not accustomed to finding himself in his own library. He put out his hand as

Thomas began to rise. 'No, please do not let me disturb you,' he said. 'Only tell me, Thomas, how is my wife's education progressing?'

'Her ladyship's progress in Greek is quite remarkable,' Thomas replied.

'But does she do as you direct her?' Lord Carberry continued. 'Is she a...satisfactory pupil?' He gave a forced laugh as he said this but though the question was addressed to Thomas, his lordship's eyes were fixed firmly on his wife.

'Lady Carberry is a meticulous pupil,' Thomas said.

'Meticulous?' his lordship repeated, as if the word had surprised and rather amused him. 'Meticulous. I must remember that. A meticulous pupil, how very gratifying. Very well, I will leave you both to your studies.' He turned and closed the door behind him with a resounding clatter. Thomas and Lady Carberry remained in silence as the sound of his footsteps receded.

They returned to their work but the atmosphere in the library had altered: Lady Carberry's concentration seemed fragile and intermittent, and the chiming of the quarter hour by the long-case clock seemed to startle her, as though she had never heard it give voice in such a manner before; the sudden alarm call of a blackbird outside the window made her frown like one who fears an act of violence is being perpetrated somewhere just out of sight. At last, sensing that they would make no more progress that day, Thomas feigned weariness and the lesson was abandoned.

He retired to his room, resolving to spend the remains of the afternoon working on an ode in praise of Laxton which he was hoping to have completed before his departure so that he might present it to Lady Carberry as a parting gift, but as the sun declined over the park he found that he struggled with the metre and the pleasure that he usually took in versifying entirely deserted him. Perhaps it was not such a good idea, after all, he decided. He could no longer be certain how his hosts would regard it. Something about Lord Carberry's reaction to his comment in the library had undermined his confidence in the whole enterprise. With a sigh he threw down his notebook upon the desk and decided instead to walk in the garden until dinner time in the hope that fresh air and exercise might help him regain his composure.

He took the path through the stand of beech trees down to the road leading to the village. He walked rapidly, hoping that the exertion might somehow quieten the nagging doubts that assailed him. Only a couple of hours ago he had been feeling entirely at ease, if not positively pleased with himself, and had seen himself as a young man standing on the brink of his life. Now, it seemed much more likely that he was nothing more than the foolish boy of his mother's estimation. On either side of him hay-meadows rippled in the breeze, their margins bright with poppies, daisies and scabious but their beauty was wasted upon Thomas. He was consumed by an unnamed fear that had been growing on him ever since Elizabeth's death. He had felt it at first as no more than the shadow of his loss but as the years went by he had begun to realise that it was not merely that he grieved for his sister; he grieved for himself as well, for the man he would not now become. That afternoon as he turned back towards the house beneath a sky at first red, then purple and finally inky grey, he realised that his fear was most of all for his own impending failure. Already he seemed condemned to forever have the physical dimensions of a child – what if he remained so in all other ways?

The Carberrys invariably retired to bed early each evening, almost directly after the meal had been eaten. 'Early to bed and early to rise, makes a man healthy, happy and wise,' Lord Carberry was fond of repeating. It was, Thomas suspected, the closest the man ever came to an appreciation of poetry.

Thomas was generally quite content with this arrangement. Unlike in his mother's house, there was always wine at the Carberrys' dinner table and Lord Carberry seemed to expect Thomas to match his own consumption, glass for glass. As a consequence, towards the end of each evening, Thomas felt himself grow clumsy, he had the sensation that he had grown an extra skin, he experienced considerable difficulty focusing his gaze, and his speech grew thick and slurred, as if his tongue and lips were no longer entirely his to command. After making his way unsteadily to his room, undressing rather carelessly and clambering into bed, it never took him more than a few minutes to drift off into a deep and dreamless sleep.

But on this particular night he was awoken abruptly by a sound which he could not at first identify but which he was aware, in that uncertain condition in which the mind finds itself upon waking from deep slumber, was somehow disturbing. Unsure how long he had been asleep, he propped himself upon his elbow, listening carefully. Then it came again: two sounds this time, one following upon the other in quick succession, the first being the sound of a slap and the second a cry, presumably uttered by the recipient of that slap. Thomas sat up in bed, astonished. A moment later the sounds were repeated, and then again and again. He could not be imagining things; it was most certainly the sound of someone being chastised.

Thomas was profoundly shocked. The only people within hearing distance were Lord and Lady Carberry, the servants' quarters being at the other end of the house. So it could only be they who were responsible for what he had just heard. Could Lord Carberry really be chastising his wife?

He lay awake pondering the implications. There was now no doubt in his mind what had happened: Lord Carberry had been punishing his wife. But what could possibly be the offence that had precipitated this course of action? Then an extraordinary idea came to him – though hitherto unadmitted, it was not entirely new. Had Lady Carberry shown too much regard for him? Was this punishment the result of jealousy on his lordship's part? It seemed so very unlikely, so out of keeping with his lordship's habitual behaviour, yet Thomas had heard that the jealous mind was never reasonable. Did not so much of literature attest to this very fact? Shakespeare's Othello, for example?

The more he considered it, the more he felt himself strangely stirred, so that it was quite impossible to compose his mind sufficiently to return to sleep. Instead, he lay on the bed, shifting from side to side. After some time he heard a noise in the corridor outside. Throwing off the covers, he stood beside his bed in an agitated state, trying to decide what, if anything, he ought to do. Then he went over to the door, opening it a crack and peering out. At first there was nothing but darkness to be seen, but then, on the other side of the landing Lord Carberry appeared, dressed in a long white nightgown. The expression on his face could only be described as jubilation. Terrified of being spotted, Thomas closed the door and got rapidly and silently back into his bed where he lay without sleeping until the birds began to sing outside his window.

Anne

Since the morning I left home in search of Mrs Dempsey's house I'd tried to put my mother from my mind. She'd thrown in her lot with Harold Lampton and there weren't no room for anyone else in her life. But now I'd learned what a fool I'd been, and how Mrs Dempsey had played upon my fears, I made up my mind to go home. After all, what did I have to fear any more?

That night, as I lay in bed looking out of the little window in my room at the clouds drifting past the moon like bits of old rag that made me think of our laundry days together, I pictured my mother's face when I returned. She'd be so happy to see me! But she wouldn't be getting her little girl back because that little girl was no more. Only a few weeks had passed since I'd left home but everything had changed. Harold Lampton was dead and I weren't a child no more.

I pictured my mother putting her arms around me and weeping for joy. Over and over again, I imagined the talks we'd have, me sounding strong and wise and her gazing at me in astonishment. The days of washing other people's linen would be over. It'd be the start of a new life for both of us. Of course the details of that new life was still a bit hazy but I'd think of something, I was certain of that. The world had taken me by surprise once but I weren't going to let it do so again. From now on, I was the *mistress of my own destiny*.

I left before anyone else was stirring, though to tell you the truth that weren't difficult to manage in Mrs Dempsey's house for no one ever showed their face until the day was well advanced. I knew my mother would be up early, getting everything in readiness for the arrival of Perk with the latest load of dirty clothes and I wanted to arrive before he did. Then, together, we could tell Perk where to stick them.

The more I thought of Perk, the more I felt rage boiling up inside me. I would make that jumped-up little maggot pay for what I'd suffered. All the way from Mrs Dempsey's house I imagined taking hold of handfuls of his hair and pulling until great tufts of it came away from his scalp and the tears came into his eyes. I would pluck him like a chicken. I pictured myself slapping him across the face, kicking him on the shins, spitting in his eye, beating him on the back with a stick and him crying out for mercy.

It was a cold December morning with a frost on the ground and the wind with a bite like the Devil's scorn but I took no notice because I was too busy lambasting Perk in my mind and finding pleasure in the thought of him blubbering, arms raised above his head as he tried to protect himself. Such speeches I spouted! I told him he was no more than a louse that lived upon the bodies of the poor, worse than a louse, for at least a louse went about its business in silence whereas Perk never stopped admiring himself and bragging of his own cleverness. I said he was as ignorant as a fly feasting on a freshly-laid turd and a good deal less useful than the turd itself.

These thoughts warmed me from the inside, and hastened

my footsteps until at last I found myself turning into the narrow lane where Mr Gillespie had led us only a few short weeks earlier, making my way through the crumbling archway and into the filthy courtyard where the smell of the cess-pit greeted me like an old friend. I declare, the inhabitants of that courtyard must have produced the strongest smelling piss in the whole of London for the air was that thick with it, it was like walking into a fog.

Home, sweet home, I thought to myself, grimly enough. But then I chased that thought away for I was returning on different terms. I was no longer little Miss Innocent. I was someone who'd seen the worst the world had to offer and was still holding my head up.

The courtyard was empty, it was too cold and too early in the day for the old crones to be standing around gossiping. So I marched straight over to the room I'd shared with my mother and rapped on the door. A tall, thin woman with red hair and a wall-eye opened it.

'What d'you want?' she demanded in a strong Irish accent.

I was taken aback. 'Where's my mother?'

'How the hell should I know?' She began to close the door.

I put out my hand and stopped her. 'Wait! Where's the woman who lives here?'

'That's me.'

'You don't live here, my mother does.'

'Listen,' she said. 'I've work to do, so just go away like a good girl before I knock your head off your shoulders.' This time she did shut the door.

I stood there for a little while, *completely flabbergasted.* Then I pushed the door open once more, for there was no lock to prevent me, and stepped into the room, but my eyes was still getting used to the dim light within when I realised the red-haired woman was standing there gazing at me with a furious look on her face and the pail that my mother and I had used for collecting piss clutched in her hand. While I was still taking this in, she raised her arm and chucked what was in the pail in my direction. There was no time to duck and the next moment I was *utterly drenched.* Before I could even catch my breath and cry out she advanced on me, swinging the pail like a weapon. I turned and fled.

I was standing, shivering, on the other side of the courtyard, still getting over the shock having a bucket of piss thrown over me and wondering what I ought to do next when I heard the sound of someone whistling. It was a swaggering kind of a whistle, the whistle of someone who thinks himself a very fine fellow indeed, and along with that whistle went the creak and clatter of a cart. A moment later I saw a familiar figure making his way under the archway, pushing a barrow piled high with soiled linen.

He was a good way into the courtyard before he caught sight of me but the moment he did so, he stopped in his tracks and his face fell. I think he would have turned and walked away if he didn't have a barrow full of shitty clothes in front of him. Instead, he just stood there, looking sheepish, until I walked over to him.

'What happened to you?' he asked.

'I'll tell you what happened to me,' I said, speaking slow and careful. 'I paid a visit to a nice, kind lady that takes in girls who are willing to work.'

'You don't mean you actually went there?'

My hand was itching to slap him but I needed answers first.

'Where's my mother?'

He stared at me in silence, a look on his face that I couldn't read.

'Where did she go?'

'You really don't know?'

'Would I be asking you if I did? Just tell me where she is or I swear I'll pluck your eyes out.' I held two fingers up to show him I meant it.

I could tell from his face he believed me. 'All right,' he said, 'take it easy. I'm sorry to tell you, your mother's dead.'

I felt like the world had suddenly come to a stop. 'What do you mean, she's dead?' I could hardly get the words out. My tongue was a piece of leather lying useless in me mouth. Pain like some great wave on the river was breaking over me and there weren't nothing I could do to stop it.

'She hung herself,' Perk continued. 'Made a rope out of linen and tied it to a rafter. It was me what found her.'

The next thing I was knew, Perk was grabbing hold of my arms and shouting,'For God's sake, stop it!'

It was only then I realised I'd been banging my head on his barrow and I did stop but I didn't want to. I wanted pain, I wanted blackness, I wanted anything that would mean I didn't have to face the truth of what he'd just told me.

Perk dragged me away from the barrow. 'You've cut your head open,' he told me.

'I don't care.'

'Well you should care.'

'She killed herself because of me.'

'That's not what I 'eard.'

'What did you hear?'

'She was going around everywhere asking for a fellow called 'arold Lampton and then someone found him dead in the churchyard. That's why she did it.'

'Then it *was* my fault.'

'Only if you killed 'arold Lampton.'

'I did kill him'

Perk gave me a hard look. 'Don't talk nonsense,' he said. 'The only person you're likely to kill is yourself.'

I thought of my mother lying in the cold clay of the churchyard alongside her parents and the brothers and sisters I'd never even met and it was like a knife going through me. I had to go and see her grave. I needed to talk to her, to tell her how sorry she was. I turned and walked away but Perk came running after me.

'Where you off to?'

'St Mary's churchyard.'

'You won't find her there.'

'Why not?'

He looked uncomfortable. 'They don't bury suicides in consecrated ground.'

I stared back at him, trying to make sense of what he'd just said but it was like he was speaking a different language. What was *consecrated*?

'I told you, she hung herself.'

'They didn't bury her in St Mary's?'

'That's right.'

'She ain't lying beside her mum and dad and all me brothers and sisters?'

No.'

It seemed like there was no end to Perk's supply of dreadful news.

'Hanging yourself ain't suicide,' I told him.

'What is it then?'

I tried to find the words to explain. 'She just didn't know what else to do,' I said at last. 'She weren't strong enough to get by on her own.'

Perk shrugged. 'You still can't put someone what's hung herself in consecrated ground.'

'So where did they put her?'

'Cross Bones.'

'Where's that?'

'Other side of the river. In the Borough.'

'Can you show me?'

Perk looked dismayed. 'I got to give Molly her washing, bring the clean clothes back to Dempsey. Then I've got another three loads to deliver.'

'What, she gets through three loads in a day?'

'She ain't the only one washing clothes for Dempsey. He's got a regular troop of washerwomen.'

'I bet he has.'

'Just go over the bridge and ask for Cross Bones. You'll find it easy enough.'

I nodded. I hadn't the strength to argue with him.

'I'm sorry, you know,' he told me. Then he took up the handles of his cart once more and carried on across the courtyard to where the red haired woman stood giving us the evil eye from her doorway.

It took me all morning to cross the river and find Cross Bones. Despite what Perk said, it weren't easy because no one wanted to give me directions. Folk just shook their heads or shrugged when I asked them. It was a doxy what showed me in the end. Well past her best, she was, her dress all stained and torn, half her teeth missing, and trying without success to catch the attention of men coming out of an ale-house.

'Someone belonging to you there?' she asked.

'My mother?'

'Got any money?'

I still had the money my mother had given me to get something to eat the first day I left home. I'd brought those few coins to Mrs Dempsey's tied up in a bit of rag in the folds of my dress and she'd handed them back to me when she took my clothes on that first morning. Like the fool I was, I took that as a sign of fair dealing but it was the only money Mrs Dempsey gave me in all the weeks I was there.

I untied the rag and handed over what I had.

Her name was Kate, she told me. She'd been walking the streets of Borough since she was my age. Had ten children of her own, every one of them dead, all buried in Cross Bones.

It was a miserable spot, closed in by broken walls and overgrown with yew trees and brambles and every kind of rank weed. There was no headstones, just humps in the ground. In a couple of places the smell of shit was very strong as if folk had taken to emptying their chamber pots there.

I looked about me. 'How will I find her in all this?'

'I'll bring you to where they dig the new graves,' Kate said and she led me round the edge of the field to the far corner where there was at least a dozen graves newly dug. 'She'll be in one of these.'

'Ain't there anyone who could tell me which is hers?'

Kate looked doubtful. 'There's a fellow by the name of Alfred what digs the graves, but I don't know where he lives. Nor do I think he could tell you if you found him. '

I started to weep again. After all my searching I still didn't know for certain where they'd put my mother's body.

'She knows you're here,' Kate told me. 'That's the main thing, dearie. You've done your best for her and I'm sure she's grateful for that. Now I'd best be getting back to work.' And with that she left me.

I hadn't done my best for her and I knew it very well. I might just as well have tied the linen rope that choked her. So I closed my eyes and begged for her forgiveness. I waited a long time there in that cold graveyard. But I didn't get any answer.

Tuah

My position in the McKerras household was never made completely clear. I was not a servant, for I was not given any wages; I was not a slave either, for I was often treated, by Archie at least, as a companion; I was simply allowed to find a place for myself like an animal that has crept in from outside. The captain, or Donald as I eventually learned to call him, no longer seemed to notice me. He slept late, left the house around midday and did not come back until the early hours of the morning, sometimes not until the following day. He had his own concerns, which I gathered from snippets of conversation that I overheard, and from the captain's oft-repeated complaints, revolved around countering the accusations that had been made by Mr Priestley and getting his hands on the money that the Company owed him. Where I slept, what I ate, what I wore, what I did with my days – all of this was now decided by Archie.

He also took over the business of teaching me English but his approach was quite different from his brother's. Both men required me to learn passages by rote but while Captain McKerras had relied upon the Bible, Archie would pick up a book at random from the tottering piles that lay everywhere about the house, glance at the title, nod to himself, then rifle through the pages and until he discovered a passage that suited his purposes, whereupon he would give one of his characteristic crooked smiles. *Of making many books there is no end; and much study is a weariness of the flesh.* Thus does King Solomon admonish us in the verses of Ecclesiastes and he was right in this as in so much else for I was often more weary from Archie's lessons than I had been on board the Laurel Bower. The passages he selected were difficult to understand and sometimes it seemed to me they had been chosen more for their effect upon the captain than for any benefit I might derive from them.

'It is of great use to the sailor to know the length of his line, though he cannot with it fathom all the depths of the ocean,' Archie would declaim, with a sidelong glance at his brother. Or, 'Revenge is a kind of wild justice; which the more man's nature runs to, the more ought law to weed it out.'

Most of the time the captain pretended to take no notice but occasionally, when Archie would make me stand before him and recite my lesson, the captain's patience would run out and he would pick up one of Archie's books and hurl it across the room before stamping out of the house in disgust while Archie only shook his head sadly and examined the book in question for damage.

Many of the qualities that had impressed me about the captain were equally evident in Archie. He was shrewd, combative, intelligent and possessed a notion of himself that considerably exceeded the condition in which life had placed him. He was also entirely fearless, as I discovered on one occasion a few weeks after my arrival in London.

The clothes that Archie sold came from gentlemen or ladies recently deceased; each week he visit the local undertaker to whom he paid a small sum of money for information about his recent customers. Then he would call at the household of each deceased person and offer to purchase unwanted garments, books and other personal effects. The grieving family was often glad to be rid of such items, finding them too painful look upon, and in their distressed state of mind the heirs naturally did not wish to haggle about the price.

A few weeks after my arrival, Archie suggested that I accompany him on one of these visits. 'Come and see how we earn our living, Abdul,' he told me with a grin.

At this stage I was still going about like someone in a daze. The sheer size and enormity of London confused me. Stepping outside the door was like throwing myself into a storm-tossed sea – it seemed to me that I could be swept away in a moment and never find my way back to safe harbour.

Almost more bewildering was the simple fact that I *could* step outside the door if I so wished. There was absolutely nothing to restrain me. Neither Archie nor the captain had laid down any conditions about where I might, or might not, go. They had given me to understand on the first night that I might sleep in the back room of the shop but other than this there seemed to be no prohibitions and had I wished to run away, it would have been the easiest thing in the world. But, of course, I had no money and no way of making any, I knew no one and feared everyone, and I had no idea where the streets led, what parts of the city were dangerous and what were safe, what passed for customary behaviour and what did not. Hence, while the thought of fleeing the McKerras household certainly did occur to me, the mere contemplation of the consequences filled me with terror. With Archie and Donald I had food and drink and a place to sleep at night and there was no longer any threat that I might be tied to a stanchion and lashed for some misdemeanour that I had not even been aware of committing. So I contented myself with carrying out whatever duties Archie saw fit to assign me – blacking boots, stirring porridge, transporting sacks of clothing up and down stairs, carrying out buckets of night soil. *The hand of the diligent shall bear rule: but the slothful shall be under tribute.*

Thus when he suggested that I accompany him to a house recently thrown into mourning, I simply followed him out of the house without question like a dog trailing its master down the street.

Archie possessed a small hand cart that was kept in the yard at the back of the shop and as we walked, I pushed the cart while Archie told me about the inhabitants of the streets through which we passed. In this street there lived mainly Irish immigrants who had not a penny between them and were full of sad stories and song; this street was full of Jews who were tailors and scholars and great keepers of secrets; in this alley a man had been found with his heart cut out and in this courtyard a woman had poisoned her husband with arsenic for sleeping with her sister. Archie was a born story teller, as I came to understand, and part of the reason he had been prepared to take me in so readily was the fact that I was the perfect audience: utterly credulous and entirely without sophistication. There is a time to keep silence, and a time to speak; our times flowed together harmoniously.

The street in which the house was situated was not more than half an hour's walk from the shop yet it seemed to belong in an entirely different city. The people who walked to and fro on these cobblestones proceeded at a comfortable pace. They did not glance furtively over their shoulders as they went, they did not feel themselves to be in imminent danger of robbery or assault (though, as events were to prove, they were mistaken in this assumption). This was a respectable neighbourhood. The house itself was in the middle of a row of identical houses: tall, well-proportioned and dignified. These were homes for people who had a part to play in the world.

We made our way down an alleyway that led to the back of the house, through a wrought iron gateway and along a path between well-tended rose-gardens. Archie knocked on the back door and it was opened by a middle-aged man in a frock-coat whom at the time I took to be the gentleman of the house – but, in truth of course, he was no more than the butler.

'Archibald McKerras, at your service,' Archie said with a nod of his head. He took a visiting card from his waistcoat pocket and handed it over. 'I understand from Messrs Heal and Glover that Mr Fielding has some items of clothing belonging to his late wife that he wishes to dispose of.'

The butler took the card and glanced at it with a show of distaste. 'I will inform the master that you are here,' he said. Then he shut the door on our faces.

Archie did not look in the least put out at this frosty reception. He merely leaned against the wall and glanced around him with a calculating air. 'Tell me,' he said after some time, 'have you ever been in love, Abdul?'

I made no reply for I had not the least idea what he was talking about. I had heard about the love of God from the captain but I had no notion of what being 'in love' might involve. Love thy neighbour as thyself?

'Did you know that in the Ancient World the god of love was depicted as a boy who went around with a bow and arrows, shooting blindly at whoever caught his fancy?' he continued, oblivious to my lack of comprehension. I suspected that he was really speaking to himself. 'I rather think that they were right, for to fall in love is to acquire a wound that is never truly healed. And when the object of one's affection is taken away at a stroke...' He made a despairing gesture with his hands.

The door opened again just then and the butler reappeared. 'You may enter,' he said.

'Wait here,' Archie instructed me. Then he followed the butler into the house and the door was closed once more.

As I tried to make sense of what Archie had been saying a hint of movement at one of the windows on the second floor caught my attention. I looked more carefully and made out the pale face of girl staring down at me. She looked about six or seven years of age, certainly no more. Perhaps it was her mother who was recently deceased. I tried to offer her a faint smile of encouragement but she only turned away and disappeared behind the curtain. I kept my eye on the window for some time, wondering whether she would return but she did not.

The door opened while I was still gazing upwards and a young man not much older than me appeared in a waistcoat and trousers. His hair was stuck to his scalp with oil and he was carrying a sack that he dumped unceremoniously in front of me. 'Your master says to put this on the cart,' he declared.

Then he returned inside and shut the door.

I picked up the sack, which I saw was stuffed with clothing, and carried it down the path and through the gateway to the cart we had left standing in the alley way. I placed it on the cart and was securing the mouth with a length of string when another young man appeared beside me. I had no idea where he had come from – he must have been lurking somewhere in the alleyway but he seemed to have simply materialised out of the air. He was a muscular looking fellow with a shaved head and a mouth full of broken teeth. I knew before he spoke that he intended villainy of some sort.

'What you got in that sack?' he demanded.

'That is none of your business,' I told him firmly, as the captain had often spoken to me.

He began pawing at the string and indignantly, I pulled the sack away from him. He turned and pushed me hard. At the same time he stuck out one leg so that I tripped and fell over backwards. As I sprawled on the ground, he landed a mighty series of kicks in my ribs that entirely knocked the wind out of me. Then he turned back to the cart and began hoisting the sack onto his back.

'Put it down!' It was Archie's voice. He had appeared in the gateway as silently and unexpectedly as my assailant. The man glanced at Archie and gave a derisive smile.

'Or what?' he said.

Archie took a couple of paces forward until he was standing right next to the man. 'Just put it down,' he said.

'Kiss my arse!' the man said and he turned and would have walked smartly away had Archie not produced a long knife from the pocket of his coat. Bending a little, and lunging forward clumsily but effectively, he drew the knife down the side of the villain's thigh. The man let out a yell. I saw that his breeches were slashed and blood was welling up out of the cut. He stared at the wound, then dropped the sack and yelled again, clutching at his leg in an attempt to staunch the bleeding.

I had by now got back on my feet. I picked up the sack and threw it on the cart. Archie gave me a nod and I lifted the handles of the cart and began to walk away with it, Archie following, seemingly quite unperturbed by his experience. I glanced behind as we turned out of the alley way to see the man down upon his knees, clutching desperately at his leg. It struck me that Archie's knife must have been as sharp as a razor and that the man might easily bleed to death where he knelt.

'The Lord giveth and the Lord taketh away, Abdul,' Archie reflected as we made our way back along the respectable street. 'So you and I must do our very best to hang onto what we have.'

Thomas

It seemed to Thomas that for Charles Lawson life was already over. The man had long ago abandoned all hope of glory, all apprehension of beauty, all pursuit of joy – if the pursuit of joy had ever been an ambition he considered worth pursuing, a possibility about which Thomas had the gravest doubts. Lawson's occupation, instead, was simply to endure the time that remained to him upon this earth, and the means he used to support that endurance was habit.

He was a square man, bald of pate and utterly devoid of humour, a man who each day ate the same meals at precisely the same times, who read the same texts from the same battered volumes, and who uttered the same dreary monologues, frowning sternly in the direction of the same unenthusiastic individuals in his audience, again and again; a man who burned the same amount of candle wax each evening, washed himself with the same meagre allowance of soap, retired to bed at the exact chiming of the same hour – and no doubt encountered the same stale dreams each and every night as his emaciated soul limped its way through the wearisome hours of darkness. He was, in fact, the very epitome of the man that Thomas wished to avoid becoming.

And yet here Thomas was, living in Lawson's house, a

member of his household, supposedly under his guidance and tutelage. Lawson's tutelage! The idea was quite simply preposterous. As if there was anything whatsoever that Lawson could teach him.

This insufferable state of affairs had come about through the intervention of Thomas's uncle, Colonel Penson, his mother's brother. The colonel's influence over the De Quincey household had been steadily rising ever since the death of Thomas's father and of late he had taken over the entire control of financial matters. Such things, in Mrs De Quincey's opinion, were the natural preserve of the masculine mind and, in the absence of her husband, she had begun to lean heavily upon her brother. Unfortunately Colonel Penson was a man who combined an extraordinarily narrow outlook with a formidable willpower, giving him all the personality of a blunt tack. A thin, sallow man with a rigorously upright bearing and the leathery look of one who has spent much of his life out of doors, his years in the British Army had taught him only two lessons: that discipline was the most important quality a man could possess and that his own instinctive opinion was invariably the correct one in every contentious matter.

Where Thomas ought to be, of course, was at the University of Oxford. He was ready for Oxford. All his schoolmasters agreed. And Thomas had no doubt that Oxford was quite ready for him.

Often, when he lay upon the narrow bed in the bleak little room he occupied at the top of Lawson's house, Thomas whiled away the weary hours by picturing himself at Oxford, chatting to his fellow students, reasoning with his tutors, or simply sitting in his rooms poring hungrily over texts. It was a wonderful dream and one that sometimes excited him to an almost unbearable pitch. The life of the mind. That was the sphere to which he aspired, that was his natural realm. Instead, he was confined to the life that Lawson saw fit to allow him and that was a miserable allowance of vitality indeed.

It was because of his uncle's parsimony that Oxford was no more than a daydream. The colonel did not believe in wasting money. Wasting money was an offence against discipline in his opinion. What was most infuriating about the whole affair was that the colonel was not even being parsimonious with his own money – it was Thomas's inheritance that he was so reluctant to release. He stood guard over the money so effectively that even Thomas himself could not lay hands upon it. When the question of Oxford had first been mooted, the colonel had listened to Thomas's arguments without a word, and had finally declared that the matter required mature consideration. Some weeks later he returned with the announcement that he had discovered a scholarship available to any individual who had resided for three years or more in Manchester. This discovery he clearly considered a very sharp piece of work on his part. He took a cigar from the box on the sideboard, snipped off its end with a pair of shears that he always kept about his person specifically for this purpose, and lit it with a spill from the cylinder beside the fire. Only after he had blown voluminous clouds of smoke about the room did he see fit to continue. On learning of the existence of the scholarship, he explained, he had recollected that his old friend Charles Lawson was the High Master of Manchester Grammar School.

Lawson, the colonel added, was as sound a man as could be found outside his own regiment and, for a scholar, he was remarkably down to earth. (That a man should be down to earth was the greatest compliment that the colonel could pay.) It had been agreed, therefore, that Thomas might board with Lawson for a period of three years. It would be a marvelous opportunity, since Lawson, as well as being entirely down to earth, was one of the most educated men in England. All this the colonel uttered with the air of a magician who has pulled a rabbit neatly out of a hat and is watching while it sits upon the table washing its whiskers.

Before another fortnight had elapsed Thomas was dispatched to Manchester, accompanied by a trunk in which his clothes and his favourite books were crammed. The journey took place amid torrential rain and he arrived at his destination, a great grey block of a house that looked as if it had been hewn out of the side of cliff, to find the High Master's household even more colourless and lacking in cheer than he had expected.

It had not taken Thomas very long to discover the limits of Lawson's erudition. The man was a complete fraud. His Greek and Latin had been learned by rote, his knowledge of all other subjects was almost non-existent. He could read the Bible, shake his head at the ingratitude of his young charges, and wield a cane with considerable enthusiasm. But that was as far as it went. His sagacity was no more than a pantomime to convince the ignorant.

For his part, Lawson quickly realised just how far Thomas's knowledge of the languages of antiquity outstripped his own and his response was to raise the drawbridge and retreat. The disinterest with which he greeted Thomas's arrival hardened very quickly into antipathy and a complete lack of communication. It was as if a treaty of mutual disregard had been drawn up between them. Thomas paid lip-service to Lawson's authority and Lawson left Thomas entirely to his own devices.

But those devices were very sorely put to the test in order

to keep him from lapsing into complete despair. The other pupils were all considerably younger than him and, though both amiable and eager to learn, they had been existing for several years in an intellectual desert, and were like a bunch of shipwrecked sailors who had lived for so long on their tiny island that they had almost forgotten their native tongue. Nevertheless, they were grateful for any knowledge that Thomas was able to share with them and in time it transpired that he found himself occupying the position of unpaid junior master. He enjoyed the respect of the younger boys and he took some pleasure in their company. Other than this, however, there was nothing for him in Manchester except prayers, routine and bad cooking.

When he was informed in a letter from his sister Mary that Lady Carberry was coming to Manchester, therefore, he could hardly believe the news – indeed, if he had been told that the Queen of Sheba had been conjured from her grave and decided to pay her respects to the North of England he could not have been more surprised. Lady Carberry and Charles Lawson seemed to occupy entirely separate spheres of existence.

The cause of Lady Carberry's visit was the continuing ill-health of her old friend, Mrs Schreiber. In order to be near the eminent surgeon Doctor White (Mary wrote as if Doctor White were a person of whom the whole world must have heard) Mrs Schreiber had taken a house in Manchester. On learning this, Lady Carberry had immediately announced that she would not see Mrs Schreiber cast adrift in a foreign town. Now, she too had taken a house in Manchester. She would be coming the following week. Lord Carberry would be accompanying her for the first few days and Mary understood that there would be others, too, in the party. Thomas must be sure to pay the Carberrys a visit once they were safely ensconced – so said Mrs De Quincey and, for once, Thomas was entirely happy to conform with his mother's wishes.

He put away the letter from his sister and looked about him as if awakening from a trance. Colour was seeping into the little room at the top of Mr Lawson's house with its iron bedstead, rusty wash basin and worm-eaten book shelves. For the last three months that room had seemed like a prison cell. Now, quite suddenly, the world was regaining its intensity, its life, its sense of promise. He was not to be rescued, it was true, but he was to be reminded that there was, after all, a world beyond the precincts of Mr Lawson's school, a world in which there was still a place for him.

Ten days later Thomas sat in a coach en route to Godfrey Hall, the house that Lord and Lady Carberry had chosen for their visit. It was not exactly *in* Manchester to tell the truth but rather a few miles outside the town. An imposing building of red brick, quite clearly newly built but with something slightly medieval in its construction so that he was not sure what to think about the architecture, concluding at last that if Lady Carberry admired it then that was good enough for him, for he trusted her taste in all things. There were no grounds to speak of, the whole building being situated in little more than an acre or two of land and girded around with a high wall like a monastery. It had been built, the coach driver informed him, by a cotton merchant, a man who owned a rapidly growing collection of cotton mills and employed hundreds of workers but was scarcely ever in the country long enough to inhabit his own house.

As Thomas's carriage drew nearer he saw that another coach was already turning into the gates of Godfrey Hall. A few minutes later the coach drew up in the drive just ahead of his own and he saw Edward Dunwoody step rather clumsily out of the door, aided by one of Lady Carberry's footmen. Mr Dunwoody had put on a considerable amount of weight in a remarkably short space of time since Thomas had last set eyes upon him. He was followed by Margaret, who must, Thomas realised, now be his wife. She, in turn, was followed by Mrs Schreiber, wrapped and shrouded in a great many garments, giving the illusion that she was a person of real substance, until a glimpse of her drawn white face made it clear that she was little more than a living skeleton. This little tableau quickly dispersed and they made their way into the house; Thomas's cab moved forwards, allowing him to disembark in their place.

Despite the fact that the Carberrys were here to support their friend whose health was quite obviously in grave decline, there was something of a party atmosphere inside the house. Lord and Lady Carberry were standing in the hall, welcoming their guests, while chattering voices and peals of polite laughter could be heard from a reception room just beyond them. Moreover, it seemed to Thomas that Lady Carberry was looking quite particularly radiant. The glint of pleasure in her eye as she greeted him was worth all the suffering that he had endured in the house of Charles Lawson.

'What a joy it is to see you, Thomas!' she declared. 'Now, at last, I shall have some enlightened conversation.'

Thomas felt himself blushing as he bowed.

'She knows she won't get any of that sort of thing from me,' Lord Carberry said, with a good-natured chuckle, taking Thomas's hand and pumping it fiercely. 'Not an enlightened bone in my body, I'm happy to say. Good to see you, young man.'

Thomas passed into the grand parlour where a small

crowd of people sat or stood clustered in little groups. Mrs Schreiber was ensconced in a chair drawn up as close to the fire as possible. Her daughter was fussing about her with a blanket. Thomas crossed the room to pay his respects and to offer his congratulations to Margaret. Mrs Schreiber only shook her head and sighed when he expressed his hope that her health might be improved, but Margaret beamed smugly at the mention of her nuptials. She immediately launched into an account of her endeavours to bring a woman's touch to Harford Hall, which Thomas understood to be the name of her new house. The place had been sadly neglected for far too long. 'A man who lives alone does not notice such things,' she declared, 'and of course Edward has so much to occupy his thoughts. I honestly think he would not notice if there were no curtains on the windows and no linen on the table. He is always conscious of his duties. You have no idea how heavily they weigh upon him'

Edward Dunwoody himself appeared just then but he did not appear to be terribly over-burdened. He was talking to a rather handsome looking man in late middle age with a very erect bearing and an impressive pair of ginger side-whiskers who was accompanied by a much younger woman with very bright blue eyes and a look of permanent amusement. Dunwoody was laughing a little too enthusiastically at something the woman had just said, and she seemed to find more humour in his reaction than in her own words. When the trio had drawn closer, Dunwoody introduced his companions as Lord and Lady Massey.

'And here is our young prodigy, Mr Thomas De Quincey,' he declared, after compliments had been paid to the ladies.

'What is so prodigious about him?' Lady Massey enquired. She spoke with the faintest hint of an Irish accent.

'Everyone declares that Mr De Quincey is destined to become one of the greatest scholars of our age,' Dunwoody replied, though he said this as if he considered the judgement – or perhaps the idea of scholarship itself – more than a little ridiculous.

Lady Massey raised one eyebrow, looking down at him. 'Indeed?'

'Oh yes,' Dunwoody declared. 'He has been teaching our hostess Ancient Greek.'

'And what kind of a pupil did she make?' Lady Massey demanded.

It was the same question that Lord Carberry had asked in the library at Laxton and as Thomas briefly recalled the air of intensity that had accompanied his host's enquiry, he found himself inexplicably blushing. 'She is an excellent pupil,' he stammered.

'As well as being very beautiful,' Lady Massey said.

Thomas felt that he had somehow been made to look foolish and he wished that he could excuse himself and wander off but to do so would only be to draw further attention to himself.

He was saved by the arrival of a short dark man with a rather business-like air who was greeted with great respect by Mrs Schreiber and with a little cry of delight by Margaret. This, it transpired, was the renowned Doctor White for the sake of whose skill Mrs Schreiber had come to Manchester. Doctor White's virtues were immediately related to the company at some length by Mrs Schreiber and then they were rehearsed all over again by Margaret while the doctor himself merely stood by, nodding every so often at these encomiums, without embarrassment or demur, but as though he weighed the compliments judiciously.

Thomas was beginning to wonder whether the list of

those who had been brought back from the brink of death by the intervention of Doctor White would ever come to an end when Lady Carberry appeared beside them with a request that Lady Massey would grace the company by playing something on the piano.

As the two women walked away together in animated conversation, Thomas could not help but compare them. Lady Massey was a good many years younger than her hostess and he had no doubt that she would be considered a great beauty by most people. In his judgement, however, she could not hold a candle to Lady Carberry. He stood there wondering what word might most succinctly sum up Lady Carberry's charm, so grave and yet so humorous, so mature and yet so girlish, so intelligent and so.... when he suddenly became aware that Lord Massey was addressing him.

'We served together in Calcutta for a year.'

'I beg your pardon?'

'Your uncle and I. We were in Calcutta together.'

'Colonel Penson?'

'The very man. An excellent officer.'

'So he assures me whenever he has the opportunity.'

Lord Massey gave an indulgent smile. 'He was never short of self-confidence.'

'I hope, for your sake, that you were not obliged to spend too much time in his company.'

Lord Massey looked thoughtful and it seemed for a moment as if he were considering saying something revealing about the colonel, when there came the sound of a chord being struck on the fortepiano and all eyes turned to the front of the room where Lady Massey had now begun to play.

The piece that she had embarked upon was unknown to Thomas but it was evident that she was an accomplished musician, and she quickly captured the attention of everyone in the room. The admiration of the company was almost universal. Only Doctor White seemed unaffected by the music, looking round the company with a faintly exasperated air, as if he were disappointed to find himself no longer the centre of everyone's attention. When the piece was over there was enthusiastic though decorous applause and Lady Massey was exhorted to play some more. She put up a suitable show of resistance before allowing herself to be persuaded and had just begun upon a second piece when Thomas turned to see Lady Carberry's butler standing beside him with an envelope in his hand.

'Lady Carberry has asked me to convey this note to you, sir,' he said quietly and with an air or discretion.

Thomas frowned at him. 'Who is it from?'

'I couldn't say, sir.'

Thomas took the note and the butler turned and walked away.

So engrossed were the rest of the company in Lady Massey's performance that this episode had passed unnoticed by any of the other guests. Thomas moved away from the company and stepped out onto a terrace where he could read the note without being observed. He had already recognised Lady Carberry's handwriting.

He tore open the envelope and read, 'I have something I would very much like to give you. You will find me at the top of the stairs in the third room on the left. S.'

S. Sarah. The sight of that single letter, standing nakedly at the bottom of the note affected him so greatly that he found himself staring fixedly at it with the blood beating in his ears like a drum until a burst of applause from inside the house reminded him of the presence of other people and the need to escape their attention. He put the note in his pocket, turned and went back into the house, making his way as quickly as possible out of the drawing room, into the hall and up the stairs. He had no idea what it was that Lady Carberry intended to give him but the prospect of a tête-a-tête was enough to overwhelm all other considerations.

The door to the third room on the left was already very slightly ajar. Thomas hesitated for an instant and then knocked. Lady Carberry's voice called out, 'Who is it?'

'Thomas,'

'Come in.'

He stepped inside and found himself in what seemed to be a large dressing room. An enormous linen closet took up much of one wall, and directly opposite it was an elaborately carved escritoire on which a great many papers were distributed along with a tall oil lamp which was the only source of illumination in the room; against the far wall was a folding wooden screen and, Thomas immediately understood that behind this screen was Lady Carberry. Along with this understanding came the realisation that she must not be fully dressed, whereupon he felt his whole body grow as weak as if he had been instantaneously stricken with fever.

'I will be with you in one moment,' Lady Carberry assured him.

Thomas remained frozen just inside the door, his gaze attracted to the screen as inexorably as an iron nail to a lodestone. It was a hinged screen, in four sections, each section divided into three panels; the top and bottom panels were painted in a complex interwoven pattern of leaves and flowers; the middle panels depicted Arcadian scenes peopled by shepherds, shepherdesses and winged cupids. But it was not to the detail of these scenes that Thomas's eyes were drawn. Instead, acting entirely of their own will, or so it seemed, they sought the crack between two of the sections where there was a vague impression of movement being carried on behind the screen. What exactly was Lady Carberry doing? In this half-light it was impossible to tell and yet Thomas could not stop himself from straining every nerve and muscle in his body in an effort to decipher those vague shapes and map them onto the picture of Lady Carberry that he carried in his head.

Then suddenly she stepped out from behind the screen and there was nothing whatsoever untoward about her appearance. Thomas felt quite certain that she must know how he had striven to gain a glimpse behind the screen and he felt his face grow hot.

But if Lady Carberry was aware of his discomfort she did not acknowledge it. Instead, she held out a book. 'I wanted to give you this book, Thomas. I was given it by a friend in Bristol and the moment I set eyes upon its contents I thought of you. Thomas would appreciate this, I said to myself.'

Thomas took the book and mumbled his thanks, still crippled by embarrassment at his earlier prurience. He opened the book and glanced at the title page: Lyrical Ballads With A Few Other Poems. He had heard of this book. He began to leaf through the pages and quickly confirmed that it was indeed the collection of poems by William Wordsworth and Samuel Taylor Coleridge that had been so loudly denounced in the pages of the Edinburgh Review.

'I must confess, it is not my kind of reading,' Lady Carberry continued. 'The language is so...so very surprising, almost like a kind of puzzle in some places but in other places, so very plain, with subjects one is unaccustomed to find in poetry. Nor do they for the most part seem to be ballads... And yet, my friend assures me that it is the coming thing. It is a riddle. And yet I am confident that you will be able to solve it for me.'

'I shall do my best, Lady Carberry.'

'Of course you shall, Thomas. And now, you must go downstairs again for people will be wondering where you are. I shall join you presently.'

Thomas backed out of the room, mumbling his thanks again. Once outside he screwed up his eyes in pain. What a fool he was! Worse than a fool. He was a filthy creature. Thank God he had said nothing while he waited for Lady Carberry to emerge from behind the screen. Of course she was not in a state of undress. She was merely looking for the book to give him. A present that he was utterly unworthy to receive. How could he have ever imagined otherwise? Yet she had written… S.

He was still berating himself when he re-entered the drawing room where the music had now ceased and the company had rearranged themselves into little clusters of individuals.

'You are deep in thought.'

It was Lord Massey.

'Yes, I'm sorry. I was miles away.'

'No need to apologize young fellow. You are not much of a socialite, I suspect.'

'I'm afraid not.'

'Mind on loftier things, no doubt.'

'Well, I'm not sure about that.'

'Modesty becomes you. Now, I wanted to ask your opinion.'

'My opinion, your lordship?'

'Please, less of the lordship nonsense. Remember, I served with your uncle. 'He gave a wry grin. 'Oh don't worry, I know exactly what you mean. He's a terrible old basilisk. Still the army would be nowhere without officers like him. Anyway, let's set your uncle aside for the time being.'

'I would be most happy to do so.'

'Quite. Well, everyone assures me that you know more about classical literature than fellows twice your age.'

'I am interested in the authors of antiquity, certainly.'

'Of course you are. The thing is, someone has offered me a copy of the Epistles of Phalaris for a rather good price. It would make the perfect gift for a fellow whose good opinion might be very valuable in the coming weeks. Politics, you know..." He smiled as if to suggest that such matters were really beneath the consideration of both of them. 'However, my wife seems to think there might be some question about its authenticity.'

'Your wife is quite correct.'

Lord Massey frowned. 'You're sure of that?'

'Absolutely certain. Bentley has established beyond doubt that it is a forgery.'

'Is that so? Well, I'm very glad I bumped into you this evening, Thomas. I believe you have saved me a sum of money. And more importantly you have prevented me from making an ass of myself.'

Thomas gave a short bow. 'I am very happy to be of service,' he said.

'If there's ever anything I can do for you in return, you must let me know.'

Thomas considered this. Perhaps he could ask Lord Massey to speak to his uncle on his behalf. A man like Lord Massey could surely exert real influence even over the adamantine will of the colonel.

Before he could say any more, however, Lady Massey appeared at her husband's side, insisting that he was needed that very instant to resolve a dispute concerning a legendary wager between the Duke of Cumberland and the Prince of Wales. He was led off complaining that he had told the story of Cumberland's wager far too many times already.

Thomas did not see a great deal of Lady Carberry throughout the remainder of that evening, a circumstance that he found at once both disappointing and something of a relief since he was not sure that he could have carried on a coherent conversation with her. Instead, he spent much of the time in the company of a couple of legal clerks with, it seemed, family connections to the Carberrys from Manchester who recounted endless dull stories of the vagaries of circuit judges. He was obliged to agree with Lord Massey's judgement that he was not much of a socialite.

When his carriage returned he was glad to take his leave. He sought out his host and hostess and thanked them for their hospitality. There was nothing in Lady Carberry's manner to suggest that anything unusual had taken place. Yet all the way home, no matter how much he tried to force his mind onto other subjects, Thomas could not help recalling the vignette of Lady Carberry behind the painted screen and each time he felt himself engulfed in a hot tide of shame.

Anne

I used to ask myself why every girl in the country weren't a moll, leastways those who didn't have the benefit of a respectable home and a dowry. It's a stupid question, of course, to anyone with an ounce of common sense but common sense was one of those things I never got my fair share of – one of the many. So it never even occurred to me that if I carried on lying with men ten times a week or more, it was only a matter of time before I found myself in the family way.

You must think I'm daft and I suppose I am. Or I was then, anyhow. But the truth was, no one ever spoke about such things at Mrs Dempsey's. It was a household that took no account whatsoever of babies. They weren't mentioned nor even thought about. Babies was as common as virgins in Mrs Dempsey's house. And, of course, I was young enough for such things not to matter at first. I hadn't even started bleeding when I threw in my lot with Mrs Dempsey. So for a while I just lay back and got on with the job whenever I had to and the rest of the time, I listened to the girls gossiping, to Suzette playing the piano and to Jeremiah's stories about the gentlemen what came through our doors and the lives they might have led outside.

But time don't stand still and I weren't at Mrs Dempsey's very long when my monthlies did start. And they hadn't started very long neither before they stopped. Naturally, I thought nothing of this, on account of me being as ignorant as a stone about everything and anything unless I'd *experienced* it myself and even then, half the time I weren't sure what it was I *had* experienced.

So I paid no mind to my condition. I never discussed it with a soul. Making the best of things, that was my great idea at the time. I'd made a big mistake by knocking on Mrs Dempsey's door and asking her to take me in. I understood that now. But there weren't no turning back and nowhere to turn back to, neither. So making the best of things was the only choice left open to me. Unfortunately, even that was about to be taken away from me.

The first inkling I had of this was when I found myself waking up in the morning with my dinner rising up out of my stomach and trying to force its way out of my mouth. Sick as a dog I was two mornings out of three, three mornings out of four, four mornings out of five, but not a word did I say about it until one morning as I sat on my bed with a bucket between my knees and a line of green stuff dangling down from my lips, I looked up to see Suzette standing in the doorway frowning down on me like the angel of the Lord on the day of judgment. 'What's all this?' she asked.

It didn't take her long to find out everything she needed to know.

'You understand what this means, Anne?'

I hadn't understood up till this point or if I had I'd refused to admit it but Suzette's face and her series of sharp questions about the last time I'd had my bleeding removed the scales from my eyes entirely.

'I'm going to have a baby,' I said.

She shook her head very firmly. 'No, Anne. You are not going to have a baby. Not if you wish to remain in this house. Mrs Dempsey has no interest in babies.'

I began to weep. It was becoming clear to me that however far I fell in this world, there was always further to fall. 'Then what am I going to do?'

'I will speak to Mrs Dempsey.' With that, she turned on her heel and disappeared downstairs.

I sat on the bed and waited for a long time. I tried staring at the stain on the wall and imagining myself sailing round that foreign country but my heart weren't in it. The other girls came in and comforted me. Charlie stayed the longest, sitting beside me on the bed, holding my hand and making soothing noises like a pigeon on a roof. I felt like I'd caught a terrible disease and it weren't at all clear if I'd survive. Finally, Suzette came back upstairs and told me Mrs Dempsey wanted to see me. So with shaking legs and a heart beating so fast I thought it'd burst out of my chest, I followed her downstairs.

I'd changed since arriving at Mrs Dempsey's. I'd gone from little girl to young woman. But in my mind I still felt like the child sitting on the grass in St Mary's churchyard looking for daisies to thread together while my mother stood in front of her own mother's grave. The tears would run down her face and she'd say over and over again how sorry she was she hadn't made more of herself. Well, now it was me who was full of apologies and it seemed I'd made even less of myself than my mother. But Mrs Dempsey weren't interested in apologies. Mrs Dempsey was a woman of business and her business was gentlemen's pleasure. There was no room in her dealings for girls whose bodies would not answer that need.

She was sitting in the drawing room, as usual, with her pack of fortune telling cards beside her. I wondered if she'd been asking the cards what lay in store for me. But I suspected Mrs Dempsey didn't need to ask a question like that. She already knew the answer.

'Sit down, Anne,' she told me.

I sat down opposite her and waited to hear my fate

The skin was stretched as tightly across the bones of her face as it was the first time I set eyes on her and her green eyes was just as cold.

'Suzette has told me what has happened. It is very regrettable, Anne.'

'Yes, Mrs Dempsey.'

'And it is not a matter that we can afford to ignore. The longer it is left, the more difficult it is to deal with. You understand?'

'Yes, Mrs Dempsey.'

'So on Friday night, Suzette will take you to see a friend of mine. Her name is Mrs Nancy. Mrs Nancy will make your problem go away.'

'How will she do that?'

'She understands these matters. But it will cost me a great deal of money, Anne.'

'I'll repay you, Mrs Dempsey. I promise.'

She sighed. 'Let us hope so.' Then she dismissed me with a wave of her hand and I went back to my room to think about what she'd just told me.

Naturally, I asked the others about Mrs Nancy but nobody could tell me a thing about her except that she was a very old friend of Mrs Dempsey's and a very clever woman. I could tell from their faces they knew a great deal more but none of them was letting on. When I asked how she would make my problem disappear, they just shook their heads.

Charlie was normally the one for explaining things but all she said was, 'That would depend.'

'On what?' I'd been following her around the house since I got out of bed, asking the same questions in as many different ways as I could think of.

'On what she thinks best.'

'But how might she go about it?'

'Mrs Nancy keeps her secrets close.'

'What's that supposed to mean?'

It means you'll find out when you see her.'

So when Friday night came round and I followed Suzette down the backstreets of Whitechapel, all I knew was I was scared. Not quite as scared as when I'd been alone with Harold Lampton but not far off. Something about the way the girls had been acting towards me all day long made me think they was cutting their ties with me, setting me adrift in very deep water. And that made me wonder if I weren't coming back.

Mrs Nancy lived in two rooms on top of a tailor's shop. She was as thin as a skeleton and her chin was as sharp as the end of a pike but she was a great deal more respectable than I'd been imagining. There was curtains on the windows, proper furniture in the living room, though for some reason the sight of the thick white cloth covering the table made my heart sink, and more candles burning than I'd ever seen in one room.

She was all business. The three of us stood in the middle of the room like we was buying fish in the market while she asked me the same questions Suzette had asked when she'd come across me being sick. She also asked my age and how long since I'd eaten, which surprised me. When I told her I'd had some bread and cheese for lunch she tutted. Then she went out of the room for a few minutes.

'Why did she want to know when I'd eaten?' I whispered.

Suzette shrugged. 'In case you shit yourself,' she said.

I was shocked to hear Suzette speak so coarsely. She was the most lady-like of all Mrs Dempsey's girls but for some reason this evening there was a hardness about her and it frightened me. 'I won't shit myself,' I said. 'Why would I shit myself?'

'I don't know.'

Mrs Nancy came back into the room before I could say any more. She was carrying a small blue china bowl. She made her way carefully across the room, trying not to spill what was in the bowl. Then she handed it to me and I saw it held muddy looking water that gave off a nasty smell. 'Drink it!' she ordered.

I did as I was told, like I always did. It tasted just as bad as it looked.

Mrs Nancy told me to sit down in a wing chair beside the table. She sat down on the other side of the table and rested her elbows on the thick white cloth. It was just like we'd come to pay a social call. She asked after Mrs Dempsey and the girls and Suzette told her that they was all in the best of health and *thriving*. Then Suzette asked if Mrs Nancy would tell us about how she and Mrs Dempsey had first met. 'For Anne has never heard the story.'

Mrs Nancy needed no further encouragement. She smiled and leaned back in her chair. 'My father had an apothecary's shop,' she told me. 'You may be surprised to learn that, Miss Anne, for you find me now living in reduced circumstances. But he was a most intelligent man, and a fine man of business, too.'

She looked at me keenly, like it was important for me to understand her father's cleverness. So I said I had no doubt of it.

'I used to clean and tidy the shop for him but after a while it got too busy and he wanted me to help him. He showed me how to preserve herbs and how to make up compounds for salves and every kind of remedy a body might have need of, and he took on another girl to keep the place tidy and that girl was Mrs Dempsey.'

That surprised me. I suppose I'd come to think of Mrs Dempsey as a person of such importance, I couldn't rightly imagine her sweeping up the shop and washing the bottles.

Mrs Nancy must have seen my surprise because she laughed. 'Oh yes,' she said, Evelyn Dempsey was a willing girl and a very good worker and she being of an age with me, we soon struck up a friendship. We had such lovely times together, me and her and her brother John. Have you ever met, John, Miss Anne?'

I shook my head.

'A fine big, strong man he was, though he was only fifteen years old. He was very sweet on me in those days. Very sweet. Then one day a customer came into the shop, pulled out a knife as long as your forearm and stabbed my father right there in front of us, right through the heart. Then he turned and ran out the door. My poor father just fell down on the floor and though we did our best to help him, we couldn't save him. He was dead within minutes.'

'But why did he do it?' I asked.

'Not right in the head. He was shouting at my father about some remedy for an ulcer that my father had sold him. That was before he pulled out his knife. Anyway, that was the end of the shop and the end of John's attentions.' She shrugged. 'I wasn't such a catch any more.' She gave a sad smile. 'After that, it was all hard going for me.'

'But did anyone ever find the man who done it?'

'Evelyn found him. Two years later. Saw him in a tavern

and knew him right away. Always was a sharp girl. Eyes like a hawk.'

'What did you do?'

'I went and spoke to John. He sorted it out.'

'Did he kill him?'

Mrs Nancy nodded. 'Put a blade right through his eye, then stamped on his neck to make sure. Leastways, that's what he told me.' She said this with a good deal of relish. Then she turned to Suzette. 'Do you see anything of John Dempsey these days?'

Suzette shook her head and started to say something about a quarrel between Mrs Dempsey and her brother but I'd stopped listening for I began to realise that something very strange was happening to me.

The first sign I had of what was in store for me that evening was when things began to turn yellow. When I say things began to turn yellow I don't mean just one or two things. Everything took on the colour of the piss in that great tub my mother and me had soaked Mr Gillespie's washing in.

I was still *marvelling* at this when I started to feel as weak as water. All the strength went out of me and at the same time I felt my breakfast rising up inside me.

'Feeling a little queer, Miss Anne?' Mrs Nancy said.

I tried to answer but my tongue wouldn't seem to work proper.

Then things started to get all mixed up. First of all Mrs Nancy was standing in front of me with a bucket in her hand and I was vomiting into it over and over, my stomach straining to bring up every last scrap. Then the next thing I knew, I was lying on the table and I felt like a great weight was pressing down on me. I couldn't move so much as a finger and I've never been so scared in all my life. Mrs Nancy and Suzette was leaning over me and talking but I couldn't make out one word of what they said. It all just seemed like noises. And there was something wrong with their faces, like they'd all been pulled out of shape. Then the pains started and after that I couldn't think about nothing else.

It was like someone had put a red hot iron inside me. That's the only way I can describe it. So sharp and so terrible it was, I thought for certain I must be dying and I could hear a woman screaming over and over and I thought how they must be killing her and someone ought to help her but of course it was me that was screaming. 'Like a stuck pig,' Suzette told me afterwards.

I never felt the same about Suzette after that day. I'd always thought she was quality before, but after that day I saw she was as hard and as cold as Mrs Dempsey herself and it was all the same to her whether I lived or died. She'd already parted company with me in her mind. It was all the same to Mrs Nancy, too. I was just another bit of business as far as she was concerned. I often thought afterwards that maybe that man who killed her father had good reason.

Whatever it was she gave me hated the baby and made me push it out of myself like I was shitting out all my insides. It came out of me in the end and Mrs Nancy collected it in her bucket, the same one I'd thrown up in. And afterwards I still kept pushing and pushing even though Mrs Nancy and Suzette was telling me it was all over, and when I could finally move my head, all I could see was blood everywhere, like a slaughterhouse and I thought at first, maybe I hadn't pushed it out after all, maybe they'd cut it out of me and I said to Mrs Nancy, 'You've murdered me.'

She just shook her head. 'I don't think so, Miss Anne,' she told me. 'If you can just stop with all this bleeding, there's a good chance you'll get out of this alive.

A good chance. The words went round and round in my head, like they had a special meaning, like they was something out of Holy Scripture and I thought to myself, 'Have I been a good girl, though?' and I wanted my mother so badly but I knew well enough we'd gone our separate ways, her and me. There'd be no help from that quarter. If I was to survive, it must be by my own strength, and there came a moment when I decided that I would survive, I'd keep my hold on life, even if it was a shitty, miserable life. I wouldn't let no-one take it away from me.

I stayed at Mrs Nancy's all that night, lying on the table where they'd put me. She covered me in a blanket and lit a fire to warm me up and the pair of them sat there talking to each other like I wasn't even there.

Sometimes I was awake and sometimes I wasn't. I dreamed about my father. He'd come back from the bottom of the sea to ask what I'd done with his map and I couldn't answer because I didn't know. All night long I kept worrying about that map. What had I done with it? Why had I let someone take it from me? I'd let my father down badly by losing it and that was the very reason he'd gone and got himself drowned.

Tuah

I did not need to be told that things were going badly for Captain McKerras in his battle with the Company. It was evident in the way he walked with his back bowed and his shoulders slumped – he who had always stood as straight as a ram rod – in the way he sat staring into space for long periods of time, neither speaking to anyone nor answering his brother's enquiries, in the way he muttered to himself sometimes, as if he were conducting an argument with an unseen adversary but, most of all, in the way he disappeared every evening and staggered back home from some tavern late at night, knocking into the furniture and cursing loudly.

The captain had always risen early but now he lay in bed for half the morning and when he rose he was exceedingly irritable, cursing whenever he found himself inconvenienced in any way. As a result, there were regular arguments between the two brothers in which voices were raised. These would invariably end with the captain storming out of the house, insisting that Archie had it in for him, just like all the rest; for he believed himself beset by enemies on all sides.

On one occasion, standing at the foot of the stairs, I heard a great crash and a moment later the captain came stamping angrily past me. I made my way upstairs and found

Archie on his hands and knees picking up the pieces of a broken jug that clearly had been full of ale. He looked at me and gave a wry smile. As I got a cloth and helped clear up the mess, I wondered where all this would end.

Then one day there came a change in the captain's manner. He rose late, as was his wont now, but he did not seem so angry with everything and everyone. There was a calmness about him, almost a dreaminess, which was as great an alteration in its own way as the shouting and cursing of the last few weeks had been. At first I thought he had found solace in faith – *come unto me, all ye that labour and are heavy laden, and I will give you rest.* This new tranquility lasted for the next few weeks. He still rose late and went out every evening, returning only in the small hours but he was in a much better humour. More than once I saw a faint smile flicker about his lips. And yet there was something about this new manner that disturbed me even more than the cursing and shouting. It did not take me long to divine what it was. At first there was a faint smell about him that tickled the edges of my memory. As the days went on the smell became stronger until there could be no doubt. The captain was smoking opium.

One morning, about a week into this new state of affairs, I was carrying a box of clothes up the stairs to be sorted through by Archie, when I became aware that the captain had emerged from his bedroom and was standing on the landing, watching me with a look of amusement.

'How are you settling in, Abdul?' he asked.

I was a little taken aback for by this time I considered myself past the settling in stage. Nevertheless, I assured him that I was settling in very well and he seemed pleased.

'That's the spirit,' he replied cheerfully. But then he frowned. 'But you must take care. You must take great care.

The city of London is an animal that devours its own children.'

I had no idea what to say to this. So I only smiled and nodded.

'We are all in the belly of the monster,' he went on. 'Not all of us will be delivered.'

I waited for a moment, for the sake of politeness, then I carried on with my errand.

The captain's good humour did not last. After a while it gave way to a dreadful vacancy. He moved about the house like a sleepwalker, speaking to no one, occasionally seeming startled or alarmed at something only he could see. He lost weight, the flesh on his face falling away and for the first time since I had met him he began to seem old.

I tried to speak to Archie about it. 'Your brother is unwell,' I told him, one morning as we were walking through the streets on one of our clothes-collecting expeditions.

'All his life Donald has been headstrong,' Archie said. 'If he is determined to kill himself, there is nothing you or I can do to stop him.'

It was about a week after this conversation that Mr Li came to our door. It was a Friday night, sometime after midnight when we were woken by a determined knocking on the shop door. I was reluctant to rouse myself from sleep for I had been deep in a dream of my uncle and such dreams were rare these days. So when I pulled on some clothes and descended I found that Archie had preceded me and was standing at the door in the midst of a discussion with an elderly Chinaman.

'Abdul,' Archie said when he saw me. 'Put on your coat and get the cart. We're going to collect Donald.'

I did as I was told. Then we set off together through the dark and silent streets, the wheels of the cart rattling loudly enough to wake the dead. I was not accustomed to being abroad after dark – *we are not of the night, nor of darkness* – but I would have imagined that at this time the streets would be entirely deserted, all the neighbourhood sleeping in their beds. I soon found this to be untrue. Eyes watched our progress from doorways and alleys, and shadowy forms kept us company from time to time. I noticed that Archie carried his long knife openly in his hand.

As we walked, I studied the Chinaman. He was small and slight, his face deeply lined, his hair completely white and a long wispy beard straggling down from his chin. I could only guess at his age but I suspected he would not see threescore and ten again. Despite this, he seemed unperturbed to be abroad at this hour. Indeed, he seemed to belong in these streets far more readily than Archie or I.

As we drew closer to the docks, the streets grew ever narrower and the houses leaned closer together, great black shadows that seemed to conspire against us. The smell of the river was much stronger than by day and although it was the smell of decay yet there was something alluring about it, even to me who had good enough reason never to set foot on a boat again as long as I lived.

At last we turned down an alley scarce wide enough to bring the barrow. Half way along the Chinaman stopped before a door and rapped it with his knuckles. The door was opened by an elderly Chinawoman. They spoke together briefly in their own language then the Chinaman turned and beckoned us to follow him inside.

The ground floor of the building was all one room, divided by rows of brick pillars and by the shadows thrown from dozens of flickering candles. The air was full of smoke and the floor was littered with mats. Upon all these mats lay the smokers, either flat on their backs or propped up on one elbow sucking at pipes that glowed like coals in the half-dark. The smell of opium was everywhere.

The Chinaman threaded his way towards the far end of the room where the captain was sitting up on one of the mats, scowling. Standing over him was a young Chinaman with an ugly expression on his face and a great wooden club in his hand.

When the captain saw us his scowl disappeared and an expression of eagerness came over his face. 'Archie,' he said. 'Thank goodness you've got here. I need some money.'

'You need to come home,' Archie said. He turned to the elderly Chinaman. 'Exactly how much does he owe?'

I was shocked by the size of the sum the Chinaman named but if Archie was similarly affected he did not show it. He merely put his hand in his pocket, pulled out a purse and counted out the required amount. Once this transaction had been completed the fellow with the club melted away into the shadows.

'Perhaps you could just pay Mr Li for one more pipe, Archie,' the captain said. 'Then I can make my own way home in the morning.'

'You're coming with us now,' Archie told him. 'We've got the cart outside.'

'I'm not sitting in the cart!'

'Then you can walk. It's your choice, but you're leaving this minute. Mr Li doesn't like customers who make difficulties. Pick him up, Abdul.'

Reluctantly, I bent down, expecting to encounter furious resistance from the captain but he was as meek as a lamb as I slid my hands under his armpits and raised him to his feet.

'Can you put one foot in front of the other?' Archie asked.

'I'm not sure.'

'Well try.'

With me supporting him, the captain made his way unsteadily across the room to where Mr Li was waiting impassively.

'You know I would have paid you in time,' the captain said, as he drew level with the Chinaman.

Mr Li gave a very slight shake of the head. 'No credit,' he said. Then he opened the door and we stumbled out into the night air.

Despite his earlier indignation at the suggestion he might be wheeled back home, the captain sat down in the cart without a murmur of protest and we set off back towards the shop.

After a while, Archie, who had been looking mightily angry, demanded of his brother what the devil he thought he was doing wasting his money in such a place.

'There are unknown lands to be found,' the captain told him, speaking as though still half in a dream. 'Continents and countries where the inhabitants and the landscape are more remarkable than anything I ever encountered when sailing the seven seas.'

'Fiddlesticks!' Archie exclaimed. 'You're a bloody fool, Donald!'

'We are all bloody fools,' the captain agreed, 'adrift on a bloody sea.'

Thomas

Thomas was sitting on his bed reading the book that Lady Carberry had given him when the Lawsons' maid knocked on the door, entered, dropped a curtsey so brief as to be little more than an overgrown twitch and informed him that there was a letter for him on the table in the hallway.

Who, in the silent hour of inward thought,
Can still suspect, and still revere himself,
In lowliness of heart.

He closed the book and set it down, then levered himself off the bed and made his way wearily downstairs. One of his mother's lengthy missives no doubt, full of admonition and reference to Holy Scripture.

Charles Lawson was standing near the foot of the stairs as Thomas descended. Thomas glanced in his direction and then looked away. He would not grace the man with a remark.

The letter was not from his mother. The handwriting was entirely unfamiliar – if Thomas had to guess, he would have said it was a woman's hand. He frowned and took the letter upstairs where he could consider it in private.

Once safely ensconced in his room, he tore open the envelope impatiently, only to discover that the letter was written entirely in French. To his dismay, he could make neither head nor tail of it, for while he was extremely well versed in ancient languages French had not been considered a necessary part of his education. Of course it ought to have been possible to work out the meaning from a careful study of the words: when all was said and done what was French but a dialect of Latin that had become horribly corrupted with the passage of time? And yet he could not. Optimisme, nécessaire, audace, difficulté, envoyage – these and several other words stood out from the page, hinting at a message of goodwill and encouragement, but to put the whole thing together was somehow beyond Thomas's skill in these circumstances for he felt so disorientated; the reason for his confusion was his almost feverish excitement at the other document that had fallen out of the envelope with the letter. It was a banker's draft for forty guineas! Someone had sent him forty guineas!

Forty guineas was a very considerable sum of money. A serviceable sum. A person could do a good deal with forty guineas. He could travel by coach. He could put up at inns. He could make his way to the Lake District – he glanced at the book lying still on his bed. A man with forty guineas in his pocket was in possession of independence.

Thomas returned to a consideration of the letter. It was signed by a Madame Sara Viguier. That much at least was clear. It was not a name that Thomas recognised. At least it was not a surname that he recognised but with a sudden burst of elation he recalled that Sarah was Lady Carberry's first name. Sara Sarah. Thomas saw then what had happened.

A few weeks earlier he had written to Lord Massey and begged him to use his influence with Colonel Penson. Lord Massey had sent an amiable reply in which he had promised to do whatever he could on Thomas's behalf but there had been no material change in Thomas's circumstances. No doubt Lord Massey had found the colonel quite impervious to reason. Instead, Lord Massey must have spoken with Lady Carberry about Thomas's situation, something that Thomas himself had always felt reluctant to do, and on hearing of his miserable condition she had seen fit to take the matter into her own hands. She had acted swiftly and decisively, making available to Thomas the means by which he might free himself from the yoke of Charles Lawson. Naturally, she could not reveal herself, so she had assumed the soubriquet of Madame Sara Viguier. The understanding of what this meant – her interest in him, her generosity towards him, the keenness of her sympathy – was almost enough to move him to tears.

Thomas's speculations were interrupted by a knock on the door of his room. He got up from the bed and opened the door to find Charles Lawson standing there with a look of naked curiosity written all over his face.

'I could not help noticing that you were in receipt of a letter this morning,' the man began. 'I sincerely hope that all is well at home.'

For a moment, Thomas considered making some sort of caustic reply but in the end all he said was, 'I thank you for your concern, sir, but all is perfectly well.' Then he shut the door, politely but firmly.

After that he sat on his bed and thought for five minutes before suddenly standing up, stuffing the letter and the banker's draft in his pocket and putting a change of clothing, the copy of Lyrical Ballads and a volume of Euripides in his leather travelling bag. With that he glanced once round the room and walked out, determined never to look at it again. He walked down the stairs, conscious of Lawson's eyes upon him once more – the man had so little to occupy his mind that even the slightest alteration to routine was enough to arouse his suspicions. Then Thomas stepped outside the front door and set off at a brisk pace for the nearest post office.

That was his mistake, of course. He should have walked into the city centre and gone to a bank. But he had been in a hurry and the post office had seemed a less intimidating prospect, though why he should have been intimidated he could not rightly have said. Yet when he arrived outside the building, far from being put at ease by the familiarity of the place, he was, if anything, more nervous than he might have been in a bank manager's office. He spent a good five minutes on the street outside, pretending to look in the window while he debated with himself whether or not this truly was the best course of action. Finally he plucked up the courage to march inside, but his manner had not been convincing. He stuttered as he announced that he wished to redeem a banker's draft. Was "redeem" the right word? Was that what people said?

The post master, with whom Thomas had exchanged a few pleasantries in the past, took the banker's draft, looked at its value and frowned down at Thomas over a pair of half-moon spectacles.

'This is a good deal of money.'

'Some might think so.' Was that another mistake? Had he appeared to be giving himself airs?

'Might I ask how you came by this?'

'It was delivered in a letter to the house where I am staying less than an hour ago.'

'I see. And might I see that letter?'

Thomas considered this request for a moment. He ought, of course, to refuse, tell the man to mind his own business and get on with his job. Surely the fellow was exceeding his authority? Instead, he took the letter out of his pocket and reluctantly handed it over. The post master studied it for some time. Then he looked up. 'This is written in French.'

'That is correct.'

'Are you aware of what is written here?'

'Of course'

'You are Thomas De Quincey?'

'Certainly. Why else have you been delivering mail to me under that name for the past three months?'

The post master nodded. 'But are you the Thomas De Quincey for whom this banker's draft is intended?'

'How dare you!' Thomas had been struggling to remain unperturbed by the post master's questions but he could no longer keep himself in check. 'Do you doubt my integrity, sir?'

The post master looked unimpressed. 'Not in the least. Pray, what relation is Madame Viguier to you, exactly?

Thomas felt himself seized by panic. Acting almost involuntarily, he snatched the letter out of the man's hands, picked up the banker's draft from the counter and walked out of the post office without another word. When he had walked a good quarter mile from the village he stopped, leaned against a tree and shook like a leaf in the wind.

But then he pulled himself together, thought the whole thing through carefully and saw what he must do. He needed some further proof of his identity. Once that had been secured he would leave the area and try once more to redeem the banker's draft but this time he would go to a large bank, where any number of such transactions took place every day of the week, instead of some semi-rural post-office where the post master did not have enough work to occupy him fully. After that, he would head directly for the Lake District and seek out William Wordsworth.

Anne

After that night at Mrs Nancy's I weren't right for a good while. Jeremiah came to fetch me back to Mrs Dempsey's the next day. I woke up on the floor, still wrapped in the same bloody blanket, to find him looking down at me with an expression I couldn't fathom. Later, I'd see that expression on the faces of all the others, and at last I understood what it was: surprise at seeing me still alive. I wondered then how many others there'd been before me who hadn't woken up on Mrs Nancy's floor.

Exactly how I got down there I couldn't tell you, since the last thing I remembered I was up on the table with someone trying to claw the insides out of me.

'Morning Miss Anne,' Jeremiah said. 'Very good to see you.'

I said nothing. My mouth was that dry it was like someone had stuffed it full of sand, and my tongue felt like a bit of old shoe leather.

'Had a bit of a rough night by the looks of you,' Jeremiah said. 'Still, you'll soon brighten up when you're back at Mrs Dempsey's. Reckon you can stand?'

I shook my head and wished I hadn't. I thought for a minute I might be sick all over again.

'Don't you worry,' Jeremiah said and he bent down, took

hold of me and lifted me up as easily as picking up a kitten. But it felt to me like I was being stabbed with a knife and I cried out in pain.

'Sorry, Miss Anne,' Jeremiah said. 'But you can't stay here and you can't walk. So what else can we do with you?' Then he turned and walked out the door with me held in front of him.

I thought he must be planning to carry me all the way back to Mrs Dempsey's but to my *amazement* there was a carriage waiting outside. When he saw us come out, the driver jumped down and opened the door. Then him and Jeremiah together got me inside, like they was putting a parcel on board. All the time I was yelling with the pain of it and I felt like my body was on fire. Somehow they got me on the seat and I sat there, holding on to Jeremiah like a woman on the edge of a cliff. Then we set off bumping and juddering down the street. It was the first time in my life I'd ridden in a carriage but I can't say I enjoyed it. I know I bit my lip so hard I made it bleed.

It felt to me like that journey would never end but when it did at last I wished it hadn't, because then we had to go through the business of getting me out of the carriage and into Mrs Dempsey's house where they was all waiting for me with the same look on their faces that Jeremiah had worn earlier. *Fancy that! She's still alive. But don't she look a state!*

Mercifully, I didn't have to make the journey to my room at the top of the house. Mrs Dempsey had a bed made up for me downstairs, in the very same room where she laid out her fortune telling cards. That was where Jeremiah put me down and that's where I stayed for a fortnight before I could climb the stairs again. And it was a lot longer before I could take up my old trade.

Those first few days I didn't care whether I lived or died.

It was all the same to me. Sometimes I was asleep, sometimes I was awake but the pain was always there.

I wept and wept, thinking upon the ruin of my life, and nothing any of them could say would comfort me. The girls was all very patient with me, now that I look back on it, though I didn't think nothing of it at the time. They took it in turns to feed me small spoonfuls of soup but I carried right on weeping even as I ate.

And yet, out of that terrible time something good did happen. Better than good. Something *marvellous*. A kind of miracle. I lost something in Mrs Nancy's house. I don't know what it was. I only know it was very important. But I also got something back. A gift.

A few days after Jeremiah had brought me back in the carriage Mrs Dempsey made an announcement. She had Suzette draw up a chair beside my bed and then she sat herself down like the Queen of England and she told me she'd decided to do something for me. It was just like the time she told me about the stain on the wall of my room. She had the same kind of air about her, like this was a *particular secret* between her and me.

'I have spoken to Archie.' she announced.

'The hunchback?'

'Do you know another Archie?'

'No.'

'Well then.'

I looked at her blankly. Surely to God she didn't want me to turn tricks with Archie now.

'There's a lot more to him than you might think,' Mrs Dempsey went on. 'He's an educated man. A man who reads.' She looked at me all meaningful when she said this.

'I see,' I said, though I didn't see at all.

'There isn't a man alive in London who knows more

about the world of literature than Archie McKerras.'

I had no idea what she meant by the *world of literature* but I didn't like to say.

'Therefore, I have asked Archie to come and read to you.'

'Read to me?'

'He will come tonight, after he has finished his business in the shop.' She paused and looked at me and I realised she was waiting for me to thank her. So I did. Then she continued. 'Do you know why it is that I am the mistress of this house?'

I had no idea what she was talking about now. 'Because you are,' I said, knowing even as I said it that it was a feeble answer.

'Because I use what is between my ears. It is time you began to do the same, Anne.' And with that she stood up and left me there, too puzzled even to weep.

That same afternoon Charlie knocked on my door with a little bottle of brown liquid that she told me was *laudanum*. I'd never had it before and I was very suspicious about taking anything of the kind after that terrible brew that Mrs Nancy had given me. But Charlie assured me it would do nothing but soothe my aches and pains. She used it very often, she told me. So I had a few drops of it in a glass of wine and at first it didn't seem to do nothing for me at all. But by and by I found I was changed into another person altogether for I no longer cared about all the bad things that had happened to me. All those hurts and sorrows, that had me tossing and turning all day long just thinking about them, floated away like rubbish floating down the river and disappearing out to sea.

Jeremiah came and carried me up the stairs to my old room and even though it hurt a good deal, I found I didn't care so very much now. When I was lying on my own bed once more, I greeted the stain on the wall like a long lost friend and for the next few hours I was content, voyaging round and about that imaginary country. It was the first time I felt like I was truly alive since the world had turned yellow round at Mrs Nancy's. From that day onwards laudanum became my daily companion.

Tuah

Captain McKerras did not return to the Chinaman's establishment for several weeks. Despite the bravado that he had shown when we went to collect him, he was subdued when he woke late the following day and he went about the house with the look of a man who knows he has shown himself in a poor light.

But this mood wore off in time. He began to be more restless and irritable. When Archie asked him a question he would make a sarcastic reply. I had seen this mood often enough on board the Laurel Bower when we had been becalmed for days on end, or after a visit to one of the Kalcut warehouses that had not turned out as he had expected. The captain could be cruel if he so wished and the opium seemed to bring out that side of his personality once its soporific effects had receded. When Archie suggested that he might bestir himself and lend a hand with the business of the shop, the captain gave him a sneering look.

'It is your business, Archie, not mine.'

'And yet here you are,' Archie observed.

'Here I am indeed, watching you crawl about the place like a crab in a bucket.'

Archie said no more but I saw his face redden and I knew

that the captain's words had wounded him.

A few days after this exchange the captain began once more to come back to the house in the early hours and the following morning I would recognise the smell of opium on his person.

On some days he was in a good humour and would talk to me, like he had done when he was captain of the Laurel Bower. On one occasion he even asked me what Archie had been teaching me that week.

'A passage from Milton,' I told him. 'About the loss of Paradise.'

He put his hand to his head in mock astonishment. 'My God, Abdul! You have come a very long way since that auction in Cape Town. '

In saying this, no doubt he meant to congratulate me but I felt immediately diminished at the reminder and the feeling stayed with me for several days therafter.

On another occasion he bade me put down a broom with which I had been intending to sweep the yard, sit down and listen while he told me of his childhood in the highlands of Scotland.

His father, he said, had been an utterly selfish man, whose sole concern was with his own comfort. 'At the age of twelve, he hired me out to a shepherd, an old bastard as mean as himself. I was made to stand in a field in my bare feet all day long, watching the sheep eating grass and trying to ignore the hunger in my belly while my father sat at home drinking whisky and acting the laird.'

Archie had come into the room while the captain had been telling this story and now he interrupted. 'You know perfectly well why our father sold you to that shepherd.'

A spasm of irritation crossed the captain's face. 'He hired me out. He did not sell me.'

'Nevertheless, you know why he did it.'

'Because he was a selfish bastard and he wanted the money.'

'Because you gave him so much rebellion and insult he could not abide your presence in the house. It was your pride that cast you out.'

The captain slammed his fist down on the table. 'Why do you always defend him?'

Archie shrugged. 'He is in no position to defend himself.'

The captain got to his feet abruptly, the chair clattering to the floor behind him. He opened his mouth and shut it again. Then he turned and stamped out of the house.

After this incident he was often absent from the house for days on end and when he did return he was almost entirely uncommunicative. His dress and his person began to deteriorate and I could tell that Archie was greatly concerned for his welfare but there was nothing he could do. The captain was a stubborn man and opium is a jealous mistress.

It was around this time that I first set eyes upon Mrs Dempsey. I had heard her name mentioned by Archie and the captain more than once, usually in some sort of ribald jest, and I gathered that she lived on the other side of the street and kept a bawdy house. I was in the shop, serving behind the counter – recently Archie had begun entrusting this job to me during quiet periods – and struggling to work my way through a book of essays which Archie had given me. He had been teaching me to read for some weeks now and I was making good headway. Nevertheless, it was one thing learning passages by rote but quite another making sense of an entire essay by Montaigne.

I looked up from my book with some relief and saw a very tall, very thin woman in a dark green silk dress staring down at me. She was much older than I had imagined, though her skin was coated with powder and her cheeks painted with rouge. She had a long, narrow face and glittering eyes.

'Good morning, madam,' I ventured.

She looked me up and down and dismissed me in a moment. 'Where is Archie?'

'He is in the back of the house, madam.'

'Well fetch him then. Tell him Mrs Dempsey has a job for him.'

I went through the door that led to the rear of the house and found Archie sorting through the endless piles of old clothing. I told him what Mrs Dempsey had said. He gave a wry smile. 'Carry on here.'

But I was far too curious for that. I waited until he had gone into the shop, then I crept up to the doorway and listened.

'What a pleasure it is to see you, Mrs Dempsey,' I heard him say.

'It has been a long time since the sight of me afforded any man pleasure.'

'A lady of such beauty and intelligence. I very much doubt that.'

'Nonsense, Archie. You know perfectly well that it is youth men desire in a woman and they dislike intelligence above all things.'

'Mrs Dempsey, in your case…'

'Please Archie. I have not come here to listen to your nonsense. I have a job for you, if you are interested. One of my girls is poorly and I am obliged to rest her. In the meantime her spirits are low and low spirits are not to be tolerated in a house such as mine. All my girls must be gay and bright.'

'And what is it you think I might be able to do to remedy this situation?'

'Read to her, of course. Will you do it?

'Naturally I would require a certain remuneration.'

'Six pence a night.'

'A shilling.'

'Ten pence.'

'Eight pence and no more.'

'Very well. When would you like me to begin?'

'This evening. After dark.'

'Is there anything in particular you would like me to read?'

'I leave it entirely up to you, Archie. Do they not call you the Scholar of Spitalfields?'

'I am called many things, very few of them complimentary. But I shall see what I can find that may interest a young lady.'

That evening, and very many evenings afterwards, Archie spent at Mrs Dempsey's and, the captain being absent, I was left to wander the house and shop by myself, peering into corners that were normally private, looking for secrets. But there were none, or, if there were, I didn't discover them. Eventually, I returned to my struggle to make sense of the book of essays. Perhaps, one day I too, could be paid for simply speaking aloud the words on a page.

Thomas

Thomas was standing in the garden of his mother's house, imagining himself well concealed behind a stone arch and considering the question of how best to attract his sister's attention without encountering any other members of the household. Since leaving the post office, all he had thought about was getting here and speaking to Mary. She would know how to lay her hands on the documents he needed. She might ask questions of course, but he was certain she could be persuaded to help.

He had entertained a vague, and, he now saw, rather improbable hope that he might encounter her walking in the garden. But he had been standing behind this arch for at least half an hour and there was no sign of her. Moreover, it was a cold day, despite being the beginning of May, and Mary had never been one to brave the cold willingly; she was the sort of girl who always preferred to be indoors.

As Thomas was thinking this he suddenly became aware that a man had emerged from a bush nearby. He was a big, broad-shouldered fellow who towered over Thomas, and how he had approached so closely without being observed was a mystery that Thomas was still pondering when the man began to speak.

'Thomas De Quincey?' He spoke slowly in a West Country accent.

'That is my name,' Thomas drew himself up to his full height, for all the good it did. 'And who might you be?'

'Daniel Hogg sir, in the service of your uncle, Colonel Penson. He sent me to ask you to come inside and talk to him.'

Thomas's first instinct was to turn and run but there was a distinct possibility that this fellow Hogg might give chase. That was not a spectacle he wished to be involved in, so he tried his best to appear unconcerned. 'I am not sure I wish to talk to my uncle at this very moment,' he declared.

Daniel Hogg looked unimpressed. 'The colonel says in that case I was to insist, sir.'

There was a certain quiet insolence about the fellow that irritated Thomas immensely. He would have liked to reply that he could insist all he liked but since these grounds were his mother's and not the colonel's, Thomas would do as he pleased – except that he knew perfectly well that his mother and the colonel would be of one mind. Besides, Daniel Hogg did not look like someone whom it might be easy to evade.

'Very well,' he said. 'You may take me to him.'

The colonel was in the library, standing near the window and making a show of reading a book, though Thomas doubted very much whether the colonel had read anything at all since his school days, unless it were a column of figures or a military order. He put it back on the shelf when they walked in.

'Thank you Daniel. That will be all,' he told his servant. 'Well, Thomas,' he continued when the fellow had left the room, 'you have certainly set the cat among the pigeons. What on earth do you mean by turning up here in the middle of term time and hanging around the place like a damned cracksman?'

'I was anxious to speak to Mary,' Thomas replied.

'Were you indeed? Well, as it so happens, Mary has gone to Ambleside.'

Thomas was taken aback. 'To Ambleside. Whatever for?'

'To look for you, of course. An express arrived from Mr Lawson two hours ago to inform your mother of your sudden departure. As you can imagine, she was thrown into a state of considerable alarm and demanded to know whether anyone had any idea of your whereabouts. After some delay Mary informed her that you had mentioned going to the Lakes in one of your letters. Whereupon your mother sent her along with the express to Ambleside to make enquiries.'

This information had such a dispiriting effect upon Thomas that he felt he could no longer remain standing. He collapsed in a chair with his head in his hands.

'You have no idea of the trouble this has caused,' his uncle continued.

'It was not my intention to cause distress to anyone.'

The colonel shook his head. 'Really Thomas, for a young man whose intellect is so highly spoken of by everyone, you do seem to have an alarming lack of common sense. What on earth did you think you were doing walking out of Lawson's house without telling anyone where you were heading?'

Thomas made no reply, keeping his eyes fixed on the dark oak table in front of him. Finally, he took a deep breath and said the thing that was uppermost in his mind. 'I am not going back to Mr Lawson's house.'

The colonel gave him the sort of look one might reserve for a sick dog. 'Come now Thomas, you must try to be reasonable.'

'There is nothing whatsoever that man can teach me.'

The colonel raised his eyebrows. 'Upon my word, you have a very high opinion of your own abilities.'

'I only wish to spend my time in the manner that would be of most use both to myself and to mankind.'

'I see. And how do you suppose mankind might benefit from today's little jaunt?'

'You mock me, uncle.'

'Not at all. I merely ask a straightforward question. What is this plan of yours to visit the Lakes, anyway?'

'It is my intention to call upon Mr William Wordsworth.'

'William who?'

'William Wordsworth!' Thomas could not help a note of exasperation creeping into his voice. 'He is the greatest poet of our age.'

'Is he indeed? Well I shall have to take your word for that. But pray, have you any reason to suppose that this fellow, William... What did you say his name was?'

'Wordsworth.'

'Ah yes, William Wordsworth. Have you any reason to suppose he wishes to see you?'

'I have written to him.' In fact, the letter was still in Thomas's breast pocket where it had resided for days. He had resolved to post it that very morning, had the visit to the post office turned out differently.

Before the colonel could make any further comment they were interrupted by a peremptory knocking upon the front door. 'I wonder who the devil that can be,' the colonel muttered. After a few moments, the library door was opened and Daniel Hogg stepped inside. Ignoring Thomas entirely, he addressed Colonel Penson.

'Begging your pardon, sir,' he said, 'but there's a gentleman at the front door from the post office in Manchester says he wishes to speak to the mistress of the house on an important matter. I told him that Mrs De Quincey was indisposed but that you might be prepared to see him.'

At these words Thomas's spirits plummeted even further. That damnable post master must have made enquiries from Lawson who had no doubt been very happy to supply the man with Thomas's mother's address.

The colonel frowned. 'I shall return presently,' he said.

Briefly, Thomas considered flight: he could leave by the door at the far side of the library, make his way round to the back of the house and be a mile away before his uncle returned; but the colonel would merely jump on a horse and set off in pursuit, it would be the kind of situation that he revelled in – action and the hunting down of a weaker creature. Thomas sighed. Only a few hours ago everything had seemed so hopeful.

The colonel returned to the library a few minutes later, his habitually genial expression entirely clouded over. 'Well Thomas,' he began, 'It seems you have not been entirely open with me.'

Thomas was silent.

'I expect you know what the fellow from the post office had to say. Unfortunately, your mother came downstairs while he was still here. She is most upset, Thomas, and also rather confused, as I confess I am myself.'

'Does she know I am here?'

'Naturally I had to tell her. She is waiting for you even now in the drawing room.' He stood by the door, looking at Thomas expectantly. Realising there was no other course of action open to him, Thomas got up from his seat and preceded his uncle out of the library and along the passage.

His mother was seated in a straight-backed chair beside the fireplace when he entered the drawing room. She was dressed in a high-waisted muslin gown, her long dark hair held back from her forehead by a hair band fastened in a bow beneath her chin, lending to her countenance an even more severe aspect than it might otherwise possess. Her eyes were red as if she had lately been weeping. 'Oh Thomas, what on earth have you been doing?' she demanded as soon as she saw him. 'What is this business about a banker's draft for forty guineas?'

'It was delivered to me at Mr Lawson's house, mother, and it was made out in my name.'

'But by whom was it drawn up?'

'It was not a name that I recognised.'

'Then why did you not make proper enquiries?'

For the briefest of moments Thomas considered telling his mother the whole story: that the money had been sent to him by Lady Carberry, that she had done so indirectly to avoid any hint of scandal and that it was a token of the esteem in which she held him. But for the first time he felt a slight anxiety about this explanation. Could he possibly have got hold of the wrong end of the stick?

'You must have understood that it was a mistake,' his mother continued. 'You must have realised that it was intended for another Thomas De Quincey. '

'I understood no such thing, mother. Ours is not a common name, after all.'

'And yet I understand that there was a letter accompanying the draft.'

At this Thomas's last hope faded. His mother was as fully informed as he might have expected.

'The letter was in French, mother. I do not speak French.'

'Exactly so. Despite all the money we have spent on your schooling, it seems there have been grave omissions from your education.'

'The classical languages are considered the basis of a sound education.'

'Do not presume to tell me what is or is not considered the basis of a sound education!' Her eyes blazed.

'Sorry, mother.'

'I should think you might be sorry, sir. Now answer me this. Do you know anyone who should have written to you in French enclosing a banker's draft for forty guineas?'

'No.'

'Of course not! Therefore, you have behaved dishonestly in laying claim to this money, and there is no greater criticism that I could make of you, Thomas. Indeed I would rather have heard that you were lying wounded upon the field of battle than that news of this kind should have reached me. I simply do not understand how a son of mine could have acted in this way.'

'I really am sorry.'

She was not to be mollified. 'Unfortunately, it will take more than an expression of regret to erase the consequences of your action. Your uncle and I must talk about this. In the meantime you are to go to your room and remain there until I send for you.'

Dismissed as if he were no more than a child, Thomas turned and made his way upstairs. Although it was a warm evening his room smelled damp and musty and he crossed the floor, intending to throw open the casement, but on reaching the window, he spied a couple talking together directly beneath him. On closer inspection he realized that the man was Daniel Hogg. Thomas was seized by an impotent fury that this man, who was no more than his uncle's servant, seemed to be everywhere, as though he had taken over all the duties of the house. He recognised the young woman as his mother's parlour maid and he heard her laugh softly at something Hogg said. Even as he stood and watched, they both turned their heads to look upwards and seemed to gaze directly at him. Dismayed, he stepped backwards, hoping that he had not been spotted. He was convinced they had been talking about him and, with this thought, he realised that his circumstances must by now be quite familiar to all the servants.

Filled with anger and humiliation, he strode about the room. He had almost resolved to leave the house that very instant without waiting to hear what his mother and uncle had decided when his eye fell upon one of the books in the bookshelf, a translation of the tales from the Arabian Nights. The sight of the book alone was enough to bring comfort and he reached out to pluck it from its place like a ripe fruit. *The Oriental Moralist…* Sitting on the bed, he opened its pages at the tale of Aladdin and his wonderful lamp and read the opening lines, recalling how he had first heard them from the lips of his nursemaid, Flossy and how eagerly he had discussed the story afterwards with his sister, Elizabeth.

At the thought of Elizabeth, he felt a pain so great and so overwhelming that it seemed for a moment as if he might fall into a dark pit of unconsciousness. Of all his siblings, Elizabeth had been the one with whom he had the most in common, although she was always much beyond him in speed and depth of apprehension and many other qualities of intellect. *She* would have been in the garden when he arrived; somehow she would have sensed his presence. He could still recall the way they had speculated together about how the magician could tell from the sound of footsteps on the other side of the world that Aladdin was the boy he sought, and he remembered Elizabeth's belief that all the inarticulate and brutal sounds of the globe must represent a secret language.

Afterwards, when Elizabeth was no longer there to lead him through the maze of thought that always seemed so impenetrable to Thomas and so absurdly simple to her, he had thought long and hard about her theory and the idea had come to him that somewhere there must be a key to that hidden language and that the man or woman who could find that key would know all that there was to be known.

Thomas put the book down and lay back upon the bed. He would never experience the same kind of intimacy with any other human being. He would always be alone with his thoughts. He was quite certain of it. His hand went automatically to touch the letter he had written to Mr Wordsworth; now though, it seemed little more than a false hope.

A knock at the door returned him to the present. He sat up in bed and called out for whoever had knocked to enter. The door opened and Daniel Hogg stepped into the room. It seemed to Thomas that his expression had grown in insolence and he would have liked nothing better than to hit the man squarely in the face but instead he waited patiently to hear the message he had brought.

'Mrs De Quincey and the colonel wish to talk with you, sir. They are in the drawing room.'

'Thank you.'

Daniel Hogg stood in the doorway as if he expected Thomas to leap up instantly and follow him. Thomas waved a hand dismissively. 'I will be down presently,' he said.

Daniel Hogg bowed and shut the door.

Thomas waited long enough for the detestable man to make his way downstairs and then he followed; as he passed the clock in the hall, he noticed that he had been closeted in his room for over an hour and yet it had only seemed like a matter of moments.

In the intervening period his mother's mood had not improved. 'Let me begin, Thomas, by saying that I am most heartily ashamed of you,' she told him as soon as he entered the drawing room, 'and I sincerely hope that you are equally ashamed of yourself. On hearing what had happened, my first instinct was to report the matter to the proper authorities and allow them to deal with it as they saw fit. However, your uncle and I have now talked the matter over at some length and he has persuaded me that another course of action might be preferable. Indeed, he has come up with a proposal which I must say, under the circumstances, is a generous one and rather more than you might have expected. I am going to leave you two to discuss it. I advise you to listen very carefully to your uncle, Thomas. He is a man of very considerable experience.' Saying this, she got to her feet and left the room.

With the departure of his sister the colonel seemed to relax a little. Standing with his back to the fire, he motioned for Thomas to sit down. 'Well now young man, you seem to have made a fine mess of things,' he said, smiling grimly. 'This is no way to heap honour on the family name, is it?'

'No, sir.'

'No sir, indeed,' the colonel continued. 'Well, we have to decide what to do for the best. Your mother, as you know, initially favoured letting you face the consequences of your action. I disagreed. A young man may behave foolishly, even reprehensibly, and still turn out well enough. That's what I told her and I've seen a few young men in my time. So, what shall we do with you, eh? It's a difficult problem. You don't want to go back to Mr Lawson's house and in this respect at least I happen to agree.'

For a moment Thomas's spirits rose. Perhaps, by some miracle, they had decided to send him to Oxford after all.

'By attempting to pass yourself off as the recipient of a banker's draft intended for someone else,' the colonel continued, 'you have committed a felony. Perhaps you are not fully aware of the significance of that?'

'I didn't take the money,' Thomas protested.

'Only because they wouldn't give it to you. That would hardly impress a justice of the peace. Even you must see that. Anyhow that is neither here nor there. The important thing now is to get you out of the way.'

'What do you mean?'

'Your mother and I are agreed that it would be the best thing for everyone if you were to take yourself off somewhere, preferably a long way from here, and disappear quietly into the background.'

'But where do you propose I go?'

'That is entirely up to you, Thomas, but you will oblige us all if you endeavour to make sure it is somewhere out of the sight of the world. Do I make myself clear?'

But what shall I live on?'

'I have persuaded your mother to make you an allowance of one guinea a week.'

'One guinea a week! How can I live on that?'

'By practising frugality, Thomas. By living quietly and staying out of harm's way.'

'But I must have more than that.'

The colonel shook his head. 'One guinea a week. You may take it or leave it. And if you ask me, Thomas, you are a very lucky young man.'

Anne

The laudanum drove everything out of my head, including all thought of Mrs Dempsey's promise. So when Suzette knocked on the door one evening and walked in with a man behind her, I was in a blind panic, thinking she was bringing up a client, and I began looking around frantically like a beast in an alley to see was there any way out for me.

Suzette understood my fear right away because she put her hand up to bid me be calm. 'Do not distress yourself, Anne,' she said. 'Archie is here to read to you, by Mrs Dempsey's invitation.'

'To what?'

'To read to you. It will help you recover your good spirits.'

'Do you like poetry?' That was what Archie asked when he'd seated himself on a chair at the foot of the bed with a pile of great thick wedges on the floor beside him that I thought at first must be bibles, on account of the Bible being the only big thick book I was *acquainted* with at that time All hunched over he was and looking to me like some kind of overgrown insect.

'Can't say I've heard any,' I told him.

'Then I shall do my best to remedy that.'

With that he set to reading me a whole string of poems.

I forget them all now but there was one about a poor boy that lived in a wood and a fine lady who fell in love with him. I didn't think that was very likely. And another about a girl who ran away with the gypsies and longed afterwards to be back home with her mother and father. That one nearly made me weep, for it put me in mind of myself. "*She thought of the home she had left far behind and wept for the promise so easily broken.*" Then there was another about a saint who cured a child that couldn't walk and brought an old man back from the dead. I weren't so keen on that one. Too holy for me, but still worth a listen. And there was one about a shepherd who was in love and all he wanted was a soft word and a smile. I considered that one downright silly. I knew well what it was men desired from a woman and it weren't just soft words and pretty smiles, neither. And there was other ones, too, that I didn't understand at all. I could make neither head, arse nor hairy tail of them.

At the end of the evening Archie asked whether I'd enjoyed the poems.

'I'm an ignorant girl,' I told him. 'How should I know what's good or bad?' But I did like the sound of the words, if the truth be told. He had a very good speaking voice, once you got used to the Scottish accent. In fact, in time I came to think that his Scottish accent made it even better. Reading voice, I should say, not speaking voice, for it all came out of those books he brought with him and he never once made a mistake. Or if he did, I didn't spot it, which I suppose ain't the same thing at all.

After that first time he turned up several times a week and when he didn't come I was very disappointed. He didn't just read poetry, neither. He read me stories about the kings and queens of England, about the emperors of Ancient Rome and about knights in armour going on long journeys.

Very often I hadn't a clue what he was talking about. There was words I'd never heard before or words I'd heard but couldn't sort out because there was so many other words around them. But Archie said not to worry. Just let it all *flow over you*. You might find you understand more than you think. And he was right about that. Once I stopped trying, I started to see the meaning in it. Not always, of course. Sometimes it was downright impossible to follow but when that happened I just let myself drift off. Sooner or later I'd come back to find my mind was following the words again.

As the weeks went by, he led me out of the darkness that had *descended* on me in Mrs Nancy's house that I thought would never leave me, and back towards a kind of *contentment*. I won't say happiness. For only once in my life did I truly know happiness and that was in the future. All the same, it was plain enough to me that Archie was a good man and I was grateful to him for being so.

I'd come to believe there was no such thing. I reckoned all men was no more than cocks walking about on legs. But Archie made me remember my own father. Not that they was in any way alike. Only that both of them was fair men that would do no harm to another human being unless they had good cause. Anyone could see that about Archie, or so it seemed to me. Life had dealt him a bad blow in making him a hunchback but he'd just turned back to life and said, 'I'll make a place for myself, a place that fits me, even if I am the sort of shape to frighten children.' And I made up my mind to do the same, however hard it was. I would find a ledge to stand on and keep standing there, whatever winds might buffet, whatever rain might fall.

PART THREE

Memento Mori

Tuah

In June the weather turned hot. For London, that is. The nights were sticky, full of the smells of the city: beer and dung, smoke and tallow, meat and tar, bread and grease, blood and fish and, hanging over everything, the great stink of the river. It was always at its worst when the nights were hot. You felt sometimes like you were drowning in a great sea of shit, and you could feel yourself turning into soil for some dreadful leprous plant to bury its roots in.

A great sadness had begun to envelop me such as I had not seen since those first days when I was captured by the Dutch slavers. *For consider him that endured such contradiction of sinners against himself, lest ye be wearied and faint in your minds.* Alone in the house so frequently, I wandered restlessly from room to room. When I sat down to read I found myself instead trying to remember my uncle's face but it was lost to me and that, more than anything, distressed me. Now I had nothing I could call my own, not even my memories.

After a couple of weeks of dull, oppressive heat the weather suddenly changed in the middle of one afternoon. The heavens opened and the sky was lit up by great flashes of lightning. It looked for all the world as though the last days had come upon us. There was nothing left for me to do in the shop and no need to wait up for Archie, so I retired to bed early with a volume of speeches and essays by Edmund Burke, but after leafing through the pages I put them aside as being far too difficult to follow. Instead, I lay there listening to the sound of the rain on the roof and indulging my loneliness until, all of a sudden, there came a loud hammering on the door. I could hardly believe that anyone would venture out in such weather. Nevertheless, I rose from my bed and went to answer.

When I drew back the bolts and opened the door I saw that it was the same elderly Chinaman who had come before. He wore a small felt hat and a coat of thin cotton tied together with string but the rain had plastered his clothes to his body. I remembered that his name was Mr Li

'I must speak to Mr Archibald,' he announced as soon as he saw me. He seemed greatly agitated.

'Mr Archibald is out,' I told him. 'I can take a message, if you wish.'

He shook his head. 'I must speak with him.'

'I've already told you. He isn't here.'

'Where is he?'

'That's no business of yours.'

He gave a sharp, decisive sigh. 'Captain McKerras is dead.'

'Dead?'

He nodded. 'You must come and take him away. We cannot keep him.'

For the third time in my life I had been orphaned. My parents had died while I was still an infant. My uncle had been murdered by Dutch sailors and now Captain McKerras, who had taken charge of me when I was to be sold in the market for the sake of my backside, was also dead.

'Mr Archibald must come and take him away,' Mr Li insisted.

Numbly, I stared back at him. I remember noticing how the raindrops were running down his face but it did not occur to me to invite him into the house.

'You must fetch him now.' Mr Li folded his arms as if to indicate that he had no intention of leaving without Archie in tow.

'Very well,' I said. I put on my coat and a hat and led him across the street to Mrs Dempsey's house where the door opened just as we arrived and a giant of a man came out, supporting a smaller, red-faced man with an enormous belly who was clearly too drunk to stand up by himself. They both stopped and stared at Mr Li and me. Then the giant spoke. 'You've come to the wrong house. There's nothing here for you.'

'I have an urgent message for Mr Archibald McKerras, who is within,' I told him.

He looked irritated. Then he turned and called over his shoulder, 'Mrs Dempsey. There's a Lascar and a Chinaman here want to see the hunchback.' Then he pushed past us, half-leading, half-dragging the fat man who was blinking at us both as if he could not make up his mind whether we were real or not.

Mrs Dempsey herself appeared then and demanded the reason for our intrusion. I explained that I had to speak to Mr Archibald and that his presence was required elsewhere but she haughtily informed me he was occupied and was not to be disturbed. So I was obliged to tell her what I had just learned.

As I was speaking a pair of young gentlemen came in the door behind me and greeted her with a show of familiarity. She looked from me to them and back to me again, clearly at a loss to know how to proceed. Finally, she told me that I might go upstairs and speak to Mr McKerras myself but that Mr Li must wait outside in the rain.

'Just mind you don't go knocking on any doors but the very last one at the end of the corridor on the top floor,' she warned me. 'Otherwise you will answer to Jeremiah.'

I took this to be a reference to the giant and I assured her I had no interest in peering into any of her rooms.

'You're a man, ain't you?' she demanded contemptuously. 'And no doubt you have a man's inclinations.'

I ignored this jibe and began instead to climb the stairs while she busied herself with welcoming her latest customers.

There was an air of respectability about the furnishing of this house, as there had been an air of respectability about the two young men who had followed me in the door, but when I looked more closely it was evident that every surface was thick with dust or sticky with grease, the paint was peeling off the walls in many places and the floors were littered with empty gin bottles, oyster shells and chicken bones. From behind some of the doors came sounds that could have been made by beasts but which I knew to be the cries of my fellow men. I was not a stranger to desire. Mrs Dempsey was quite right. I was a man and did have a man's inclinations but whenever the heat of longing arose in me, into my mind came the image of Tarjong, the girl from my village whom the Dutch slavers had used all that long night when they came to our island. Everything else I had forgotten but I could not forget Tarjong. I believe the sound of her sobbing will be with me on my death bed.

When I reached the door behind which Archie was to be found I knocked, and after a moment a female voice bade me enter. I opened the door and found myself in a small musty-smelling room with a sloping ceiling. Much of the room was taken up with a bed upon which a young girl who looked no older than Tarjong was sitting with a rug drawn up about her legs. She had long brown curls and her skin was extremely pale. She was looking at me out of large, liquid eyes and at first I could do no more than gaze back at her, entirely entranced.

It was Archie who broke the spell. 'What are you doing here, Abdul?' he demanded.

I told him what Mr Li had said. He did not respond, but the colour drained from his face. Then he closed the book he had been reading and got to his feet. 'I'm afraid I must leave you,' he told the girl on the bed.

She made a vague gesture with one hand. 'If someone close to you has died…' she began.

'My brother,' Archie told her.

'Then of course you must go.'

Archie nodded and left the room.

I bent down and gathered up the books. Then I straightened up, taking one last look at the girl. She was gazing at me with wide-eyed curiosity.

'Where are you from?' she asked suddenly.

'I don't know,' I replied for indeed I did not know. I did not know the name of the island where I grew up. It was always just the place where we lived until I was taken away by the Dutchmen. To the crew of the Laurel Bower I was a Malay or a Lascar, but I later learned where Malay was on a map and saw immediately that it was far too big to be my home. I think perhaps I shall never know exactly where I came from.

She laughed at my confusion and then immediately clapped her hand over her mouth. 'I'm sorry,' she said.

'Leave the books!' Archie called impatiently from the landing outside. 'Hurry up!'

I tried to give her a smile but I suspect it was more of a grimace. Then I turned and followed Archie down the stairs.

Outside, we found Mr Li soaked to the skin, still waiting

patiently. He nodded when he saw Archie. 'You must come with me, sir,' he said.

I thought Archie would have all sorts of questions but he followed Mr Li in silence and I brought up the rear, the three of us picking our way as quickly as we could through the river of mud and filth that the street had become.

As we made our way towards the docks I found myself thinking of the girl on the bed at the top of Mrs Dempsey's house, the paleness of her skin, the large liquid eyes, the way she had laughed when I confessed that I did not know where I came from and then her dismay when she realised that this was not a time for laughter. All of this had worked upon me strangely and I felt that I would have liked very much to see that girl again.

At the same time I was aware that my thoughts should be with Captain McKerras. He had been my saviour. He had re-made me into the person I was now. That person had no place he could call home, no memories save a few fragmented pictures and of those most were terrible: a man's with his throat cut open, a sobbing girl being repeatedly raped, a man with his head on fire. Nevertheless, here I was alive and walking through the streets of London in the cold, insistent rain.

The scene in the opium den was exactly the same as at our last visit. The door was opened by the same elderly Chinawoman, as small and as wrinkled as an apple in February. She said something to Mr Li in her own language, speaking quickly and urgently and he replied softly, nodding his head several times, as if to reassure her. Something about the way they addressed each other made me think they must be husband and wife and then, for the first time, it struck me that this was not just some anonymous den of vice. It was their family business. The death of the captain was a stain upon that business and it needed to be erased as quickly as possible. Even here, which I had thought to be near the bottom of the many-layered heap of humanity that was London, appearances were important. A dead man on the premises did not look good.

I had expected to find the captain stretched out on a mat among all the other smokers, as he had been before, but Mr Li led us to a small room at the end of a long dark hallway. It was little more than a cupboard without windows or furnishings. The captain lay on a sheet upon the floor. A quick glimpse was enough to show that Mr Li had not been mistaken. The captain's soul had departed his body and all that was left was a lifeless husk. *While we look not at the things which are seen, but at the things which are not seen: for the things which are seen are temporal; but the things which are not seen are eternal.*

We stood around the body in silence. I did not know how to behave on such an occasion. Were there prayers that should be said? Were there certain sentiments that ought to be uttered? Had he truly believed in the God of his Bible? I glanced furtively at Archie and saw him shake his head sadly but that was all.

It was only then that the problem of what to do with the body occurred to me and I thought that I should have brought the barrow, although the prospect of wheeling the captain's corpse through the dark, rain-sodden streets was enough to make me shudder. However, I need not have concerned myself. Mr Li was prepared to make all the arrangements. He knew of an undertaker. An Englishman, he assured us, not Chinese. A very good man. Very respectable. He would take the body that night. All he needed was payment in advance.

Archie nodded his head. 'Can you bring him here now?'

'He is here already. In another room. I take you to him.'

I waited with the captain's body while Archie went off with Mr Li to talk to the undertaker. I would have liked to sit down for it was late and I was tired but there were no chairs and for some reason it did not seem right to sit down on the ground beside the corpse. Instead, I stood there with my hands clasped in front of me, thinking about the change in fortune that had brought the captain, who had once seemed to me to be the most powerful of men, to such a wretched and undignified end. I felt very alone there with his empty body.

Eventually Archie returned and tapped me on the shoulder. 'Come along, Abdul,' he said. 'We have done our best for Donald. But he has placed himself beyond our reach.'

Mercifully, it had stopped raining when we went back outside. The dense blanket of clouds that had covered the night sky was all blown away and the stars were showing. As we walked home, my thoughts turned once more to the girl on the bed.

'Why were you reading to that girl?' I asked.

I knew the answer to this, of course, for I had overheard the conversation between Archie and Mrs Dempsey but I wanted to speak of the girl.

He looked at me in surprise. No doubt he had been thinking of his brother and I wondered whether he would be angry with me for asking about the girl at a time like this but he merely said, 'She has been gravely ill and Mrs Dempsey believes that my reading may help her recover.'

'But can reading really help someone recover from an illness?'

He thought about this. Then he said, 'It has cured me of my hump.'

I was astonished at this statement and only looked at him in confusion.

He smiled wryly back at me. 'You are tempted to point out that it is still there,' he observed.

'I don't… I mean … it is not my place.'

Archie put up his hand to stop me. 'Literature is the great leveller, Abdul,' he told me, 'for when I read I stand as straight and true as any man.'

Thomas

It had taken Thomas four long months to get as far as London, crisscrossing the country on carts and wagons of every kind but most of the time condemned to travelling by foot. He had washed in springs and under parish pumps, slept in barns and outhouses – even on one occasion in a dry ditch beside the road – refreshed himself with meagre fare in the lowest class of inns and had his pocket picked twice, once while standing in a market-place near Crewe and once while eating at a chop house in Stafford. He was no longer the young innocent who had once sat in a wing chair opposite Lady Carberry and discussed Greek tenses; though neither was he the worldly-wise traveller he believed himself to be.

The worst of it was that he now found himself unable to claim even the miserly allowance that his mother and uncle had agreed upon. Ever since a post master in Bedfordshire had regarded him sternly and asked a great many searching questions when he applied for his monthly guinea, he had been unable to summon up the courage to enter any Post Office. The shadow of his earlier disastrous attempt to redeem the bankers draft lay over all his dealings with authority. He told himself repeatedly that he was behaving unreasonably: the one guinea allowance was his by right;

there could be no doubt upon that score; therefore he should not have had any hesitation in claiming it. But another voice within him pointed out in reply that although the post master had yielded up the precious guinea in the end, he had clearly been suspicious of Thomas.

Yes, Thomas conceded, the post master had not trusted him but the man's misgivings had been solely on account of Thomas's ragged and unkempt appearance. Sleeping beneath the stars night after night and traversing the roads of England mile after weary mile leaves its mark upon a man.

Perhaps that was true, the former voice continued, but what if the news of Thomas's earlier attempt to lay claim to money never intended for him – he had come to accept the truth of his mother's assessment of the forty guineas by now – what if news of this attempted felony had travelled across the country from post master to post master? He would not be so hard to describe – short, bedraggled, and young – and his name was distinctive. What if he were to enter another Post Office tomorrow and find himself suddenly placed under arrest? The thought of it made him dizzy with terror.

These fears were ridiculous, surely? The authorities had more important things to concern themselves with than scouring the countryside for a young man who might or might not have tried to claim the sum of forty guineas dishonestly? Yet Thomas could not be certain, for he could no longer trust his own judgement.

He was desperately hungry. The holes in his shoes were growing along with the hole in his stomach, and he had nowhere to sleep. For these reasons he had decided to adopt a new strategy and apply to a money lender whose name had been mentioned by a corn merchant he had met upon the road a week ago. The man had given Thomas a lift from Newbury to Reading and as they travelled he had talked of business, mentioning a Jew called Dell who lent money to a number of men with whom he did business. 'Though Dell is no doubt not the fellow's real name,' the corn merchant declared, 'for it is far too honest and English sounding. Nothing about these Jews is as it seems.' Having said this, he spat voluminously to emphasize his disgust.

'But would he lend money to me, do you think?' Thomas asked.

The corn-merchant laughed. 'He would lend money to Judas Iscariot if he thought he could get it back with interest.'

It was with this expectation that Thomas stood on the corner of Greek Street and Soho Square and stared at the house in which he had been told that Dell's agent, a Mr Brunel, conducted his affairs. It was a large, double-fronted building, no doubt a most desirable residence once but now so neglected and decrepit, so much in need of paint, so moss-bedecked and thoroughly bedraggled looking that it seemed a most unlikely situation for the transaction of any business. And yet it was indisputably the address he had been given.

Ragged curtains of uncertain hue were drawn across one of the windows downstairs but the other casements stared blindly back at Thomas. He stepped closer and peered through one of these. It was difficult to see anything very much except for dirt and cobwebs until he rubbed a little circle clean with his sleeve and pressed his nose against the cold glass. The room within was entirely empty, the walls and floor bare. He stepped back, shaking his head. There must have been some mistake. He had misheard the address or else he had been tricked.

A wave of self-pity engulfed him. The money-lender had been his last hope; now even that slim chance seemed to have eluded him. But as he turned to walk away, he saw, standing regarding him ominously, a great ape of a man with such a barrel of a chest that his coat and waistcoat seemed stretched across his frame, with such long arms that they appeared to hang down beyond his knees and yet with such a small head as to be grotesquely out of proportion to the rest of his body.

'Are you in the habit of peering into other people's houses?' the stranger demanded, in a most unfriendly tone.

'I was looking for Mr Brunel,' Thomas replied.

'Were you now? And have you any reason to suppose that Mr Brunel might wish to see you?'

'I believe there is every chance of that since I have come upon a matter of business.'

'And what business might that be?'

Thomas decided that this fellow's manner was not at all to his liking and he saw no reason to talk about his private affairs out here in the street. 'My business is something I intend to discuss with Mr Brunel and with no-one else,' he said.

'Is that so? Then I bid you good day.' Without further ado the fellow stepped up to the front door of the house, took a key on a long chain out of his pocket and unlocked the door.

'Wait!'

The stranger paused upon the doorstep.

'Am I to understand that you are Mr Brunel?'

The stranger shook his disproportionate head. 'You are to understand nothing of the kind,' he replied. Then he stepped inside the building and closed the door firmly behind him.

For a moment Thomas was quite at a loss to know what he should do next. Then he stepped up to the front door and knocked vigorously. After a moment the door was opened a crack and the same hulking, pin-headed ruffian stared out at him.

'I wish to see Mr Brunel,' Thomas said.

'Have you an appointment?'

'No but …'

'Then come back when you do.'

The door was shut firmly in his face.

Thomas stood looking at the door for some time as a wave of impotent rage broke over him. At last he turned despondently and began to walk away. However, he had not gone far before he spied two gentlemen coming towards him. One of them was a solidly built man with a brick-red complexion and great bushy side-whiskers. He was wearing a canary yellow waistcoat. The other was a thin, weasel-faced man whose eyes were constantly darting from side to side even as he listened to what Canary Waistcoat was telling him, and nodding his head gravely.

As they passed, Thomas overheard Canary Waistcoat say, 'It cannot be before six weeks, whatever Dell may say. These things take time and the circumstances of the sale are not within my power to amend.'

At these words hope surged in Thomas's breast once more. He turned back and accosted the pair. 'Begging your pardon sirs,' he began, 'I hope you will not consider this to be an impertinence, but I believe I overheard one of you mention a certain Mr Dell.'

Canary Waistcoat gave him a hostile glare, as if he did indeed consider this interruption to be a very grave impertinence, if not something far worse. Weasel-Face, too, considered him suspiciously. 'And if we did mention that gentleman,' he asked, 'of what account is that to you, sir?'

'I have come here today to speak on a matter of considerable urgency with Mr Brunel, who, I have been given to understand, acts on behalf of Mr Dell.'

'And who might you be, sir?' Weasel-Face enquired.

'Thomas De Quincey at your service.'

Weasel-Face nodded.' Well Mr Thomas De Quincey, I am Mr Brunel and I do act for Mr Dell upon occasion.'

A spasm of intense irritation crossed Canary Waistcoat's face at these exchanges. 'Look Brunel,' he said, 'I cannot stand here all day long while you conduct your business in the street. Just inform Dell that he will have his money when the sale is completed but not until then. It cannot be before six weeks. The matter is out of my hands.'

'I shall tell him what you say, Mr Butterworth,' Brunel replied. 'As to what instructions may follow, I cannot comment.'

'He can do what he likes,' Butterworth declared.' There is no blood to be got out of a stone. Not in England at least. Perhaps in the Middle East, I cannot say. But not in England. We are a civilised nation, Mr Brunel. You can tell that to your Jew master.' As he said these last words, his face contorted.

Brunel merely nodded gravely, as if these were important facts that must be weighed carefully and taken into account before any opinion was passed. 'I shall tell him what you say, Mr Butterworth,' he repeated.

Mr Butterworth now turned and walked rapidly away, as if he could not wait to place as great a distance as possible between himself and his erstwhile companion. Brunel stood looking after him for a moment, whistled softly to himself, then turned to Thomas. 'I presume you come upon financial business?'

'Certainly.'

'Then you had better come into the office.'

Brunel led the way back to the dilapidated house, produced a key from his pocket and unlocked the door. Inside, the place seemed no more salubrious than its outward appearance had suggested. The hall smelled dank and musty and there was a graveyard chill about the air. Brunel stepped into the room on the left of the hall, the only one in the house to boast a set of curtains. These had now been drawn back and a pale, cheerless fire was burning in the grate. In front of the window stood an enormous wooden desk which was piled high with dog-eared ledgers, invoices, legal documents and correspondence. A wooden chair was drawn up behind the desk and another faced it. A brass candlestick with the stub of a candle still in it stood in the middle of the floor. Other than this, there was no furniture of any kind, nor any decoration. Brunel walked over to the desk and sat down, motioning Thomas to do the same.

'Now then, Mr De Quincey, to business.' He looked at Thomas expectantly.

'I have been informed that Mr Dell might be prepared in certain circumstances to advance money to individuals whose expectations have for one reason or another been deferred,' Thomas said.

Brunel leaned back in his chair and clasped his hands together. 'Well now Mr De Quincey, that may be so and then again it may not. But let us assume, purely for the purposes of furthering our discussion of course, that the gentleman in question might indeed be induced to act in such a manner. Am I to understand that you are just such an individual as you have described, one, I mean, whose expectations have been – how did you put it? – oh yes, whose expectations have been deferred?'

'Yes sir, you would be correct in such an assumption.'

'I see. And what exactly are your expectations, Mr Thomas De Quincey?'

'I shall come into an inheritance of some four thousand pounds in four years' time.'

Brunel shook his head and from his expression it was clear that he regarded such a statement as lamentably short of what was required. 'Four years, Mr De Quincey! Four years.' Suddenly he called out at the top of his voice, 'Pyment!'

There was a scuffling sound in the passage and a moment later the pin-headed giant stepped into the room.

'Mr De Quincey here is under the impression that Mr Dell might be prepared to advance money upon the expectation of his inheritance in four years' time, Pyment. Four years! What do you think of that?'

'I'd say it's not very likely, sir,' Pyment replied.

'Not very likely!' Brunel echoed in a tone of indignation, as if his clerk's reply had only added insult to injury. 'It is more than unlikely, Mr Pyment. It is quite out of the question. Not open to negotiation. Mr Dell would not consider it. He cannot wait four years. Mr Dell is a man of business.'

'Yes sir,' Pyment agreed.

Brunel let out a long, steady sigh, as if this was yet one more in an endless chain of disappointments he had been forced to endure that day. He turned back to Thomas. 'Think upon it, Mr De Quincey,' he continued. 'In four years' time both you and I may be dead and buried, food for the worms, all mourning ended. What would Mr Dell do then? Eh? No, I'm afraid Mr Dell will need rather more in the way of surety than your inheritance can provide. Is there nothing else that you can suggest?'

'What sort of thing did you have in mind?'

'Well surely a... gentleman such as yourself is not completely without connections? Surely there is someone of quality who can vouch for you?'

Thomas shook his head.

'Consider my position, Mr De Quincey,' Brunel continued, 'I have no proof other than your own word that you are the person you say you are. And yet you would have me approach Mr Dell on your behalf with a request for money. It ain't practical. That's my objection. It ain't manageable. It ain't businesslike.'

He looked down at his desk, picked up a document from the pile that awaited his attention and began to read.

Thomas sat there uneasily for a moment. 'You will not reconsider…' he began.

Brunel gazed at him over the top of the document, as if surprised to find Thomas still there. Then he shook his head. 'It cannot be done, I am afraid. I bid you good day, Mr De Quincey.'

As Thomas closed the door of Mr Brunel's offices behind him he knew exactly what it was that he must do, yet he walked the street for another hour before accepting his fate and settling upon a shop. Peering through the windows he saw that the inside of this establishment was stacked with bookshelves and that each bookshelf was positively groaning under its weight of printed knowledge. As he stood outside on the pavement, still hesitating, a hunchback came out of the shop clutching a parcel of books under his arm, gave him a brief nod and then shuffled off down the street with a limping gait.

Thomas gazed after the hunchback for a little while, envying the man the ease with which he belonged in this city; Thomas felt that his every word, his every gesture, his every act declared him to be an outsider; a provincial; a country bumpkin. At last he turned back to the shop, took a deep breath and plunged inside.

The bookseller was a tall, thin, stooping man with a shock of white hair, a ragged looking beard and very bloodshot eyes set close to a long, straight nose. Thomas wished him good morning and placed his Thucydides upon the counter.

The bookseller picked up the book, opened it at the title page, checked the date of publication, flicked through the pages rapidly, then, to Thomas's surprise, put the book to his nose and smelled it before setting it down upon the counter once more. 'I have a whole shelf full of these,' he said.

Thomas's heart sank. It seemed that there was no end to the chain of disappointments. 'There is always a demand for Thucydides,' he asserted.

'There is always a supply of Thucydides,' the bookseller replied. 'What is the other book you hold in your hand?'

Reluctantly, Thomas handed over his copy of Lyrical Ballads. The bookseller's countenance brightened. 'This, I can sell,' he declared.

It was as if the man had reached inside Thomas and begun ripping something out from the very core of him: this copy of Lyrical Ballads had become a token of his hopes and his dreams, both a comforting reminder of Lady Carberry's affection and a beacon summoning him towards the world of letters. He would much more willingly have parted with the clothes on his back except that he knew they were in such a condition as to be entirely worthless.

His attempts to negotiate a better deal than the bookseller was prepared to offer were without success and eventually, he was forced to part with the book for the price of a couple of nights' lodging, a few scraps of food and a small bottle of laudanum to keep the hunger at bay when that had run out. With the heaviest possible heart, he turned his back on the white-haired vulture, opened the door of the bookshop and stepped out once more onto the street.

Anne

The day after the boy knocked on our door with the news about Archie's brother Mrs Dempsey decided it was time to put me back to work. And who was my first gentleman caller? Mr Bayliss of course, puffing and wheezing his way up the stairs like a pig up Primrose Hill. He'd heard I'd been *indisposed*, he said sitting on the bed, sweat running down his face and his eyes almost popping out of his face. So he'd brought me a little present to cheer me up. He put his hand in one of his pockets – Mr Bayliss's coat was as big as a ship's sailcloth and his pockets was as deep as the Thames itself. I think he could have carried me around in one of those pockets and no doubt he would have liked to – and he pulled out a china doll with a painted face, handing it over with a *flourish*, like he was delighted with his own cleverness.

Not that long before, I'd have been very pleased for I'd never had nothing like that when I was little girl. But I weren't a little girl now. So I just stared at the doll until Mr Bayliss asked me if I didn't want to pick it up. Truth be told, I didn't want to. Something about it sent shivers down my spine but I did what he wanted. That was my job, after all.

'You'll have to think of a name for her,' he said. He looked at me.

'Jenny,' I told him. It was the first name that came into my head.

'A very good name.' He put the doll at the head of the bed where it could watch me singing nursery rhymes and stroking his cock.

After Mr Bayliss it was business as usual. One gentleman after another came to visit me. The first time one of them stuck his cock inside me properly – an old sailor covered in tattoos with a scar on his face that looked like someone had tried to cut his cheek off once upon a time – I was frightened it would hurt me so badly I wouldn't be able to bear the pain. But as it turned out the worst part was thinking about it. The deed itself didn't last long enough to cause me much distress. All the same, I was bruised and sore at the end of the evening and not at all well-disposed towards Mrs Dempsey.

That was how things carried on for a week until the morning when I woke up to hear a fierce banging on doors and Jeremiah's voice shouting something I couldn't make out. Now that was unusual enough to get me out of bed for Jeremiah weren't one for shouting. If one of Mrs Dempsey's guests had a bit too much to drink and started causing difficulties, Jeremiah would *escort him off the premises*. If the toss pot tried to put up a fight, which very seldom happened, Jeremiah twisted his arm up around his back until he saw sense and not a few tears. And, of course, if the worst came to the worst, Jeremiah's cosh could do the talking for him. I had never so much as heard him raise his voice before. So I jumped out of bed, threw on my gown and opened the door of my room.

I saw Muriel and Estelle coming out of their room at the same time. So I called out to them, to ask what was going on but neither of them seemed to know. They looked worried, though, and that was enough to make me properly alarmed.

All three of us hurried downstairs to Mrs Dempsey's room where the noise was coming from. Charlie, Cecille, Suzette, and Jeremiah was already there, standing in the middle of the room staring at Mrs Dempsey with shocked faces. She was sitting at her card table with her fortune cards spread in front of her, staring back at them and I could see right away that something was up. Her features had gone all out of shape – one side of her face was drooping and her eyes was as glassy as the eyes of the stuffed bird on the shelf behind her.

No one was saying a word. I didn't think it was my place to interfere but since it looked like nobody else was going to speak, I said, 'Are you alright, Mrs Dempsey?'

'For God's sake, Anne, she's dead,' Suzette said.

She can't be dead, I thought to myself. They're making a mistake. But at the same time, another part of me was taking in the news. Mrs Dempsey was dead and that could only mean one thing. I was about to be *cast adrift* on the world once more.

'The question is, what are we going to do now,' Jeremiah said.

'Everyone looked at Suzette. 'I think you should go and tell Mrs Nancy,' she said.

'Right you are.' Jeremiah turned on his heel and walked away.

'Should we lay her out somewhere?' Cecille suggested.

Suzette raised a finger to her lips and waited until the front door had closed. Then she looked at us one by one, and there was a very calm, very *determined* look on her face. 'Listen to me, everyone,' she said. 'We have to think about ourselves.'

'What do you mean?' Cecille asked.

'This shop belongs to John now. '

I couldn't think who she meant at first but then I remembered Mrs Nancy's story. John was the one who had put a knife through someone's eye.

'I've heard all about John Dempsey,' Suzette said, 'and from what they say, he doesn't care for anyone or anything. So if you ask me, the first thing he'll do when he hears she's dead is get rid of us.'

'How can you be sure? Charlie asked.

'Because Mrs Dempsey told me he was always trying to get his hands on her money.'

'You think we'll be in his way?'

'Of course we will. He'll want to sell the house. So he won't want us here.'

'Well there ain't much we can do about that,' Cecille said.

'Maybe there is and maybe there isn't,' Suzette said. 'Either way, we don't have a lot of time. As soon as she hears the news, Mrs Nancy will send a message to John. They could both be here within half an hour.'

'So what are you suggesting?' Cecille asked.

'Every week Mrs Dempsey takes her money out of the strong box and delivers it to her bank,' Suzette went on. 'Only she didn't go last week because she was feeling poorly.'

'So that's a fortnight's money in there,' Charlie said.

Now everyone was nodding and looking interested.

'And by rights it's ours. We earned it but all we ever see is the little bit of pocket money Mrs Dempsey gives us.'

Mrs Dempsey giving out pocket money was news to me but no-one else seemed surprised so I guessed that it was another example of my *simplicity*.

'What we have to do,' Suzette went on, 'is find the key before they get here.' She looked at each of us in turn. 'Agreed?'

Everyone agreed, including me, though I didn't know if it was for the best or not.

'Any idea where the key might be?' Charlie asked.

'It's in this room somewhere, I know that much.'

'Maybe it's round her neck,' I suggested. They all looked at me as if they was surprised to see me still standing there. Then Suzette gave a crooked kind of smile. 'Perhaps you'd like to look, Anne.'

'Me?'

'Well someone's got to do it.'

So that was how I found myself searching Mrs Dempsey's corpse for the key to her strong box and a very *unpleasant* task it was, too, because she was cold and stiff and heavy. Somehow I had to move her this way and that without her falling off the chair. I looked round her neck, down between her breasts and up her skirts – which felt like a shocking thing to be doing – and in every part of her clothing but with no result. Meanwhile Suzette and the others was tearing the room apart.

I was struggling to put her shoes back on, though goodness knows why since she was hardly going to be doing much walking any more, but that was me, always paying attention to the wrong thing, when Muriel suddenly gives a little shriek. She'd found a key in a glove in the bottom of a cupboard. She held it up and Suzette nodded. 'That's it,' she said and she put out her hand.

Muriel hesitated for a moment then she handed it over. Suzette went to the corner of the room, uncovered the strong box where it was hidden under a piece of purple damask, and put the key in the lock. It turned without any difficulty and she opened the lid.

The money was in a small leather bag. She emptied it out onto the floor and we all watched her count it. There was five pounds and a penny altogether which was a great deal more than I expected but clearly not as much as Suzette had hoped for. That came to exactly sixteen shillings and ninepence each.

'Now,' Suzette said, when we'd all got our share, 'I don't want to know where any of you is heading but I will say this much. Be sure it's long way from Whitechapel because, make no mistake, if John Dempsey finds you he will cut your throat as soon as look at you.' Then, without another word, she walked out of the front door and that was the last I ever saw of her.

The others didn't delay, neither. They just grabbed whatever clothes they could carry and went out the door after her. I was the last one, not because I was busy gathering up my belongings. Belongings! All I had was the blue dress that Mrs Dempsey had given me when I first arrived and another one in dark red with a pattern of flowers what Archie brought round a few weeks after my visit with Suzette – but because I was so frightened I stood for ages in the middle of my room wondering where on earth I would go to hide myself from John Dempsey.

But I didn't want to be still standing there when he walked in the door so in the end I bundled the two dresses and a spare shift into a canvas bag and followed the others out the front door. I had the money in my purse on a bit of string round my neck and that was both *comforting* and *terrifying* but I had no idea where I was going. I just walked and walked, heading west and hoping for the best.

Tuah

A good name is better than fine perfume, and the day of death better than the day of birth.

Captain McKerras's funeral was a dismal affair. It was the first Christian burial I had attended and, although I had not known what to expect, I had imagined something grander than this, something that would give meaning to the captain's life and to his death. Something that would set a mark upon the world equal to his ambition and determination.

Instead, I witnessed a shabby little clergyman stutter his way through the wretched ceremony before a congregation that could be numbered upon the fingers of two hands. Archie was the only family member present. Of the crew of the Laurel Bower, only Mr Gilbert and Mr Priestley turned up. In addition to these, there was a small group of black-veiled women whom I later learned were to be found at every funeral in this parish, attending funerals being a kind of recreation for them.

While the candles were being lit I noticed an incongruous figure slip into the back of the church dressed in a long blue padded coat without lapels, and white baggy trousers, a soft black hat clutched respectfully in his hand. It was Mr Li, of course, though for a moment I failed to recognise him in such an unlikely setting. One or two of the black-veiled ladies glanced in his direction before looking away again quickly and the undertaker who stood at the back of the church presiding over the arrangements gestured for Mr Li to take a place in one of the benches but he shook his head and shrank back into a corner. Shortly afterwards, the service began.

I knew that the captain had held the Bible in the greatest reverence. Indeed, he had encouraged me to learn many passages from it by heart while I was on board the Laurel Bower. Nevertheless, the words of the service meant nothing to me as I stood and watched the other members of the congregation, dutifully murmuring the responses. I had expected this whole thing to have a profound emotional effect upon me but to my disappointment I found that I felt nothing whatsoever.

Before the service had begun the undertaker, himself so cadaverous as to suggest he had only recently arisen from his own grave, had approached Archie and asked whether any member of the family wished to be among the pallbearers. Archie had suggested to me that I should volunteer and I had, of course, agreed. So when the church service was over, I walked up to the coffin and, along with five of the undertaker's men, put my shoulder underneath the coffin.

It was surprisingly heavy – that was my first impression. The captain had not been a heavy man, especially towards the end of his life, and it had been no great effort to wheel him in the barrow back from the opium den in Limehouse, but carrying him upon one's shoulder was a different matter. The edge of the coffin dug into my flesh, on account of the fact that the other pallbearers were all bigger than me. So I was glad when we reached the hole that had been dug in the graveyard and we were able to set the coffin down upon the ground before lowering it on ropes into the grave.

We stood around the grave while the clergyman continued with his prayers. I felt a little ashamed of myself for complaining, albeit inwardly, about the weight of the coffin. Without the captain, I dreaded to think where I might be now. There was much mention of our lord and saviour by the clergyman but the captain had been my lord and saviour.

We are orphans and fatherless.

Again.

After the prayers were finally over, Mr Gilbert came over, shook hands with Archie and nodded to me. 'He was a good man,' he said. 'There will not be another like him at sea or on land.'

Mr Priestley waited until Mr Gilbert had moved away before he approached. He offered his hand to Archie but ignored me entirely. 'My name is Priestley,' he began.

'I know who you are,' Archie said.

'Good. That makes my job somewhat easier.'

'Your job?'

'I am here in a personal capacity, of course, Mr McKerras, but also as a representative of the Company.'

'I see.'

'We wish to convey our deepest sympathy.'

'And how deep would that be, exactly?' Archie replied. 'Would you measure it in fathoms, I wonder?'

'I understand your feelings, Mr McKerras.'

'I very much doubt that, Mr Priestley.'

'You blame the Company for your brother's death.'

'You are quite wrong. I blame the Company for my brother's life.'

Mr Priestley was clearly taken aback by this remark but it did not take him long to regain his composure. 'The Company has authorised me to inform you that it will not continue with its proceedings against your brother.'

Archie uttered a mirthless laugh. 'They might have trouble pursuing him where he has gone.'

'Or against his estate.'

'There is no estate. Every penny has been spent.'

Mr Priestley raised one eyebrow as if to suggest that in different circumstances he might have been prepared to dispute this. Then he made a grimace that perhaps was intended to be a smile. 'In addition, we are prepared to take the boy off your hands.'

'I beg your pardon, sir?'

'The Company is prepared to relieve you of the burden of the captain's cabin boy.' He gave the slightest of nods in my direction. 'We will find a place for him on board one of our vessels. I am authorised to take him away with me forthwith.'

I looked at him and then at Archie whose expression was entirely unreadable and I felt my legs grow weak so that I feared I might fall down into the grave and land on top of the captain's coffin.

'That will not be necessary,' Archie replied.

'He will be treated well, if that is what concerns you. I will attend to all the arrangements personally'

'I said it will not be necessary.'

'Well, if you should change your mind, I can easily be contacted at the Company's offices.' He gave a short bow and walked away.

'Thank you, sir,' I said. I wanted to kneel down before Archie and throw my arms around his legs. 'I cannot begin to tell you…'

'Never mind all that,' Archie said. 'Let us go home. There is nothing further we can do for Donald now.' He began to limp away and I followed gladly.

'You know, Abdul,' he told me, as we made our way back towards the shop, 'if there is one thing I hate more than churchyards, it is the people one meets in them.'

Thomas

Thomas stood once more outside the door of Mr Brunel's offices. He reached out his hand to take hold of the knocker but was momentarily seized by a spasm of coughing which seemed to rack his whole frame. It had been little more than a week since his last visit but the change that had come over him in the intervening period was clear enough for anyone to see. He looked gaunt and pale and there were shadows as dark as bruises below his feverish eyes. He recovered from his coughing fit at last, took hold of the knocker and let it fall heavily upon the door. There was a long delay before the door was opened a crack and an eye surveyed him. A moment later the door was opened fully to reveal Pyment standing on the threshold, looking disdainfully at him. 'You again,' he said.

'Will Mr Brunel consent to see me this morning?' Thomas asked.

'I shall have to enquire.'

The door was shut once more and there was a long delay before Pyment returned and reluctantly granted him admission. 'Mr Brunel is at his breakfast,' he declared, 'but he has agreed to see you as an act of kindness.'

'I am most grateful.'

'I should hope so, too.'

Mr Brunel was seated at his desk behind the great mound of correspondence that appeared only to have grown in the interval. He had a hunk of bread in one hand and a mug of ale in the other. He put down the ale and motioned with his free hand for Thomas to sit.

Thomas did as he was bid, his eyes firmly fixed on the bread, the smell of which seemed to fill the room. He could imagine exactly how it would feel to place a piece of that loaf in his mouth, the precise texture of it, elastic and melting at the same time, and the taste, a little salty at first perhaps but then beneath that, the great wide open flavour of bread, broad and satisfying as the fields of wheat from which it was made.

'I didn't expect to see you back so soon, Mr De Quincey,' Brunel said, now that he had swallowed the mouthful he was chewing.

'I have considered what you said to me and I have remembered something that may have a material bearing on my case,' Thomas told him.

Mr Brunel wiped his mouth with his sleeve. 'A material bearing on the case?' he said in a tone that suggested he thought this very unlikely indeed. 'And what is that, pray?'

Thomas put his hand into his breast pocket and produced the letter from Lord Massey, thanking him for his assistance with the authentication of the Epistles of Phalaris and promising to do whatever he could to assist Thomas in his present difficulties.

Brunel examined the letter with the aid of a pair of pince-nez. Then he nodded and looked up. 'I believe you may be right, Mr De Quincey,' he declared in a tone of mild surprise. 'This does indeed have a material bearing on your case. You should have showed it to me before.'

Of course he should, but Thomas had not wanted any suspicion of his current destitution to reach the ears of Lord Massey, or even worse, the ears of Lady Carberry. But of late he has begun to believe that he might easily die upon the streets of London and therefore he had no other recourse.

'If I may have your permission to show this letter to Mr Dell?'

Thomas had not expected this. 'You wish to retain it?'

'Mr Dell will need to see it for himself.'

'I see.'

'And, naturally, we will need to examine your father's will at Doctor's Commons, to ascertain that your expectations are in accordance with the claims that you have already made.'

'Of course.'

Brunel returned the letter to its envelope, looked about him on the desk, located a metal box underneath a pile of papers, opened the box and put the letter inside. 'Of course it will be necessary for you to persuade Lord Massey to guarantee any sum which Mr Dell might be prepared to advance,' he continued, 'but since he addresses you so warmly in this letter, I do not anticipate any difficulties in that respect.'

Thomas frowned. 'Are you saying that I cannot have the money here and now?'

Mr Brunel shook his head sadly and smiled. No doubt it was the same weary smile he reserved for all those supplicants who came before him with such unrealistic expectations. 'These things take time, Mr De Quincey.'

'But surely the letter alone is proof of my acquaintance?'

'Of course it is. I understand that, but the noble lord must be contacted. It must be ascertained beyond doubt that he is prepared to recompense Mr Dell in the event of your being unable to do so.'

'There will be no such need,' Thomas protested. 'You have my word upon that.'

'I appreciate that Mr De Quincey and I realise that while a gentleman such as yourself lives and breathes there is no doubt whatsoever that his word is good enough for every eventuality; that point is not even open to dispute. But what if something untoward should happen? Accidents may occur. Unforeseen circumstances may arise. We can never be prepared for what Fate itself may thrust in our way. And for that reason Lord Massey must be contacted.'

'But how shall I live in the meantime?'

Brunel sucked the air through his teeth as he considered this knotty problem. 'It's a difficult question Mr De Quincey. Surely a young man like yourself must have some friends in London to whom he can turn when he finds himself at a low ebb.'

Thomas shook his head. 'There is no one. I am reduced to sleeping in doorways, Mr Brunel,' he said. 'And at night it is so cold, I am not sure how much longer …' He faltered. Tears began to run down his face.

Mr Brunel looked dismayed. 'Now come along Mr De Quincey, this will not do. A gentleman like yourself doesn't carry on in this way.' He lowered his voice. 'You don't want Mr Pyment to see you like this, now do you?'

Thomas shook his head but the tears continued to flow freely down his cheeks and now he began to sob.

Mr Brunel looked very unhappy indeed. Clients had sat or stood in this office and raged at him, they had used language that would disgrace a dockside inn, they had threatened him with violence, with litigation, with everlasting damnation but never, until now, had a gentleman sat opposite him and wept. Mr Brunel did not consider himself to be a bad man. There had been, and there would continue to be, certain negotiations, certain transactions, certain disclosures or failures to make disclosure, which would not bear too much scrutiny from the appropriate authorities. These things were necessary in order that a man might make his way in the world. Furthermore, there had been times when Mr Brunel had been obliged to harden his heart and take actions which had resulted in unpleasant consequences for the persons against whom those actions were directed. On occasions he had even been forced to allow Pyment, or some of his associates, to act in a very direct manner indeed in order to make his clients see the importance of attending to Mr Dell's requests. But he had never before been confronted with a young gentleman of evidently keen intellect and delicate constitution who had sat opposite him and wordlessly wept in this fashion. Mr Brunel was at a loss to know what he should do next.

It seemed to him that Thomas De Quincey was singularly unprepared for the teeming, villainous, bustling, cunning barbarity that was the nation of London. He was a child in a man's body. Brunel was not accustomed to dealing with children. At last, he resolved upon a solution. 'Listen to me, Mr De Quincey,' he began. 'I'll tell you what I'll do for you. Within a week I shall have examined your father's will. Within a fortnight, perhaps less, Lord Massey will have been contacted. In the meantime you may sleep in this building during the hours of darkness but only on the condition that you are gone before I arrive in the morning and that you do not appear until after I have left at night. Obviously, I cannot offer you lodgings without charge because in doing so I would be neglecting my own interests and that is something that no man who hopes to hold his own in the world should ever do. However, I am prepared to wait for my money until such time as a loan has been negotiated with Mr Dell.'

Thomas opened his mouth to speak but Mr Brunel held up his hand to defer any show of gratitude and to make it clear that he had not yet finished. 'This is an offer which I make you out of Christian charity, Mr De Quincey and there are many who would pronounce me very foolish indeed to do so. No doubt they would be correct in that estimation. But a man cannot be always thinking of business. Sometimes he must reach out and give a fellow creature a helping hand. So, Mr De Quincey, you have heard my offer. Have you anything to say?'

'I am most grateful to you, sir,' Thomas stammered.

'Very well. I'm pleased to hear it. And now, if you don't mind, I should like to finish my breakfast in peace before setting about my work, which as you can see, grows greater by the day.'

Thomas nodded but he did not move from his seat. His eyes were fixed upon the remains of the loaf resting on the desk. Brunel followed the direction of his gaze and then he raised his own eyes to heaven. Picking up the loaf he held it out in Thomas' direction. 'Here, for God's sake take the bread and go before I come to my senses and realise what a fool I am making of myself.'

Thomas sprang forward like some wild animal and seized the loaf from Brunel's hand. 'Thank you so much Mr Brunel,' he said, bowing repeatedly as he backed away towards the door. 'You are very kind, sir, very kind indeed.'

Anne

The money didn't last long. For one thing, rooms was a great deal more expensive up west than down around Whitechapel. For another, nobody was buying my meals for me now. Every time I wanted to eat I had to part with some of Mrs Dempsey's money and it was like pouring water into a hole in the ground. It was clear to me I had to start earning or I'd very quickly be in trouble and there was only one way I knew how to go about that. But it weren't going to be as easy to arrange now that I didn't have Mrs Dempsey to find me gentlemen.

After a few weeks I got into conversation with a girl that lived in the room below me. Her name was Daisy and she was tall and strong-looking with fair hair and freckles and a friendly sort of face. She looked like she knew her way around.

Daisy had been in London for nine months, she told me. Before that, she'd been in service in Lincoln until the lady of the house had caught her in the linen press with the master. 'As if it was my fault,' she said. 'And him as ugly as a toad and sixty years old if he was a day. What could I do if he followed me in and shut the door? Anyway, that was the end of waiting at table for me. Out the door that very afternoon.

And you needn't expect a reference, the old bat tells me. So I made my way to London. Green as anything when I arrived here but I soon learned.'

The place to go for trade, according to Daisy, was Oxford Street. 'There's no shortage of gentlemen with money in their pockets, every one of them in search of a good time.'

'But do you bring them back here?' I asked for I'd seen no sign of gentlemen coming and going.

Daisy shook her head. 'Perish the thought!'

'So where *do* you do it?

'Doorways, alleyways, basements, courtyards - anywhere we can find a bit of dark and a bit of quiet. The gentlemen don't care. So long as they get to stick it in you, they're happy.'

She invited me to go out with her that very night. 'For there's safety in numbers,' she said. 'We can look out for each other, like a pair of sisters.'

I agreed, of course. What else could I do? So now I was a street-girl. Like I said there's always another rung below you and with the death of Mrs Dempsey I'd been forced to take a step downwards.

We was catering for men of a lower class than at Mrs Dempsey's and there weren't nothing fancy about it. Up against the wall, stick your arse out and hope there ain't no constable about – although some of *them* weren't above taking a turn if they thought no-one was looking.

It was hard work. When I weren't on the job I was walking up and down the street, wearing my shoes out. And no-one had a good word for me. Respectable people crossed the road to avoid me. Cheeky kids threw vegetables at me, men who'd spent all their money spat at me. Even the men who used me cursed me as they handed over their money. And, of course, I was always scared. There weren't no

Jeremiah to protect me now. I could very easily run into another Harold Lampton and that might be the end of me.

During the day there weren't much to do except get yourself a bit of something to eat and a sup to drink, then sleep or sit about gossiping with Daisy. Most days I had a drop or two of laudanum around the middle of the day and I found it brought me comfort. Daisy, too, had a liking for the linctus, as she called it. Oftentimes, the pair of us would lie down together in my room, me on my mattress and her on the floor, dreaming companionably.

The thing I liked best was the feeling that came over you when the laudanum first started to work. You'd be all cranky and tired and every bone in your body would be complaining from overuse and then all of a sudden, the laudanum would start to make itself felt like an angel's whisper. All that weariness, all that misery, all them aches and pains would melt away and then you'd start remembering.

It was remarkable what you found you could recall. Tiny little things that had dropped down the cracks of your memory rose up to the surface and you felt the force of them all over again. I remembered sitting on my father's shoulders and it was as if I was doing it all over again right then and there. I felt myself to be a little girl with his great strong shoulders supporting me. Some days I could even talk to him and he would talk right back to me, though afterwards, when the dream had vanished, I couldn't remember a single thing he'd told me.

I remembered my mother washing me and dressing me and sitting me on her knee, and I remembered her telling me what a precious little girl I was. That filled me with joy but also with sadness for no one else had ever called me precious and I had no expectation anyone ever would.

Not all the memories that laudanum awakened was pleasant ones. Plenty of times I saw Harold Lampton's face suddenly leering up at me or the great sack of Mr Bayliss's belly as he sat down on the bed and waited for me to bring him to a froth. But I would willingly endure the nightmares for the moments of happiness that came with them.

Some days I might go for a walk in the afternoon if the sun was shining. It was pleasant to walk the streets without plying my trade. Instead, I would simply look upon the crowds of people buying and selling, drinking and gaming, all of them going about their business without a thought for me. I liked to gaze at their faces and try to imagine their lives. I saw villains and pick-pockets, clerks and constables, gentlemen and ladies and one day I saw Suzette.

It was somewhere in the neighbourhood of Golden Square. I don't even remember where now. I was just standing on a corner watching sparrows eating seeds out of a pile of horse dung. I'd started having a drop of laudanum before breakfast and this morning I'd taken a little too much so I was half in a daze still.

When I saw Suzette walking on the other side of the road, dressed like a lady and leaning on the arm of a stern-looking gentleman, I thought at first I was imagining it but the closer she got the more certain I became that it was really her.

Of course I should have paid her no heed. That was what we'd all agreed but I weren't thinking clearly. I weren't thinking at all if the truth be told. I was just dizzy with joy at seeing a familiar face. So I crossed the road smartly and called out her name.

But Suzette weren't going to be caught out like that. She took no notice of me whatsoever, just sailed right past on her gentleman's arm without so much as glancing in my direction. Like a fool, I ran after her, calling out, 'Suzette, it's me, Anne,' until finally, she and her gentleman came to a halt. 'You have mistaken me for someone else, girl,' she said, looking at me like

I was a piece of shit that she had just stepped in.

'Sorry, madam,' I said, as she walked off again. She was right, I told myself as I watched her disappear down the street, I had mistaken her for someone else. I'd mistaken her for a friend, which she'd never been. I walked home then feeling very sorry for myself. Suzette was no more than a whore when all was said and done but I was that far below her that she might call me girl and I must call her madam. As soon as I got indoors I had another dose of laudanum to take away the pain and I lay down on the bed to wait for sleep to carry me off.

But there weren't no refuge there for I dreamt I was dead and buried and lying in my coffin. I could feel the worms devouring my flesh but I couldn't move so much as a finger to help myself.

Tuah

A week after the captain's funeral, we were sitting down to our breakfast of oatmeal when Archie put down his spoon with a clatter and announced that we would have to do something about my legal status.

I had no idea what this meant.

'As far as the law of England is concerned, you do not really exist, Abdul.'

'Why not?'

'There is no record or your birth. We do not know for certain how old you are, or even your proper name.'

'My name is Tuah.'

'Abdul Tuah?'

'Just Tuah.'

'Then where did the Abdul come from?'

I shrugged. *And whatsoever Adam called every living creature, that was the name thereof.*

'I see. Well, anyhow, it is customary for a man in England to have at least two names – a Christian name and a surname.'

'I could choose another name.'

'It is not as simple as that. We will go to see Mr Duncan this morning. He is a legal man. He will explain what needs to be done.'

I imagined that Mr Duncan, being an authority upon the law, would be a very grand person indeed and I was more than a little nervous about the prospect of encountering him. When we arrived at his office an hour later, therefore, I was surprised to find it was no more than two rooms above a print-shop in Paternoster Row.

Mr Duncan himself was an untidy man in his late fifties. His moth-eaten wig sat crookedly on his head; he had no beard yet he was not exactly clean-shaven either; his eyebrows were so wild they looked as though they might be trying to make up for the shortcomings of his beard; his belly would not have been out of place on a woman expecting to give birth within the week. He was surrounded by piles of papers and his fingers were stained with ink. In repose, his features took on the expression of a man with a particularly bad toothache. However, he seemed not displeased to see Archie, wishing him good afternoon and bidding him take a seat. Me, he frowned at uncertainly but, after hesitating, he made a gesture suggesting that I, too, might take a seat if I so wished.

'What can I do for you, Mr McKerras?' he asked, sitting back in his chair and clasping his hands over his belly.

'Allow me to introduce Abdul,' Archie replied. 'He returned with my late brother from his last voyage and has been living in our house ever since. I am told that he was taken from his home by slavers when still a child and bought by Donald at auction. He has no documents of any sort, not even a date of birth. We wish him to become a person whom the law recognises.'

Mr Duncan's eyebrows rose higher and higher until it seemed they might disappear beneath his wig altogether.

'A puzzle,' he said, at last. 'Indeed a puzzle.'

'But not beyond your very considerable ability to solve, I have no doubt.'

'Your confidence is gratifying. 'He took up a quill and wrote something in the notebook that lay open on his desk. Then he looked up. 'What is his full name?'

'My name is Tuah,' I said.

Mr Duncan looked at Archie and he nodded.

'How do you spell it?' Mr Duncan asked.

'I have never seen it written down.'

'Then we shall have to do our best. He hesitated for a moment, then wrote down the four letters that I have since come to recognise as my name and handed the book to me. I studied them, trying to recognize myself in those unfamiliar characters. Then I handed it back. 'Thank you.'

He took a pipe out of a drawer, lit it and puffed out a long cloud of smoke. 'We need a point of entry.'

I looked at Archie. My name I could manage. But everything else was a mystery.

'Do you mean the date when he came on board my brother's ship or the date he returned to England?' Archie asked.

'Neither. The law is a trail of paper, Mr McKerras, and it always leads backwards. Each document refers to an earlier document which refers to an even earlier document and so on right back to the start of the whole process, in this case, that is the point at which this young man's existence was first confirmed in writing.'

'Then it must be today.'

Mr Duncan shook his head. 'It is not strong enough. If we begin with today, then the proceedings could extend themselves for years. Letters will be sent back and forth, objections raised, enquires made, affidavits sworn, hearing adjourned. You and I could be dead and buried before the whole thing was concluded.

'Then what do you suggest?'

'The law does not take kindly to novelty. The familiar is always to be preferred. Grooves are worn in stone steps by clerks of the court. It is my opinion, therefore, that my learned friends will look much more favourably upon Mr Tuah here if he has been baptized into the Church of England and is in possession of a certificate to that effect.' He turned back to me. 'Do you think you could see your way to that?'

I nodded. I had no idea what I was agreeing to, of course, but I remembered the words with which the captain would begin his address every Sunday as the men all stood on deck with their heads bowed: *And he said unto them, Unto what then were ye baptized?* And I understood that until these words encompassed me, I would always remain a slave.

'Then I think our business is concluded for the time being and I wish you both good day.'

Archie rose to his feet and I immediately followed him. A few moments later were out in the street once more.

'So you are to become a Christian,' Archie said as we made our way home. 'How do you feel about that?'

'I don't know.'

He gave a wry smile. 'You may have to display rather more enthusiasm, you know. Zeal, I believe that's the word, Religious zeal.'

'I do not understand what it truly means.'

'None of us does.'

The following day I began taking lessons from the very same clergyman who had officiated at the captain's funeral. His name was Reverend Hewitt and he was a timid kind of a man, not above forty years of age, with thin reddish-brown hair and watery blue eyes. The lessons were conducted in a room in the vicarage next door to the church and we sat facing each other across a bare wooden table.

The Reverend Hewitt began by telling me how God had made the world in seven days, how he had placed Adam and Even in a garden and told them not to eat the fruit of the Tree of Knowledge of Good and Evil and how they ate it nonetheless and were cast out of paradise where they were forced to earn their bread by the sweat of their brow. I also discovered that we are all of us descended from Adam and Eve and so share in their sin of disobedience. For some reason, this was not something the captain had read to me, though Archie had made me learn passages from Milton which I saw now referred to these events.

I found it hard to concentrate on what the Reverend Hewitt said for he had a habit of blinkıng excessively whenever he looked in my direction and much of my attention was taken up with trying to ignore this behaviour. Moreover, I could not help noticing that his fingernails were bitten down to the quick and I found myself wondering what it was that made him so fearful, for he was a man of God and that must mean he was someone of considerable importance.

He told me of the Great Flood and how Noah had saved the world by building an ark and bringing two of every creature on board. Finally, he told me how God had spoken to a man called Abraham and commanded him to kill his only son but then changed his mind and sent an angel to save the boy just in time and how he then made a covenant with Abraham and his descendants that they would be his chosen people. I wondered if the Reverend Hewitt was afraid that God might ask strange and awful crimes of him too. Perhaps God already had.

At the end of all this I asked him whether there was much more for me to learn. He looked startled and began blinking even more violently so that I wished I had held my peace.

'We have but barely begun,' he told me, sounding quite indignant. 'Every child in England is taught as much as this before he is six years old.'

I apologised and took my leave of him. On the way home I wondered greatly at the behaviour of the Reverend Hewitt's god. Surely he could have guessed that Adam and Eve would eat the apple? And what was I to make of his commandment to Abraham that he should kill his only son? But I recalled what Archie had told me, that no one understands Christianity properly. So I resolved to think no more about it. I must be baptized if the law was to recognise me and before I could be baptized, I must listen to the Reverend Hewitt's stories without asking too many questions.

On my return I saw that a hearse had drawn up outside Mrs Dempsey's house and I immediately thought of the pale young girl in the room at the top of the house. I was certain that it was she who was in the coffin being carried out at that very moment. I hurried into the shop where Archie was sitting behind the counter, reading.

'Who has died in Mrs Dempsey's house?' I demanded.

Archie looked up, surprised at the urgency of my tone. 'The old woman herself,' he replied and I felt a great sense of relief. 'Died in her sleep. The doorkeeper told me so himself. And apparently all the girls are gone.'

For the former things are passed away.

'Gone where?'

Archie shrugged. 'Who knows? In search of a new employer, I expect. But, tell me, what did you learn from the Reverend Hewitt today?'

'That God is indecisive and that I must not listen to snakes.'

Archie gave one of his wry smiles. 'Well, that is very good advice. You would do well to remember it.'

But for me, the Reverend Hewitt's lesson had been entirely eclipsed by the news of the death of Mrs Dempsey. I felt an odd sense of disappointment at the disappearance of the young girl in the room at the top of the house. Of course, I knew perfectly well that this made no sense for we had scarcely spoken and I was quite certain she had given no further thought to me once I had left the room. And yet I had nursed a secret hope that I might see her again.

Later that afternoon, when I was minding the shop, a man dressed in black clothes and a black hat came into the shop. His hair and his beard were close-cropped and grey and he looked as if he might have been sixty years of age; but he was well-built and good-looking with a fine set of teeth for a man of his age and a great deal of confidence about him so that his presence seemed to fill the shop.

I asked him how I might be of service.

'You can tell me where the bunch of whores who lived on the other side of the street has gone.' He said this with a smile that was merely a display of teeth, and at the same time his eyes flashed with menace and I felt immediately that he was a dangerous man.

'I'm afraid I have no idea.'

'Where is the hunchback who owns the shop?'

'Mr McKerras is upstairs,'

'Tell him John Dempsey wants to see him.'

I went and found Archie and told him about the visitor.

'That all right, I'll deal with him,' he told me.

I followed him downstairs and listened from the back, peering through a crack in the curtain.

'Mr John Dempsey,' Archie began.

'That's me.'

'May I offer you my commiserations on the death of your sister?'

'I thank you. But your commiserations are not what I came here for. I am told you had dealings with the pack of whores that infested my late sister's house.'

'I had dealings with them, certainly.'

'Meaning what, exactly?'

'Meaning that they bought clothes here from time to time and a few weeks ago your sister asked me to read to one of the girls.'

'Read to her?'

'Yes. She was in low spirits and your sister was of the opinion that being read to might cheer her up.'

'Then my sister was more of a fool than I took her to be. Listen to me, now. Those whores have made off with money that is rightfully mine and I would very much like to know where they went.'

'I'm sure you would. Unfortunately, I have not the least idea.'

'You wouldn't be lying to me, would you?'

'I am not in the habit of lying to anyone.'

'I am very pleased to hear it. However, if you should come across any information, perhaps you would be so good as to pass it on to me. I shall be staying in my late sister's house for the time being.'

'I very much doubt that I will hear anything that may be of value to you,' Archie assured him.

'Well just in case.' And now he lowered his voice so that I had to strain to hear. 'If I find you are lying, I will put your fucking eyes out. Do you understand me?'

'Perfectly.'

'Then I bid you good day.'

After he had gone I asked Archie whether he was afraid that John Dempsey would do him harm – for I most certainly was. He shook his head. 'I doubt it very much,' he said. 'He does not really believe I had any part in the whores' disappearance. He just wanted someone to threaten.'

'What if he finds the whores?'

'Oh, if he finds the whores he will certainly kill them, but we are not whores, Tuah.'

Since the visit to Mr Duncan's office he had called me Abdul twice and each time he had looked unhappy with himself afterwards. For several days after that he had simply avoided addressing me directly. This was the first time he had called me by my true name. For the rest of the day I kept remembering how it had sounded.

Thomas

That same evening, after spending the day walking the streets, Thomas returned to Brunel's office and found the lawyer as good as his word. He showed Thomas upstairs to a tiny room at the top of the house. There was no bed, nor even a chair. Nevertheless, Thomas lay down gratefully upon the bare boards. After Brunel had left the building he took a small green bottle from his jacket. It contained the last of his laudanum which he swallowed gratefully.

Very soon he felt himself begin to relax. The cold of the streets and the weariness of his body were sloughed off, all his thoughts were turned inwards, and it seemed as if a theatre was opened up within his brain across the stage of which vast and stately processions passed, friezes of never-ending stories as sad and solemn as if they were drawn from times before Oedipus or Priam.

Several hours later he was awoken by a scratching sound. He opened his eyes but at first he could see nothing at all. He was aware that he was lying on a wooden floor but he had no idea where he might be. Then he remembered. Gradually his eyes adjusted to the darkness and, by the faint glimmer of moonlight shining through the uncurtained window, the outline of the room began to take shape.

The scratching sound commenced anew. He understood what it was now: rats. He sat up and banged with his fist on the wall; the noise ceased abruptly. He got to his feet, hugging himself and stamping to try to restore the feeling to his toes. He was dreadfully cold. There was nothing here that might serve him as bedding of even the most rudimentary sort, nothing that he could wrap around himself against the dreadful chill. The room was entirely bare.

Mr Brunel had made it clear before he left that his tenant was to restrict himself to the top floor of the house but now Thomas considered searching the rest of the building for something that might alleviate the cold in some way, some heap of rags perhaps; even the thought of creating a nest for himself beneath a mound of documents seemed attractive. Before he could begin to act upon this decision, however, he became aware of another noise coming from somewhere in the house. This time it did not sound like rats. It was louder and there was something deliberate about it. He stood very still and listened and as he did so, he realised that someone was coming up the stairs.

There was something about those footsteps shuffling inevitably nearer that made every hair on his body stand on end and filled his mind with an overwhelming dread. Since he had left his home several months ago, Thomas had been quite alone in the world; he had slept in the open air and been woken in the night by the screech of an owl; he had come to his senses at the break of day to find a bull staring down at him; he had been sidestepped by respectable folks, threatened by suspicious farmers, accosted by drunken ruffians, but never until now had he felt stalked by something that was not of this world, plagued by a spirit… Yet that was the conviction that now began to grow upon him.

From the crack beneath the door, a ghostly, flickering light was stealing into the room and now the handle of the door began to turn. Thomas tried to cry out, to ask who was there: but his tongue would not move. He could only stand rooted to the spot as the door swung slowly open and his dead sister appeared in the doorway gazing in at him.

Nothing in his life had prepared him for such a horror. In the light of the candle she held in her right hand, Elizabeth's face was strangely distorted. Her eyes were wide open and she stared without speaking, as if accusing him of some unspeakable crime. He could only stare back without breathing. Suddenly she turned and the door slammed shut behind her.

Released from a spell that had bound him more tightly than the strongest cords, he rushed down the stairs, opened the door and fled into the night.

Anne

Daisy and me was walking along Oxford Street one night. She was telling me all about what it was like being in service, when I saw a young man sitting on a step outside the door of an ale-house looking completely *bewildered*, like he'd gone to bed on nice soft sheets somewhere and woken up to find himself robbed and lying in a ditch. That was the first time I ever set eyes on Thomas. He was that small and slight, I thought he was a nipper at first.

He didn't notice me, of course because that was what he was like. He looked at the world but all he ever saw was his own strange thoughts. Sometimes he'd try to explain those thoughts to me. I never had much idea what he was talking about, though he always made out I understood him better than anyone.

Anyway, there he was, wild-eyed and ragged but, even so, you could tell he was quality, when all of a sudden the door of the ale-house spilled open and two men come staggering out onto the street. One of them, a great big brute with a scar that ran from his right eye all the way down to his chin, stumbled over Thomas and was only saved from losing his balance by his companion, an older man, who caught and steadied him.

The man with the scar was furious, pointing at Thomas and calling him every name under the sun. Thomas had got to his feet by now and was backing away, stammering out apologies. But the man with the scar weren't interested in apologies. He pushed Thomas hard and sent him *sprawling* backwards. At the same time the older man slyly stuck out his foot, causing Thomas to fall to the ground. Now the pair of them began raining kicks on him while he curled into a ball, yelping like a beaten dog.

I don't know why I decided to get involved. The sensible thing to do would have been to walk on by but I couldn't do that. Something about the look of that young man just drew me in. I ran over and shouted at them to leave him alone.

'What's it got to do with you?' the fellow with the scar demanded. I could see he was the kind to strike a woman as easily as another man but I stood my ground even when Daisy came over and started trying to pull me away. Then all of a sudden a pair of constables appeared on the scene. Big fellows they was with stout wooden staves in their hands and I felt a good deal safer as soon as I saw them.

Right away, the fellow with the scar began coming out with a pack of lies. 'This here shagbag's been lying in wait outside the ale house, tripping people up as they leave in the hope of robbing them,' he declared.

'That ain't true at all,' I told them. 'The poor lad's done nothing wrong. He was just sitting on the doorstep taking a rest, when these two come out and set about him.'

'You don't want to listen to her,' Scar-face said. 'You can see what kind of woman she is.'

'Take him away and lock him up,' his companion demanded. 'What's he want to sit there for if he ain't planning to rob the customers when they come out?'

Everyone looked at Thomas who had sat up by now and

was holding his sides and groaning.

'What have you got to say for yourself, boy?' the constable asked him. 'Were you intending to rob these gentlemen?'

'Of course not. Surely you can see that I am the injured party?'

The way he spoke!

The constables must have recognised he was a gentleman because they straightened up, looked around, and told the two drunks to go on home.

Scar-face was *outraged.* 'It's a poor state of affairs when a decent law-abiding person can't go about his business without fear of assault and robbery,' he complained but the constables began giving him threatening looks and his companion dragged him away, muttering loudly about thieves and villains.

'You'd better get up now,' one of the constables told Thomas. 'You can't go on sitting there all night.'

He got to his feet though he looked very shaky.

'And I should try to stay out of trouble from now on.'

'I intend to, sir.'

'And the same goes for you two,' the other constable told me and Daisy.

'Of course we will,' Daisy said, giving him her cheekiest smile. 'We're good girls, ain't we Anne?'

'That's right.'

'We're very, very good,' Daisy went on. 'And we're always happy to assist the officers of the Watch.'

'All right, that will do.' The constable shook his head. 'Let's not waste any more time here,' he said to his companion. And off they went.

Thomas was gazing at me like he thought I'd *descended from heaven* specially to save him. 'I am eternally grateful to you, madam,' he said, at last.

Daisy giggled. 'You and a lot of other men,' she said. 'Was you looking for a bit of fun, then?'

'I beg your pardon?'

'A good time, you know.'

'I'm not sure…'

'Come on Anne,' she said to me. 'I don't think we're going to get any custom here. 'Try not to trip anyone else up,' she told Thomas. Then she set off down the street and I followed her but I couldn't help glancing back over my shoulder at him. He was still staring at me with the same dazed look. I gave him a little wave and he looked even more *astonished* than before. Then he raised his hand and waved back, ever so gently.

For the next few hours I was busy. One customer after the other came rolling out of a tavern looking for a bit of fun. Daisy was right when she said there was no shortage of men with a bit of money in their pocket looking for pleasure in Oxford Street. After a while, I decided I'd had enough. I hadn't made as much money as I generally did but I didn't care.

Daisy didn't want to go home yet. You've got to strike while the iron's hot, she told me. But I was still tired from taking too much laudanum earlier in the day. So I left her to it and made my way homewards, ignoring the men swaggering up to me, made brave by drink and the few pennies in their pocket.

Half way home, I saw Thomas again, asleep on a doorstep just a few yards from where we'd left him. I knew what'd happen if he stayed there. The constables would be back within the hour and they'd drag him off to the lock-up. It weren't no business of mine and yet, when I thought about the way he'd waved to me, somehow I found I couldn't leave him there. So I walked across and gave him a shake. 'You can't sleep here,' I told him. 'You'll only get yourself in trouble again.'

Only he wouldn't wake up. And he was terrible cold. I bent more closely over him and it seemed to me he weren't even breathing. A terrible sorrow come over me even though I didn't know him from Adam. Just an hour ago I'd been talking to him and now he was dead. Or very nearly. It seemed so cruel.

No, I decided, I wouldn't let it happen. I wouldn't give him up without a fight. I shook him, over and over, but he didn't open his eyes.

I let go of him and ran to the nearest tavern. I flung some coins down on the counter and asked for a jug of port wine and spices.

Then I ran out with it, ignoring the potboy's complaints, lifted up Thomas's head and held the jug to his lips. 'Come on,' I urged him, 'Drink some of this.'

Some of it must have gone down his throat because he suddenly began to cough and his eyes flew open.

'That's more like it,' I told him.

'What is it?' he asked, all in a panic. 'What's happening?'

'Don't worry, it's only port-wine. I'm not going to poison you. You have another sip, now.' I put the glass to his lips again and after a moment he did take another sip.

'Do you think you can sit up?'

'I believe so.'

Take it easy. Don't go leaping to your feet. Just wait till your strength comes back. Here, drink the rest of the port.' I handed him the jug but he was too weak to hold it and only succeeded in spilling it. So I took it back and held it for him, like you might do for a child.

'I seem to be making a habit of running into you,' I told him.

'It is most kind of you,' he replied. Then, all of a sudden he looked alarmed and pushed the jug away. 'I cannot take any more of this!'

'Why not? It'll do you good.'

'Because I have no money with which to reimburse you.'

That made me laugh. 'I don't want no rebursing,' I told him. 'Just get it down you and then see if you can get to your feet, only slowly mind, because you don't look to me like you've got the strength to take it any other way.'

He finished the port and I helped him to his feet.

'Listen, I need to take this jug back,' I told him. 'You just wait here and I'll be back before you know I've gone.'

I took back the jug and when I returned he was leaning on the wall, looking like a ghost. I wondered how old he was. Not much older than me, I reckoned.

'So where are you going now?' I asked him.

'I confess, I had no particular destination in mind,'

'You do talk fancy!'

'I suppose I do.'

'You'd better come along with me,' I told him. I don't know why I said it. It just came out.

'Thank you,' he said, as if I was doing him a great honour.

Then, the two of us set off back down Oxford Street, arm in arm, like a gentleman and a lady taking the night air.

Tuah

A month after I heard the story of Adam and Eve I was baptized a Christian. *For as in Adam all die, even so in Christ shall all be made alive.* The only people present apart from me were the Reverend Hewitt, Archie and Mr Duncan, the solicitor. By this time I had been taught all about Jesus Christ. Many questions had come into my mind as I listened to the accounts of Christ's miracles, his crucifixion and his resurrection from the dead but I had learned that the best way to proceed with the Reverend Hewitt was not to interrupt. Questions caused him to go red in the face and blink excessively.

The name I took was James. This was Mr Duncan's idea. 'You can still keep your own name,' he told me, 'but it will become your surname.' So I was James Tuah in the eyes of the church. Afterwards, Archie, Mr Duncan and I went to an inn to toast my conversion.

I had never been inside an inn before and I was nervous about accompanying them, suggesting that it might be better if I went home and left them to enjoy their celebration together. But Archie only laughed and told me that I was going to become an Englishman now and no Englishman is ever afraid to enter a drinking establishment. So I followed them inside and found that no-one took any particular notice of me. Indeed, there were plenty of other customers whose looks or clothes proclaimed they had been born far from London, including a sailor whose face was as black as coal but who laughed as loudly and confidently as any other.

We chose a corner table and when the mugs of ale and the glass of golden whisky for Archie (the true holy spirit he said, thus confusing me considerably) arrived, Mr Duncan raised his up and offered a toast to 'Tuah who was, to James Tuah who is, and to James Tuah McKerras who shall be.' But he cautioned that there would be a great many steps upon the way to that final outcome and that every step would be made of paper and ink. Despite Mr Duncan's cheerful confidence and Archie's continual quiet benevolence for which I was immensely grateful, I did not feel entirely at ease about this transformation. Whatever name I adopted, I was not an Englishman; nor would I ever be one.

One evening a few days after this celebratory drink, I stood regarding myself as best I could in the looking glass that hung upon the wall of the room in which Archie sometimes allowed customers to try on items of clothing. The image it showed produced within me a deep sense of despondency.

The following day, in the middle of the morning, I told Archie that I had an errand to run and I set off for Limehouse. When I knocked on the door or Mr Li's establishment it was opened by the young, strongly-built Chinaman who had stood over the captain when Archie and I had come to collect him on the occasion of my first visit. He said nothing but regarded me enquiringly.

'I wish to speak with Mr Li,' I told him, 'on a personal matter,'

He frowned and nodded. 'You wait here.' Then he closed the door.

After a few minutes the door was opened again and Mr Li himself stood there, regarding me. 'You are Mr McKerras, his servant,' he said.

I considered this, then I said. 'I am James…' I paused. 'I am Mr McKerras's companion.'

He looked surprised. 'My apologies. Please come inside.'

He led me into a small bare room, furnished only with a rug on which a number of cushions had been spread around. Then he gestured for me to sit down. So I did. He sat opposite me and regarded me expectantly.

'Firstly, I would like to thank you for attending the captain's funeral service,' I told him.

He nodded.

'I am also here to ask for your help.'

'My help?

'Please allow me to explain something about myself, Mr Li. I did not come to England of my own volition. I was forcibly taken from the island of my birth by slavers. I was sold in a market and bought by the captain who gave me my freedom. His brother, Mr Archibald, has made me a part of his family.'

'Then you have been fortunate.'

'Yes indeed. I have been most fortunate. May I ask you a question, Mr Li?'

He made the faintest of gestures, barely moving a finger but I took it as an agreement that I might proceed.

'Do you consider yourself to be an Englishman?'

He shook his head. 'Chinese,' he said.

'That is what I would have expected. I do not consider myself to be an Englishman either. But since I was made a slave I have not met another man or woman from my island, nor do I ever expect to. I doubt that I could even find my island again if I set sail in search of it. All of the life that I had as a child has been lost to me. They have given me a name, the name of an Englishman, and yet still, I am not an Englishman'

I was surprised at how difficult it was to say all this. It was as though these thoughts had been locked within my heart for so long that taking them out and displaying them before another human being was like reaching inside my chest and pulling out some part of my vital organs. But though I spoke haltingly, Mr Li made no attempt either to stop or encourage me.

'What I want is to have some clothes made,' I continued.

Mr Li frowned. 'I do not understand. I am not a tailor.'

'No. But you do not wear the clothes of an Englishman.'

'You want Chinese clothes?'

'No but I am looking for someone to make me some clothes that are not English, not European. I thought, perhaps, the person who made your clothes—'

'My wife make my clothes.'

'I see.' For some reason I had not expected this.

'You want I ask her to make clothes for you?'

'Could she do that?'

'Why not?'

He went out of the room and came back a few minutes later with his wife. So small she was, like a child in stature, with little black eyes burning with a keen intelligence and knowing. She bowed to me, then spoke to her husband in her own language. He turned back to me. 'These clothes you want, describe them to me.'

Once upon a time I would have found this task entirely eyond me but now I was working with clothes on a daily basis. So I explained that I wanted a jacket of undyed broadcloth without lapels and with a collar like Mr Li's, fully-lined and with frog fastenings but that I wished it to be shorter than his. I also wanted a white shirt of finer cotton with a similar collar, a pair of loose undyed canvas trousers and a white felt hat, similar in shape to Mr Li's.

He relayed all this to his wife who nodded then produced a measuring tape and a slate from somewhere about her body and moving swiftly and confidently, began taking my measurements. Afterwards, she spoke to her husband and he turned to me.

'She need some money to buy cloth.' He named a sum, which seemed entirely reasonable to me and I handed it over.

'When shall I come back?' I asked.

'I let you know,' Mr Li told me. 'I pass your shop very often.'

'Do you?' I had not imagined Mr Li emerging from his den for anything less important than the death of a customer.

'I have a son. He live not far from you.'

This news also surprised me. Mr Li was far more a part of London than I had imagined, far more a part of London than I could ever imagine myself becoming.

I thanked him and walked home feeling even more alone than when I had set out. As I turned onto the Mile End Road I saw a group of men coming towards me, all of whom were clearly the worse for drink. Among them I recognised the figure of John Dempsey. Had I been less deep in thought I might have had the sense to step into a doorway and thereby avoid them but they were upon me before I realised, jostling me and jeering until I felt myself tripped and I was sent tumbling into the gutter.

Then Dempsey put up his hand. 'Gentlemen, please!' he said, speaking with mock gravity, 'this is one of our neighbours lying distressed by the side of the road. We should not pass him by.' He bent down and stretched out his hand.

I declined his assistance, getting to my feet unaided.

Dempsey immediately began to brush the front of my coat. 'Dear, dear, dear, sir! You must watch where you're going.'

I tried to move away but he held me by my coat front and put his face so close to mine that the smell of strong drink was almost overpowering.

'Any word from those whores?' he whispered.

I shook my head.

'Don't forget to let me know if you hear from them.' With that he rejoined his fellows and they continued to make their unruly way down the street.

Thomas

When Thomas opened his eyes he found that he was lying upon a straw mattress, gazing up at the crudely-cut wooden beams and knot-ridden planking of an unfamiliar ceiling. Confused, he tried to raise himself on one elbow but he was dreadfully weak and the sudden motion made his head throb so violently it felt as though something inside his skull might burst.

'No, don't get up, rest now.'

A girl was kneeling beside him, putting out a hand to gently restrain him.

At once, the events of the previous night came rushing back: the vision of his sister, the flight from Mr Brunel's office, the men who had attacked him and the girl who had intervened. The girl. She who was kneeling over him now. She had brought him back here last night. This was her room and he had been sleeping on her mattress. He looked at her more closely. She was no older than himself, with very pale skin and dark eyes, deeply shadowed and rimmed with red. Her mouth seemed a little too wide for her face. That and a slightly pointed nose gave her a kind of half-wild look that reminded him of Elizabeth. She managed to look both kind and reckless at the same time.

'I'm afraid I don't know your name.'

'It's Anne.'

'I am Thomas.'

'I know. You told me last night.'

'Did I? What else did I say?'

'That your mother and uncle have thrown you out of home and that you want to be a poet.'

He groaned. Why on earth had he told her that?

'I cannot stay here.'

'Off you go, then,'

He struggled once more to raise himself from the mattress but without success. The girl only laughed. 'You ain't got strength enough to stand,' she told him. 'I don't know how I ever got you back here last night. What you need is rest. Wait a minute.' She went over to a corner of the room and rummaged around amid a pile of clothes. Then she turned, holding up a blue glass bottle triumphantly. 'An angel's kiss!'

'Laudanum?'

'That's it. The cure for every pain and every sorrow.' She knelt beside the mattress once more and held the bottle to his lips. 'Not too much, now.'

Thomas swallowed a mouthful and sank back upon the bed.

'That's better. You get some sleep now. Don't you worry about a thing. Let it all just drift away like shit in the river. You're safe with me. Safe and sound.

The next time Thomas awoke it was to the most delicious smell he had ever encountered. The room was darker so he guessed it must be evening. The girl – Anne – was sitting on the floor beside him and in her hands she held a meat pie. Never in his life had anything looked so inviting.

'Come on,' she said. 'Ain't you going to take it?'

'I haven't any money.'

'I ain't selling it. I'm giving it to you.'

'What about you?'

'I've already eaten.'

Thomas took the pie, bit into it and closed his eyes to savour the taste. No, the tastes for there were so many different flavours: the buttery, salty pastry, the deep, earthy gravy, the pungent, spicy meat. Then there were the textures: crisp and crumbly, firm and chewy, thick and syrupy.

'Enjoying it?'

'Yes, thank you.'

Thomas did not stop eating until he had finished the pie. Then he gave a deep sigh of satisfaction and licked his fingers. Beside Anne on the floor were a jug of ale and two mugs. She poured some for both of them.

'I'm going to work in a short while,' she told him.

'To work?'

'Yes.'

'What is it that you do?'

She looked at him suspiciously. 'You know perfectly well what I do.'

'No, I don't.'

'What do you think I was doing when I brought you back here?'

Thomas shrugged. 'Going for a walk?'

'Come off it! You can't be that innocent.'

'I don't know what you mean.'

There was a flash of anger in the girl's eyes now. 'I'm a doxy. There, you've made me say it. Satisfied?'

'A what?'

'A drab, a trollop, a street girl.'

Thomas's eyes opened wide. 'Oh! I'm sorry. I didn't realise.'

She still looked angry. 'How could you not have realised?'

'I don't know. You just seem so….'

'So what?'

'So good.'

She gave him a long look as if trying to decide whether he was mocking her. 'I must have given you too much of that laudanum,' she declared at last.

'You could have left me in the street.'

'I could have.'

'But instead, you brought me back here and you've fed me and let me sleep in your own bed.'

'Not much of a bed.'

'Yes, but why did you do it?'

She shrugged. 'I've never met a poet before.'

'I'm not a poet. I haven't written anything.'

'Not yet, Thomas.'

'Maybe I never will.'

'Maybe. But you want to, don't you?'

'Yes.'

'Well that's a start. Now I've got to go. If I was you I should go back to sleep. The more you rest, the sooner you'll get better.'

In truth, the act of eating had exhausted him. He lay back on the bed and closed his eyes. Almost immediately he slipped back down the velvet tunnel of sleep.

The next time he was aware of Anne was when she woke him, coming back some time in the early hours of the morning. The room was dark and he could only see her silhouetted form but he was aware that she was taking off her dress. He knew he ought to look away. Nevertheless, he found himself unable to stop watching her shadowy form as the dress slid to the floor and she stood there clothed only in darkness until she picked up a shift and pulled it on over her head. Then she came over to the bed.

'Are you awake?' she whispered.

'Yes.'

'Then move over.' She lay down beside him.

Never before had Thomas lain on a bed with a young woman. She was so close to him that he could feel her heat and smell her sweat. *She half enclosed me with her arms, She pressed me with a meek embrace* – Coleridge's words came unbidden to his mind, though in fact they lay separate and untouching. Nonetheless... He lay there for a long time, rigid with anxiety until he became aware from her breathing that she had fallen asleep. Then he, too, slipped back into oblivion.

In the morning he woke to find her sitting in a corner of the room fully-dressed, watching him. This could not continue, he told himself. This very evening, he would return to Mr Brunel's offices.

But when evening came he found that he was simply not strong enough to face the prospect of shivering all night in the room above Mr Brunel's office. And on each of the following days it was the same. He suffered agonies of guilt every time Anne brought him food but he quieted his conscience by telling himself that when he had received the money from Brunel he would pay her back.

More importantly, perhaps, he did not want to return to his solitary condition. For the first time in his life he had a friend. It was so enjoyable just to sit on the floor together, with their backs against the wall and talk. Thomas told her about his childhood and she told him about hers, and much of what they said was the pure and unvarnished truth. But there were some things they did not talk about, of course. She never told him anything about the men who paid for her services; he did not speak of the banker's draft that had been his downfall nor of the death of his sister, or the visit she had paid him in Mr Brunel's office.

A good deal of the time they passed in companionable silence, made richer and more pleasurable by the sharing of a little laudanum. Sometimes they went for hours together without speaking, eyes closed, gaze turned inward upon endless seas of reminiscence and invention – for at times the images seemed to come from some place deeper or older than memory; Thomas saw visions of strange and magnificent buildings, vast pillared monuments, great bridges across measureless chasms; he wandered through the ruins of colossal cities, stopping to gaze at inscriptions in unknown characters whose meanings he could not even begin to guess at.

Yet it was not all awe and wonder. Often he found himself breaking out into laughter at the smallest thing, and sometimes Anne's friend, Daisy, joined them and all three of them laughed together, falling into fits of giggling that left them with aching ribs and tears running down their faces. There was a new lightness about his life which Thomas had never imagined might be possible.

Of course sharing a single room presented difficulties: there was the business of washing, of dressing and undressing, of using the chamber pot. Thomas tried to do all this only when Anne was absent and whenever Anne began to remove her clothes or picked up the pot, he would quickly leave the room and stand in the grimy hallway observing the crumbling plaster and the beetles that scuttled across the walls, or wander around the filthy little courtyard where the same three or four old women always stood in a knot talking in low voices and ignoring the same solitary cripple who sat gazing determinedly down at the ground as if doing penance or perhaps considering vengeance for some dreadful crime.

On the afternoon of the fourth day when Anne returned to the room from the pump with a jug of water for washing, Thomas began getting to his feet but she held out her hand. 'You don't have to leave, you know. I ain't bothered.'

Thomas paused, kneeling before her like a supplicant. 'I cannot remain here while you…'

'While I wash myself?'

'Yes.'

'Is it such a terrible thing?'

'Of course not.'

'Then what are you afraid of?' She raised one eyebrow and began unlacing her dress.

Thomas immediately turned his face to the wall but he was aware of Anne's continued movements behind him and of the rustling sounds of her dress falling from her body

'Turn round, Thomas,' she said, softly.

Thomas shook his head.

'Do I disgust you? Is that it? Is it because I'm a whore?'

'No! Of course not!'

'Then turn round and look at me.'

Still kneeling and trembling like a leaf, Thomas slowly turned.

She was completely naked, her dress in a crumpled heap about her feet.

Thomas had thought he knew all about desire. Experience had taught him that that it could be mastered by ignoring it, by refusing to listen to its insistent whispers, by thinking of higher things. But the desire he felt as he gazed upon Anne's nakedness was so intense that he could no longer think of anything at all. It consumed him like a flame. All he could do was gaze on and on, like a beggar confronted with a horde of stolen gold. 'I may have been bought and sold,' Anne said, 'but I am still a person.'

'I know you are.'

'Do you? Do you really?'

'Of course I do.'

'Then be brave, Thomas. Be the man you really want to be.' She stepped out of her dress and began to walk towards him.

She drew level and stood looking down into his eyes and he made a decision – or it was made for him. He reached up, put his hands upon her hips and drew her body towards him.

He did not know what he was doing. He had no experience, he had not read of such things, nor had anyone ever spoken to him of how to go about the act of love. Love... He almost laughed. He knew nothing, had read nothing and so there was nothing to consider, no advice to heed or disregard. He acted purely upon instinct, placing his cheek against her thigh and holding it there. She shuddered and gave a small moan that was so like a sound of pain he almost checked himself but she placed her hands upon his head, encouragingly so that he rubbed his cheek against her, like a cat rubs up against its owner. Sensing what it was she wanted he began to explore her body with his lips and tongue, putting his face between her legs, seeking out the part where all the pleasure was locked up, waiting to be released. He gave himself completely to the task until he was entirely at one with her body, creating a rhythm of pleasure which gathered itself and quickened through every part of her until she suddenly stiffened, held herself rigid for a moment then, gripping his head firmly, cried out, an exclamation that started like fear but ended with joy.

That night Thomas awoke in the darkest hour feeling certain he had just heard his sister's voice. But he was not afraid this time. He understood with complete certainty why she had come to visit him in Mr Brunel's office. She had wanted him to find Anne, or for Anne to find him – it amounted to the same thing. With this thought came another understanding that was so intense and so liberating that it was all Thomas could do to stop himself from laughing out loud and waking Anne.

He finally understood the nature of the secret language that his sister had spoken about when they were children, the language that had enabled the magician to recognise Aladdin as the one boy in all the world who could retrieve the magic lamp. It was the very same language that had brought Thomas and Anne together. She had recognised him and brought him back to her room. He had recognised her and stayed. It was the alphabet of heart's desire. Had not Anne tried to tell him this herself? Follow the wishes of your heart and you will become the man you have always wanted to be. From now on he would learn the language of heart's desire and he would listen to no other.

The following day, after they had breakfasted on a stale loaf and some hard cheese, Thomas set off to call on Mr Brunel. Pyment admitted him more readily now, though always with the kind of look that might normally be reserved for something that had crawled out from under a stone.

Mr Brunel was in a cheerful mood and offered Thomas a cup of chocolate from a pot on a tray beside his desk. It was an offer that Thomas gratefully received, taking it as a sign that he had risen significantly in Brunel's estimation. The chocolate was deliciously thick and sweet.

'We have missed you, Mr De Quincey,' Brunel declared. 'It seems you have found some lodgings, after all.'

'It is to inform you of my new address I have come to see you this morning,' Thomas replied

Brunel picked up a pen, turned a leaf in his ledger and gazed at Thomas enquiringly.

'I can be contacted courtesy of Miss Anne Chambers, number eighteen De Lacey Court, which is but a short walk from here,' Thomas told him.

One of Brunel's eyebrows moved almost imperceptibly. 'Miss Chambers is a relation of yours?' he enquired.

'She is a very dear friend.'

'Well thank you for that information, Mr De Quincey. '

'You have had no reply from Lord Massey as yet?'

Mr Brunel put his head on one side and made an equivocating gesture with his hand. 'Nothing definite as yet, but we shall know how to find you the instant we have news.'

'I see.'

Mr Brunel's gaze fixed itself upon the cup of chocolate in Thomas's hand. Thomas drained the dregs which were incompletely dissolved and not entirely enjoyable to consume. Then he got to his feet. 'I bid you good day, then.'

'Good day to you, too. Oh, and Mr De Quincey,'

'Yes.'

'Do take good care of yourself around De Lacey Court. It is not an altogether salubrious area.'

But as Thomas walked back to Anne's room he thought how much he disagreed with Mr Brunel. Yes, the area around De Lacey Court was broken down and dirty. Yes, it was inhabited by a population of street-girls and beggars, drunkards, rogues and bare-footed urchins. Yes, he suspected that vagabonds and cut-purses lay hidden in every second doorway. But there was also a freedom to be found here that was quite intoxicating.

He stopped for a moment to watch a blindfolded man juggling a set of wooden hoops and as he stood there a group of young women came along the street, walking arm-in arm and singing loudly. A little knot of men staggering out of an inn stopped to admire them, some calling out encouragement, others making suggestions of the coarsest kind, but the women were quite undaunted. They were followed by a group of laughing children chasing a flock of geese. Somehow it felt to Thomas as though all this had been arranged for his own entertainment.

When he returned at last to Anne's room she was standing by the window gazing out into the street. She turned to look at him and he saw for the first time that she was not just pretty. She was beautiful – in a way that he did not entirely understand. There was a kind of grace about her, and the fact that she could possess it despite the terrible circumstances of her life took Thomas's breath away.

He crossed the room and stood beside her, gazing deep into her eyes. Putting his hand to her face, he gently traced the outline of her cheekbone with his finger. She smiled, slid her arms inside the coat and wrapped them around him. Then he brought his lips to hers, closed his eyes and poured his whole soul into a kiss.

Anne

I know you'll say it ain't likely. You'll tell me that every girl must find it out for herself when she's growing up. Especially a girl what grows up to be a whore. But what you choose to believe is your concern. I'm telling you the truth when I say I didn't know there was such a thing as a woman's pleasure before I met Thomas.

Or perhaps you think it a fine joke, that all the time there was this other half of love-making, the woman's half, and I knew nothing at all about it. Well you'd be right. It is a joke. One of God's jokes upon the world and proof that what the clergymen say is true: God is a man and all his jokes is made at the expense of women. My mother always said that Lord told women to submit, nothing more.

Of course once I learned what I'd been missing I set about making up for lost time. Now that Thomas had unlocked the door, I made very sure it stayed unlocked. We enjoyed ourselves, let's just say that. It weren't one bit like it was with all those other men. For one thing it was all about giving, not about taking, and for another - and when I tell you this you'll have a right good laugh but I don't care – for another, it really was about love. A lot of people will tell you there ain't no such thing. It's just a story to entertain young ladies, a way of painting the world in prettier colours than it really owns. I'd have said as much myself before I met up with Thomas but I'd have been wrong. Love is a kingdom all on its own, the most beautiful kingdom ever *established* upon this earth, and Thomas and me had stumbled right into it. It changed the both of us. It made us into different people. Better people.

I ain't going to pretend it was all straightforward because it weren't. We come from different worlds and while you could forget about that a lot of the time there was other times when you couldn't. Like when Thomas would get on one of his hobby horses and start trying to explain what some philosopher thought, or tell me all about the Ancient Greeks.

I never had the slightest idea what he was talking about and I sometimes wondered if he did himself, especially when he'd had a drop or two of laudanum. I'd put up with it for a while because I liked to hear the sound of his voice but then I'd put my finger to his lips to make him stop. 'I don't care about the bloody Ancient Greeks, Thomas,' I'd tell him. 'They're all dead and gone hundreds of years ago. You and me is alive now. So let's make it worth our while.' With that I'd give him the look. And believe me, by then I knew how to look at a man in a way that put everything else out of his mind, however lofty a mind it might be.

Some days Thomas would get an attack of conscience. Those days was the hardest to put up with. He'd spend hours just staring at the wall like a man who's been sentenced to death. Or else he'd start to lecture himself in words as long as your arm. I learned to leave him alone when he was in one of these moods. He'd always come round in the end.

One day, when we'd been together for a month, Thomas decided he didn't want to see me working on the street no more. We was sitting on the bed with our backs to the wall sharing a loaf of bread when he come out with it.

'That's all very well,' I told him, 'but what do you propose we live on? They don't give bread away for nothing, you know.'

That was when he told me about his allowance of a guinea a week and how he hadn't been collecting it. Well, that didn't make no sense to me at all. So, naturally, I asked him why he hadn't collected it and the whole story come out.

'Six guineas is mine by right,' he said, 'and I intend to collect it this very day.'

'But I thought you was worried they'd lay hands on you and bring you before a magistrate?'

'Did you not tell me to be brave?'

'I did.'

'Then that is what I intend to be.'

'Well this is excellent news, Thomas. Six guineas may keep us for a month if we're careful. And then there'll be the weekly guinea on top of that. Perhaps I *can* stop working, or at least, cut it back to once or twice a week.'

'Wait, Anne! My allowance is just the beginning.'

'The beginning of what?'

'You will recall, I explained that I am waiting upon the decision of a moneylender.'

'So you said.' He'd told me about this the day after I brought him back to my room.

'Well, he has given his agreement in principle to furnishing me with the sum of three hundred pounds.'

'Three hundred pounds! Thomas, are you serious?'

'Perfectly. Provided I can persuade Lord Massey, an acquaintance of mine, to guarantee the payment upon my coming of age, the money is mine.'

'You didn't tell me you'd asked him for three hundred pounds! And you didn't say you had a friend a lord, neither.'

Thomas shrugged. 'The fact of him being a lord is neither here nor there. What matters is that when I get the money…'

'If you get the money.'

'I will get it, I am sure of that, and when I do…'

He hesitated and suddenly a cold feeling began creeping up my spine. 'When you do, you'll be a rich man,' I said, to fill up the empty space that was growing between us.

'Hardly rich, Anne, but I shall have wealth enough for what I plan to do.'

It was like listening to a death sentence. I could see in my mind's eye exactly what would happen when he laid his hands upon that money. He'd walk away from me, back into the world of lords and ladies where he rightly belonged, and I'd never see him again. I felt like my heart was breaking when I understood this but I told myself I should have expected nothing else. So I leaned over and kissed him on the lips. 'And I hope that when you've set yourself up as a gentleman you'll think of me from time to time.' I said, trying to sound as bright as I could, though I couldn't help a catch from coming into my voice. It was all going to be over so much more quickly than I'd thought.

And then the *miracle* happened. He leaned across and took my hands in his. 'You mistake my meaning altogether, Anne,' he said. 'I fully intend to leave this misery and squalor behind me, but when I do so I shall be taking you with me.'

My heart leapt but just as quickly it sank again, for I knew it couldn't happen. Not in the real world. 'Don't be foolish, Thomas,' I told him. 'You won't want to take me with you. Let's not pretend.'

'But I do, Anne. I want that more than I have ever wanted anything in my life.'

'Be sensible, Thomas. You know what I am.'

'I know that you are generous, kind-hearted and sincere.'

'That's not what I mean. You can't bring me into respectable society, you must know that.'

'Listen, Anne, all that sunders you from the respectable society of which you speak is money. Nothing else. Money creates respectability. And three hundred pounds is enough to procure that respectability for both of us.'

'But where would we go?'

'Away from London altogether. I thought perhaps the Lake District.'

'The Lake District?' I didn't even know where that was.

'Right now it is the very centre of the literary world. I could write. You could keep house for me. No one would ask any questions. No one would find us there unless we wanted to be found.'

He was holding both my hands in his and looking deep into my eyes.

'You're not trifling with me, are you?' I asked, 'because I couldn't bear it.'

'I would never trifle with you, Anne. Do you believe me?'

I nodded. I couldn't trust myself to speak.

But Thomas was not satisfied. 'Then tell me you believe me.'

'I believe you, Thomas.' Now I began to weep in earnest.

He put his arms around me and I let the tears come. 'I never thought I'd see this day,' I told him, between sobs. 'I never thought I'd find my way out of all this.'

And so that afternoon Thomas went to the nearest Post Office to claim his six guineas and while he was gone, I called in to see Daisy. I'd been neglecting her ever since Thomas had arrived. Daisy didn't hold it against me, though. She was good like that. We spent our time just gossiping. She asked a lot of questions about Thomas. I wanted so badly to tell her of his plan to take me away and make an honest woman of me. I thought I'd burst from holding in the news. But I knew better than to go blabbing my mouth off. This was too important.

"Well he's certainly cheered you up, that's all I can say,' Daisy told me. 'If by any chance he's got a friend that's looking for company, don't forget to point him in my direction, will you?' She laughed as she said this but underneath, I could tell, she envied me my new-found happiness and I thought to myself, when I'm a lady, I will try my best to do something for you, Daisy.

When I went back to my room later I found Thomas sitting on the bed reading a book. He looked up and gave me a great big smile. 'The first part of our plan has been a success,' he said.

'Well, that's good news. What's the book?'

'Lyrical Ballads. It's my own copy. I pawned it before I met you and now I've managed to get it back. I thought it was gone for good.'

'That's nice.'

'Sit down a minute and listen to this. *Strange fits of passion have I known…*' There and then he started reading poetry to me and I admit, it did sound very fine, though much of it went over my head and, to tell you the truth, he didn't read quite as well as Archie. Sometimes he went too fast and sometimes he stammered but I didn't let on I'd noticed. After he'd finished he looked at me like he'd just given me a wonderful present so I told him it was very beautiful. That pleased him no end.

'The finest literature transcends all barriers of rank and reaches into the soul of those who know how to listen,' he said, very solemn and grand. He went through the pages like a dog after a rat. ' "Poetry is the spontaneous overflow of powerful feelings: it takes its origin from emotion recollected in tranquillity..." '

'I'm sure it does,' I told him. Now what do you say we celebrate your success with a couple of bottles of laudanum?'

'A capital idea!' He closed the book.

First of all we took ourselves off to Jack White's Pudding Shop in Oxford Street where we dined on pease pudding and eels with a mug of good ale. Next we visited the apothecary for our laudanum and then straight home where we took our pleasure with even more delight than usual.

I'll tell you something strange. When Thomas and me took laudanum together it was always much stronger than when I took it by myself. We'd lie on the bed, side by side and it was like our two souls was *entwined* together. Go on, laugh. I know it sounds like something out of one of Thomas's books of poetry. But it's the truth. I'd close my eyes and first there'd be the feeling. Like your body was filling up with warm water. It always started in the toes and then crept up the rest of me. Soon enough I couldn't feel the bed beneath me no more. I'd just be... floating. Like a flower in a puddle. Next would be the colours. Little spots of colour, floating in the darkness, like more flowers, petals or something. I'd look at one of them and it'd get bigger and brighter and all of a sudden it'd come to life and my heart would jump like it was ready to burst. Then there'd be a rush of pictures, like sitting on a merry-go-round with all the people flashing past. Faces of every kind, and not all of them friendly neither, changing and growing into other things. Next minute I'd be in there with them, part of them. I'd leave myself on the bed behind and I'd be back there in my childhood, talking to my father and watching his face or maybe I'd be flying down the street above the heads of the people, or I might be climbing some stairs that went on and on and sometimes I might be dressed up in strange clothes and there'd be people all around me in a procession muttering in some strange language. Things I didn't understand at all.

Then would come the bit that never happened with no one else but Thomas. I don't rightly now how to talk about it. All I can tell you is, things got deeper and faster and stronger and I'd be scared but I'd try not to let it stop me because I knew something inside me was struggling to get free. And it was like coming up through water until all of a sudden there was nothing but light, an ocean of it, and we was there together him and me floating on that ocean. Our two souls together. And I could talk to him without words but there weren't no need to talk. Because it was enough just floating. And I knew what it was, this ocean. It was love.

And so we passed our time together like children at play. If you was to ask me what we did all day, I couldn't rightly tell you, other than talk – that was mostly Thomas, he did love to talk – and dream and bring each other comfort. Sometimes, if we'd been moderate with the laudanum, we'd walk the streets together for hours just for pleasure and London seemed a kind of fairy-land to us, put there for our entertainment.

The only cloud on the horizon appeared the week after Thomas told me about his allowance when he went to the Post Office to collect what he was owed. I called in on Daisy again but as soon as she saw me she frowned.

'There's been a fellow round here asking about you?' she said.

I felt an icy hand clutching at my heart. 'What fellow?'

Daisy shrugged. 'He wouldn't tell me his name. He was an ugly brute.'

John Dempsey. It had to be. 'What did he look like?'

'Big. Like an ape. All arms and legs with a head too small for his body. You ain't done something to upset him, have you, Anne?'

I just shook my head. I'd never told Daisy about Mrs Dempsey's money. 'Probably just someone after a good time,' I told her. But I didn't say it with much conviction and I could tell she didn't believe me.

Tuah

On Sundays I attended St Mary's church and joined in the service with the rest of the congregation, though none of them ever spoke a word to me. The Reverend Hewitt, who always stood outside in the churchyard when the service was concluded and greeted the parishioners by name, only nodded to me. I strongly suspected that he considered me an embarrassment to the parish and that my presence had only been made possible by strenuous efforts on the part of Mr Duncan. Yet, had not the Reverend Hewitt told me that Christ himself instructed his followers, *go ye into all the world and preach the gospel to all creation*?

The difficulty I presented, of course, was that I was neither fish nor fowl – or rather, I might be one of them, but it was doubtful whether I was truly human. In the eyes of the Reverend Hewitt and his flock, I was a savage who had put on the airs and graces of an Englishman and, as such, I was an affront to everything they held dear.

Thus it was, whenever I had dealings with the ladies and gentlemen of London. Among the poorer people my comings and goings were scarcely noticed, but anyone with a position in society wished to have as little to do with me as possible, with the exception of Mr Duncan who continued to coax and cajole the law into accepting me.

After my baptism Archie formally appointed me as his heir. He informed me of this over breakfast one morning. 'In the event of my death, you will inherit the house and the business,' he declared. 'Mr Duncan will see to it.'

'I am deeply honoured,' I told him, 'but I sincerely hope that you will live for a great many years to come.'

'So do I, Tuah, for there are still at least as many books to read as when I first began to learn my letters.'

Unlike the captain, Archie scarcely ever drank. He had no friends. There were men and occasionally women whom he encountered for reasons of business – undertakers and the bereaved individuals whose names they passed on to him, rag-buyers and haberdashers, bankers and their clerks – but there was no friendship in any of these associations. To all of them he was just a hunchback who bought and sold second-hand clothes.

He lived extremely frugally, spending nothing on his own attire or his appearance beyond what was necessary to preserve a degree of respectability, or on furnishings for the house and shop. Reading was his sole recreation. He bought books and he read them. In time, I came to appreciate the wisdom of this way of living and to make it my own. Between us we sought to work our way through the great piles of books that littered the upstairs of the house. But we never came anywhere near to exhausting the volumes in Archie's makeshift library for their number was always growing.

Despite, or perhaps because of this frugality, Archie had acquired rather more wealth than I had imagined, for now that I was to inherit the business it became necessary for me to understand its workings properly: the money that was taken in, the money that was spent, and the difference between the two small but steady streams. It was necessary for me also to learn how profit and loss were recorded on paper so that the health or sickness of the business might be comprehended at a glance, where the money was held on our behalf and how it was invested.

Because the captain had been so downcast I had concluded that the McKerras fortunes had been dealt a mortal blow, but it had only been the captain's pride that had been wounded. Yes, he had not profited as he had hoped. Equally, the Company had pursued him for what it considered to be revenues lost by his negligence. But Archie had always kept the business of the shop entirely distinct from his brother's speculative ventures. There would have been enough to have provided them both with a living, had they been careful. The captain's despair and descent into addiction was like the tantrum of a child who has been denied a promised treat.

Archie came to rely upon me more and more. It was often still necessary for him to deal in person with the bereaved gentlefolk since for the most part they refused to even countenance the idea of dealing with me. But I collected the clothes and any other possessions belonging to the deceased that were included in the bargain once they had been made into anonymous bundles that no longer rebuked the survivors with their echoes of the lost loved one.

One afternoon, when much of London was swathed in a fog that was born of the river and crept across the face of the city like a disease as the day steadily progressed, I was returning from a house near Moorgate, pushing the barrow in which were two large bundles of clothes of very fine quality indeed. Before setting out from the house of the deceased, however, I had taken the precaution of wrapping them in cheap cloth and throwing a great many rags in beside the bundles, so that no-one would give me or my cargo a second glance. The fog was so dense in places that I imagined myself wandering through a city made empty and desolate by one of those plagues that the god of the Bible had visited upon the people of Egypt. I had often heard the story of the plagues from the Reverend Hewitt and in telling it, he had shown an uncharacteristic animation. His eyes had widened and it seemed to me that he relished the idea of Jehovah punishing the enemies of Israel with such inventiveness and cruelty; he would often repeat the words of the cursing: *the Lord shall smite thee with madness, and blindness, and astonishment of heart: And thou shalt grope at noonday, as the blind gropeth in darkness, and thou shalt not prosper in thy ways: and thou shalt be only oppressed and spoiled evermore, and no man shall save thee.*

When I reached the shop, I brought the barrow round the back entrance and was opening the gate that led into the yard when I realised that for some time I had been aware, or perhaps half-aware, of a regular tapping sound following me, though exactly how long this had been going on I could not have said. At the same time a strong feeling of being watched came over me.

I turned around, peering this way and that into the fog but I saw nothing at first and I began to conclude that I had been imagining things. The fog has unnerved you, I told myself. But then a faint breeze stirred and the fog shifted slightly, allowing me a glimpse of a figure in a doorway and I was immediately sure that he was the one who had been watching me. The man was a cripple and he supported himself on crutches. I could not think where I might have seen him before. Yet there was something both familiar and threatening about him. I put down the handles of the barrow and took a couple of steps towards him.

Immediately he turned and began walking away on his crutches, making surprising speed.

'Wait!' I called out but my cry only drove him to greater efforts. Abandoning the barrow, I set off in pursuit even though I felt that there had been something threatening about him. I told myself that I was being ridiculous. A one-legged man could not present any kind of a serious threat to me. Yet, even as I pursued him, a sense of dread stole over me and I shivered. At the end of the road he turned a corner and disappeared from sight. I broke into a run but by the time I reached the corner there was no sign of him. I ran back and forth, looking down side-streets and peering into doorways. It seemed impossible that he could have disappeared so completely. And yet he was gone as surely as if he had never been there at all.

It suddenly occurred to me that I might have been the victim of a trick, that the cripple might have wanted me to become aware of him so that I would abandon the cart and set off in pursuit. Mortified at the thought of being caught out so easily, I hurried back to the shop but the barrow was exactly as I left it. The bundles of clothes was quite untouched.

I pushed the cart through the gateway and shut it behind me. The sooner I was indoors, the better I would like it, I decided.

It was only when I was lifting out the first of the bundles that it came to me where I had seen the cripple before. Wasn't he the same man that Archie had stabbed in the leg and we had both left to bleed to death in the alleyway? No, I told myself, I was allowing my imagination too much rein. I had not seen his face properly, after all. There was no way that I could be certain, or even half-certain, that it was the same man.

And yet, as I carried the bundles of clothes inside the house an awful sense of foreboding came over me. Things had been going too well for too long. Perhaps my run of good fortune was coming to an end.

Thomas

Thomas leant back against the well-padded upholstery of Lord Massey's coach and told himself that everything was going to be all right. His luck had changed.

On the night he had collapsed in Oxford Street his life had reached its nadir. He had very nearly sunk without trace but Anne had reached out her hand and pulled him to the surface and his transformation had begun. Now he was on an upward path and it was all going to turn out for the best. His suffering had all been for a purpose.

Yesterday morning when he had paid his regular visit to Brunel's office to enquire whether there had been any developments, the man had actually smiled at him. 'We have had a response from the noble lord,' he declared almost as soon as Thomas had put his head around the door.

'He has agreed to guarantee the money?' Such elation coursed through Thomas's body that it was all he could do to prevent himself jumping for joy.

'Not quite.'

The elation subsided as quickly as it had arisen.

'No doubt that will come in time,' Brunel continued, 'but first he has asked to see you.'

'To see me?'

'Yes. He will meet you at White's tomorrow morning at eleven o'clock.'

'But why does he wish to see me?'

Brunel shrugged his shoulders. 'I understood that you and he were friends.'

'And so we are.'

'Well then.' He waved his hand dismissively. 'His coach will arrive to pick you up from outside this building at half past ten.'

As Thomas walked home afterwards he considered Lord Massey's response. Now that he came to think about it, it was entirely reasonable. If the earl was going to guarantee a loan, he merely wished to meet up with Thomas first and ascertain the purpose for which the money was to be used. Very well, Thomas had already explained that his uncle was not as accommodating as might be wished, and he would tell Lord Massey that in consequence of his uncle's inflexibility, he had decided to take charge of his own destiny. The loan was simply a necessary step on the way. Once he came into his inheritance the money would be promptly returned. Lord Massey was a man of action; he would surely approve of such a bold strategy.

Before Thomas was half way back to Anne's, however, a difficulty presented itself to him. He could not meet Lord Massey looking like this. He had been living rough for some weeks before meeting Anne and even now he had not been paying a great deal of attention to his appearance. At the very least he would have to get hold of some new clothes. But he did not have a great deal of money left – they had been rather profligate with the laudanum of late. The six guineas were nearly all spent.

Anne supplied him with the answer. She knew a shop in Whitechapel that sold second-hand clothes. Whitechapel was a good four miles away, Thomas pointed out. Perhaps there were other second-hand clothes shops nearer to hand. Anne was adamant. The clothes in this shop were of extremely good quality and they were sold at very affordable prices; the proprietor would certainly be able to provide Thomas with suitable attire; and it was essential that he make a good impression upon the noble lord.

Unfortunately, although Anne gave him clear directions, she could not accompany him to the shop, for, as she explained, there was a man whom she did not wish to meet living close by. The thought of this thug, whoever he was, made Thomas angry, but Anne reassured him that the man had not harmed her and as long as she stayed away from the area there was no chance that he would find her.

So he had set off for the shop himself and it had taken him a good part of the day to find it, and more than once he had mistaken the way. But find it he had, and on entering he had been surprised to find the business of the shop entirely in the care of a young Lascar or Malay, or perhaps a Hindoo, not a great deal older than himself. The fellow had very little to say for himself, though he did appear to speak excellent English, and Thomas had quickly concluded that his day had been wasted. Nevertheless, he explained that he was in need of clothes suitable for meeting an important gentleman at White's Club in Piccadilly. The fellow looked neither impressed nor unimpressed. He simply took Thomas's measurements then disappeared into the back of the shop for so long that Thomas was on the point of giving up, when he returned with a very decent looking kerseymere coat, nankeen waistcoat and buckskin breeches.

'If you would like to try them on, sir, there is a room just within,' the fellow said.

He showed Thomas a store room full of bundles of

clothes tied with string and left him to try on the clothes, all of which turned out to be a perfect fit. He suspected that they showed up the poor state of his boots but decided that those would have to do. The fellow named a very reasonable price and while he was tying the old clothes up into a bundle Thomas noticed a few items of jewellery lying in a wooden box upon the counter. Among them, was a small heart-shaped silver locket. He picked it up and held it out.

'How much is this?'

The fellow looked uncertain. 'A shilling?' he suggested.

Thomas frowned. No doubt it was a good price but it was more than he could afford.

'Sixpence,' he said.

'The fellow shook his head. 'It is worth more.'

'Sixpence or you can take back the clothes.' It was a dangerous ploy and Thomas thought for a moment that he had over-reached himself but finally the fellow nodded.

Thomas smiled as he walked out of the shop. He had got the best of the bargain, he told himself.

Anne was greatly impressed with his new clothes, telling him that he looked every inch the gentleman and that he might have no fears whatsoever about walking into White's, whatever White's might be and however grand its owners considered themselves. When he pulled the locket out of his pocket she was gratifyingly delighted, throwing her arms around him and kissing him repeatedly.

'No one's ever bought me nothing like this before,' she told him. She had run downstairs to Daisy to borrow a pair of scissors so that she could cut off a lock of Thomas's hair which she had placed carefully inside the locket before slipping the chain around her neck.

'I shall wear it next to my heart,' she told him. 'Always.'

At the time, Thomas had allowed his anxieties about the

forthcoming meeting to be entirely swept away by her enthusiasm for his new wardrobe. Now, however, as he sat in Lord Massey's carriage and the appointment with the noble lord drew nearer those anxieties reasserted themselves. It would be most unwise to mention Anne: Lord Massey would only ask questions that Thomas would find difficult to answer. The best policy was to keep it simple. He had decided he would not wait to attend the university; the money was necessary to support him in finding lodgings, paying fees, living expenses and so forth. And what of his plans after the university? Surely Lord Massey would not enquire about those, they were in the very distant future. But what if he did? Thomas would say that he was considering applying to the East India Company, though of course in reality he was considering no such thing. On the day of his father's funeral Thomas had made up his mind that he would not follow the path his mother expected him to take. He would not be a stranger to his family; he would not devote himself to acquiring wealth in some god-forsaken corner of the world; he was going to pursue the life of the mind instead. That was where both his strength and his inclination lay. But none of this he would convey to his lordship – indeed, the less said about the future, the better.

The coach drew up outside the entrance to White's and Thomas dismounted. He made his way up the steps, through the double doors, gave the fellow behind the desk his name and told him that he was here to meet Lord Massey.

'Ah yes,' the man replied. He was a tall fellow with something remarkably horsey about his countenance. 'We received a message from Lord Massey just a moment ago. He sends you his apologies. Apparently, he has been unaccountably delayed. But he requests that you await him in the morning room and he will endeavour to be here as soon as he possibly can.'

Thomas nodded. 'Thank you. The morning room?'

'On your left, sir. Would you care for some refreshment while you wait?'

'No, thank you.'

'Very good, sir.'

There were a handful of gentlemen in the morning room – an elderly man by himself reading a letter, two middle-aged red-faced men who looked like brothers and who seemed to be arguing about whether the Duke of Portland possessed the qualities necessary to lead a government. Two somewhat younger men had spread what looked like a set of architect's drawings out upon a table and were examining them closely. In the far corner of the room an enormously fat man seemed to be asleep. None of these individuals paid Thomas the slightest attention as he sat down at a table near the doorway and commenced the business of waiting patiently that he had studied so hard under the tutorship of Pyment and Brunel. The time passed slowly. A waiter came and asked Thomas whether there was anything he wanted. Thomas told him he was waiting for a friend and the waiter sallied forth instead towards the red-faced brothers who called enthusiastically for claret. Then he approached the younger men intent on their drawings but was waved away irritably.

A group of half a dozen gentlemen came in together talking animatedly. As they passed Thomas, one of them, a tall man with a long nose and eyes like a bird of prey, observed to his fellows that it was not a question of whether such a ministry was a good idea but rather whether it was even possible. 'All the talents, indeed,' he said, sniffing, and one of his companions chuckled. The political sphere was not one that had ever held much attraction for Thomas. He watched the new arrivals as they disputed with great earnestness. Every now and then one or other of their number would grow angry at the refusal of the others to see things from his point of view. They too called for claret and soon their voices were all being raised at the same time.

The hands of the great clock above the doorway moved with painful slowness as if there were some invisible force within the room holding back the passage of time. After half an hour Thomas rose from his seat and went to speak to the fellow at the door. Had Lord Massey given any indication as to how long he would be? Even as Thomas spoke the words he knew the question was futile. Lord Massy had only said that he had been unavoidably delayed and that he would get here as soon as he possibly could.

Thomas went back to the morning room and resumed his wait. The waiter came into the room twice and each time he glanced enquiringly in Thomas's direction but Thomas ignored him. He had almost no money left and however much a glass of wine might cost at White's, he was quite sure it was more than he could afford.

An hour passed with still no sign of Lord Massey. The two red-faced brothers had long gone. The three younger men had rolled up their map and walked past Thomas, talking about billiards. The political men were still arguing volubly, the speeches of some among them replete with condescension, while others thumped their fists upon the tables and others still looked on in cold disdain, each in accordance with political and social alliances that were no doubt known to everyone in the room except Thomas. He was not so much ignored by them as entirely invisible.

How much longer ought he to wait? That was the question. Of course, the answer was obvious. He would wait as long as was necessary, for he could not afford to do anything else. If he were to walk away now and Lord Massey were to arrive a few minutes later, it would be a complete disaster. However intolerable the delay, whatever ignominy he had to suffer in order to procure this loan, he would not leave the club without talking to Lord Massey.

Anne

I went with Thomas as far as Brunel's office to see him off and to give him courage. Afterwards, I walked back home, dreaming of the life we'd build together in the country. I could see that little cottage with the sun shining above it and flowers growing in the front garden. Thomas had read something that made me see it clear as day – *It is the first mild day of March, each minute sweeter than before, the red-breast signs from the tall larch that stands beside our door.* Though I wasn't sure what a larch was until Thomas told me.

Daisy was sitting on a step in the courtyard when I returned and I stopped to pass the time of day.

'They've been asking for you on the street, you know,' she said. 'What's happened to your little sister? That's what they keep saying I tell them you'll be back when you're ready.'

'I won't be back.' I didn't mean to come right out with it like that but I couldn't help myself. The picture of Thomas and me in our little cottage was still fresh in my mind.

'What, never?' I could tell from the look on her face she thought I was fooling myself.

'I've made a decision, Daisy. My life is changing.'

'What you going to live on then?'

I wanted so much to tell her about my plans. But I knew I had to keep quiet. The dream was so close now and I didn't intend to ruin things by blabbing. So I just said, 'I'm going to find a different way to live.'

'Well let me know when you do. I'll come and join you.'

There was bitterness in her words. She was disappointed in me for I no longer spent my days with her and she felt I'd cast her over. But I couldn't tell Daisy about my plans. She wouldn't have believed in them. No one would but Thomas and me.

I sat on the floor of my room and a great *urge* came over me to take some laudanum to make the time pass more quickly before Thomas's return. I resisted for as long as I could for we were almost out of money now and we had to be careful with what we had. But at last I allowed myself just *the smallest sip*. Then I sat back to allow it to do its work.

No sooner had it begun to take effect than there came a knock at the door which startled me greatly for no-one ever knocked on my door. The first thought in my mind was that John Dempsey had caught up with me and I grew so weak with terror I couldn't speak. But then the door was pushed open and a nipper of about ten years stuck his head inside.

'Are you Miss Anne Chambers?' he asked.

'What's it to you?'

'I got a message for you.'

'Go on then. What's your message?'

'Mr Thomas De Quincey asks you to meet him at the corner of Golden Square and Lower St James Street.'

This surprised me greatly for it was less than an hour since I'd parted with him. Surely he couldn't be back already? 'When does he want me to meet him?'

'Now. He is waiting for you at this very moment.'

I told myself it was a good sign. Lord Massey must have agreed just like that and perhaps the deal was already done. This could be the beginning of my new life. The boy disappeared without another word and I got to my feet a little groggily, grabbed my shawl and set off to meet my future.

It weren't far from where I lodged to Golden Square and as I drew near to the corner of Lower St James Street I looked for Thomas among the crowds of people strolling back and forth but I could see no sign of him.

I was standing, looking about in confusion when a lady and a gentleman came up to me. 'Miss Chambers?' the gentleman said.

'That's me.'

'My name is James Patterson. This lady is Mrs Sedgwick. We are friends of Thomas De Quincey.'

Right away I smelled a rat. What I should have done, of course, was turn and run but I was still slow-witted from the laudanum and, like a fool, I let them draw me into their trap. 'Where is he?' I asked. 'I'm supposed to be meeting him here.'

The woman smiled. 'We will take you to meet him, if that is what you wish. We have a carriage drawn up nearby.' She pointed a little way down the road to where a grand-looking carriage was drawn up with a fancy looking footman beside it.

I didn't like the look of this. 'Tell me where he is, first,' I demanded.

'You know where he is,' she said in a soothing kind of voice. 'He has gone to White's to meet with Lord Massey. But there is a great deal that we need to inform you about in relation to both your futures and it would be easier to discuss the details in the carriage where we can be both private and undisturbed.'

Then the two of them set off walking towards the carriage and after a moment's hesitation I followed, trotting along behind like an obedient child. I didn't know what else to do. As I drew nearer I saw a crown painted on the side of the carriage and I knew then that these were more of Thomas's aristocratic friends, whatever they chose to call themselves. So maybe I was doing the right thing by getting into the carriage with them. Maybe this was what it'd be like from now on.

The footman sprang to life as soon as he saw us, opening the carriage door smartly, and they *ushered* me in. Then the lady followed and the gentleman came after, shutting the door firmly behind him. A moment later we was all seated and the carriage was in motion.

It was Mrs Sedgwick who began. 'Now then, Anne,' she said, looking me up and down and smiling. 'I hope I may call you that?'

I nodded.

'I believe I can see why you have made such an impression upon our Thomas.'

It was meant to be a compliment, of course, but it only annoyed me. He wasn't her Thomas, he was mine. 'You know nothing about me,' I told her.

She wasn't the least bit put out by my tone. She just carried on smiling like a queen at a beggar. 'We know more about you than you imagine, Anne. Mr Brunel's man has been carrying out some enquiries on our behalf. We know how you earn your living, for example.'

She might as well have said, *we know you're a filthy whore*. But I weren't going to let her humiliate me. 'That's all in the past,' I said. 'Anyway, Thomas doesn't care. So why should you?'

'Thomas is a very principled young man,' she went on. 'Unfortunately, he can also be somewhat rash in his judgements at times. His family and friends have been deeply concerned about his welfare.'

'Is that right?' I said. 'Well, that's not what he told me.' She was starting to make me really angry now. I knew all about Thomas's family and it weren't a pretty story. Hadn't they kicked him out of home? Where would he be now if it weren't for me? Six feet under, that was where.

'What exactly *did* he tell you?' Mr Patterson asked.

'That his mother and his uncle threw him out and that they don't care a straw what becomes of him.'

'My dear girl,' Mrs Sedgwick said, 'I am a good friend of his mother's and I can assure you that she cares a great deal what happens to him.'

'Then why did she throw him out?'

'Thomas had some… difficulties. Did he tell you that?'

'He made a mistake, that's all.'

Mrs Sedgwick nodded. 'That is also my opinion, though not everyone will see it like that. However, the fact is, Thomas placed himself in a difficult situation – difficult for himself and difficult for his family.'

'So they turned their backs on him.'

'No. That is not what happened. His mother and his uncle put their heads together and they decided it would be best for him to keep his head down for a while. In the meantime he could travel, see more of the world, learn to stand on his own two feet.'

'Well now he *can* stand on his own two feet. So that's all right then, ain't it?'

Mrs Sedgwick sighed. 'I'm not so sure it is, Anne. Are you aware of how much money Thomas is trying to borrow?'

'Three hundred pounds.'

Mr Patterson leaned forward again. 'And how much of this has Thomas promised you?'

I felt the blood rush to my cheeks as surely as if he had hit me across the face. 'He ain't promised me nothing!' I told him.

'Really?' I could see he didn't believe me.

'He said he was going to look after me,' I told him. 'That's all.'

Mrs Sedgwick gave him a warning look and he sat back in his seat without saying any more. 'We must apologise if we seemed to be impugning your motives, Anne,' she went on. 'I have no doubt your friendship with Thomas is entirely disinterested.'

'I never asked him for a penny, if that's what you mean. The cottage in the country was all his idea.'

Her eyes opened wide and I knew right away I'd made a mistake. What did I have to go and mention that for?

'A cottage in the country?' She spoke very softly, as if she could hardly believe what she'd just heard.

'That's right.'

'You and he living together under the same roof?'

'I don't see what that's got to do with you.'

'Let me be entirely frank with you, Anne. Whatever Thomas believes, whatever you yourself believe, your friendship with him cannot continue.'

She was so sure of herself, so certain she knew what was best for Thomas, I wanted to scream at her to leave him alone but I was that upset I was struggling to breathe.

'If you really are a friend to Thomas, you must see that his association with a woman in your position can only bring harm to both of you. Doors are closed to you and they will always be closed because of what you have been, because of what you are. The question is, do you wish to bring shame and dishonour upon Thomas as well as yourself? Do you wish to bar him from respectable society as well?'

'It was his idea, not mine. I didn't ask for any of it.' I was crying now and I could hardly get the words out.

'We understand that, Anne, but Thomas is not like other people. He is a young man for whom ideas are as vivid and as tangible as reality, someone who dreams and does not always understand the practical necessities. It is up to those of us who are his friends to help him understand the difference.'

I didn't know what she was talking about any more and I didn't care. I was too busy sinking into a *swamp of misery and despair.*

'I must entreat you, Anne, for Thomas's sake, to be a true friend and not to meet with him again.'

'Not to meet with him again?' It was as though she had stuck a knife into my heart. 'How can I do that?'

'We can help you,' Mrs Sedgwick said. She nodded to Mr Patterson and he brought a leather purse out of his pocket. 'There are ten guineas in this purse,' he said, holding it out to me.

I knocked his hand away and the purse fell to the floor of the carriage. 'I don't want your money!'

'Don't be foolish, Anne,' Mrs Sedgwick told me. 'We mean to help you.'

'You can help me best by stopping this carriage and letting me out!'

'The money is only a part of what we offer you,' Mrs Sedgwick went on. 'Wait until you hear what else we have to say.'

I wanted to spit in her eye.

'I have a friend called Lady Dugland who lives in Kent, in the neighbourhood of Plumstead Manor. She has been a widow these past ten years and the principal concern of her life is serving her creator as best she can through charitable work. She is a high-minded individual and she has agreed to take you into her service on my recommendation. You will be given a good home and treated fairly. Naturally, you will be expected to earn your keep but your duties will be no more or less than any other maid up or down the country would expect to encounter. You will never have to return to the streets. You can begin anew and put all this behind you.'

Even as she was saying this, I glanced out of the window and saw that we was approaching London Bridge. I felt myself beginning to panic and I thought about opening the door and flinging myself out. Mr Patterson must have seen me for he put out a hand to bar the door. 'Do not be foolish, Anne,' he said. 'You do not need to add injury to your list of difficulties.'

'What do you say, Anne?' Mrs Sedgwick asked me.

'I don't want to go into service,' I told her, 'and I don't want to put this behind me.'

'Naturally,' she said. 'It has been an adventure for you, a wonderful adventure, but it is over now.'

'I love him!'

'If that is true, then you will not want to hurt him.'

'Of course I don't want to hurt him!'

'But if you cling to him that is exactly what you will do. You will ruin him, Anne. Is that any way to treat the man that you love?'

Now I could see the dark brown river out of the carriage window, and the boats that plied their trade back and forth. I thought of the country I'd imagined on the wall of Mrs Dempsey's house and I understood then that this was the only kingdom I would ever own.

'You must give him up, Anne. For Thomas's sake, you must let him go free.'

Mr Patterson bent down then and picked up the purse. He held it out to me once more.

'Take it, Anne,' Mrs Sedgwick urged. 'Recognise your true station in life and be grateful that you have been offered a second chance.'

Tuah

I awoke in the night from a dream in which I was a child once more, hiding behind the rocks while the Dutch slavers sat around their fire, laughing and eating and taking it in turns to rape little Tarjong. Afterwards, I sat up in bed with my heart thudding and the memory still vivid in my mind. Gradually, however, the images faded, the beating of my heart slowed, and as I sat there, recovering my composure and wondering how much of the night remained to me, I became aware that there was a peculiar quality to the darkness in the room. It seemed to be changeable, at some moments a little less dense, at some moments a little more so: even *darkness which may be felt.*

I realised that this unnatural quality, whatever it was, was being caused by something outside the house, rather than inside. So I rose from my bed, shivering slightly, and pulled back the curtains. My room was at the back of the house but I could immediately tell from the red glow in the sky and the showers of sparks flying past the rooftops that one of the buildings on the street must be on fire. I called out for Archie and quickly began pulling on my clothes. When I went out into the hallway, he was emerging from his bedroom, doing up his coat.

'Dempsey's house is ablaze,' he told me.

We ran downstairs and out of the house. Other residents were coming out of their houses too and shouts were being raised for water. It was clear that the fire was already well advanced and that the flames were at their worst towards the top of the house. Archie immediately sent me back indoors for buckets and I ran around inside the house a little frantically, barking my shins against objects in the dark before locating two good buckets and rejecting one with a broken handle.

When I went outside again the crowd had swollen. Many of them were simply standing about, watching helplessly, but some of the younger men had begun to organise a human chain to pass buckets of water from hand to hand. When I ran over to offer my assistance I saw that the water was being thrown on the buildings on either side, rather than on the house that was in flames. Hope of saving that had already been abandoned.

As I took my place in the chain, I looked around for any sign of Archie but he was nowhere to be seen. Then a cry went up from the crowd, a mixture of excitement and terror. A figure had been seen at one of the top storey windows. Like everyone else, I craned my neck upwards and for a brief instant saw, silhouetted against the flames, the outline of a man. Very likely it was John Dempsey and if so then I had little reason to feel kindly disposed towards him. Nonetheless, the prospect of being trapped at the top of that building with the flames rapidly advancing towards you was one that made me pity him.

One man had fetched a hammer and he now began trying to break open the front door but it had obviously been well built and well locked too for despite strenuous efforts he was making little headway. Another individual was more successful breaking in the windows but when he attempted to clamber inside, the heat and the smoke were too much for him.

Archie appeared at my side just then. 'Let's try round the back of the house. It may be easier there,' he suggested. It seemed to me that any attempt at rescue was doomed to failure but it was not my policy to question Archie so I left the chain and followed him down the street to the alley that ran along the backs of the houses.

We easily got into the yard behind the house but it was difficult to approach the house more closely for the area was full of thick black smoke. Archie tied his neckerchief across his face and I did the same. Then we advanced towards the back door, trying to breathe as evenly as possible. Naturally, the door was locked but it was nothing like the barrier that the front door had presented. A few good kicks and it flew open.

The heat was considerable as we stepped inside, like putting one's head inside an oven, but it was the smoke and the darkness that were our chief obstacles. Almost immediately I found I had completely lost sight of Archie. I called out to him and he called back.

'I have found the stairs,' he said when I had located him once more. 'I am going to see if it is possible to reach the upper rooms.'

I wanted to object that if the way were at all passable anyone upstairs would already have come down but I was prevented from speaking by a fit of coughing. When I had recovered Archie was already gone. I stumbled forwards until I, too, had located the stairs. Then I began gingerly to make my way upwards.

As I reached the first landing, the stairwell grew noticeably brighter and I could make out Archie's figure just a little way ahead of me. The reason for the improvement in visibility was of course that the rooms above the ground floor were ablaze and the blast of heat on my face felt like a powerful warning. *And they shall be afraid: pangs and sorrows shall take hold of them; they shall be in pain as a woman that travaileth: they shall be amazed one at another; their faces shall be as flames.*

We should not be in this place, I was certain of it. This whole venture was madness. We could not hope to rescue Dempsey and we would meet our deaths in the attempt.

I determined to take hold of Archie and reason with him but there came a tearing sound and suddenly burning timbers were raining down upon us. One of them struck me on the shoulder with enough force to knock me off my feet. I lay on the floor for a moment, stupefied, then a sense of the peril of my position forced me to struggle to my feet. The whole of my right side hurt but when I flexed my arm it did not seem to be broken. I looked around for Archie and saw him lying on the floor just ahead of me, pinned to the ground by a smouldering beam.

I stumbled forwards and pulled the beam off Archie, burning my hands in the process. Then I bent over him and called his name. At first it seemed to me that he might be dead and my courage almost failed me but then he gave a groan. I shook him and called his name again and he mumbled something incoherent in reply. Somehow I got him to his feet and began dragging him down the stairs. Getting down the stairs without the pair of us tumbling headlong was a slow and painful process and though Archie was not a heavy man he was almost more than I could manage. All the time I feared that the whole building would fall down upon us.

My eyes must have adjusted to the gloom, or perhaps the flames from above had grown stronger. Either way, I found it easier to see where I was going and when we finally reached the foot of the stairs I blundered my way to the door, dragging Archie behind me. At last we were outside again. The air in the back yard felt fresh compared to what we had endured inside the house. Archie was moaning with pain and asking to be allowed to lie down upon the ground but I would not let him rest until we were well clear of the building.

'That was madness,' I told him, when we were both finally sitting down in the alley with our backs against the wall. 'We were both very nearly killed'

'It is thanks to you that we were not,' he admitted.

I was pleased that he acknowledged this but still irritated at the foolhardiness of the whole endeavour. 'But why sally forth into a burning building in the first place?' I demanded.

He turned to look at me, his face soot-streaked and bloody. 'Because, despite the joke nature has played upon me, I would be a man, like any other man.'

So that was it. He wished to prove himself, and in the process he might have killed us both. I stood up and reached out my hand. 'Any other man would have seen that such an attempt was folly,' I said, pulling him to his feet. 'Come on, let us go back to the shop and discover how seriously we have hurt ourselves.'

We limped back down the alleyway and out into the street once more. The crowd was still gathered where we left them and the top storey of Dempsey's house was entirely engulfed by flames. No one would come out of there alive now, I thought to myself. Water was still being thrown onto the walls of the adjoining buildings but otherwise the conflagration was simply a public spectacle. I would not have been surprised to find someone selling pies or chestnuts.

I was still supporting Archie and by now my right

shoulder and arm were beginning to throb insistently. As we drew nearer to the shop I began to imagine how pleasant it would be to lie down upon my bed and surrender to sleep. Once I had done so, even if the entire street were to burn to the ground around me, I should not stir.

At that moment I became aware that what had seemed no more than just a denser pool of darkness within the shadows ahead of me was in fact a person, seated on the ground and just as this truth dawned upon me, the individual in question shoved something out that tangled in Archie's legs and brought first him and then me tumbling heavily to the ground.

It was a crutch. I realised this at the same moment that I hit the ground and with that realisation came an instantaneous understanding of who the seated figure was: the man I had seen watching the shop when I had returned home in the fog, the same one whom Archie had once left for dead so many months earlier. It was clear, moreover, that he was intent on repaying the compliment, for despite his missing leg he was now crouched over Archie and I glimpsed the blade of a knife flash in his hand. I yelled and launched myself towards him but before I could reach him something very hard hit me on the back of my head and I descended into blackness.

I returned to wakefulness to find that I was being rudely shaken by a big, burly fellow with a huge black beard who was leaning over me and saying something I could not understand. Convinced that this was the man who had hit me on the head I lunged at him but he easily caught my arm. Then another, equally burly fellow appeared and laid hands upon me so that between them they held me pinned to the ground.

'Now listen to me, you murdering bastard,' the first man

said. 'You are under arrest and if you put up any further resistance it will not go well with you. Do you understand?'

'What am I under arrest for?'

'You know perfectly well. Now shut your mouth and get to your feet.'

'Where is Mr McKerras?' I demanded but my question was cut short as I was dragged to my feet and both my arms wrenched up behind my back so that I cried out in pain.

I looked about for Archie but there was no sign of him. A small crowd of onlookers was standing watching my humiliation, their faces lit up by the flickering light of the flames that were still busily consuming Dempsey's house, but of Archie I could see no sign.

'You have made a mistake!' I shouted. 'Mr McKerras was set upon by a man who was lying in wait for him.'

'We know who set upon him,' the bearded fellow told me.

'I was trying to protect him when someone hit me on the head.'

'You can tell all that to the magistrate.'

'I want to know what has happened to Mr McKerras,' I insisted.

The bearded fellow forced my arm even further up my back so that I screamed in agony. 'Shut it!' he said. 'Or else I'll break your fucking arm. Now come on.'

As they were dragging me away, I suddenly glimpsed the face of Mr Li among the bystanders. 'Mr Li!' I shouted. 'Find Mr Duncan, Paternoster Row. Tell him what has happened, I beg you.'

But Mr Li only stared back impassively, his face betraying not the slightest hint of emotion. Then we had left the crowd behind us and I was dragged away, still vainly protesting my innocence

Thomas

It was two full hours before Thomas finally accepted that Lord Massey was not going to appear and neither was any word going to be received from him. He felt angry, confused and near to despair. Had he been the victim of some kind of prank? It seemed unthinkable. Had something happened to Lord Massey of such import he had entirely forgotten his appointment? Had he been struck down with illness or injury? Thomas had plenty of time to consider each of these options as he sat in the morning room, studiously avoiding the supercilious looks of the waiters and the occasional curious glance from one of the regular patrons, but he could come to no fixed conclusions beyond that he had in some way been treated somewhat shabbily.

At the desk in the lobby he asked for a sheet of notepaper and wrote the date, then considered for some time before adding, 'I was sorry not to see you today.' He thought a great deal about adding something more, something that might convey the urgency of his situation and the insult he had received, but in the end he merely signed his name and handed the note over to the clerk.

As he walked unhappily back towards Oxford Street, he considered his options. He only had enough money left for a few more days. A week at the most. It was essential, therefore, that Brunel advance him something, no matter how small. He would go to see the fellow this very afternoon. No, that would not be a good idea. He needed to recover his composure first, for it was imperative that he adopt the right tone; were he to visit Brunel now, he would be disadvantaged for he would be unable to prevent himself from seeming daunted by Lord Massey's absence. He must treat the whole thing as if it were of no consequence whatsoever. Lord Massey was a busy man. He was unable to keep his appointment for one reason or another; there was nothing to be read into this, no personal slight, no lessening of regard. There would be another appointment shortly. This was what his manner should proclaim. In the meantime he had need of a small sum to defray his current expenses. It was entirely reasonable; it was entirely businesslike.

Anne would be disappointed. Of course she would. Anne did not understand what the lives of people like Lord Massey were like, and she would see this as a deliberate insult. It was important that Thomas let her know he did not consider it in that light at all; we are each of us at the mercy of circumstance, that is all, he would tell her. Lord Massey would be back in touch and in the meantime Thomas would ask Brunel for something to tide them over. Above all, he did not want Anne going out on the street again. The very thought of it made him shudder.

He would not tell Anne that he had received no word from Lord Massey. He decided this as he turned into the court where she had her room. He would say only that a note was delivered to the club explaining that Lord Massey had been unavoidably delayed for reasons of business but that he would be in contact with Brunel to arrange another meeting very shortly. Would it be better to say the delay was occasioned by family reasons? No, that would suggest an accident or an illness, perhaps even a death, which might prove difficult if by any chance Lord Massey and Anne should ever converse…

It was not likely that they would converse, of course, but if Lord Massey were really to take an interest in Thomas's affairs, then it was within the realm of possibility. So it had to be taken into account. Nevertheless, it was hard to conjure up a mental picture in which Lord Massey and Anne addressed each other as equals. Best not to think about it. Thomas wiped the slate of his imagination clean as he ascended the stairs. The door of Anne's room was unlocked, as usual, and he pushed it open. The room was empty. Thomas felt at once both relieved that he did not have to explain what had happened to Anne and disappointed that he had been deprived of her sympathy. He sat down with his back against the wall and prepared to wait for her return but after only a few minutes he got to his feet again and rummaged around in a pile of clothes in the corner until he discovered the bottle of laudanum. There was less in it than he had expected, almost nothing really – almost but not quite. He put the bottle to his mouth, threw back his head and waited as every last drop of the precious liquid trickled down his throat. Then he sat down again and waited for it to take effect.

The trick with laudanum, Thomas had discovered, was to do two contradictory things at the same time. First, he must empty his mind of all thought; even the thought of thought must be ignored. Simultaneously he must concentrate as hard as he possibly could, focusing all his mental power in one point, as if he were sending forth a beam of light from the very centre of his mind. It helped to stay perfectly still and fix his gaze upon a single spot in the room. In time the enchantment would begin to steal over him, altering the contours of the room subtly and indefinably. He would begin to see, behind the filthy, fly-blown plaster, the flickering characters of the magical language appear; the alphabet of desire would reveal itself to him bit by bit and then the squalor of his surroundings would be of no consequence.

But today there was simply not enough laudanum. No matter how thoroughly he emptied his mind, no matter how determined his concentration, the magic would not answer to him, and although he was teased by faint glimpses of its secrets, hints and promises of its potency, all were withdrawn as quickly as they were offered.

Exasperated with this day that had delivered nothing but disappointment, Thomas got to his feet again. He would go in search of Anne. It was her company that he craved most of all. She would be with her friend Daisy, no doubt. Thomas tolerated Daisy but he did not really like her. There was something about her of which he instinctively disapproved, though he could not quite put his finger upon what it was. He would not say as much to Anne of course for Daisy was Anne's only friend. Perhaps it was that beneath the dismissive way she talked about her customers, she seemed not altogether unhappy in her work. No, it was wicked of him to think this! She was an unfortunate victim of circumstances, like Anne. But she was more hard-edged, nonetheless, coarser-grained.

Thomas knocked upon the door of Daisy's room and when he heard her summons, he pushed it open and stepped inside. Daisy and another young woman whom Thomas had not seen before were sitting on the floor on opposite sides of the room, smoking clay pipes. A bottle of gin stood open between them. They gazed at him with bleary-eyed curiosity, as if waiting for him to begin juggling, or eating fire.

'I was looking for Anne,' he said.

'Well she ain't here, that's for certain,' Daisy said.

'No. I don't suppose you would have any idea where I might find her?'

The mouth of Daisy's companion had opened and her eyes were wide with astonishment. 'Is this Anne's fellow?' she asked and when Daisy nodded she added, 'Don't he talk fancy for such a little 'un?'

Daisy smiled at her and then turned back to Thomas. 'No idea,' she said. 'I seen her going up to her room a couple of hours ago, maybe more.'

'Well she's not there now.'

'Gone to take the air, I expect. Mind you…' she paused.

'What?'

'Well, it don't mean nothing, I expect, but she did tell me as how she had come to a decision.'

'A decision about what?'

'Her life was changing,' she said. 'Probably just had a little sip too much of sauce.'

'Thank you.'

'You're very welcome. This here, this is Alice. Ally between friends.'

'I'm very pleased to meet you.'

'Likewise I'm sure.'

'Why don't you sit down and have a drink?' Daisy suggested. 'I'm sure Anne will be back soon.'

'That's very kind but I think I'll take a stroll down Oxford Street.'

'Good idea. Only don't go getting tempted by any pretty face, now.'

The vulgarity of this remark filled Thomas with indignation and his feelings must have been written across his face for the two women laughed out loud.

'Only joking, Thomas,' Daisy said.

'I see. Good day, then.'

Thomas backed out of the room, conscious that he had been made to look a fool.

He walked from one end of Oxford Street to the other and back again, peering into every doorway, searching the faces in every crowd. He dismissed what Daisy had told him about the decision that Anne had come to; she surely had been talking about their plan to go to the Lakes together once Thomas had secured the loan; what he feared was that she had lost faith in his ability to raise money and gone back to her trade. The thought of this was like a physical pain. But he told himself that right now she was probably back in her room waiting for him and he hurried back as quickly as he could, only to find that the room was still empty.

He was ravenously hungry but he could not bear the prospect of eating by himself. Instead, he settled down on the floor of the room and tried to occupy his mind by reading Thucydides but he could not concentrate upon the text. As dusk drew on he could not help the feeling growing within him that something calamitous had taken place: first Lord Massey had failed to appear and now Anne was missing. Could the two events be connected? When night came on, Thomas went out once more and walked the length of Oxford Street without success. He bought a pie and brought it back to the room. It tasted of dust and ashes.

Anne

Plumstead Common seemed to me as *dismal* a place as I'd ever set eyes on. Nothing but scrubby old heathland on all sides, then Mrs Dugland's house looming up out of the dusk like a great ship at anchor. The very sight of it was enough to fill my heart with dread.

For the last hour of the journey none of us had spoken. Many more times since we'd crossed London Bridge I'd considered opening the door of the carriage and throwing myself out. What stopped me every time was Mrs Sedgwick's warning: 'You will ruin him, Anne. Is that any way to treat the man that you love? For Thomas's sake you must let him go free.'

Mrs Dugland herself was the nearest thing I'd ever seen to a skeleton walking. She looked me up and down with two little black eyes like buttons when Mrs Sedgwick introduced us – only, as I guessed, she weren't Mrs Sedgwick at all because I heard Mrs Dugland call her your ladyship when we first arrived. But that was all I heard because they very quickly bundled me into a room full of so much furniture and so many ornaments there was scarcely room for a body to breathe while the three of them went off to another part of the house to discuss my future.

I sat on the chair where they put me, as stiff as if I was made of stone. I hadn't even the strength to weep. All my thoughts was on Thomas. I kept imagining him coming back to the room and finding me gone. I could see his face lost and *bewildered*, like when I'd first found him on Oxford Street. He would think I'd run out on him. Worse than that, he'd think I'd stopped believing in him. He'd come to the conclusion he'd misjudged me all the time and I was never the girl he'd imagined me to be. And maybe I weren't, or else what was I doing here?

I would never see him again, that was what I kept telling myself. From now until the end of the world Thomas and me would be *sundered* and he'd never learn the truth about me.

I felt worse even than when I'd come back from Mrs Nancy's and understood for the first time that no-one in the house cared a brass farthing about me. When I'd understood that Suzette and Charlie and Cecille and Muriel and Estelle and even Jeremiah had all expected me to die, I'd swallowed down that knowledge like I was eating cold porridge. They'd accepted my death, mourned my passing and gone about their business in the blink of an eye. Anne? Oh yes, she used to work here for a bit but she's gone now. Shame, really but it can't be helped. That's what they'd have said if anyone had asked after me, but of course no one would have asked. So I'd come to terms with my *insignificance* and I had no further *expectations*. I would do my job and Mrs Dempsey would provide my board.

Then Thomas had come along, with his belief in a finer world and his poetry and his old Greeks, looking at me like I was a proper person, talking to me like I was a lady. The memory of those looks he gave me made me ache all over with sadness. When his eye fell upon me he did not see a street girl. I had to tell him that was what I did, for God's sake! He looked at me and saw a person.

And he loved me. He actually loved me. No one will ever believe that but it's true. He knew what I was and he loved me; it was obvious even from the way he touched me, as if I was the most *delicate* of creatures. Mrs Sedgwick or whatever her bloody name is, she just thought I was a greedy little trollop who'd got her claws into Thomas. I was a problem to be solved in the easiest and the quickest way possible, a mistake Thomas had made what his friends had got to clear up. But I weren't a mistake to Thomas.

I sat on the chair, thinking of what I'd lost and I wished I'd died on Mrs Nancy's table. I wished all the blood had run out of me in a great dark puddle on the floor and left me without sense or feeling. I wished I'd slipped away into the darkness where there ain't no more sorrow, no more pain and no more love.

After half an hour I heard the front door close and the carriage drove away. Then Mrs Dugland came into the room. Beside her was a great big woman with a face so red and raw it looked like she'd been scalded, and a pair of shoulders as broad as a man's. I got to my feet and stood there meekly, waiting to hear what would happen next, though in my heart I didn't care if they'd made a decision to have me hanged. I would have gladly tied the noose myself.

'Mrs Sedgwick has told me all about your background, Anne,' Mrs Dugland began, speaking very quiet but in a voice hard as iron. 'I hope you understand how fortunate you are to have been given this opportunity to start anew.'

'Yes, ma'am.'

'And I hope you are truly grateful.'

'I am, ma'am.'

'We shall see. It is deeds that matter here, Anne, not

words. If you carry out your duties faithfully then you will demonstrate your gratitude. Now I have given Dora the responsibility for your training so you will do exactly as she tells you at all times.'

'Yes, ma'am.'

'Our Lord extends his mercy even to the most wicked of sinners, Anne, but they must be prepared to do their part in return.'

'Yes, ma'am. I shall do my part'

'Very well. You may go.'

Dora led me up several flights of stairs to a tiny room not much bigger than a cupboard at the very top of the house. It was just like at Mrs Dempsey's all over again except that in this room there was two beds and two washstands, two chamber pots and two small tables, with a copy of the Bible on each one. So it seemed I was to have company.

On one of the beds lay a plain black dress which Dora told me to put on, and while she stood and watched, I took off the blue dress I'd brought from Mrs Dempsey's. She put out her hand and took it away. Then her eyes fell upon Thomas's locket. 'What's that?' she demanded

'Only a lock of my mother's hair,' I told her. 'It's all I've got left of her.'

She nodded and I made sure not to let the relief show on my face. Then I pulled the coarse black dress on over my head and down the stairs we went once more.

I hadn't eaten a thing since that morning and I was weak with hunger but I weren't going to ask for so much as a crust of bread. I knew how any request would be received and I weren't going to give them the satisfaction of scolding me. Instead, I just ignored the rumbling in my stomach and kept my mouth firmly closed while I was led to a big laundry room and set to work washing clothes in a wooden tub with a dolly stick.

This ain't so hard, I told myself. You know all about washing clothes and at least there's plenty of soap this time and no soaking the dirty things in piss, neither. Dora stood and watched me until she was satisfied I could be trusted to get on with the job. Then she went away and left me to work my way through a mountain of dirty clothes.

The minute I'd finished, Dora appeared again and I realised she must have been spying on me from somewhere. She put me mopping the hallway. After that I had to beat a carpet and polish the silver until tea-time. There was never a moment when I weren't busy.

I took my meal by myself in a room at the back of the house. A bowl of mutton soup and a piece of bread and lard. It weren't much but I was used to surviving on what the sailors called short rations, so I ate it up and didn't complain. I could hear the other servants in the kitchen having theirs and from time to time I caught glimpses of them but no one spoke to me that afternoon or even so much as gave me a nod, and I took no notice of them in return.

After everyone had eaten and gone about their business, I was led into the main kitchen and told to wash the pots and pans. Then there was the kitchen floor and the pantry floor to be swept and mopped, the coal scuttles to be filled and a great basket of kindling to be brought in from the shed outside so that it would be ready for the morning. When that was all done Dora *presented* me with a pile of mending and stood and watched me tackle it.

She weren't greatly impressed with my needlework and I can't say I blame her. After a while, she took away the finer articles, leaving me with a selection of socks, aprons and overskirts. That should be enough to keep you busy until bedtime, she declared. Finally, when the clock struck ten, she told me I could go to my room, but I should be sure to wash myself thoroughly and say my prayers, thanking God in his *infinite mercy* for delivering me to a safe harbour. She spoke as though I had no more understanding than a little child.

I didn't care how she behaved towards me. I had other things to think about. My mind was full of pictures: Thomas kissing my fingers one by one, Thomas putting out his hand and stroking my cheek, Thomas sitting on the other side of the room with his knees drawn up to his chest, looking at me like he wanted to learn every detail of my face. This was my pain but also my *consolation*.

When I went into to the bedroom I found a young girl already there, putting on her nightdress.

'Hello,' I said, 'I'm Anne.'

She looked down at the ground.

'Don't you want to tell me your name?'

'Betty,' she whispered. Then she turned her back on me and knelt down beside her bed to pray. I got undressed and splashed a bit of water on my face. I didn't bother with the prayers. God never had much time for me so I didn't see why I should get down on my knees before him. Besides, there weren't much to thank him for right now except a bowl of soup and a lot of housework.

I climbed into bed and hugged my knees against the cold. Betty took a long time finishing her prayers. Then she blew out the candle and climbed into the other bed.

'How long you been here?' I asked.

She said nothing.

'Ain't you going to talk to me, then?'

Not a word.

'Please yourself.' She didn't look very entertaining company, anyway. I turned over and tried to still my thoughts but even sleep didn't want to be my friend and it was a very long time before the darkness claimed me.

I woke to the most terrible screaming I've ever heard in my life. It was like someone was being murdered and it was right beside me. I sat up in the bed with my heart hammering, trying to work out where the hell I was but the screaming went on and on so that I couldn't think properly. It was as though I'd died and gone to hell. At last I remembered that I was a servant in a house in Kent and I realised that the noise must be coming from the girl in the next bed.

Suddenly the door burst open and in walked Dora with a candle in her hand. The screaming stopped and in the candle light I could see Betty sitting up in bed with her eyes wide open but even as Dora crossed the room, she took another breath and began to scream anew, so piercingly I put my hands to my ears to block out the sound. Dora stopped in front of Betty's bed, drew back her hand and slapped the girl hard across the face. Instantly, the screaming stopped. Betty shook herself like an animal and then the sense came back into her eyes and she hung her head.

Dora looked at me. 'If it happens again, you know what to do. Now lie down and go back to sleep, both of you.' Then she turned and walked out of the room.

Betty whimpered for a while before she went back to sleep. I lay there a little longer until I, too, drifted off. In the morning when we was woken by Dora, I saw the mark of her hand on Betty's cheek but the incident was not spoken of by anyone.

Over the next couple of days I learned the names of the other servants and I came to see that there was something wrong with every one of them. There was Mrs Lavender, the cook, who had one leg a good deal shorter than the other and limped about the kitchen most clumsily. She was a bitter woman, always complaining about something. The very first time she had occasion to speak to me she told me that she knew very well what kind of girl I was and if she had her way I'd be locked up in prison, not working alongside decent people.

Then there was a boy called George who had very bad skin and couldn't speak proper on account of being half deaf. Dora referred to him as the footman, though as far as I could see he spent most of his time in the stable looking after the horse so that he had hay seed in his hair and smelled like a horse himself.

There was also an elderly Irishman called Reilly who did the gardening and split logs for the fire. He didn't live in but took his meals with the household. He spoke to me from time to time though I could never understand a word he said. I couldn't see what was wrong with him at first but then one afternoon when I was coming in from the wood store with a pile of kindling I saw him standing in the middle of the lawn, without his shirt on. I stopped in surprise and saw he was bare-foot too. His boots, his shirt and his jacket was all in a neat pile on the ground beside him and as I watched, he began to unlace his breeches. Suddenly Dora come marching across the lawn, calling out his name.

'Put your clothes back on this minute!'

Reilly looked at her. Then he looked down at his clothes as if surprised to find them on the ground beside him. Dora stood there with her hands on her hips and waited until he did as he was told.

We was all shoddy goods, the lot of us, badly made or else spoilt in some way. No doubt there was some great secret about Dora, too, though I never got to the bottom of it. I didn't mind being counted among them. Who was I to give myself airs and graces? But why couldn't we all have been a bit more cheerful? I'd hazard a guess that there was more joy to be found in a prison cell than in that house. The very air in the place stank of shame and defeat. So much so that Dora didn't even need to *rebuke* us. We was always ready and willing to *reproach* ourselves.

I didn't see much of Mrs Dugland but every now and then I caught a glimpse of her watching me work from some hiding place. On the Sunday we was all summoned to the drawing room where she made us stand together while she led a kind of service, reading out of a big black bible. She chose the story of the prodigal son. I'd heard it before in church but I'd never liked it because it just didn't seem fair how the other brother was treated. But that's God for you – he has his golden boys and girls. Then she read out a lot of prayers and the rest of us mumbled our way through them. I could feel her eyes on me all the time and I kept my lips moving even though I weren't sure of the words. Lord protect us, lord guard us, lord deliver us from temptation – too bleeding late for that now.

This was what my life had become and I knew I must get used to it. I began to lock away my thoughts and give myself completely to the tasks that was put in front of me. When Betty woke up screaming again the following week, I stumbled across to her bed and shook her awake. It took a little longer than a slap but it worked in the end. When Mrs Lavender complained that I hadn't washed the dishes properly I told her I was very sorry and washed them all over again. If I had reason to say anything to George, I spoke slowly and clearly and looked him right in the eye, like I was dealing with a half-wild dog. And if Dora gave me an order I carried it out promptly and to the letter, making sure she had no reason for complaint.

None of this was because I was grateful to Our Lord for

extending his mercy to me, or to Mrs Dugland for giving me a second chance, but only because I couldn't see no other road before me. Like all the rest of Mrs Dugland's sorry household, I trod the path of shame because it was the only path there was. I could have walked back to London, I suppose, but it was a long way and I was too deep in misery to consider such a plan.

And then one day my saviour did appear. Only he weren't the one from Mrs Dugland's bible. I was in the kitchen mashing turnips. Mrs Lavender made a kind of pudding out of dried peas, turnips and eggs, only to tell the truth it were mostly turnips, so there was lots of them to be mashed. I was staring out of the window, thinking to myself that there weren't really that much difference between Mrs Dempsey and Mrs Dugland – both of them put me in an attic room, both made me work for my keep, and both made themselves out to be finer creatures than they really was – when a cart pulled up outside. The driver, who was all muffled up in a great coat and scarf and a battered three-cornered hat, jumped down and rapped on the back door.

'Well, get off your backside, girl, and see who that is!' Mrs Lavender said.

So I went and opened the back door and who should be standing there, as large as life but my father's old drinking mate. He'd gone downhill since I last saw him. His nose was so red and angry it looked like it might burst into flames at any moment and his hair had turned grey at the sides. But it was the same old Hawk and, as if to prove it, he spat a great gob on the path beside his feet. I stepped outside and pulled the door nearly shut behind me.

'Hawk!' I said, keeping my voice as low as I could. 'Is it really you?'

He frowned. 'Do I know you?'

'Course you bloody well know me. It's Anne.'

'Anne? Well, I'll be damned. You've grown up.'

I was tempted to point out that time had left its mark on him as well and it hadn't been kind but I wanted Hawk on my side. Something inside me was suddenly coming back to life. Maybe all my dreams was *shattered*. Maybe I didn't know what to do with myself any more. But the arrival of Hawk out of the blue seemed like a sign that I couldn't just ignore. Someone was stretching out a hand to me in the darkness and I knew I'd be a fool not to take hold of it.

'What are you doing here?' I asked.

'Selling baskets. Mending pans. Sharpening knives. Perhaps you'd be so good as to recommend me to the lady of the house.'

'I will,' I said, 'but in return I need you to do something for me.'

He looked at me warily. 'What sort of thing?'

'Give me a lift to London.'

'I ain't going to London.'

'I'll make it worth your while.'

'You ain't got the money.'

'Three guineas.'

That surprised him. 'You've got three guineas?'

'Yes I have. Come back again tonight at eleven o'clock. Wait down the road for me under that tree.'

'I don't know...'

'Four guineas, Hawk.'

The door opened behind me and Dora appeared. 'Who is this man and what does he want?' she demanded.

Hawk gave his most winning smile. 'I have a selection of baskets for sale, madam. All kinds and all sizes. Whatever you might want to store, I have a basket to suit.'

'We don't want any baskets. Good day!'

'Also pans at very good prices.'

'I said good day. Anne, return to the kitchen immediately.'

I gave Hawk one last pleading look and went back to the turnips.

Tuah

No one would listen to my protests. Whenever I tried to speak my arm was twisted behind my back or I was hit around the face with the back of a gloved hand and threatened with worse.

They took me to the House of Detention in Clerkenwell where I was locked in a small, dark room with just one barred window at the very top of the wall, a straw mattress for me to lie upon and a bucket for me to shit and piss in. I felt as though I had gone back in time to the days and nights I spent locked in the hold of the slavers' ship. Then, however, I had been confined with other souls and there was a kind of miserable consolation about that. In the House Of Detention – the *Nask*, I heard it called, an evil sounding word if ever there was one – I was solitary. There were plenty of other inmates of course and from time to time I would hear their cries, but I was kept separate from them. This was a personal hell into which I had been plunged and I would have to bear it alone. A phrase came to me from the captain's bible and I repeated it again and again to myself as I sat on the straw, gazing up at the window and the tiny glimpse it provided of the outside world. *Turn thee unto me, and have mercy upon me; for I am desolate and afflicted.*

I did not know whether Archie was alive or dead. If he was dead, I would surely hang for his murder unless Mr Duncan could save me. But every time I thought about my desperate appeal to Mr Li, I saw his face staring back at me, utterly impassive. There was absolutely no reason why he should involve himself in my misfortune. He was a Chinaman who ran an opium den and had no doubt survived this long by staying out of trouble, but the authorities would have no hesitation in crushing him beneath their heel if he caused them difficulties. I reminded myself, also, that he had a son. So he had much to lose – not just his own security but that of his family. I told myself all this and yet I could not help but cling on to the tiny thread of hope that he might have sought out Mr Duncan on my account.

The hours passed slowly. The chink of light grew dull and then dark. A warder unlocked the door to my cell, put a plate with some bread and a mug of ale upon the floor, then retreated once more without a word. The bread was as hard as a stone and I was obliged to soak it in the ale before I could eat it.

Night descended and with it utter darkness. Now the noises of the prison seemed both louder and more miserable. I heard the sound of sobbing and of vomiting and of one man chanting over and over again, 'I call upon Satan, lord of the earth. I call upon Beelzebub and all the princes of hell. I call upon the powers of darkness and of death,' before footsteps ran down the passage, a door was unlocked and his litany was cut short with a cry of pain.

The tiny opening at the top of my cell was growing light once more before I finally fell into a shallow kind of sleep but even that was filled with scenes from the blazing house and the crippled assassin waiting in the darkness.

I was woken by the warder bringing a bowl of porridge which was thin and cold but which I ate gratefully nonetheless. After that I sat with my back against the wall and prayed once more, using the words that I had learned from the Reverend Hewitt. I listened for an answer but all that came back to me were the groans and curses of my fellow-inmates, the footsteps of the warders, the turning of keys and the opening and shutting of heavy doors. Beyond this, my day was like a blank slate and there was nothing to do but endure the passing of the hours.

That night I lay upon the straw and in my desperation my mind reached out for that other world my uncle had told me about when I was a child. For a long time it seemed to me that there was nothing of it left to me. Then I noticed a star shining in that tiny patch of sky the window let me see and on a sudden the locked door of my memory was opened. I saw my uncle sitting by the fire outside his hut and I heard his voice, deep and strong.

Long ago, long ago, he was telling me, the Sun had to leave the Moon to go on a journey. He knew that his wife, the Moon, was expecting a child and, before he left, he said to her in his sternest voice, 'If the baby is a boy, keep it but if it is a girl, you must kill it.'

The words were like a knife in the Moon's heart but she made no protest for she knew that she could never stand against the strength of the Sun. Instead, she bowed her head and considered what she should do.

The Sun had still not returned from his journey when the time came for the child to be born. So there was no-one to see the Moon give birth, no-one to hear her cries of pain. But the pain turned to joy when she was delivered of a beautiful girl. As soon as she saw the child's face she vowed she would not kill her. Instead, she hid her in the big box where she kept her clothes.

As soon as the Sun returned, he asked to see the baby.

With her eyes full of sadness, the Moon told him that it had been a girl. 'I killed her just like you said.'

But that night a boy with white hair came to the Sun in a dream, saying 'Your wife has hidden a girl child in the box where she keeps her clothes.'

The Sun awoke and immediately began searching for the child. When he found her he flew into a rage and slew her with his knife. Then he cut her body into tiny pieces – as many as the grains of sand that lie along the seashore – and tossed the pieces out of the window. But as they tumbled through the sky they began to shine. At last each little piece came to rest in its own place and there it continued to sparkle as a reminder to the Sun that for all his strength he could never truly destroy the daughter of the Moon.

The memory of my uncle's story brought me peace and I slept then until the morning when a warder opened the cell door and told me to pick up my bucket and follow. I did as I was told and he led me along a corridor with another warder close behind. Out we went into a yard, at one end of which stood a great cess-pit. The two warders waited in silence while I emptied my bucket, then they led me back. On the way back to my cell I asked, 'Am I to be brought before a magistrate soon?'

'No questions!' I was told.

Then I was locked back into my cell. In the afternoon I was brought a bowl of stew and in the evening a piece of the same hard grey bread and a mug of ale. Night fell. I lay for a long time listening to the grim music of the prison and then I fell asleep.

On my third day in prison I began to wonder whether I would even be taken before a magistrate at all. My appearance was against me. Despite Mr Duncan's efforts, I was no Englishman and perhaps I would not be considered worthy of Englishman's justice. I might simply be locked away and forgotten. I recalled the prisoner who had called upon Satan and all the lords of hell and I understood the despair into which he must have sunk. Did not Satan mock the Lord, saying, *Skin for skin, yea, all that a man hath will he give for his life?*

Then late in the day, when the light was beginning to fade once more, the door of my cell was opened and the warder ushered Mr Duncan inside. He shook his head when he saw me. 'I have come to take you out of this place,' he announced.

Mr Li had not let me down after all. He had gone to Mr Duncan's office first thing in the morning and told him what he had seen. Mr Duncan had immediately set about making enquiries. The first thing he had discovered was that Archie was indeed dead; he had been stabbed through the heart and his body taken away to a nearby workhouse until it should be claimed for burial – and I was to be charged with the murder. The hearing was due to take place on the following Monday and in the meantime the particulars of the case were being recorded.

'I did not have much time in which to act,' Mr Duncan told me. 'If you had once been arraigned, it would have been a devil of a job untying all the knots. I spoke to everyone who lived in your street and fortunately for you more than one of them saw what happened.'

'What did happen?'

'You were hit over the head by the cripple's accomplice, who has been identified as a man called Jeremiah Norton.'

The name meant nothing to me.

'He was in the employ of Mrs Dempsey for a good many years and known to everyone in the street as a notorious blackguard and cut-throat. I am told that you should consider yourself especially fortunate.'

'Fortunate?'

'Other folk who crossed him were never seen again.'

'Perhaps my skull is harder than other people's.'

'It seems more likely that he was distracted by the number of possible witnesses. Both he and the cripple left the scene of their crime as speedily as they could manage. No sign of either of them has since been reported.'

'But I am no longer to be accused of Archie's murder?'

He shook his head. 'The constables have accepted that they acted in haste.'

'I can return to the shop?'

'That is where I am taking you now.'

By now we had reached the front gate of the building and it was only a matter of signing my name upon a register and waiting a few moments while the great door to the street was opened and then I was outside breathing the air of freedom once more. I could scarcely believe my own swift deliverance and I do not know how long I might have stood there, looking about me at the people rushing past and savouring the joy of freedom, but Mr Duncan had a carriage waiting and he bundled me inside and we set off without further ado.

'There are some legal niceties to be attended to,' Mr Duncan told me as the carriage wound its way through the streets of Clerkenwell but ownership of Mr McKerras's estate will pass to you, eventually. In the meantime, you can continue to live in the shop and even conduct business, though you should be careful and exact in your accounting, in case there should be any enquiries.' He reached into his pocket and produced a set of keys. 'These were recovered from Mr McKerras's body.'

'What about Archie's funeral?'

'That can take place as soon as the coroner's inquiry has been held. It is scheduled for tomorrow morning.'

'And Archie's body?'

'Is being held in a nearby workhouse where they have provision for such eventualities.'

'I should like to see him.'

'I shall do my best to arrange it.'

It was very strange returning on my own to the shop. Archie had never made a great deal of noise but somehow his presence had filled the place. Now it seemed both vast and utterly devoid of purpose.

'Will you be all right?' Mr Duncan asked, as he prepared to leave me.

'I think so.'

'Have you any money?'

I went and unlocked the strong box that Archie kept in a back room. There was plenty of money for my present purposes.

'Come to my office tomorrow morning at ten. There are some papers to sign. Afterwards, we can go to see Mr McKerras's body, if that is still your wish.'

He left me then and I wandered from room to room trying to accustom myself to this new state of affairs. Then I fetched water and soap, stripped off all my clothes and did my best to wash away the smell of the prison. After that, I gave myself a shave with Archie's razor. I had one that I had purchased for myself but for some reason using Archie's seemed the right thing for me to do. Then I went out to a chop house where I spent more upon my meal than I had ever had occasion to before. Yet I enjoyed my meal no better than the prison food and pushed it away half-eaten. I had no idea who I was any more or what the world expected from me. I drank more than I was used to and walked unsteadily back to the shop where I lay down upon my bed and wept.

Thomas

Thomas asked every individual who lived in Anne's court whether they had any notion of her whereabouts. No one could help him; very few of them had even noticed her presence. They listened to his attempts to describe her and shrugged. There were lots of girls like that, they told him.

Those who knew her were instinctively hostile. It was clear that they believed he intended to do her harm and when he tried to assure them otherwise he only confirmed his guilt.

Many of them sought to interest him in other girls: cheaper, better, younger, older, fair girls, dark girls, red-heads, girls who would take him in their mouths, girls who would take it like a boy, girls he could beat, and girls who would punish him. These were good girls, girls they could vouch for. They knew how to satisfy a man and they would not run away as soon as they had a few shillings in their hand.

Others laughed and slapped him on the back. She will come back when she needs money, they assured him. It was the one thing he could rely upon. As surely as the sun rose and fell, she would be back. She was a street-girl. What else was she to do?

Every day he walked back and forth along the length of Oxford Street, scanning the crowds for a glimpse of her face. In the evening he returned to her room and ate, just enough to stay alive.

Daisy came to call, clucking sympathetically like a mother hen with a wounded chicken. She brought half a bottle of gin and sat herself down beside him. 'You're going to have to stop this,' she told him. 'You're wearing yourself away to nothing. Have a drink.'

Thomas drank directly from the bottle. It was like drinking liquid fire and he fell into a fit of coughing that quite exhausted him.

Daisy tutted and shook her head in dismay. 'What a state you've got yourself into!' she said. 'Have another drink, only this time take it slowly.'

Thomas did as he was told. It still burnt but this time he managed not to give way to another spasm of coughing.

Daisy took the bottle from him and swallowed a generous measure. 'It's a terrible shame the way she's treated you,' she said.

'No!' Thomas protested. 'It isn't like that at all.'

'If you say so, Thomas, though there are some people who would call her downright ungrateful.'

'She saved my life!'

'Well, I'm not sure you was exactly dying when we found you. But yes, she helped you get back on your feet again, that's true. But you've done lots for her, as well.'

'What have I done for her?'

'What have you done? A man of your class taking up with a girl like that! Come on, now, Thomas, anyone with any sense would say you was doing her an honour.'

Thomas shook his head angrily. 'I wasn't doing her an honour!'

'If you say so, darling boy. Here, have another drink.'

She passed the bottle to Thomas and he swallowed another mouthful. A wave of tiredness began to make its way over his body. He had tried so hard to find Anne, asked so many people without even the slightest hint of success.

'I've got a spot of the old Tender Mercy in my room,' Daisy told him. 'What do you say to a drop or two?'

'Laudanum?'

'The very same.'

'Yes. Yes, thank you. I'd welcome that.'

Daisy stood up but when Thomas tried to do the same the room seemed to lurch around him. Daisy laughed. Then she reached down, took Thomas's hands in hers and raised him up. She was surprisingly strong.

'Do you think you can walk?' she asked.

'Yes.'

But outside on the stairs, he would have stumbled if Daisy had not caught him. She held him against her body just a moment longer than Thomas felt was necessary before she released him and they continued on their way downstairs to her room.

Daisy's room was no different from Anne's except for a tattered rug that she had hung against one wall.

'D'you like my tapestry?' she asked him.

'It is most…' Thomas hesitated.

Daisy laughed out loud. 'Don't worry. I know what you must think. A fellow what was throwing it out of his shop give it to me when I took a fancy to it. He had it on the floor but I like it on the wall. Sit yourself down and I'll find the Tender Mercy.'

Thomas sat on the mattress while Daisy rummaged around in the piles of clothes until she came up with what was very nearly a full bottle of laudanum. She pulled out the stopper, then swallowed some and handed it to Thomas. He had not taken any for some days and the smell alone was enough to fill him with the excitement of remembered pleasure. He put the bottle to his lips and took a careful dose.

'Go on, have a bit more!' she urged him and Thomas allowed himself to be persuaded.

When it took effect, it was overwhelming. One moment Thomas was sitting upright, listening to Daisy telling him about an apothecary she knew who would make up a special tincture that was nearly twice the strength when he was in the right mood and how she knew exactly how to get him in the right mood, and the next moment he was lying flat upon his face, feeling as though the whole building had fallen down upon him and was pressing him into the mattress. He was aware that Daisy was asking him if he was all right but he was unable to answer: his body was no longer his to control; his thoughts were no longer his own; he was being whisked along a great shadowy corridor; he had entered the habitation of giants. He closed his eyes and surrendered to the drug.

For a very long time it seemed to him that he wandered through the ruins of some vast and ancient building, searching for something precious that had been lost here long ago. He could not recall exactly what it was but he knew that wars had been fought over it, lives had been ruined, men had been driven mad in their quest to uncover this great secret.

At last, understanding what was required of him, he lay down flat with his ear to the ground and listened. At first it was no more than a whisper, like the sound of the wind breathing through the sedge beside some ancient and forever sunless sea. But gradually the murmur grew and Thomas knew it then for what it was: the footsteps of all those who had ever walked, or ever would walk upon the face of the earth. He listened harder, knowing there was a meaning in those endlessly changing patterns, if only he could understand it. All the secrets of the world were repeated, over and over, in an unfolding rhythm of desire and satisfaction. And if a man would but surrender to the dance of syllables, accept the paths he was ordained to tread from long, long ages past, he would surely find within his grasp the lamp that lights the world, and gives the bearer his every hidden wish.

After what might have been weeks or days or only hours, he opened his eyes and he understood that he was back in Daisy's room, staring at the most wonderful, the most richly patterned tapestry. Daisy was at the other end of the mattress, sitting at right angles to him and gazing into his eyes with a look that was so knowing and so gently mocking that Thomas felt sure she saw right through to his soul.

'So, Thomas,' she said, speaking slowly and teasingly, 'you are back in the land of the living once more.'

'Yes.'

'You never really noticed me before, did you?' There was a note of accusation in her voice but this was belied by the wide smile that spread across her face.

Thomas hesitated, unsure what he ought to say. She was right, of course: he had disregarded her entirely until now; he had not done her justice. But all that was altered now for he found he could not take his eyes from her, and he seemed to be aware of her whole being and yet to seek more.

She moved closer to him. 'I have my charms, Thomas. Don't you think so?'

'Yes, you do. Certainly.'

She was wearing a red silk dress fastened at the front and while Thomas watched, fascinated by her liquid movements – as if she inhabited an alien sphere surrounded not by air but by some other magical substance that invested her with the grandeur of a river goddess – she reached up with one elegant hand and released the fastenings. Moving more slowly than seemed possible, the dress swung open to reveal her large, heavy breasts with their dark purple nipples that looked to Thomas like some unknown and exotic fruit.

She leaned further forward and put her hand upon his leg and immediately he felt himself stiffening.

'Don't be afraid, Thomas,' she whispered. 'The world is a cruel place and we must find our shelter where we may.' She moved her hand higher until it rested in between his legs. 'I see you do appreciate me, after all.' She laughed softly.

Thomas could no longer speak. The power to do so had been taken from him, the words all stolen. His whole body felt as if it were about to burst into flame.

Daisy began to unlace his breeches. She bent her head in concentration, her long hair brushing his thighs. Then she bent lower still and took him in her mouth.

An involuntary cry escaped from Thomas. Without taking him from her mouth, Daisy raised her eyes and regarded him gravely and then she moaned as if this act gave her such pleasure she could not restrain herself. She bore down upon him, taking more and more of him within herself. Thomas forgot everything else as the pleasure burst forth from him.

When he awoke he knew immediately that he committed a terrible sin and groaned with disgust as the memory of his deed tumbled vividly into his mind. He who had sworn to learn the language of the heart and speak no other!

He sat up in bed and discovered that he had the worst headache he had ever known. A great iron ball rolled ponderously from one side of his skull to another and lightning bolts of pain lanced across his forehead. But somehow he had to force himself off the mattress, crawl across the floor towards the bucket in the corner. Once there, he was violently sick.

Afterwards, he stayed kneeling over the bucket, shivering, the sweat growing cold upon his forehead while he waited for his pulse to steady. But he welcomed the sickness. It was a good deal less than he deserved.

'Feeling a bit rough?' Daisy's voice enquired from behind him.

He could not bring himself to reply.

'I'll go and get us something to eat,' she continued. 'You'll feel better with a bit of something solid inside you.'

Another spasm of retching seized him, like an iron hand clutching at his innards, but all he could manage to bring up was a string of green bile.

Daisy brushed past him and opened the door.

'Empty the bucket when you've finished,' she told him. Then she was gone.

It was some time before Thomas felt strong enough to get to his feet, and take the bucket out to the cess-pit. With every step he took the world reeled around him but he forced himself onwards. Afterwards, he rinsed the bucket under the pump and put his own head beneath the jet of water. It was so cold that it was as though someone had hit him with a cudgel. He withdrew his head quickly and stood there, bent over, gasping with pain and shock. 'That will teach you,' he whispered as he gradually straightened his back once more.

He retraced his steps to Daisy's room where he replaced the bucket. Then he went upstairs to Anne's room, the very sight of which was an accusation. He retrieved his coat and set off once more. He did not wish to be anywhere near the building when Daisy returned.

At first his footsteps began taking him towards Brunel's office but then he stopped and considered another destination. It would be a long, weary walk and he was in no condition to make such a journey but it would be a kind of penance.

It was the middle of the day before Thomas reached the Mile End Road by which time he was almost ready to lie down upon the street like a beggar or again curl up in a doorway. There was something different about the place, that much was obvious, though at first he could not make out what it was. Then he saw that a house just up the street from the second-hand clothes shop had been burnt to the ground. Charred beams still littered the street, the smell of ash and soot was still in the air.

The shop was closed but there was no sign indicating why this should be. Frustrated, Thomas stood back and looked the building up and down but he could glean no information. He stepped up to the front door once more and hammered hard with his fist. There was no answer, so he tried again but with the same result. At his third attempt a window opened on the floor above. The Malay who had sold him his clothes stuck his head out. 'I am sorry but we are closed for business,' he said.

'I do not come on business,' Thomas replied.

The Malay frowned.

'Then what do you want?'

'I would rather not discuss it out here in the street.'

The Malay withdrew his head and closed the window. A minute later there came the sound of bolts being withdrawn and the door was opened. He gestured for Thomas to step inside.

It was dark in the shop for the wooden shutters were fastened and the Malay made no move to unlock them. 'What is it you want?' he asked again.

'I came here the other day and bought some clothes.'

The Malay frowned. 'A lot has happened to me of late,' he said. 'I'm afraid I cannot remember…'

'It does not matter,' Thomas told him. 'I am not here about the clothes. I am here because I was originally given the address of your shop by a young woman called Anne.' He scrutinised the Malay's face carefully, searching for some sign of recognition, but there was nothing.

'She is a… a street-girl,' Thomas continued. 'I understand she used to live near here.'

The Malay nodded, understanding dawning upon his face. 'One of Mrs Dempsey's girls.'

'Mrs Dempsey?'

'She died some weeks ago. That was her house that but lately burnt to the ground. While she lived it was a house of pleasure.'

'I see. Yes, that may be where she lived. Have you seen her?'

The Malay shook his head. 'They all left when the old woman died. No one knows where they went.'

Thomas had not expected anything different, yet all the same he felt his spirits sink even lower than before, if that were possible. 'If by any chance you should see her,' he continued, 'I would be grateful if you would tell her I was looking for her and that I can always be contacted at Mr Brunel's office. Perhaps I could write a note?'

The Malay shrugged. 'I do not even know which girl you are referring to. There were a number of them.'

'Her name is Anne,' Thomas repeated. 'Do you have a piece of paper and a pen?'

The Malay went into the back room and returned with some writing paper, a pen and inkwell. Thomas thought hard, then wrote:

My Dearest Anne. Whatever your reasons for disappearing, please be assured that my wishes for both of us have not altered. You can reach me at any time through Mr Brunel. Yours in hope. Thomas.

He waited for it to dry, then folded it and handed it to the Malay. 'If you do encounter her, perhaps you would be so kind as to give her this note.'

The Malay took the note but he continued to look doubtful.

There was nothing for Thomas to do then except turn around, walk out of the shop and set off back the way he had come. He would go to see Brunel and beg him for a small advance. If the man would not cooperate then Thomas had no idea what he would do next.

It was very hard to walk back to Brunel's office. Thomas felt like someone who has been castaway upon some isolated shore and lost to his fellow man for scores of years. His throat was dry, he was faint with hunger, and his head hurt so much he wanted to bang it against the walls of the houses that he passed but he made himself place one foot in front of the other until at last he found himself knocking upon the door of Brunel's office.

The door was opened by Pyment who looked at him and shook his head. 'Talk of the devil!' he said. 'You'd better come in.'

He led Thomas into the room where Brunel conducted his business and there, to Thomas's astonishment he saw Lord Massey seated opposite Brunel, both looking very comfortable in each other's company.

'Thomas!' said Lord Massey, rising to his feet. 'How very good it is to see you – but you do not look at all well! Pray take this seat.'

Thomas considered declining the offer out of politeness

but in truth he was not entirely convinced his legs would continue to support him for very much longer, so he thanked Lord Massey and sat down heavily.

'Pyment!' Brunel ordered. 'Another chair for his lordship.'

Pyment disappeared without complaint and returned a moment later bearing another chair.

'Perhaps some small refreshment for our friend,' Lord Massey suggested. 'He looks quite done for.' He gave Pyment his most winning smile and Brunel nodded his agreement.

'I'll see to it, your lordship,' Pyment said.

Lord Massey turned back to Thomas. 'I cannot apologize enough for failing to appear at White's,' he said. 'You must have thought me an absolute scoundrel.' He waved aside Thomas's attempts to protest. 'I was detained on unavoidable political matters, which I am not at liberty to discuss, I'm afraid. The whole affair was the most unconscionable waste of time. But there you are. Very few of us are the masters of our fates. However, here I am at last and I have some news which I believe you will find most agreeable.'

Thomas was finding it difficult to keep Lord Massey's head in focus. He could see a second, shadow head and he found himself wondering whether his lordship's soul was not beginning to drift free of its bodily moorings. But he knew this notion was no more than the after-effects of the laudanum and he forced himself to concentrate on what Lord Massey was telling him.

'No doubt you have been aggrieved at my silence, Thomas,' Lord Massey continued. 'You felt that I had not lived up to the promise I had made. No, no, it would be entirely understandable. But it would not be correct. For in truth I have been working devilishly hard behind the scenes and the upshot is that I have convinced your uncle and your mother that the very best thing would be to send you to Oxford.'

'What?'

Lord Massey chuckled. 'I see I have taken you by surprise. But wait. In addition, they have agreed to make you an allowance of a hundred pounds a year. It is not much, I know, not enough you will say but, remember, your board and lodging will be provided and I'm sure we can come to some sort of an arrangement about books. So what do you say, Thomas?'

Thomas stared back at him in disbelief. It was what he had wanted so badly, until he had encountered Anne.

'Ah! Here is Pyment and unless I'm very much mistaken he is clutching a meat pie and a jug of ale. Not exactly elegant fare but substantial, nourishing, and just what you need to set you up.'

Pyment handed the pie to Thomas and set down the jug of ale on the corner of Brunel's desk. 'Time for the prodigal son to return, Thomas,' Lord Massey said and all three men beamed happily in Thomas's direction.

Anne

The heath was covered in a low, creeping mist that chilled you right through to the bone. Hawk was dressed for travel in his great coat, muffler, and three cornered hat but I was only wearing the thin dress that Dora gave me and before long I was shivering *violently* as I sat up on the driving seat beside him.

Hawk shook his head as if he'd expected better from me. Then he reached behind, pulled out a blanket and handed it over. It smelled strongly of horse but I was too cold to care. I wrapped it around me as tightly as I could and eventually I began to warm up.

'I thought you'd left the country,' I said when we was clear of Mrs Dugland's house and I felt brave enough to speak out loud.

'That was the general idea,' he agreed. 'I needed to disappear in a hurry and if folks thought I'd taken ship for foreign lands, then so much the better.'

'You left me and my mother well and truly stranded.

He shrugged. 'I didn't have no choice, Anne. Ever come across a fellow called John Dempsey?'

'I don't think so.'

'You'd remember him if you'd met him. Nasty piece of work, I can tell you. A right bleedin' turk. Anyway, I owed him money so I had to make myself scarce or he'd have put me in the ground.'

'Well you could have given us warning, that's all I'm saying.'

Hawk shrugged. 'Would have put you in more danger than saying nothing.'

We was right in the middle of the heath now and it was so bleak and empty I could easily have imagined I'd died and was crossing the border that leads a soul to *purgatory* – or maybe worse. Even the horse shivered.

'How's your mother getting on, these days?' Hawk asked.

'She's dead.'

'What?' He gave a sharp jerk on the reins and the carriage came to a halt. 'Dead? Marjorie? What happened to her?

'Hanged herself.'

He sucked in his breath. 'Oh my good God! I'm very sorry to hear it, Anne. I really am. Your mother was a good woman.' He made the sign of the cross, and muttered a prayer. Then he took up the reins again and we started off once more, both of us considering my poor mother's fate. I couldn't help thinking that things might have turned out a lot better for her if my father and Hawk hadn't been so fond of drinking together but I said nothing about that. I just watched the moon dip in and out of the few rags of cloud and wondered what she would have had to say about the way my life turned out.

After a while Hawk coughed up a big gob of oyster green and spat on the road. Then he said, 'So whereabouts you heading?'

'I'll tell you that when we get a little nearer London.' The truth was I still hadn't made my mind up. I was running away from Mrs Dugland and the infinite mercy of God but I didn't know where I was running to.

'You been working for that woman long?'

'Just a few weeks.'

'What was you doing before, then?'

'Well I weren't making baskets. That all fell through after you scarpered.'

'I suppose it did. Sorry about that.'

'We was doing washing for a bit, me and mother.'

'Oh no! Who was you washing for? Don't tell me it was that bastard, Gillespie?'

'Who else?'

He shook his head in disgust. 'So what made you pack that lark in?'

'My mother took up with a fellow called Harold Lampton.'

'Not Lightning Lampton?'

'The very same.'

'He's another nasty piece of work.'

'He was. He's dead now.'

'Is he? Well I don't suppose he'll be missed.'

'My mother missed him. It was on his account that she hanged herself.'

'I don't believe it! That miserable fucker wasn't worth a second thought.'

We was passing through the village of Plumstead now – though village was too fine a name for it. There was no more than two or three cottages huddled together for company and the place was as quiet as a graveyard. Not like London, I thought to myself. Day or night there was people on the streets of London. A doxy wouldn't get much trade here.

Just outside the village a stupid little dog ran out into the road barking at us and I got scared he'd rouse someone from their beds but the horse just ignored him and after a while he turned tail and slunk off back home. Good riddance! I said to myself. We was on the main road to London now and even if I didn't know where I was bound, I knew I weren't going back to Mrs Dugland's.

'So what happened to you after your mother died?' Hawk asked.

'I had to support myself, didn't I?'

'And that's when you went into service?'

'Something like that. Anyway, what about you?'

Hawk shrugged. 'I been living in Kent mostly, going about from place to place, getting a bit of work here, selling a few bits and pieces there. Went back to London for the first time a week ago. Can't say it'd changed much.'

'How come you went back if you was so afraid of John Dempsey?'

'Dempsey's in the same place as Harold Lampton.'

'What d'you mean?'

'Burnt to death in his sister's house.' He chuckled. 'They say there was celebration from one end of Whitechapel to the other.'

'Burnt to death? Are you sure?'

'Sure and certain. I went there myself to take a look. Nothing but a pile of ashes left.'

'Mrs Dempsey's house, in the Mile End Road?'

'That's it! I thought you didn't know him.'

'I knew *her*. I knew the house. I worked there, Hawk.'

He looked at me suspiciously. 'How do you mean, worked there?'

I suppose I should have kept my mouth shut but a kind of *defiance* rose up in me. So I said, 'I was one of Mrs Dempsey's girls.'

'Wait a minute! Are you telling me you was a doxy?'

'That's about the size of it.'

'Oh, Anne! I can't believe it!'

'What else was I supposed to do?' He was making me

angry now. 'I didn't have no family. I didn't have no friends. I couldn't just lie down and die.'

'There's other ways, though,' Hawk muttered.

'Oh yeah? What are they, then? You tell me about them other ways.'

Hawk said nothing for a long time. Then he shuffled a bit further away from me. 'I'm not sure I should be sitting up here with you beside me,' he said.

'What?'

'Well, I have my reputation to consider.'

'Your reputation!' I swung back my arm and fetched him such a hard clout across the side of the head he almost tumbled down onto the road.

'What the hell was that for?' he said, when he'd recovered himself.

'What do you think it was for? Your reputation, indeed! As what, exactly? As a travelling tinker? Or as a drunken sot, maybe? Or a man who doesn't pay his debts? Or a fellow what lets his friends down?'

Hawk shook his head sadly. 'That ain't fair,' he murmured. 'That ain't fair at all.'

'It's perfectly fair,' I told him. 'You're all those things and a good deal more, Hawk. And don't tell me you ain't never been with a doxy!'

'I most certainly…'

'Give it a rest!' I told him. 'I know the kind of man you are. You ain't wicked, but you ain't no saint either. So don't start acting all holy. It don't suit you.'

By way of answer Hawk drew a great draught of green out of the back of his nose and spat noisily onto the road.

'And you can stop doing that, an' all.'

'What?' He looked at me in *amazement*.

'It's disgusting, Hawk. Ain't no one ever told you that?'

'No one's said nothing.'

'Well I'm telling you now. It's a disgusting habit.'

After that neither of us felt very much like talking. We carried on in silence for a long time with just the odd hoot from an owl to keep us company. After a while we saw another cart on the road up ahead but it turned off about half a mile later. Then a fellow came galloping up behind us on horseback and for a terrible few minutes I thought Mrs Dugland had sent someone to fetch me back but he just carried right on past and I breathed again.

I asked myself why I'd told Hawk about working for Mrs Dempsey. I could just as easily have made out I'd gone straight into service. Some childish notion of honesty from all the bible stuff I'd heard as a little mot, I suppose. I never seemed to be able to grow up in the way that other folks did.

But now all I could think was that if a man like Hawk didn't want to sit beside me when he learned what my life had been, how would the gentlemen and ladies in Thomas's world behave? It seemed *highly unlikely* they'd be more generous than Hawk. Thomas kept telling me that *respectability* was only a matter of money and perhaps it was true as far as he was concerned, but the rest of the world didn't look at things the way he did.

Hawk's horse had only two speeds: dead slow and stop. So dawn was coming up when we finally reached the city. London Bridge was smothered in fog, just like the heath I'd left behind, but somehow I didn't find it half so threatening.

'You still ain't told me where you want to go,' Hawk pointed out.

Suddenly I knew. 'Mrs Dempsey's house. I want to see it for myself. After that, you don't have to set eyes on me again.'

'Don't talk like that, Anne,' Hawk said, sorrowfully. 'I

shouldn't have said what I did. I was wrong.'

I shook my head. 'You was right,' I told him. 'I ain't respectable. I never will be respectable again. Your best bet is to have nothing more to do with me.'

'I'll always be your friend, Anne,' Hawk said.

'Thanks, Hawk.' But I knew his words meant nothing. Hawk hadn't saved my father when he'd fallen in the Thames and he couldn't save me, neither. No more could Mr Thomas De Quincey. I was beyond saving. I thought of that old crone I'd met when I was looking for my mother's grave and the miserable plot of land she'd brought me to where all the fallen women lay, and I knew there was no way back for me. A doxy is a doxy until the day she dies.

Hawk set me down opposite Mrs Dempsey's, or what used to be Mrs Dempsey's but what was now no more than a pile of ash and charcoal. He wouldn't stop for long for there was others he owed money to, not murderous buggers like John Dempsey but still the kind to kick up a fuss if they clapped eyes upon him. So I got out the four guineas but he refused to accept it. 'For your father's sake, and your mother's too,' he said, 'I can't go taking your money.'

I thanked him and watched him ride away. The last I heard of him was a great snort as he disappeared into the distance.

I stood and *surveyed the ruins* of Mrs Dempsey's house for a good while. It was hard to believe that this was where I'd grown from a little girl to a woman. I wondered what had become of all the fine furniture, the piano, the ornaments. Had it all turned to ash or had the neighbours come snuffling through the embers, picking out anything of value what was left? That was more likely.

In the end, there was nothing to do but turn around and walk away. Only where was I to go now? I still hadn't decided. Then my eyes fell on the second-hand clothes shop and I thought of Archie, who'd read to me when I returned from Mrs Nancy's, and given me all those new and useless words. I wandered down the street towards the shop. I'm not sure exactly what was in my mind. I just felt the need to gaze on a familiar face.

It was much too early for the shop to be open but when I peered through the glass I saw someone sitting behind the counter, reading. I thought at first it must be Archie so I knocked on the glass but when the figure looked up I saw it was the boy who worked for Archie, the one who'd come into my room with news of Archie's brother's death. He came out from behind the counter and opened the door.

'Sorry to trouble you,' I said. 'I was looking for Archie. I used to live across the road at…'

'I know who you are,' he said. 'You are the one he read to.'

'That's right. It helped me, the reading. It helped me a great deal. Anyway, I was in the neighbourhood so I thought I'd just pop in and say hello. '

He shook his head. 'I'm afraid that Archie is dead.'

'Not him, too!'

'He was attacked on the street three weeks ago and stabbed.'

For some reason this was the last straw. Everyone I ever cared about was either dead or parted from me. A great sob burst out of me and then another. I wept for Archie and for Thomas and for my father and my mother but most of all I wept for myself.

The poor fellow didn't know what to do with me. He went and fetched a chair and sat me down but I just couldn't stop weeping. I'd been a fool, I knew that. I'd made a terrible mess of my life. All I'd ever wanted was to be out of harm's way but all I'd done was walk into one trap after another.

Tuah

Of course I knew who she was. I had watched her from the shop window, standing for a long time staring into the remains of Mrs Dempsey's house. I was reasonably sure, too, that this was the girl the young man with the pale face and wild eyes had been talking about. I could have told her about the note he had left with me and no doubt you will say that I should have done, but I did not. I was under no obligation to him. I was under no obligation to anyone except Archie and his brother, both of whom were dead.

I fetched a chair and waited for her to compose herself. While she wept, I asked myself why she had come into the shop to begin with and why she wept so bitterly to hear of Archie's death. I considered everything I knew about her circumstances and an idea came to me. It was bold, much bolder than anything I had ever done before and I was frightened by its audacity. But I tried not to show anything of this. Instead, I waited until she was calm. Then I said, 'I did not realise you were so fond of Archie. You must have known him very well.'

She shook her head. 'I'm sorry. I hardly knew him, at all. I don't know what you must think of me.'

'It does not matter in the least what I think,' I said. 'I am no one of consequence.'

She frowned. 'Do you mind if I ask – why is the shop still open when Archie is dead?'

'It is my shop now.'

'Is it? Then you are someone of consequence, after all. Well it's an ill wind that blows no good to somebody.' She got to her feet. 'I should go. Thank you for putting up with me.'

I saw that even as she said this, she was reluctant to leave. So I said, 'Forgive me for asking, but have you somewhere to go to?'

'Course I do.'

Her response came back so quickly that I knew she must be lying. So I made up my mind that I would make my offer. After all, what did I have to lose? *Two are better than one; because they have a good reward for their labour.*

'I only ask because I have need of someone,' I told her. 'You see, I cannot manage the shop by myself.'

'You want someone to help you run the shop?' There was a spark of interest in her eyes now whereas before they had been dull and lifeless.

'Exactly.'

'Are you offering me a job? Is that what you're saying?'

'Would you like one?'

'I've never worked in a shop before.'

'It is not that difficult.'

She hesitated, thinking about it. At last she said, 'I haven't anywhere to live, right now. I had a room but….'

'You could live here.'

'In the shop?'

'Above the shop. There are plenty of rooms. You could have one of your own. You would be quite safe. I would not interfere with you. You have my word on that.'

I haven't any money for rent.'

When I first came here,' I told her, 'I had no money for rent. Archie and his brother Donald did not charge me rent. In return I worked.'

'You're offering to let me live here for free?' She still looked suspicious.

I knew I had to be entirely honest with her. Nothing but the truth would convince her. 'I have no one in the world,' I admitted. 'I am quite alone. It is very hard to continue by yourself. If you were here, it would make life more bearable. For if they fall, the one will lift up his fellow: but woe to him that is alone when he falleth; for he hath not another to help him up. That is what is says in the Bible."

'Never mind the Bible. What about what I did in Mrs Dempsey's house?' she said. 'And all the men I did it with?'

'That is not important to me.'

'It seems to be important to everyone else. What about your reputation? What about your customers? What would they think?'

'I have no reputation. Maybe I will have no customers. But I think people will always need clothes and they will not always be able to afford to buy them new.'

Still she hesitated. 'I don't understand. Why are you offering me all this? Why me?'

'I've already told you, I am alone in the world and I thought, perhaps, you might be, too. But if I'm wrong…'

'You ain't wrong,' she said. 'I am alone.'

'Then what do you say? Will you join me?'

She still hesitated and I bit my lip to stop myself saying anything further. At last she made up her mind. 'I will. With thanks. Only I don't know your name.'

'Tuah.'

She repeated it. 'I ain't never heard that name before. I'm Anne.'

'I know,' I said. 'I came into your room in Mrs Dempsey's house once to tell Archie of his brother's death.'

'When Archie was reading to me. I remember. I loved to listen to him read.'

'The rooms at the top of the house are full of books,' I told her.

'Pity I can't read.'

'You could learn.'

She laughed. 'Is that part of the job, then?'

'It is the best part.'

The unexpected visitor finally disappears behind the cluster of cottages at the end of the lane but Thomas continues to stand at the window, the locket clutched in his hand. On the desk behind him are the writing things he had set out that morning with such hope, believing himself to be inspired, as if his mind's eye were a lighthouse beam cutting a swathe through inner darkness. Now he feels like a man returned to the everyday world from the land of faerie, very much older and yet no wiser, those great truths that had dawned upon him earlier all vanished. It seems instead that something has been stolen while his attention was ensnared for the lamp of his imagination is suddenly nowhere to be found.

White clouds sail across the sky and as he watches they shape themselves into visions of beds with white lawny curtains; in the beds lie the sick and the dying, tossing in anguish and weeping clamorously for death. God, for some mysterious reason, cannot release them from their pain. Instead he suffers the beds to rise slowly through the heavens towards him.

The vision passes and, like an immigrant who stands bewildered on the shore of a new country, hearing all about him a language of which he possesses only the merest fragments, struggling with half understood words and phrases, Thomas at last begins to understand what the man's visit signifies: he has failed in the first great trial of his life. With this knowledge comes the certainty that he will never be the man he has always wished to become until he can put this day behind him, until he can find a way to encase it in narrative.

He turns from the window and, weaving through the piles of books, sits down at his desk and picks up his pen. But where to start? Then his eye falls upon the empty vial of laudanum. There is a druggist not ten minutes walk away whom he has always found to be very accommodating. Perhaps, after all, a walk is what he needs.

Author's Note

Thomas De Quincey did not become a poet, though he did become a good friend of Wordsworth and Coleridge. Indeed, he seems to have been something of a favourite with Dorothy Wordsworth. After the Wordsworths left Dove Cottage, where William wrote so much of his most famous poetry, Thomas took up the tenancy and remained in the cottage for the next ten years.

He made his name firstly as a journalist and essayist but he is best known as the author of first ever celebrity autobiography in the English Language, the scandalous *Confessions Of An English Opium Eater,* a best-seller when it was first published.

In the *Confessions* he describes the unfortunate affair of the banker's draft, his time spent living rough, his encounter with Anne in Oxford Street and her subsequent disappearance. He also gives an account of the appearance at the door of his cottage, much later in life, of a mysterious foreigner whom he describes as a Malay, though there is no indication that these events might be somehow related.

In writing this book I have allowed myself to take very considerable liberties with known facts, or with facts as they have been presented by Thomas. I make no apologies for doing so since this is a work of fiction, not a biography. Moreover, Thomas himself was by no means a reliable source of information. He was an opium addict and like all addicts he experienced the world through the prism of his addiction. He was also a storyteller who could not resist embroidering an event for his own purposes.

There is no doubt that Thomas was greatly affected by the death of his sister and it seems to be true that her skull was cut open after her death by doctors who wished to understand the nature of her illness.

It is also undeniable that Thomas was greatly affected by the story of Aladdin, though where he got the bit about the magician putting his ear to the ground and discerning from what he heard that Aladdin was the only person who could touch the lamp, nobody knows. This detail, which fascinated Thomas, does not seem to exist in any known version of the story.

Thomas was certainly invited to Laxton by Lady Carberry to arrange her library and, according to Thomas, she did ask him to teach her Ancient Greek. He was also acquainted with Lord Massey, though it was from another aristocratic acquaintance that he sought to borrow money.

Anne did disappear without trace and though he was finally force to accept this and continue his life without her, he regularly returned from Oxford to walk the streets of London in the hope of bumping into her. Even in his old age he wrote that whenever he found himself in a crowd he could not help scanning the faces of those around him in the hope that she might be among them. Sadly, she never was.

Acknowledgements

In writing this novel I have been encouraged and assisted at almost every step of the way by Kathleen Ktorides and Rosemary Keaney, to both of whom I am extremely grateful. I would also like to thank my editor, Robert Peett, whose input has been invaluable.

About the Author

Brian Keaney is an award-winning author, best known for his young adult and children's fantasy novels *Jacob's Ladder*, *The Hollow People* and *The Magical Detectives*. For a number of years he was Royal Literary Fund Fellow at Goldsmiths College and at the London College Of Fashion and he taught creative writing on the Pembroke College Cambridge summer programme. He has a house in the west of Ireland where he spends as much time as possible. His writing has been translated into twenty languages.